Bump and Run

Also by Mike Lupica

Bump and Run

mike lupica

G. P. Putnam's Sons
New York

This is a work of fiction. Names, characters, places, and
incidents either are the product of the author's imagination
or are used fictitiously, and any resemblance to actual per-
sons, living or dead, business establishments, events, or
locales is entirely coincidental.

G. P. Putnam's Sons
Publishers Since 1838
a member of
Penguin Putnam Inc.
375 Hudson Street
New York, NY 10014

Library of Congress Cataloging-in-Publication Data

Lupica, Mike.
Bump and run / Mike Lupica.
p.   cm.
ISBN 0-399-14647-4
1. Football players—Fiction.   2. Football teams—Fiction.
I. Title.

PS3562.U59 B86   2000   00-038719
813'.54—dc21

Printed in the United States of America
1   3   5   7   9   10   8   6   4   2

This book is printed on acid-free paper. ∞

BOOK DESIGN BY AMANDA DEWEY

For Taylor, of course

And for Thomas J. O'Neill,
who lived an awful lot of this,
laughing all the way

PART ONE

go team

one

I was known in Vegas as the Jammer. My real name is Jack Molloy, which most football fans know as well as the point spread by now. But nobody on the Strip ever called me Jack for long. If you've ever been on the Strip and don't know me or what I used to do there, then you're the new target audience for the Chamber of Commerce, which wants to turn the place into some kind of Disney wet dream.

You want to bring the wife and kids on the four-day, three-night weekend package and say things like, "Jesus, Myrtle, an indoor volcano!"

People say now that Las Vegas was more fun before they tried to de-Bugsy it, make it more wholesome for a new millennium than Kathie Lee's kids. But the fun was still out there for you once you got past room service. You just had to know the right people.

Like me.

"Jammer," my boss Billy Grace liked to say, "you're one of the last guys left who don't think having a cocktail and getting a hard-on are against the law."

I'd always tell him to stop then, he was starting to make me blush. Of course that was before the National Football League in general and the New York Hawks in particular took me hostage, as if pro football was the guys with the towels on their heads and I was the U.S. Embassy.

I'll get to that in a minute.

If you want to know the whole story of my season in tabloid hell, how it happened that I became as well known as Jerry Jones or George Steinbrenner or any of those other celebrity owners, you have to know where it all started, and it started when I was still the Jammer.

My official title at Billy Grace's hotel, known as Amazing Grace, was Casino Host. It's like saying Michael Jordan's position was guard. I was Billy's go-to guy. Some reporter from the *Las Vegas Sun* once asked him what I did and Billy said, "Whatever it is, he's indispensable." Sometimes Billy—who wanted to be the king of Vegas as much as Kirk Kerkorian and Steve Wynn ever did—just described me as his Director of Logistics.

I set up what needed to be set up, arranged what needed to be arranged, fixed what needed to be fixed. I didn't particularly want to know if you were a good guy or a bad guy, just if you had money in your pocket and wanted to spend it in Billy's bar or at Billy's tables.

If you were staying at Amazing Grace and needed to be hooked up, I was your man. And let me explain something right here, just so there are no misunderstandings. When I say hooked up, I don't mean hookers. Though I must say that most of the working girls I know, especially the ones in Vegas, are a much better class of people than a lot of the high rollers and socialite scum I've met in what has passed for my adult life.

When I say hook you up, I mean just that, whether it's a tee time at Billy's golf course—God's Acre—or the best odds on the Georgia-Florida game, or a showgirl who'd not only laugh and look at you the way Siegfried always looked at Roy, but who wouldn't ask you for five hundred dollars afterward to help out with her acting classes.

The real tourists and the amateurs still had this idea that Vegas was some kind of high-class whorehouse. I never looked at it that way, not from the first day Billy brought me out from New York. I always looked at Amazing Grace as the world's classiest frat house, one with so many good-looking women around, you thought they'd put blackjack tables in Hugh Hefner's grotto.

Say a star athlete is in town for a big prizefight and he wants to play God's Acre. Billy'd had it built because he just had to have a better course than Shadow Creek, which was Wynn's pride and joy before he sold it to Kerkorian, along with The Mirage, a few years ago. Maybe you remember, it was one of those periods when you got the idea that everything and everybody in town was suddenly on the market.

We'll call the guy Mr. Perfect, football hero. Mr. Perfect's guys would call Billy, and Billy would call me and he'd say what he always did.

Handle it.

The regulation stuff—the tee times, the comps at casino, the cigars that tasted like they'd come straight from Castro's own humidor, the reservations for the shows—that was as easy for me as lying is for the President. But usually with stars, even ones who had an image as squeegee-clean as a sitcom dad, there'd probably be a nanny in the package somewhere.

Nanny is the polite way of describing what Billy just calls discreet pussy, in Vegas or anywhere else.

It worked this way for jocks, for politicians and movie stars and CEOs and university presidents and presidents of your favorite sports teams, even the Secretary General of the U.N. one time. It's also how I worked, at least before pro football car-jacked me.

So let's say that in addition to trying to break par and break the bank at Billy's tables, Mr. Perfect—even with Mrs. Perfect back home, organizing another charity auction—also wanted to get laid. Most of the high rollers did. Even the God guys.

Especially the God guys, if you want to know the truth.

A few years ago, when the whole world was in town for a Tyson fight, I accidentally walked in on a famous Christian quarterback just as his nanny finished up with something that seemed to fall under the general heading of an oil change. When she'd left the room, I said, "If you don't mind me asking, how does what just went on here fit in with your religious beliefs, exactly?"

The quarterback shook his head sadly, and sighed.

"Jammer," he said, "we've all got needs."

If my latest football hero was feeling needy that weekend, I was supposed to help him out. The real trick was getting the girl into the hotel and around the hotel and finally out of the hotel, keeping her discreet while still making sure she enjoyed her free time. That way she wouldn't end up feeling like a love slave who'd sell her story someday to the *National Enquirer* or *The Star* and eventually end up as a featured selection on Oprah's Book Club.

If the drill went the way it was supposed to, and it usually did, the only people who ever saw the quarterback and his nanny together were his guys and my guys and me.

The drill went like this: She'd register at the concierge desk with one of Perfect's security guys. The two of them would check into their room, which the security guy would end up using. There'd be an adjoining room next door, which would stay empty. And on the other side of that would be one of Billy's Temple of Gold–type suites, which are equipped with everything except a helicopter pad and indoor rain forest. That's where our perfect hero was waiting. The suite would have a private elevator, outside phone lines, even a personal chef on twenty-four-hour call, one of the more versatile guys from what I called my A Team.

The only guys working that floor would be from my own Casino Host staff. Jammers in training, I called them. I'd also have alibis set up in advance, around the golf and the gambling and the fight, even a log I could produce if I had to, one that would show my star at God's Acre between noon and five o'clock, say, then eating dinners with friends—all male, of course—at a certain time. Then at a particular blackjack table from the time the fight ended until four or five A.M.

All in all, it would be a timeline that would make O.J. hot, just in case a suspicious wife or some asshole reporter came around looking to ask questions afterward.

Maybe you're starting to understand the irony of my nickname now: I didn't get you into jams, I kept you out of them. Unless, of course, you rubbed Billy or me the wrong way and a compromising situation—another of my specialties—was required.

Then I got your ass into a jam, sometimes with snapshots to prove it.

Billy liked to pick the girls either way. He did this because (A) it made him feel like a sheikh, and (B) he said he didn't want anybody to ever call me a pimp.

"Let's face it, Jammer," he'd say sometimes, "I'm no good and can prove it."

I don't mind telling you, in the interest of full disclosure, that Billy's career in business began with a job that involved him taking $500,000 from New York to Miami in a suitcase in 1957. He didn't tell me a lot about some of his other duties in those days, but when he did, it would all come out sounding like the first season of *The Sopranos*. When he got drunk enough sometimes, he'd hold up his hands, which were big enough and beat-up enough that they could have belonged to some old baseball catcher like Yogi Berra, and say, "You don't want to know where these hands have been. . . ."

He was right, I didn't, but I did know that particular routine the way cops know Miranda.

Anyway, that would be Mr. Perfect's weekend at Amazing Grace, courtesy of the Jammer. If one of Billy's girls ever did go public, it would be her word against ours. When you came right down to it, it would be hard for her to prove she was ever on the premises in the first place, unless she clipped the complimentary robe or the remote for the big-screen TV.

Put it this way: We never needed our VIPs to fill out a Satisfied Guest card to let us know they'd had a good time. Some guys might get busted by their wives somewhere else along the dusty old trail, but never on my watch. It's why they all came back, and when they did, treated me like we'd pledged the same fraternity in college and knew the secret handshake. It is also worth pointing out that every time they did come back, they dropped enough money to buy a G-5 at Billy's tables, which he thought was the real national pastime, not baseball or football or sending dirty e-mail.

I was thirty-five. An old girlfriend said I reminded her of the way Harrison Ford looked when he used to wear the hat. I had stock options from Billy as high as the volcano he'd built in the main lobby. I was still single, living just off the fifteenth green at God's Acre, carried a five-handicap in golf, still drank Scotch, smoked the cigars I hadn't given away to whoever was my new best friend that week. When everything happened that changed my life and the course of pro football history, at least for a little while, I had just broken up with Stacy, who made Cindy Crawford look like a boy.

Stacy was a dancer in our Show Tune Revue and an aspiring actress.

"Let me ask you something, Jammer," Billy said the first time I described Stacy as an actress. "Aren't they all?"

I'd worked in television, bartended for a while in New York, invested in a couple of places there, even opened a place of my own. When that finally went bust, Billy'd offered me the gig at Amazing Grace and I became the Jammer. There I was. I knew everybody, drove a cream-colored Mercedes convertible, and generally felt like that if I ever did retire I'd have to come out of retirement to do it. Billy said I was the closest thing to a son he ever had. The only thing his ex-wife, Roxanne, had ever given him was a daughter who'd turned into a Rodeo Drive junkie and was currently married to a tattooed mutant from a rock band known as Fourth Level of Hell.

I had my secrets, but who doesn't?

Life was good for the Jammer.

That was before God became such a cutup.

Usually on Monday I didn't do anything except pretend I was still sleeping when Stacy woke up wanting to play Wounded Soldier/ Naughty Nurse.

That was before she'd informed me one morning, the Vuitton bags I'd bought her packed by the front door, that I was hampering her growth as an artist and as a woman.

"Face it, Jack," she said in her exit scene. "You're a controller. Hopi told me that even after the breast reduction and I just didn't want to listen."

Hopi was her yoga instructor and inner trainer.

Weekends for me, especially weekends when Billy had a big fight going, were as close as I ever got to hard time. And we'd had the fight of the year on Friday, between TruValue Jones, the reigning heavyweight champ, and his number-one challenger, White Trash Bobby White. The two of them had been ducking each other for years, but Billy'd finally thrown so much money at them that even the bed bugs who managed them couldn't say no. The fight seemed to be dead even by just about everybody's accounts going into the twelfth and final round, then thirty seconds before the end, White Trash Bobby White kneed TruValue in the balls as they were being told to come out of a clinch. White Trash was disqualified, and as soon as he was, his walk-around guys—all wearing militia outfits—had a World Wrestling Federation death match with Tru-Value's boys, who wore Los Angeles Laker road jerseys, snap-brim fedoras and jack boots. By the time Billy's security broke everything up, the two managers were already underneath the ring setting a date for the rematch.

At Amazing Grace, of course.

Billy and I celebrated in his penthouse that night with a guest list of usual suspects that might have looked this way on the official scorecard later:

- Two U.S. Senators, one from each side of the aisle.
- Three members of the NBA's all-time top fifty players.
- One network morning host, male.
- One network morning host, female, a frisky little thing who we all agreed afterward had become the fifty-first member of the all-time NBA team.
- Two studio heads.
- A microchip billionaire who would end up winning all the Hot Tub Awards.

- Two members of the 1999 U.S. Women's World Cup soccer team who wanted to take off a lot more than their team jerseys.
- The previously-thought-to-be-gay leading man who was the silver medalist in the hot tub.
- Four Laker Girls.
- Half the chorus line from the Show Tune Revue, minus Stacy, who was already in L.A. auditioning for a sitcom about a Playmate-turned-meteorologist and her zany friends.
- The precociously young country star who admitted after drinking up all the margaritas that she'd lied about her age, and apparently hadn't spent nearly as much time in that church choir back in Nashville as *People* magazine said she did.

I left before the morning prayer and got about six hours of sleep before eventually dragging my own remains over to the spa at the hotel in the late afternoon to continue a daily regimen of torture that the doctors had all assured me would hold off a knee replacement for at least a few more years.

The injury had happened my sophomore year at UCLA, in the fourth quarter of our game with USC, which used to decide a trip to the Rose Bowl before the computer nerds from the NCAA ruined college football. I'll tell you more about the play later and why it broke down the way it did for our quarterback, Bubba Royal, and me. Just know that it ended with a steroid-crazed 327-pound football terrorist named Mountain Montoya doing everything to my anterior cruciate ligament except drive over it with the Grand Cherokee the Southern Cal boosters had given him.

I never played another down of college football, but did earn the right to make walking up a flight of steps feel like an Olympic event forever.

I hated exercise, but I didn't want a knee from Home Depot, either.

So I found time every day to make a tour of the Nautilus equipment in Billy's gym. I figured I'd give it my usual tour and then spend an hour in the sauna trying to remember why I'd ended up playing White House intern with one of the senators' wives. By then it would be time to watch the preseason Monday night game between the Hawks and the Dallas Cowboys.

Billy came through in dark glasses about five o'clock. He's got thick black hair that is either a tribute to his Sicilian ancestors or Grecian Formula, a washboard chest that has cost him hundreds of thousands in personal trainers over the years, a nose that he's broken seven times as a young middleweight, and coloring that even I now describe as dark-complected after hanging around him all these years. In the half-light of his own lounges, you could even call him ruggedly handsome, in a sort of five-crime-families way.

"Was that you I saw going into the screening room with the senator's wife?" he said.

"I felt bad for her," I said. "The potential-next-vice-president of the United States had disappeared with a Laker Girl by then."

I groaned through another leg lift.

"Two," he said.

"Two?" I said. "Like hell. This is my third rep."

"I meant two Laker Girls," Billy said. "By the way, how can you be working out when I know you feel like the same brand of shit I do?"

I said, "A man without structure in his life is just a smaller version of White Trash Bobby White."

"Good point. Where we watching the game?"

"How about your home away from home?"

I was talking about the penthouse suite Billy kept here, in addition to his real home, a rather amazing replica of the Vatican that took up pretty much of the whole front nine at God's Acre. The first time Billy took me through it, I only had one question afterward: "Where's the gift shop?"

"I'll see you at six," he said, which was the time *Monday Night Football* came on in the West.

I did another leg lift that must have sounded like some kind of Swedish movie to the rest of the gym.

"I want your solemn word on something," I said. "No girls."

"Is this some kind of allergic reaction to the senator's wife, or just a love of the Hawks?"

"You know me. Despite everything, I love my Hawks. Now leave me alone."

"I never figured this Hawks thing," he said.

"Don't try," I said. "It's like cracking one of those World War Two codes that they have in really bad spy novels."

He walked out past the aerobics class, where a lot of girls in no clothes, most of them from the Show Tune Revue, were working out to old Donna Summer disco music. He cocked his head toward them as if maybe he wanted to invite the whole class to *Monday Night Football*. I gave him the finger and he was gone.

I looked up at the clock. I was a half hour from being finished. After I went through the machines, I liked to sit on the exercise bike and watch blue-haired girls try to beat the shit out of their parents on afternoon talk shows. But on this day I decided to watch CNN's *Headline News*, in case I had missed any terrorism or stock market crashes overnight.

Some shrieking kid had just done the sports when the "Breaking News" screen came on.

The next thing I saw was his face.

It wasn't up there because he'd won the Nobel Prize.

They let the boy anchor handle it.

I was fumbling with the volume switch on the headphones I was wearing, so I missed the start of it.

". . . in his luxury box at the stadium when he was stricken," the boy anchor said. "He was taken by ambulance to nearby Montefiore Hospital in the Bronx, but was pronounced dead on arrival."

There was a live shot of the inside of the stadium now, where the Hawks-Cowboys game would be played later. Behind the girl twink doing the standup, I was pretty sure I could see Bubba Royal, now the veteran quarterback of the Hawks, light-tossing to someone whose number I couldn't recognize.

I didn't even notice that I'd gotten off the bike now and was right on top of the television, or that Billy had come back and was standing next to me.

I took off the headphones.

"The set was on in my office," he said.

I nodded and started to put the headphones back on, but Billy waved me off and just turned the volume up loud enough to be heard over the machines.

Some fat guy started to bitch from the rowing machine and Billy turned and gave him a look and said, "Shut up or check out."

". . . one of the most popular owners in the National Football League and certainly one of the most colorful," the boy anchor was saying.

Now he looked straight into the camera, trying to play two parts all at once: Frank and Earnest.

"The one thing he never did across a long career during which he became one of the most beloved figures in the game was win a Super Bowl. This was supposed to be his year. Now it ends two weeks before the Hawks play their first regular-season game."

He paused here for the big finish.

Bring it home.

"Big Tim Molloy," the boy anchor said. "Dead at the age of seventy-seven, survived by his second wife Kitty and the Molloy twins, Ken and Babs, who were with their father in his luxury box when he suddenly collapsed, and a third child . . ."

"Me," I said out loud. "Jack Molloy as the Beaver."

two

hadn't spoken to my father in five years. My choice, not his, though it's not as if he'd held on to my leg when I was leaving his office at Molloy Stadium for the trip to Kennedy and the flight to Vegas.

One of the last things he'd said that day, as I recall, went something like this: "Molloy"—it's what he'd always called me—"you've apparently grown up into having all of the qualities of a real dog. Excepting loyalty, of course."

It was one last heartwarming family drama for the two of us.

I'd always told myself that I'd make things right with him before he finally grabbed his chest or pulled the queen of diamonds at his annual physical. But as usual, he was was one step ahead of me.

Here was something else he'd told me in his office that last day, one last parting gift of Words to Live By, courtesy of Big Tim Molloy:

"You're not going to figure out that I actually knew what the hell I was talking about until the cardinal's giving the eulogy and Kitty's inherited my half of Palm Beach."

Kitty was my stepmother. She'd walked right in about fourteen months after my mother had died and scooped up all the goodies before the old man knew what hit him. She was the interior decorator he'd hired to fix up his new house in East Hampton, because the old one, he said, was my mother's, down to the dust on the books.

Decorator to the stars turned up to be nothing more than a cover for Kitty Drucker-Cole. The only real ambition she'd ever had, as far as any of us could ever tell, was Second Wife.

"Good heavens, Jack," she'd said at the wedding, after a little too much champagne, "any fool can arrange the deck chairs."

It is probably worth mentioning here that before my father, Kitty Drucker-Cole had screwed about half of the eligible bachelors on the Forbes 400, and more than a few who weren't. Eligible or bachelors, I mean. The old man didn't care. He was like every rich old fool I've ever met.

He was sure she loved him.

The old man had made his money in real estate, the generation before Trump came along and acted as if he'd invented all the tall buildings. Big Tim Molloy was the son of a bookmaker who'd operated out of a saloon in East New York, when that wasn't the burned-out-building capital of the world. Francis Timothy Molloy, my grandfather, known as Frank, was one of the Brooklyn characters of his time. From everything the old man had told me and even some things I'd read in the newspaper clippings the old man had kept, I must have gotten at least some of the Jammer in me from him. He ran with the sports crowd at Toots Shor's, owned a piece of a few fighters, knew everybody from Dempsey to Joe DiMaggio. My grandmother had died giving birth to my father, and after that Frankie Molloy had decided he wasn't going to wait around for the fun in his life to start.

He always told my father, "There isn't going to be any inheritance, because I plan to spend it all."

He was lying a little bit. He died during my father's senior year at Fordham, where he was majoring in legitimate business. There was about a million dollars left, and Big Tim Molloy immediately started buying up great chunks of lower Manhattan in the Wall Street area, way before that's where all the money was. He was always a step ahead. It would be that way his whole life. In the sixties, he managed to buy up about half the potato fields in the Hamptons, before everybody else figured out that was the play out there. He bought his first house out there for $85,000 and eventually sold it for six million and change.

Somewhere along the way, he decided he wanted to have a football team. He told me that Frankie Molloy wasn't around very much when he was a kid, that he was raised by a succession of Irish nannies, but that Sundays were the magic day for him, because Sundays meant Giants football games at the Polo Grounds. Frankie used to show him off in his church clothes and the camel topcoat that was a miniature version of Frank's and tell everybody on the 50-yard line, "This is my son Timothy, who will grow up to be president someday, providing he can't find something on the level to do first."

The old man was always on the level, with the right politicians and the right charities and a front seat at St. Patrick's on Sunday, and any time there was a big-ticket funeral. But he always carried around those Sundays with Frankie Molloy. The old man always had it in the back of his mind that he'd own a football team someday.

That way he could show off on his own kid on the 50.

He tried to get the Jets right before Joe Namath invented the Super Bowl, but by then Sonny Werblin and Phil Iselin and Leon Hess were dug in, and everybody knew that when the other two were gone, Hess would be still standing, which he did until he died at about the age of ninety-seven owning all the oil and all the gas stations. He knew he'd never get a shot at the Giants, even though it pissed him off when Robert Tisch, one of the New York real estate guys in the old man's weight class, got half after Tim Mara died.

So Tim Molloy settled for the Memphis Marauders, out of the old American Football League, one of the teams that made the cut when the AFL and the NFL merged in 1967. He bought them in 1977, and had moderate success with them over the next ten years, even making the AFC championship game—the game before the Super Bowl—one year against the Dolphins. When Hess took the Jets over to Giants Stadium in New Jersey in the eighties, the old man made his move.

"They call themselves the New York Jets," he said. "The New York Giants. Playing their home games in New Jersey. What kind of bullshit geography is that?"

The old man always had a way of making New Jersey sound like Iran or Iraq or one of those countries they came up with after Russia got cut up into more pieces than the phone company.

It took him about five years of finessing two NFL commissioners, his fellow owners, Leon Hess, his dear friend Wellington Mara, Bob Tisch, the television networks, and every politician in New York City with a private bank account. The Memphis Marauders became the New York Hawks. Molloy Stadium got built, mostly with the old man's money, up the Deegan Expressway from Yankee Stadium, where the old Yonkers Raceway once stood. When everybody bitched that there was no place to put a third game for a New York/New Jersey team on Sunday, the old man showed them how they could move the first game of the traditional doubleheader back to noon in the east, then have the next kickoff be at 3:30, then have three or four Sunday night games starting at 7:15.

That way, the old man reasoned, you could have three major networks in play on Sundays and let ABC keep *Monday Night Football.*

Barbara Walters interviewed the old man on *20/20* one time and asked him what his secret was and the old man quoted Frank Molloy: "I've never come across a single roadblock in business that couldn't be eliminated by a suitcase full of money."

His dream was that I'd go off to Notre Dame and score touchdowns for Jesus and then end up playing for the Hawks someday. I decided on UCLA when I took a good look at the UCLA song girls while their basketball team was winning another national championship.

Tim Molloy never did understand why I wanted to play in front of the Polynesian-looking girl, third from the left, and not the prancing leprechaun at South Bend.

Maybe the failure to communicate started there.

When I blew out my knee, the old man decided to put his money on a different dream. His, not mine. He hadn't grown up to be president, as Frank Molloy used to tell the boys at the Polo Grounds he would. But I was going to be president of the New York Hawks, even if I had never suggested for a minute of my whole life that I had any interest or ambition to be part of the family business.

"I wasn't ever any good being on a team," I told my father. "Now I'm supposed to run one?"

"The alternative is J and Crew," he said, which is how he referred to the evil twins, Kenny and Babs.

"They've been sucking around the team since they started dressing alike," I said. "They want this. I don't. Give it to them and watch them finally turn on each other. It'll be like watching killer tropical fish try to rip each other to shreds."

"They don't like football," he said. "They like being famous. I think it's some course they must have taken at whatever sissy school it was they went to."

Vassar, I reminded him.

"Jesus," he said, "Vassar. Who're they playing this week?"

"I'm not ready to be a grownup," I said.

"You're never going to be ready, goddamit!"

"Excuse me for wanting to screw around for a while instead of going right to professional screwing like you did."

"At least the kind of screwing I did was lucrative," he said.

"I don't want to work for you."

"You could have skipped the part at the end, Molloy. You just don't want to work."

"I'm producing games now. What do you call that?"

"A new way for you to impress bimbos."

"At least I've managed not to marry any."

That was another night, at a place I had a small piece of, called T.J. Tucker, that ended up with a chalk line around it.

I wasn't sure what I wanted to be. But I knew I didn't want to be Little Tim Molloy. And having grown up around the team, watching things from the inside, I had already figured something out: Football was becoming less and less about the games than it was about the owners, and the revenue streams, and all the shit that grownups had started wearing, like going to a game was going door-to-door on Halloween. It was owners who wanted the whole thing to be about them, general managers who wanted the same thing. And coaches. And the cockroaches passing themselves off as agents. And every spiffy wide receiver who came out of college with $10 million in bonus money and a contract to write a book before he'd actually read one.

So I tried television for a while, worked my way up through the ranks, thought I had actually shown enough to get a crack at being on the No. 1 team at CBS, which meant sitting in the truck on Super Sunday. Except one day Rupert Murdoch's network, Fox, came along to blindside CBS and everybody else with an offer of $400 million a year to televise National Football Conference games, and just like that, CBS was out of the football business. I didn't want to change sports, or change networks.

I decided to hang around New York for a while, while I reviewed my options.

One night I lost a bet to Johnny "Shirts" Hughes, a bartender at Peartrees on 49th and First, and had to take his weekend shift for a month. And all of a sudden, everybody I knew from football and television and various modeling agencies and just hanging around started showing up at Peartrees on Saturday and Sunday nights. Sundays were normally pace nights in Manhattan. But now Peartrees was a place where you could find a tight end from the Hawks in deep conversation with a soap opera actress, who'd be complaining that the producers had threatened to kill her in a car crash if she didn't lose weight. You'd hear the director of *Monday Night Football* saying that he couldn't decide which of his announcers to kill first.

We made big news one night when Jimmy (the Greek) Snyder, who was still working the pregame show on CBS in those days, took a swing at his partner, Brent Musburger, after both of them had been more than slightly overserved.

It was basically what we were all looking for in those days, which meant one large permissive room.

When Tommy O'Neill and Tucker Frederickson opened up T.J. Tucker, down on 59th and First, I went in with them. Then I had my own place up on Third Avenue, one block over from Elaine's, called Montana. Montana became the new hot place for a while.

Then a funny thing happened, as I was on my way to being the new Toots Shor:

It wasn't the hot place anymore.

It had happened to a thousand other places in New York and now it was happening to mine. There were about a thousand good reasons, and the only one that mattered was this:

People wanted to go somewhere else.

I accepted that about as easy as some of my partners accepted cocaine not being the smartener they told themselves it was.

Pretty soon my partners were gone, and so were the profits I'd made from T.J. Tucker, and so were the profits I'd made the first year at Montana, and I was starting to turn my trust fund into an ATM machine.

By then everybody in town seemed to know that Montana was on its way to being a Korean grocery except me.

That's when Billy Grace, who'd been a regular with me all the way back to Peartrees, mostly because he said I had this way of attracting tits and legs and hair and faces, asked me if I wanted to go to Las Vegas with him. We were sitting around Montana at about 4:00 A.M., waiting for our dates to come back from their two hundredth trip to the ladies' room.

"Jack," he said, "maybe you and the big city need a trial separation."

I grinned at him, and made a gesture at a front room that was empty at that moment except for the two of us, the two Deltas in the ladies' room, and my bartender, Joe Healey.

"What," I said to Billy, "and give up show business?"

Billy lit up an unfiltered Camel, when he was one of the last guys left doing unfiltered Camels.

"I love you like a son, Jack, but I've got to level with you here: It's not like being a free spirit is working out so fucking great for you."

I had the place sold within two weeks, sold my apartment two weeks after that. Finally came the day when I went over to the old man's office at Molloy Stadium to tell him that I was going to work for Billy Grace instead of him.

"What," he said, "all the Gottis were spoken for?"

There was nothing for me there.

"Casino host," he said, looking at me over his thick black reading glasses, nodding.

The old man had gotten a little jowly by then, and his hair had turned white, and there were mornings, after he'd had a few too many the night before, when what was once a classic leading man's nose now looked as if it had a battery inside it. But you could still see the good-looking bastard he'd been when he was younger. I remember my mother looking at him one night at the other end of the dinner table and saying, "My very own Cary Grant, just shorter."

"Your mother would have been very proud," he said, still nodding. "She'd actually hoped you'd grow up to be a croupier."

"I just need a change of scenery, is all," I said.

"How about an office?" he said.

I stood up, shook his hand.

"I'll stay in touch, Pop," I said.

"You used to be a better liar, Molloy," he said. He shuffled some of the papers on his desk, looking everywhere now except at me. "Now you're not even good at that."

Now he was dead. In the gym at Amazing Grace, Billy shut off the television set, tossed me a towel.

"I don't suppose anybody here would like to go up to the suite and get completely shitfaced, would they?" he said.

The funeral was at St. Patrick's Cathedral and had everything except the floats and Rockettes they give you in the Canyon of Heroes when the Yankees win the World Series again. But when you'd overtipped as many bishops and politicians as the old man had, they sent you off with all the trimmings. There were certain bullshit traditions in New York that never seemed to change, and hero funerals were still one of them.

Even if the only truly heroic thing Big Tim Molloy had ever done outside buying and selling with both hands was somehow convince everybody that having pro football back within the city limits was more important to New York than more cops.

"Look around," he said one time when I was a teenager. We were in St. Patrick's that day for the funeral of a Bronx borough president who'd once stolen everything except the Deegan Expressway. "Spread it around enough, and they all cry at your funeral."

It was the last Thursday in August, and the place was packed. Vince Cahill, the Hawks coach, had brought the whole team. The inside of the church felt like a hot plate, but the players looked happy, mostly because they weren't at practice.

Tony Bennett sang "Ave Maria."

The cardinal said with a straight face that he was sure Tim Molloy was up in heaven petitioning the Lord to make every day a New York Sunday in the fall.

I nearly barked out a laugh on that one before I managed to turn it into something that sounded like a coughing fit from my seat in the second row, behind Kenny and Babs. Kitty, sitting next to me, drove one of her high heels into the toe of my buckled Cole•Haans.

The commissioner said, "Some people called Tim Molloy a visionary, but I always thought of him as a dreamer."

The mayor was next. He still had the combover of thinning hair that I remembered from before I'd left town, which meant that his hairstyle still brought the word "drape" to mind.

The mayor described the old man's memory as "a permanent part of the skyline of the city."

I whispered, perhaps a little too loudly, "Jesus . . . H. . . . Christ."

Kitty, with a ventriloquist-like control of her mouth, whispered back "I mean it, Jack, shut . . . the . . ." just as Babs interrupted her by standing up right in front of us and beginning her drama-queen walk to the pulpit.

She was wearing a black dress that I guessed had cost more money than the coffin. I hadn't seen her in five years, either, and noticed that she seemed to have been on some kind of all-you-can't-eat contest since I'd left. She was about two minutes into a presentation about the connection between God, family and football when she talked about the awesome responsibility she and Kenny felt to "honor Daddy's memory by taking the Hawks into the next football millennium."

Babs started blubbering then, the cardinal had to come over and console her, and it was here, for some reason, that the chorus broke into a medley that began with "Nearer My God to Thee" and ended with a rousing version of "New York, New York."

They'd selected a number of current and former Hawks to carry the coffin out. Babs and her husband, Chappy, and Kenny and his wife, Ashley, were next down the aisle.

Kitty and I were next. She was dabbing away imaginary tears.

She said, "How long are you in town for, Jack?"

I nodded up ahead to Kenny and Babs. "I thought I'd just stick around for the tag team match between your lawyers and theirs."

By the time we got outside, they were loading the coffin into the back of the hearse for the ride up to the Gates of Heaven Cemetery in Valhalla, which had been the most exclusive address for dead New York celebrities all the way back to Babe Ruth.

Kenny and Babs got into their limo, Kitty and I got into ours. When I sat down next to her, she gave my knee a squeeze that I thought was somewhat more than motherly.

"You're still a bad, bad boy, aren't you, Jack?"

Before I could say anything, she sighed.

"God," she said in a throaty voice. "I love bad boys."

three

here were enough lawyers in the conference room to form a conga line. The only ones I recognized were from cable television. I had become convinced over the past few years that there was a repertory company of them, on twenty-four-hour call every time there'd be an O.J. or a JonBenet or a Monica.

One of them, from Kitty's team, was a Georgetown guy named Paul Janzen. I remembered him doing a lot of Geraldo and Larry around the time when anybody who'd ever practiced law was on television asking the age-old question about whether or not a blowjob in the Oval Office was considered sex or just the president unwinding a little bit.

Janzen had red hair that he wore in bangs and a red beard and a bow tie. He had the jacket to his suit off and I noticed he was wearing suspenders that had the Hawks logo—a sleek hawk flying past the top of the Empire State Building—all over them.

I noticed he also seemed pretty friendly with Kitty Drucker-Cole Molloy.

"Good morning, Jack," Kitty'd said when I arrived.

I grinned at her.

"Mommy!"

Now she gave me a sigh that landed like a bowling ball.

"Do you know Paul Janzen?" she said.

Janzen stood up now. He was smaller than I thought he'd be, just because he had a voice he'd borrowed from James Earl Jones.

"Your father was a dear friend," he said.

My father, I remembered, thought of lawyers as slugs with brief-cases.

"I used to hear a lot about you," he said.

"Well, we have something in common, then," I said. "I used to hear a lot about me, too."

I went to the other end of the long table and began counting the house. There were three lawyers with Kenny and Babs. Kitty had Janzen and a black guy who looked like a road-show Johnnie Cochran. Modest Afro, gangster pinstripes, blue shirt with white collar, and a tie that looked like a mustard stain.

I idly wondered when all the lawyers, black and white, started dressing like pimps instead of undertakers.

The black guy peeled away from Kitty and Janzen, came down and introduced himself to me. Darnell Winfield was his name. He seemed to be in charge. He went to the head of the table at the other end, smiled brilliantly, dramatically clicked open his briefcase and said, "Okay, boys and girls, let's see what's under the tree."

He went through the estate laws of New York in so much detail my hair started to hurt toward the end.

Then came all the charitable donations, the biggest chunk going to Special Olympics, just because the Special Olympics meant the Kennedys, and that was always good enough for the old man.

Kitty didn't get half of Palm Beach, but she did get the house in East Hampton and the apartment on Central Park West.

The grandchildren—Kenny and Babs each had one daughter—got trust funds like the one I had gotten, which means they couldn't even sniff the money until they were thirty.

Even before Darnell talked about the Hawks, Kitty, Kenny and Babs got what I considered a heartstopping amount of money.

"Wait, Darnell, there must be a mistake," Kenny said sarcastically. "You haven't said anything about Jack."

"You just sit there and be nice, Kenny," Babs said, and made Kenny sound sincere.

"Yeah, Ken," I said. "Sit."

"Finally," Darnell Winfield said, ignoring us all, "we come to the last part of Tim Molloy's last will and testament, which involves the ownership of, and dispositon of, the New York Hawks football team."

He went through what felt like five minutes of "whereas," and then said, "Appropriately, Kenneth and Barbara will receive fifty percent of the team, and that fifty percent will involve all marketing, ticketing, parking, rights fees related to those areas, and concessions."

Kenny said, "But . . ."

Darnell held up a hand.

I noticed Kitty squeezing Paul Janzen's furry little hand on top of the table.

"The entire football operation of the Hawks, all football-related matters and complete and final authority in matters of personnel and payroll, I hereby leave to . . ."

Darnell paused here, looked briefly at Kitty, and then said, ". . . to my oldest son, John Francis Molloy."

There was a bit of chaos then, though not as much as the *New York Post* would report the next day. I was there, and can tell you that Kitty did not bite Paul Janzen as she climbed across the table and attempted to rip the will out of Darnell Winfield's hands before Babs, coming from Darnell's blind side, could beat her to it.

Kenny had pulled his knees up against his chest and was making what sounded like hen noises.

When order was finally restored, Darnell managed a grin.

"I've always thought about making one of these a Pay-Per-View deal," he said.

He cleared his throat, either for effect or because of a pretty solid shot Babs had landed below the ear, before one of Darnell's partners had cut her off.

Darnell said, "There's one last line here at the bottom, directed to Jack from his father. I will read it exactly as written, in his own hand:

" 'Okay, Molloy. You're up.' "

four

I guess my favorite headline, if I'd had to pick one, was in the *Post* and read this way:

"CRAPS!"

The smaller headline underneath, next to what looked like my prom picture, said: "Black Sheep Casino Boy Inherits Hawks."

The *News*, the other tabloid in New York, went this way:

"OH, BROTHER!"

Underneath theirs was a smaller headline about the prodigal son returning, next to an adorable picture of me standing in front of Amazing Grace with Billy and some of his friends, most of whom *News* readers probably thought had been wiped out about halfway through the first *Godfather* movie.

This was the morning after the reading of the will. I was doing coffee in the living room of the suite I'd decided to spring for at the Sherry-Netherland. I'd told the switchboard operator to hold my calls unless a man named Grace called. I had the New York papers, plus *USA Today*, spread out all around me on the floor, just in case I couldn't make it to the bathroom in time.

On page 3 of both tabloids was the same picture of Kenny and Babs standing outside the Sony building, where Darnell had his offices. Kenny looked as if he'd been shot with one of those sedative darts they use on animals that have escaped from the zoo.

Babs looked as if she'd just swallowed bees.

"I loved Daddy very much," she was quoted as saying in the accompanying story. "But clearly his mind gave out before his heart did."

Down further in the story Kenny said: "If my brother Jack was Dad's first choice to run the Hawks, I'm just wondering who was second, the parking attendant at the Mirage?"

Kitty also said that the only surprise bigger than me getting the team was that our father had actually remembered my name.

The NFL commissioner, Wick Sanderson, told the *Times* that the league would be running a routine background check on me.

"Of course," the commissioner said, "we always hope there won't be any organized crime issues, especially with Las Vegas and casinos and gambling on Mr. Molloy's résumé."

Coach Vince Cahill, bless his heart, went on ESPN and said, "I'm used to dealing with [bleeped out] children, I suppose I can [bleeped out] work for one."

Later in the same interview, which was being replayed from the previous night's *SportsCenter* on ESPN, Cahill said, "What's he been doing out there, anyway, besides hitting on [bleeped out] sixteen and staying on seventeen?"

The twink doing the interview threw it back to the studio, saying what an irascible old character Vince was.

Kitty Drucker-Cole Molloy told Cindy Adams, the gossip columnist for the *Post*, "My husband is more full of surprises dead than all my other husbands combined were alive."

Liz Bolton was the president of the Hawks, the only woman with that title in the National Football League.

She was unavailable for comment.

The only person who didn't treat me like someone who'd spent the previous five years checking slot machines for spare change was Pete Stanton, the general manager of the Hawks. He went all the way back to Memphis with the old man.

"You know who didn't do many dumb things?" Stanton said on Channel 4. "Mr. Tim Molloy didn't do many dumb things. I'm going to assume he knew what he was doing on this until it's proven otherwise."

This was the local news that came on before *The Today Show*. The sports guy looked into the camera after the sound bite from Pete Stanton and smirked.

"Sounds to me like somebody looking to hold on to his job. Back to you, Abdul and Chi Lin."

I waited until seven, when I knew somebody would be working the switchboard at Molloy Stadium. I didn't have Pete Stanton's extension, but I remembered from the old days that he liked to get to work when the coaches did.

He picked up on the first ring. I told him to get his ass over to the Sherry before he started cutting whichever defensive backs had tested positive in training camp.

"How about our Number-One goddam bonus-incentived-up-the-ass draft choice from Notre Dame?"

"No shit?"

"A possible, not a definite. I'll know by the end of the week. Maybe his pee pee was just cloudy because he has a urinary tract infection. Or because he's been screwing around like a sailor on leave since he escaped from South Bend."

Stanton paused.

"Am I really being summoned?"

"Actually," I said, "you could stay there and wait for Kitty to show up. I heard her say something about wanting to meet with you and Liz Bolton first thing this morning."

Pete Stanton said, "I'm on my way."

"When you get to the front desk, just ask for the bunker. Eva and I will be waiting for you."

He brought the Hawks' public relations man, Brian Goldberg, with him. Goldberg had red thinning hair, a freckled face, horn-rimmed glasses and looked to be the captain of the high school debate team.

"Don't worry," Stanton said. "He can drive a car and drink legally and everything."

"Plus, you can trust me," Goldberg said.

"Tell young Mr. Molloy what you call his brother and sister."

The kid grinned.

"Pit and Bull."

Pete said, "Brian's gonna be the guy in charge of convincing people your father didn't leave the team to Wayne Newton."

Pete Stanton was even more darkly complected than Billy Grace. He had thick black hair that kept falling into sleepy eyes, and looked as if he already needed to shave again. He was wearing the same thing he'd been wearing when they interviewed him on television and what he seemed to be wearing every time I saw him interviewed on television: blue blazer, open-necked golf shirt. He was out of Baltimore, where he'd started out as a sportswriter, and then moved on to a columnist's job in Memphis. The way I'd always heard it, he and the old man ended up drunk one night in the bar of the Peabody Hotel. They got into it about the team and the way the old man was running it and finally the old man said, "If you know so goddamned much about football, why don't you try making a living at it?"

He started out as the Marauders' p.r. man and then worked his way up to assistant general manager and then got the big office when the team moved to New York.

We moved out to the terrace, which overlooked Central Park. Down to our left was the studio for Bryant Gumbel's version of *Today*, next door to FAO Schwarz. The show must have just gone off the air, because the crowd of people who'd come to watch from the street as Gumbel's co-host tried to get a word in was starting to disperse.

I had poured more coffee for everybody.

"Well," I said brightly, "how do the linebackers look?"

"Overrated, overpaid, and occasionally sociopathic," Stanton said. "But it's early, of course."

"Okay, enough small talk," I said. "What the hell do I do now?"

Brian handled that one.

"Pete and I were talking about this all the way over in the car, when we weren't going through the papers hoping there'd be another picture of Babs looking like she wanted to gnaw Kenny's arm off. And there's only one important question: Do you actually want to do this?"

Billy Grace had asked me the same question when he'd finally gotten through about midnight.

"I've watched more sports news than a couch geek," Billy'd said on the phone. "And from what I can gather so far, the league don't want you, your coach don't want you and your family wants you freaking dead. Other than that, and what the estate taxes are gonna do to you, you've come out of the blocks like the prince of the city."

"I know this is supposed to be every red-blooded American boy's number-one jerkoff dream," I told him. "But what the hell do I really know about running a football team? I could put my half up for sale tomorrow. What did the candy-ass Saints go for a couple of years ago? Eight hundred million? Help me out here, what's half of that?"

"Now who's a candy-ass?" he said.

"But an extremely wealthy one," I said.

Billy Grace said, "I'll leave you with one thought, and then I've got to go, because I've got some issues with the senator."

"He's still there?"

"He's decided he's in love with either Bambi or Thumper, I can't remember which one."

I reminded him he was going to leave me with one thought. Billy got off on what he called tangibles sometimes.

"You're the Jammer," he said. "You've handled bigger assholes than these guys with one hand," and hung up.

I told Pete and Brian what Billy Grace had said. I told them about Billy and Billy's life and explained to them what it meant to be the Jammer in Vegas. I told them about how shitty things had ended between my father and me. I told them I'd always felt like more than a bookmaker's grandson than Tim Molloy's son.

I also mentioned in passing that I knew more about the Hawks and Hawks history than anybody living, now that the old man was dead.

I talked for a long time and then I stopped.

"It's a race to see who can screw you the fastest, the way I see it," Pete said.

"Or who hates you the most, the twins or the commissioner," Brian Goldberg said.

"Or the other owners," Pete said.

I asked whether they'd stolen this pep talk from Rockne or Lombardi.

"You know what everybody would really like?" Brian Goldberg said. "For you to end up with nothing."

"They've got between now and the Super Bowl to figure out the best way to bust you," Pete Stanton said.

He stood up.

"So," he said, "you about ready to go to work?"

five

ince Cahill was in his second season as the Hawks' coach. The old man had hired him away from the Saints after Cahill had won the Super Bowl with them, telling the reporters he didn't want to go out like Leon Hess.

When they asked him what he meant, he said, "Waiting until next season doesn't help you a whole hell of a lot if you die this season."

The old man gave him a whole pile of goodies, everything Cahill wanted except the title of team president. Pat Riley had gotten it in basketball, along with a piece of the team. Jimmy Johnson had it with the Miami Dolphins. Bill Parcells had the same deal when he coached the Jets. It was the same kind of dick-swinging I saw with athletes all the time. There was a golf tournament in Vegas one time for all the NBA coaches, and a few of them were having lunch one day at God's Acre. Tariq Mooh-Motum, the coach of the Pistons that season, got to talking about why this tattooed point guard had forced a trade so he could go somewhere else and make the same kind of money one of his teammates was making in Minnesota or Portland or some fucking place.

"It's the 'Wanna Be the Man Disease,'" Tariq said. "Number-one killer virus we got, running through the whole league the way the clap used to."

Big Tim couldn't let Cahill be the man with the Hawks, because they already had a woman. Liz Bolton was team president when Cahill was hired and she still had the job. According to Pete, it made Cahill mad enough to eat jockstraps that hers was bigger.

"Her what?" I asked.

"Title," he said. "Power. Office. You name it."

He was showing me around the downstairs offices at Molloy Stadium.

"She having something going on with my father?"

Stanton grinned.

"You sound like Vince."

"Did she?"

"There's a lot of bastards around here who want to believe it. Vince is just the one who makes the most noise, at least when she's not around. But I'm going to tell you straight up: I think he gave her the job because she's smart."

"But she is pretty good-looking."

He said, "Oh yes."

"Married?"

"Divorced."

We were passing the large area, set off by cubicles, where Vince Cahill's assistant coaches worked.

"Jesus," I said, "how many coaches do we have?"

"Twenty," he said.

"What do they all do?"

"It's like trying to figure out what sportswriters do," he said.

To our left, past the coaches' area, I saw a nameplate on the door that said, "Dr. Gerald Crenshaw, Team Psychologist."

I pointed to it.

"Team psychologist?"

Stanton said, "Yes sir."

"We have a team psychologist?" I said.

Stanton said, "Where have you been, Jack? You say you follow the league? Everybody's got a team psychologist now, even if not everybody calls them that." He lowered his voice. "It's just one more thing I have to work around. I go out and find some absolute running/throwing assassin at Jerkwater A&M, some guy who's so big and strong and fast I can't decide whether to make him the next Walter Payton or the next Peyton Manning. But it doesn't mean shit around here if it turns out he wet his bed or has mommy issues."

"Jesus," I said, "a team psychologist. Where's the anger-management counselor?"

A female voice behind me said, "I think you already passed his office."

I turned around and there she was.

I tried to give her the killer smile that always worked with tourist women. "I don't suppose you'd . . ."

"Even be here if Pete hadn't asked me to blow off a breakfast meeting in the city," Liz Bolton said.

I started to put my hand out, but she was already past us, saying, "The elevator is this way."

Pete leaned close to me and said, "As long as you don't make any sudden movements, you should be fine."

L iz Bolton was about five-eight, with short blond hair and blue eyes and the kind of perfect, classic nose that can take generations of WASP inbreeding to produce. She wore some kind of dark gray Italian suit, with pants, one of those high-fashion deals where the jacket was long enough to be a skirt. She had the sleeves rolled up to her elbows. The only jewelry was a man-sized Swiss Army watch.

She sat down behind her desk and didn't say anything for a couple of minutes, as if she couldn't decide what to do first, call in the loan or just go ahead and foreclose on the farm.

Behind her, out a huge bay window, was the field at Molloy Stadium, one of those new retro parks made to look like something as old as leather helmets. The old man had wanted the old Polo Grounds, those Sundays with Frankie Molloy, and that is exactly what they gave him. Every time I saw a Hawks home game played there, I thought the whole thing should be in black-and-white.

I said, "Is this a bad time?"

She said, "Are you talking about this morning, or just a generally rotten thoroughly shitty time?"

I leaned forward and set the coffee mug I had with me down on the desk. Without saying a word, she reached into the middle drawer of her desk and slid a coaster across to me, like we were starting a game of air hockey.

"Listen," I said, "if it's any consolation to you, this all shocked me as much as it seemed to shock everybody else."

"Really. That's very reassuring."

"Really," I said. "The way things had gone with my father and me, I wasn't expecting him to leave me anything, except maybe one more lecture."

She was sitting as straight as a model in her chair, one forearm on top of the other. Behind her, out the window, I could see some of the guys on the grounds crew working on what seeemed to be a chewed-up area at midfield.

"So you had no idea he planned to do this?" I said to her.

"None."

"He never even hinted . . ."

"Never."

"So you have no theories about why he did it?"

She leaned forward.

"So you're asking if I have some insight as to why your father gave away something that became his whole life to the biggest disappointment of his life? No, Jack, I can't answer that."

I looked over my shoulder, then turned back to her.

"Sorry," I said. "I just wanted to see if you had your secretary or somebody standing back there with a sign that said, 'Please bust this asshole's balls.' "

"Do me a favor, will you, Jack?" she said. "Go back to Las Vegas with all your colorful gambling friends and showgirls and leave the football operation to the grownups?"

Brian Goldberg had given me her résumé. She had started out as on-air talent at ESPN, switched over to management, finally worked her way up to number two in programming there about the time Disney bought the company and started trying to see if it could make the ESPN logo as famous as mouse ears. Rupert Murdoch hired her away when Fox got football, and then the old man hired her away from Murdoch. She knew football, television, could cheat her way around the salary cap like a champion, was tough as a nose tackle and made every other owner in the league—with the exception of Bitsy Aguilera, the former showgirl and *Price Is Right* appliance girl who'd inherited the Chargers when her husband, Emilio, died in a suspicious boating accident—want to throw her on the table every time she walked into a conference room.

Brian said that Liz Bolton had a way of making Kitty disappear, mainly because Kitty lived in a constant state of fear that someone would mistake her for Liz's mom. The old man had once confessed to both Brian and Pete Stanton that there was no proper dollar value he could put on a skill like that.

Now the old man was gone and she was acting as if the last thing he'd ask her to do was to baby-sit me.

"We've got a chance to win this season," she said. "You at least know how much your father wanted to win a Super Bowl, don't you?"

I told her I vaguely remembered something about that.

"We're not there yet, despite what the geniuses in the media seem to think," she said. "There's still a couple of missing pieces, if Pete can find the players and I can find the cap room. You know how a salary cap works in the NFL, Jack?"

I asked her if she meant the way it was supposed to work, or the way it worked with people like her, who could hide money in bonuses and deferred payments and side deals the way millionaire gangsters hid money in Switzerland. I asked her that if the cap was supposed to be harder than the top of her desk, how come Jerry Jones seemed to find room to sign a Deion or a Rocket every time he needed to?

And how come a team could be under the cap one year and then $20 million over the next year with the same players?

"You mean that salary cap?" I said.

I thought she almost smiled, but it might have been wishful thinking.

"Leave this alone, Jack," she said. "Go away. Or put your half up for sale. Even if you start the process now, it will take the whole season, and by then we'll have had whatever shot we're going to have to win it all this year. You won't be subjected to background checks that are going to be no fun at all for you, you won't drag your brother and sister down with you. Or drag this team down with you. Your father said you never worked at anything. Don't feel as if you have to start now."

Pete said that if I said anything to piss her off, she might quit on me, and that I shouldn't want her to quit, because he needed her, and so would I if I decided to stick around.

I told him I would try to be good.

I stood up now and picked up my mug and slid her coaster back across the desk at her.

"I'm glad we had this chat," I said. "I'll let you know as soon as possible what I plan to do."

When I got to the door, I turned around.

"You know what's kind of amazing?" I said to her.

"What?"

"That I lived in New York City as long as I did and was never married to you."

six

he old man's office, which looked like another one of Kitty's auditions for *Architectural Digest*, was on the 50-yard line, home side of Molloy Stadium, the level below where the luxury boxes were. Most of those, I remembered, were as big as tour buses.

It had to be the 50, that's where he'd come in.

He'd stood up here watching practice one day and said, "Molloy, the only way I can describe it is that it's like owning your first car, just every single day."

It looked as if nobody had been in here since he'd died in his own luxury box upstairs. There was a dead Cohiba in the ashtray, a half-bottle of designer water next to the phone, a yellow legal pad next to the stand for his Mont Blanc fountain pen. He'd never got off fountain pens. Every time he ever put one of his cigars to his mouth, there'd always been ink stains on his fingertips.

Jesus, I thought, the shit you remembered.

I looked at what he'd written on the legal pad. It was a call list. The mayor's name was there, the commissioner's, an agent's name I recognized from the sports section.

And mine.

He'd put three big stars next to mine, as if reminding himself it was important.

What was so important, after all these years, that he had to call me?

"Molloy," I said, my voice sounding as loud as a megaphone, "you're just full of goddam surprises, aren't you?"

I moved around the room. The walls were covered with photographs of him and what looked to be every Big Guy he'd ever known or met. There was Tim Molloy with popes and actors and actresses and Broadway producers like David Merrick, with heads of state and mayors and governors and ex-players going all the way back to his first season in Memphis.

There he was flanked by Joe Louis and Ali, by DiMaggio and Mickey Mantle, by John and Robert Kennedy.

There he was in a tuxedo, looking like a jockey standing between Bill Russell and Wilt Chamberlain.

There he was with my mother, Katherine Conner Molloy, when the two of them were students at Fordham, the old man wearing a letter jacket and my mother in a sweater and plaid skirt.

There he and Kitty were with George and Barbara Bush, apparently at some golf tournament, the old man actually allowing himself to be in the same picture with a Republican.

And there was a whole section, one that must have been added after I left, devoted to me. Me at UCLA, walking off the field at the Rose Bowl after the USC game.

Me on the field with the old man before a Hawks-Giants game.

And one of us together after a high school game I'd played for McBurney.

The one right next to that was a grainy old black-and-white of him and Frank Molloy down on the field at the Polo Grounds.

I went and stood where he used to stand at the window and watched the Hawks do stretching exercises down near the end zone to my right.

"Well, we've moved right in, haven't we? When do Daddy's pictures come down and the ones of the ring-card girls go up?"

Babs.

"We can check after he leaves to see if anything valuable is missing."

Kenny.

They were standing a few feet inside the doorway, apparently trying to glare me through the window and into the mezzanine.

"Hey, sis," I said. "Hey, asshole."

Kenny must have had a haircut after he'd left Darnell Winfield's office. Either that, or he'd spent the night pulling it out.

"Nice look, Ken," I said. "I saw that exact same cut on last month's cover boy for *The Advocate*."

"Yeah," he said. "Right."

Babs said, "We heard you were lurking around the stadium."

"I don't have to lurk," I said. "I'm the boss. It was in all the papers, along with those very attractive shots of you."

She was wearing a short-sleeved summer dress. Her arms, I noticed, looked like swizzle sticks. Her cheekbones looked sharp enough for her to file her nails on.

"You're the boss for now," she said. "We'll see for how long."

Kenny said, "Don't think you're going to get away with this."

He was wearing what he always wore under his dark suit: white shirt, suspenders, rep tie.

I said, "Get away with what, exactly?"

I sat down behind the old man's desk.

"Really," I said. "You're both reasonably intelligent, in your own twisted way. What's the scam here? What's the hustle? We were all in the room yesterday. Johnnie Cochran read the will. I got my half."

I picked up the Mont Blanc and held it the way the old man would have held one of his fat cigars.

"And you got yours."

"Let me ask you something, Jack," Babs said. "Do you really believe that the other owners are going to approve the likes of you to run Daddy's team? They're not."

"What makes you think they'll approve you two?" I said.

"If they decide this ugly little family feud of ours is paralyzing the organization," she said, "they might not. Which would probably give you some sort of perverse pleasure."

Kenny said, "As if you have any other kind."

"What pisses you off the most here?" I said. "That the two of you obviously wasted all these years kissing his ass, or that he passed you over for me?"

Babs came across the room and fell into one of the chairs on the other side of the desk as lightly as a leaf falling to the ground. Kenny stayed right where he was, still trying to look rugged from a distance. He had always been more afraid of me than the dark.

"Daddy obviously had some sort of . . . episode when he did this," she said. "There's no other explanation."

I said, "Maybe he just liked me better, even if he did have a rather unusual way of showing it."

Babs leaned forward and said, "He would have been better off leaving the team to Kitty."

I noticed she still couldn't say her stepmother's name without acting as if a skunk had suddenly sprayed the whole room.

"Now," I said, "you've gone too far."

"You don't want this team, Jack," she said. "You've never wanted any part of this team. Or this family, for that matter. You only played football in the first place because you thought it would be easier to get cheer-leaders into the backseat of your car. Daddy said you were actually happy out in Las Vegas, doing whatever sort of greeting thing you do out there."

Kenny cleared his throat and came right out with it.

"Let us buy your half," he said. "It's our best chance to keep the team in the family."

"If you decide you don't want to be here," Babs said, "we don't want to take the chance you'll sell your half to somebody else."

Kenny said, "It would be the same as selling the family out."

"We're not just willing to pay you to go away, Jack," Babs said.

"We're willing to overpay," Kenny said.

"After all," Babs said, "we are talking about a New York football team here."

"One with a privately owned stadium."

"We just want to keep the team in the family. Is that so difficult for you to understand?"

"And as far as you're concerned," I said, "I'm not family."

"Not so anybody would notice," Babs said.

"We believe we could come up with investors willing to put up five hundred million," Kenny said.

Babs said, "You could ride off into the sunset and keep your streak alive of never really having worked a day in your life."

No one spoke now. I closed my eyes and imagined myself sitting in my office at Amazing Grace, getting ready for a big fight, all my usual balls in the air, every line into my office blinking, trying to finesse Jack Nicholson out of the Presidential Suite on Line 1 because I had just found out that Tom Cruise was coming in from London, asking Harry Connick on Line 2 if he could add a show on Friday night, just this one time, as a personal favor to Mr. Grace.

But I was here instead with the evil twins, wondering where my Jammer was now that I needed one. When the old man would get into his cups and start getting weepy about the Kennedys, he'd tell me that Bobby's problem when he finally ran for president was that he didn't have his own Bobby to run his campaign for him the way he'd run Jack's.

He considered it a badge of honor to be on a first-name basis with both Bobby and Jack even after they were dead.

I got up from his desk now and stood looking out the window at practice, where Bubba Royal had just thrown one about seventy yards on the fly to our star wide receiver, A.T.M. Moore.

"It's the best thing," Kenny said.

"For everybody," Babs said.

"For the team."

"For the league."

"For the family."

"Even for you."

I was afraid that if I didn't stop them, it was going to turn into some kind of yuppie rap.

I turned around, smiling Jack now, and said, "I don't think so."

Babs threw her skinny arms into the air and said to Kenny, "I told you he wouldn't listen to us."

"You're going to play this whole thing out, Jack," Kenny said. "And at the end of the day you're going to look like a deadbeat when the league votes you down and you have to sell."

"Take a look at some of the other people they've turned down over the years," Babs said.

"You think they're going to approve *you*?" Kenny said.

I looked over at the two of them, standing by the door, then over at the black-and-white of the old man and me.

"You know what I really think?" I said. "That it's time for both of you to get out of my office."

I called Pete Stanton from the old man's phone and told him I was ready to inspect the troops.

seven

"I used to be a Boy Scout when it came to picking players," Pete was saying. "But I've turned."

We were standing at the end of the Hawks' bench. On the field, Bubba Royal and the offense were practicing their two-minute drill. It had been a long time since I'd been on this field, but it was the same as it had been the first time the old man had taken me down there when I was a kid. This close to the action, there were two things that never changed: how big these bastards really were, and how loud all the snorting, grunting barnyard noises were once they started trying to beat the shit out of each other.

"Now I just basically look for four things in a player," Pete continued. "Speed, intensity, instincts and an acquittal."

"Like with A.T.M.," I said.

In front of us, Bubba Royal threw a ball from about his own 40-yard line that was supposed to be one of those Hail Mary passes you see on the last play of the game, where all the fast guys on offense and defense end up in the end zone. The defensive backs try to knock the ball down and the wide receivers try to bat the ball around like a volleyball until one of them can catch it in a play that will be replayed about six thousand times before the next morning. I had read somewhere that one of the teams just called the Hail Mary play "SportsCenter."

This one was no contest, because one of the guys going for the ball was A.T.M. Moore, who made everybody else jumping look like midgets. The ball disappeared into his huge hands like a coin going into a parking meter.

Then he did his trademark move, as if punching out his personal code on a real A.T.M. machine and then grabbing his money.

"Like with Automatic Touchdown Maker Moore," Pete said.

"What was his real birth name? I forget," I said.

"Ahmad Taj Mahal Moore," Pete said. "His old man played on the Vikings with Ahmad Rashad and the kid was conceived in Atlantic City. He had it legally changed to Automatic Touchdown Maker at one of his colleges, I can't remember which."

Pete Stanton had drafted A.T.M. out of South Carolina when no one else in the league would touch him. There was some question about his exact age by then, because there seemed to be multiple birth certificates, but Pete said that when they started tracking just his college career, they figured he couldn't be any younger than twenty-five. He had been to eight colleges in all, but only if you counted New Mexico State twice.

A.T.M. had started at the University of Arizona, in Tucson, but had to leave five games into his freshman season when it was discovered that the white BMW he had purchased, in cash, had somehow only cost him $375.50.

"What," A.T.M. had told *The Arizona Republic*, "I'm not allowed to use my Wildcat discount?"

Wildcats was the U of A team nickname.

From there he went to Oregon State, until it was discovered that his entire course load for his first semester—which had produced a 3.2 grade average, a personal best—had been handled by a thirty-two-year-old female teaching assistant named Oretha Keeshon. A.T.M. did not have to pay Oretha for his classwork, but she had convinced him that a fair trade-off for his eligibility would be for him to marry her, which he did.

"This marriage is nullified, as far as A.T.M. is concerned," he told *The Oregonian* newspaper, making his and Oretha's union sound like a holding penalty. "I'm tellin' you straight: Goin' to class woulda been a piece of pumpkin pie compared to being married to that bitch Oretha."

On the field at Molloy Stadium, Pete Stanton said, "You take the word 'straight' away from A.T.M. and he'd have to use sign language to communicate his innermost thoughts."

A.T.M. had announced that when he got his eligibility back in a year, he'd be transferring to Florida State. Once he got there, he helped the Seminoles win a national championship, in what the NCAA—admitting it was using some guesswork—classified as his sophomore season. But the Seminoles' dreams of repeating were dashed when A.T.M. shot up the burgundy BMW he'd gotten at Oregon State outside a popular campus hangout one night. The athletic director would tell Pete later that he would have been able to keep a lid on the incident if Oretha hadn't been inside the car at the time.

"Well," A.T.M. told the FSU student paper, "there goes the Theismann Trophy."

When his probation ended, he went to West Virginia, where he caught twenty-five touchdown passes in nine games. A.T.M. would have played the first full, eleven-game schedule of his college career if it hadn't been discovered before the Boston College game in late November that he had, in just one semester, rung up $12,000 in long-distance calls on a phone card belonging to the team's Wellness Coach.

"I just thought it was some of that '10-9-8-7000' shit," was A.T.M.'s explanation to the investigator the NCAA had sent to Morgantown.

He was six feet eight inches tall, taller than most tight ends, but with a sprinter's speed. One time, Pete forgot which college on this one too, he had run a charity 200-meter race against Michael Johnson, then the reigning Olympic champion. When A.T.M. blew by him going into the last turn, Johnson grabbed his hamstring as if he'd been hit by a sniper's bullet.

I remembered how much heat Pete had taken when he'd drafted A.T.M. with the nineteenth pick of the first round a few years before, especially since he was still on work-release at the time, because of a beef with Oretha on back child-support payments.

"I'm not payin' her a dime until I see the results of the D.E.A. tests," A.T.M. told *The Washington Post*. "Oretha's the type's gonna end up having three kids with four different fathers before she's through."

Pete drafted him anyway, with the full backing of the old man, who got into some trouble with the commissioner for saying that maybe A.T.M. was good enough to have caught all the women Jim Brown used to throw off the balcony.

A.T.M. caught 127 passes his rookie year, eighteen for touchdowns, despite being double- and triple-teamed constantly after the third week of the season. After every game, A.T.M. would thank God and Big Tim Molloy, who'd not only gotten a restraining order against Oretha but had also hired a full-time bodyguard for A.T.M., the legendary former Hawks linebacker Tire Iron Timmons.

Tire Iron, now a fully ordained minister in what he called the World Holy Unitarian Preachership church—WHUP for short—had a deal with the old man that worked this way: For every month that A.T.M. was not questioned by the police or charged, the old man would write a $10,000 check to WHUP.

Pete said that when he would run into Tire Iron during the off-season, on one of those days when A.T.M. was at the stadium for the team's conditioning program, Tire Iron would say something like, "Thirty thousand down, thirty thousand to go."

He meant until the start of the regular season.

Tire Iron was on the other side of the field from us, just standing there watching A.T.M., with his massive arms folded in front of him. He was about six-six himself and didn't seem to have lost much off his playing weight, which I remembered as just under three hundred pounds. The old man had told me one time that Tire Iron, whose skin was the color of a light coffee, was so tough that nobody ever even had the nerve to ask him whether or not he was white or black.

"If we make the Super Bowl and A.T.M. still hasn't gotten into trouble, WHUP gets a million bucks, tax free," Pete said. "It's why he has a better attendance record at practice than our quarterback."

He meant Bubba, my old college teammate.

"Bubba still drink as much as ever?" I asked.

"Only when it's dark out," Pete said.

"How many years you think he's got left?"

Pete said, "Not nearly as many as him and his agent think he does. Between us, if he can get us to the big game, I've got this thing set up that we go with the kid next year. He's ready."

The kid was Tucker O'Neill, Bubba's backup, out of Brigham Young, who'd won the Heisman Trophy as a sophomore, gone off to Guam after that to do two years as a Mormon missionary, and was already the father of four at the age of twenty-three. He'd been backing up Bubba the last two seasons. When Bubba'd gone down with a knee the year before, the team had won five games and lost just one with Tucker at quarterback.

"Tucker's a little different from Tire Iron," Pete said. "He actually seems to love Jesus for himself, and not the money."

"How's Bubba feel about Tucker waiting in the wings?" I asked.

"About the same as your brother and sister feel about you," Pete said.

Now on the field, Bubba threw A.T.M. a little screen pass and he ran through the Hawks defense as if his name should have been Crazy Legs Nagurski or something.

"Lesson number one for the new owner of the team," Pete Stanton said, "and it applies to this business as much as it does any other: Stars change everything."

I told him to stop, he was going too fast for me.

We stayed until the end of practice. A pretty redhead whose microphone had "Fox Sports Net" written on it came over with her camera guy and asked if I'd like to give her a couple of minutes. I politely said no, telling her that Brian Goldberg had set up some kind of press conference the next day.

The press credential hanging around her neck said her name was Vicky Dunne. I recognized her from all the Sundays when she'd stood on the sideline breathlessly telling us which lineman was out of the game and which one might return.

I'd always assumed that television people became sideline reporters because all the good jobs were taken.

"You could do a girl a favor and give her your first interview," she said. "Can't you work on him for me, Pete?"

"He's one of those twisted-type owners you still run into sometimes," Pete said. "He doesn't want to be on TV."

"Two minutes?" she asked.

"I don't think so," I said, "but thanks for the offer."

"We could do it right here," she said.

"Listen," I said, "we're opening with the Saints. Why don't you call the little prick who just bought them. He's already on television more than *Seinfeld* reruns."

Bobby Finkel was his name. He was twenty-eight years old and had made his fortune in some kind of dot com, I just couldn't remember which one. I'd read a piece about him in *USA Today* a couple of weeks before. The first time Bobby Finkel had addressed the Saints players, the paper quoted him as saying, "I'm young, I'm rich, and I'm an a———."

The article said he was already in negotiations to have his own local show in New Orleans, the kind most coaches have.

"You'd be a much better get than Bobby Finkel," Vicky Dunne said now. "God, he's done everything except Ricki Lake."

I shrugged. She walked away pouting. As soon as she was out of earshot, Pete said, "But, listen, good luck with the cookie drive."

In the last twenty minutes of one of the Hawks' last practices before the start of the regular season, in what Pete said was a relatively normal day at the office, here is what we saw:

- A vicious helmet-swinging and finally eye-gouging fight between one of our defensive ends, Raiford "Prison Blues" Dionne, and our All-Pro offensive tackle, Elvis Elgin, both of whom weighed in at 320 pounds. We didn't see how it started, but it ended with all four of the linebackers from our 3–4 defensive set holding back Raiford, and the rest of the offensive line restraining Elvis Elgin, who was still yelling at Raiford as they pulled him away.

"I'll kill your nigger ass," Elvis said.

"But they're both black," I said to Pete.

"I know," he said. "Cute, huh?"

"You and your whole nigger-assed family," Elvis said.

Raiford, who'd calmed down now, spit in Elvis's direction and said, "Hey, bitch, I got an idea for you. Why don't you run your own nigger ass over to Taco Bell when we done here today and see if it fits through the drive-through window any better'n it did when you was in college."

It was one of the most famous stories in college football history. It was Elvis's senior year at Iowa State. Distraught over a late holding call against Nebraska, one that cost his team the game, Elvis decided to do what he always did when he was feeling a little blue:

Eat.

So he drove his pickup over to a Taco Bell near campus and made his usual order: half-dozen beef burritos, half-dozen tacos, large fries, large Coke. But when he drove away from the window, he realized that they'd left out the fries. Somehow, it was, as Elvis would tell ESPN, "the straw that broke the coffin's back." Enraged, he threw the pickup into reverse, jumped out of the car and tried to go through the drive-through window at the kid who'd taken his order.

Elvis, who was six feet four, was heavier then, weighing in at 355 pounds. He was able to make it halfway through the window before getting stuck.

It pissed him off even more, that and the sound of the sirens in the distance. He began to scream expletives as he tried to wriggle himself free. Two things happened then, both unfortunate:

1. His baggy blue jeans came completely off, revealing that Elvis Elgin had forgotten to throw on any underwear before leaving his dorm room.

2. The wall on that side of the Taco Bell collapsed on top of him, as if an earthquake had suddenly hit this particular stretch of strip malls in Ames, Iowa.

From the time the Hawks had drafted him in the second round, opponents had found that the best way to get under Elvis's skin was to evoke the incident, or just use the nickname the sportswriters did when he gave up a lot of quarterback sacks, which was Drive Thru.

All we could hear now from Elvis's side of the field was nigger, nigger, nigger.

"This is the fourth time in training camp those two have gone at it," Pete said. "One more time, and they don't get to room together anymore on the road."

Vince Cahill became so enraged himself after rookie running back Bobby Camby missed a block, causing Bubba Royal to get leveled by Raiford Dionne, that he called the entire offense together, pulled down his gray sweats and his jockstrap, then grabbed himself with both hands.

"You know what I'm showing you here?" he screamed.

I mentioned to Pete that I didn't get a great look, but it seemed to be a penis, only smaller.

"Balls!" Cahill screamed. "Just in case you pussies have forgotten what a real pair of them look like!"

It was here that Bubba officially ended practice for the day.

"Yeah," he yelled, "and if you pussies want to know what those balls feel like, just ask Tucker there!"

When everybody except Tucker O'Neill laughed, Cahill cursed them out a little more and then told them he was tired of looking at them and then proceeded to faggot them all the way off the field and through the tunnel.

"Maybe I'll wait until tomorrow to say hi to the coach," I said to Pete Stanton.

We were walking off the field ourselves. It was real grass at Molloy Stadium, kept in better shape than the fairways at one of the old man's country clubs. When they were building Molloy Stadium and somebody'd asked him whether or not he was going to use artificial turf, he'd said that he was putting down a playing surface for football, not new carpeting for hell.

I had picked up one of the practice balls, and suddenly wanted to hand it to Pete and tell him to hit me, I was going long.

As we went through the goalposts, I looked up and saw Liz Bolton standing in her window, arms crossed, staring at us.

"Bubba shouldn't have said that about Tucker," Pete said.

"It did seem a little out of line, frankly."

"No, that's not what I meant," Pete said. "Anybody who wants to know what Vince's balls feel like should actually ask Vicky."

eight

I had planned to spend the night at the Sherry with the reading material Pete and Brian had given me. They had put together a package of basic stuff on the collective bargaining agreement, the salary cap, the roster moves we still had to make, the number of playoff teams we had on the schedule. They figured that I might surprise people if I showed up the next day and didn't sound dumber about pro football than the dumbest guy calling sports radio in the middle of the night.

Or the host.

"Think of it as 'Football for Dummies,'" Brian Goldberg had said in Pete's office. "I've spent the whole day telling people you know at least as much about football as Vicky Dunne."

"Make us proud," Pete had said.

I was going to shut off the phones, again, and do about $200 worth of room service from Harry Cipriani, the restaurant downstairs.

But there were two messages waiting for me, one from Billy Grace and the other from Bubba Royal. Billy said he was staying around the corner at the Four Seasons, and that if I missed him there he'd be up at Elaine's restaurant about eight.

Bubba left his pager number on my voice mail and said that unless he heard from me, I'd know where to find him later on.

Billy had fallen in love with Elaine Kaufman, the owner, the first time I'd ever taken him into her famous joint at 88th and Second. Elaine was at our table, in the middle of a story, when Billy decided he had to use the men's room. He stood up to go and realized he didn't know where it was. He also didn't want to interrupt his host just as she was getting to her punchline.

So he's standing right behind her, waiting, and without even looking at him, Elaine points and says, "Go down to Michael Caine and take a right."

When I walked in, he was sitting at one of the prime tables along the right-hand wall, by himself, watching a Yankee game on television. About twenty feet away, in the area behind him where the room opened up, were two of his walkaround guys, Johnny Angel and Vinny Two. They both had real last names that sounded like towns in southern Italy, but no one could ever remember them.

Billy said there had once been a Vinny One, but he wasn't at liberty to talk about it.

"It was part of the agreement," he said.

What agreement? I'd asked.

"The agreement that said I couldn't even talk about the agreement," he said.

Johnny and Vinny both wore silk sports jackets, one white, one black, both roomy enough to cover up the holstered guns I knew they had. They both had black t-shirts on underneath and had plates of pasta in front of them as big as wastebaskets.

Billy didn't get up.

"I thought you might need some moral support and shit like that," he said.

He waved for the waiter. I noticed he was wearing the huge Super Bowl ring that Al Davis, the Raiders owner, had given him. Billy said that he and Davis had gone to Erasmus Hall High School in Brooklyn together, at least until he had to leave because of the gun rap.

"Plus," he said, "I wanted to tell you in person that it took exactly one day for there to be guys crawling all over Vegas asking questions about my boy the Jammer."

"From the league?" I said. "I hear they do a series of background checks."

"From your own team," he said. "At first I thought Ken and Barbie had sent them, but it wasn't."

Ken and Barbie is what he'd always called the twins.

"So who?"

"The broad that runs your team, that's who."

"Liz Bolton has hired her own investigator to do a background check on me?"

I turned and motioned to Tommy, the bartender, to send over a backup Scotch to go with the one I had in front of me.

"I saw this Liz Bolton on television after the funeral," Billy said. "Goddam, she's good-looking. You sure the old man hadn't gone Viagra over her?"

I told him I didn't think so.

"Shame," he said.

He lit a cigarette. Elaine's was one of the few places left in New York where you didn't have to get a court order to open a pack of Marlboros. He offered me one and I took it.

"You keep saying you quit," he said.

"For five years. That just shows me I've got it licked."

I told him about my meeting with Liz then, and about the twins offering to buy my half, and about Pete Stanton being the only guy in the whole organization who didn't look at me like I was there to steal parking passes.

"So," I said finally, "if the league can't make it look as if we're more mobbed up than a Scorsese movie, she's going to try to do it."

"Maybe."

"And you're telling me that before any kind of shitstorm begins for us, I shouldn't take the money and run?"

I noticed that Vinny Two had moved to the end of the bar near the front door and was talking to a Heather Locklear look-alike wearing a dress cut down to her navel, where it was being held together by either Krazy Glue or just sheer willpower.

"Now you listen to me," Billy said, "and excuse me if I hurt your fucking feelings the way your old man used to. But you are not walking away from this because of me. That's point number one."

I asked him what point number two was.

"That you aren't walking away from this because of me, *asshole*," he said.

I started to say something and he waved me off. "I just want to tell you where we are here before you make up your mind about any of this," he said. "As soon as I see the message that somebody from NFL Security wants to talk to me, I pick up the phone and call Mr. Wick Sanderson, the commissioner, whom I fixed up last year when he was on his way to a Monday night game in San Francisco, even if he would like me to forget such a thing ever happened."

I felt myself smiling, remembering the sight of the five-six commissioner with Carole Sandusky, who was known to all of us in Vegas, affectionately, as Hollywood Tits. She was at least six inches taller, so that when the two of them hit the dance floor for a waltz, Wick Sanderson's head would disappear almost completely into her cleavage. She had once been a Playmate of the Month, back in the early eighties. Ever since, she had supported herself by running what she persisted in calling an escort service, even though she was the only employee. As far as Billy and I had ever been able to tell, her only overhead was monthly pager costs and an annual visit to her plastic surgeon in Beverly Hills for the ten-thousand-mile tune-up on her face and breasts.

"Very cute couple," I said.

"Anyway," Billy continued, leaning closer, "I just let him know that he better be careful as to how I was portrayed by the league or in the newspapers in relation to Jack Molloy, the new owner of the Hawks. I reminded him that I have already been investigated thoroughly by the Nevada Gaming Commission, and everybody else except Judge Judy. He started to say, No, no, no, Billy, you don't understand, this is just normal league policy. I said, No shit, that's funny because I have a policy too. He says, What policy is that? And I say that it's the one that if you push my friends around, I push your friends around. He says, Now what does that mean, exactly? I say it means we get a lot of football owners pass through town. Now the commissioner says, Are you threatening us? I try to sound offended and say, Threaten you? I don't make threats."

I made a motion like I was hitting a game-show buzzer.

"You make promises," I said.

"There you go."

"You happen to bring up Carole's name?" I asked.

"I might have mentioned that she said to say hello if I ran into him," he said. "And that she said something about keeping a bottle of special foot lotion just for him."

"So you basically put the muscle on the commissioner of the National Football League?" I said.

"Even if I did, it doesn't mean shit," he said. "Because he's not the one you have to worry about. He's just an errand boy for the owners. Them you got to worry about. In the end, this isn't gonna be about muscle, it's gonna be about getting enough votes from what they call their Finance Committee."

"Votes," I said. "I can do that."

"Don't be so fucking sure. I had Oscar make a few calls today."

Oscar Berkowitz was his lawyer.

Billy said, "And what Oscar found out and which you are about to find out is that these bastards can pretty much do anything they want to. It used to be it was pretty routine if somebody inherited a team—they go through the motions, but the thumbs-up was pretty much a given. But then that guy with the Cardinals died a few years ago and left the team to the broad he called his soul mate and the league called his former house-keeper? Esmeralda Lopez? Remember her? Somehow the league got word that he was going to do it before he kicked, and put more teeth in the rules while the bastard hung in there on life support. So now any transfer of any kind has to be approved. Which means they can approve your brother and sister and tell you to sell. Or they can approve all a' you. Or tell all a' you that you gotta sell to a Rupert or Ted or Billy Gates of their choice, which is all you're gonna get at these prices. You still get your money. So do the twins. But the owners get what they want too, which is another Old Boy—of their choice—for the Old Boys Club. You ask me, that's the way I think they'll go, even if Ken and Barbie probably do not."

"They can do that in your United States of America?"

"Jesus, Jammer, wake up," he said, "this isn't America, it's the National Football League. They can keep you out, the way they keep their own wide receivers out of their country clubs."

Billy looked at Vinny Two and made a slight tilt of his head that meant get the car, pay the check, bring the girl.

He said, "The next owners' meeting is the week of the Super Bowl, in Phoenix. That's when the shitbirds'll decide. It means we got the season to come up with the votes on the Finance Committee. Oscar did a little checking. The full ownership has never gone against what the committee recommended. Pass the committee, you're in like fuckin' Flynn. Or you're gonna end up the same kind of joke as Esmeralda, the Mexican Hazel."

"Hazel?" I said.

"She was a maid on television," he said, "before your time."

He patted me on the cheek.

"Have a nice night," Billy Grace said.

nine

The first time I'd ever seen Bubba Royal in person on a football field was his sophomore season at UCLA, at about the same time America was starting to fall a little bit in love with the Louisiana kid who had Terry Bradshaw's arm and goober ways and the looks of a young Robert Redford. I'd signed my own letter of intent with UCLA by then and the old man had finally given up trying to change my mind.

It worked out that the Hawks were on the road to play the Cowboys the same weekend that UCLA was playing the University of Texas in the Cotton Bowl. Texas was ranked No. 1 in the country in both the AP and UPI polls. UCLA had lost a couple of games early, but that was before Bubba became the starting quarterback.

Texas led the game 24–7 after three quarters, but it was here that Bubba Royal—"Number 22 in your program and Number One in your heart," was the way he always described himself—went to work. He threw for one touchdown and scrambled forty-seven yards for another.

Texas managed to kick a field goal in between all that. So it was still Texas ahead 27–21 when Bubba and the Bruins' offense got the ball on their own 10-yard line with one minute and two seconds left.

It is probably worth mentioning here that Bubba was out of timeouts and playing on a sprained right ankle that he'd hurt when somehow hurdling Texas defensive back Baskerville Homes on his touchdown run.

It took Bubba eight plays, six completed passes and two runs, for him to win the game for UCLA that day. The one that is still replayed is the pass he threw to his tight end, Doak Burden, with thirty-three seconds left. Texas, even rushing just three men, seemed to have Bubba trapped in the backfield. Somehow he escaped to his left, outrunning the pursuit even on his ruined ankle. It seemed he would be able to get out of bounds and stop the clock, until he spotted Doak Burden breaking open about ten yards up the field.

Bubba put on the brakes and set himself to throw. Except at the last second he spotted Texas's All-America defensive end, Bonzie Fasullo, not only catching up with him but taking what appeared to be a perfectly aimed swipe at Bubba's right hand, the one holding the football.

What happened in the next moment became a permanent part of the legend of Eldrick "Bubba" Royal, as much a part of that legend as the drinking and serial marriages and car wrecks and allegations about gambling that he always denied.

Most people in the stadium, watching in real time without benefit of instant replay, missed it, but not me.

Even Bonzie Fasullo would say he didn't believe it until he saw it on the eleven o'clock news.

But just as Fasullo reached for the ball, sure he was going to cause a fumble and stop the UCLA drive and preserve his team's shot at a national championship, Bubba pulled the ball down and still managed to deliver a perfect strike to Doak Burden.

Behind his back.

Like it was Magic Johnson to Kareem on a fast break in basketball.

Burden caught the ball and he stepped out of bounds and the drive stayed alive, until Bubba, with six seconds left, knowing this was the last play because he'd never get another chance to stop the clock, took the ball up the middle on a quarterback draw that only he knew he was going to run, finally running over Baskerville Homes at the goal line.

As soon as he did, Bubba Royal was officially famous.

The old man knew the UCLA athletic director, so we got to go into the UCLA locker room. We were standing outside later when the Texas coach, Jerry Raye Hightower, who came from the next bayou over from where Bubba had grown up in Redneck, Louisiana, asked one of the equipment managers if he could bring Bubba out.

When the kid came out, still wearing his powder-blue Number 22 with what looked like most of the dirt from the Cotton Bowl still on it, Jerry Raye said, "Hey, Bubba."

"Hey, Bubba," Bubba said.

It's what he called all guys, and why he had the nickname. Girls he called "Hon."

"Good'n," Jerry Raye said.

"Thank-ee."

"Ask you something about that one?"

"Shoot."

"You throwed that one behind, didn't you?"

"Sure."

Jerry Raye nodded.

"Thought so. Yeah."

"Yeah," Bubba said.

Jerry Raye Hightower started down the hall toward his own locker room, still nodding, stopped and came back.

"You the best football player I ever seen," he said.

Bubba Royal said, "Thank-ee."

A lot of people thought Bubba should have won the Heisman the next year, even though he missed the last three games of the regular season and the Rose Bowl when he lost control of his Mustang in Beverly Hills one night and put it through the front window of The Ginger Man restaurant, where Carroll O'Connor, the owner, was sitting at the bar having a drink with his bartender, Marvin B. Cohen.

"When I pulled him out of the front seat," Marvin told the *Los Angeles Times*, "I told him it was first and men's room."

There were those who said that the first time they started wondering about the LAPD was when Bubba turned up with a blood-alcohol level way below the legal limit. But he tore up his left knee pretty badly and didn't come back to play until the fourth game of his senior year, by which time I was a star sophomore tailback. And the two of us had already put our Bruins in the Rose Bowl when I started one way on a play we called Student Body Right and then cut back the other way, with Bubba suddenly the only blocker ahead of me in the open field. But then he slipped on the muddy turf and there was Mountain Montoya coming straight for me.

The last thing I remembered before I passed out on the five-yard line at the Coliseum, where we were playing the game, was Bubba standing over me with tears in his eyes saying, "I owe you one, Bubba."

He was sitting at a back booth at a place called The Last Good Year, on 50th Street and Second Ave. According to the owner, Joe Healey, who'd been my bartender at Montana, 1956 was the last good year. The Giants had won the NFL championship, led by Frank Gifford and Chuckin' Charley Conerly. The Yankees had won the World Series and Mickey Mantle had won the Triple Crown and Don Larsen had pitched his perfect game in the World Series. The Brooklyn Dodgers were still in town and so were the New York baseball Giants, and Eisenhower was president.

So Healey had opened The Last Good Year not long after I left town and turned it into a time warp, with an old-fashioned jukebox and only pictures of fifties ballplayers on the wall, and big old Sylvania television sets and front pages from all the old New York City tabloids under the glass tabletops.

The pay phones were rotaries.

There was a back room beyond the back room where athletes knew they could come and get drunk if they wanted to, and sit with either Bad

Girls or Very Bad Girls and not have to worry about being hassled by fans or sportswriters or gossip columnists.

I found Bubba Royal at a table in the way back, sitting with two blondes he introduced as Micki and Misty.

"These two ladies love football and me," he said. "But if they don't leave now, they both gonna miss bed check."

He handed them hundred-dollar bills and said, "Good luck with finals." Then they were gone and it was just Bubba and me. Sinatra was singing, because Sinatra was all Healey had on the jukebox. I asked Bubba what school Micki and Misty went to and he said it was the College of Hair and Styling, Brooklyn campus.

"I'd marry both of 'em if I could," Bubba said, "but my accountant says I can't fit no more wives under the cap."

He meant his own personal salary cap.

I hadn't been able to see his face at practice, because he'd never taken his helmet off. But now even in the half-light of the way-back room, I could see that the years had been just as mean to Bubba Royal as alimony had. You could still see the golden boy he'd always been, and still could be when somebody'd backlight him the way they did aging actresses. But there was a thickness to his face, the start of a double chin. Worse, there was a sourness he gave off, stronger than the smell of the whiskey, the kind you picked up from losers in a casino, even if they were all the way across the room.

"I saw you at practice," he said.

"Our coach is crazy," I said.

"Only when you can settle him down," he said.

He wasn't as drunk as he'd acted when I showed up. I knew that game from college. It was easier for him to play Bubba Royal, was all.

"You talk to all the tightasses and green eyeshades over there?" he said.

"Ever' one," I said in his accent.

They'd just left him a bottle of Johnnie Walker, which he'd been drinking since college because he'd read somewhere once that Joe Namath said once that he liked his women blond and his Johnnie Walker Red. He poured us some and we clicked glasses and he said, "To old pals."

He put down his glass and said, "You know something, Bubba? I've been drinking like this pretty much ever' night for the last twenty years."

"No shit," I said, "I hadn't heard that one."

"You decided whether or not you're gonna actually ride this horse?" he said.

"What do you think I should do? This team has pretty much been your whole life."

"I think you should run like an agent chasing a dollar," he said. "Like you used to for the alma mater."

He groaned as he straightened up and limped off toward the men's room like he should have been attached to a walker. When he came back, he made a motion like someone trying to shake himself awake.

"C'mon, pill," he said. "You never took this long to work before."

When whatever he'd taken finally did kick in, he cried and told me how much he loved the old man. He nearly cried again when he told me how much of the money was gone and what it was like to have to prove himself in the last year of his contract after every goddam thing he'd done for the goddam New York City Hawks. By God, he said, he'd be a lot closer to being even if just one of his ex-wives would remarry. He said he thought we had just the right mix on the Hawks, which meant that your God guys and your straight-arrow types were pretty much balanced off with the guys who liked to piss in the sink in the ladies' room and spend as much time figuring out ways around drug testing as they did learning their playbooks.

Bubba said, "No lie, those of us who need a little pick-me-up are using more masking agents than East German swimmers."

I told him that, just watching the games on television, a lot of the boys still seemed pretty frisky to me, especially early in the game.

He leaned across the table and said, "Get out while you can, Jack."

Jack always meant he was serious.

"You don't stand a chance against them," he said.

"Who's them?"

"The tightasses. The bottom liners. Assholes from the network who act like they're the ones playing the game. Sissy boys like the commissioner. Owners, mostly. It ain't our game anymore, it's theirs. They say we're the stars and we're the goddam show and they still pay us like we are, least the ones of us who can still get guaranteed contracts out of them, so's they can't cut us loose the first time they feel like we's used up. They stand up there in their luxury boxes and say that it's all about what happens on the field. But it's like we're workin' in a field to them. We're just product to them, a cut above those action figures they make us out to be in their video games. It's all about marketing now and rights fees and how many luxury boxes you got and how much you can get for them. You've got your top tightasses and bottom liners owning the team and then you got tightasses under them running the team and then you've got general managers and coaches scared shitless of all of them. And you know what it all comes down to? They've all of 'em figured out that we're a way for them to reach the audience they want, which is every goddam Bubba sitting out there with his remote in his hand and money in his pocket."

I looked around and noticed that it was just the two of us now in the way back and just a few stayers in the other back room closer to the bar. On the Sylvania above us, I heard one of the twinks, a black guy, saying it was the 2:00 A.M. *SportsCenter*.

"You know I still owe you one," he said.

I told him that was a long time ago, he didn't owe me anything.

"All's I got to give you is advice," he said. "Get out now, Jack. Get out with your money before they fuck with you the way they do everybody else."

I told him that people had been telling me to get out all day, and it had now officially worn my ass out.

"You think you know what the game is here," he said, lowering his voice. "But you don't know the half. Remember what I'm telling you. You don't know half. Even your daddy didn't know. You think everybody wants to win and . . ."

"And what?" I said.

He leaned back and closed his eyes and it was a couple of minutes before I realized that the quarterback of the New York Hawks was fast asleep.

Joe Healey said not to worry, when he came back and saw that Bubba, still upright in his chair, had done the head-back. Healey said it happened all the time, that he would usually call the driving service when he saw Bubba getting near the bottom of the bottle. He said he could tell the driver to drop me at my hotel if I wanted. I told him I'd walk home.

I walked up to 59th, past where T.J. Tucker used to be, then over to Fifth. It had gotten colder, unusually cold for August. Football weather, really. I could feel my knee stiffening up the way it always did about five minutes after the temperature dropped. I thought about what Billy had told me and what I was in for and thought about the deal the twins were offering and how I could probably get more from somebody else. Billy Grace was telling me to stay, but he was the one who'd always told me that there was only one thing we were all looking for and that was easy money. Now here it was, in the middle of the table, more easy money than I could ever spend, the score of a lifetime.

I wondered whose side Liz Bolton was on, besides her own.

You don't know the half, Bubba had said.

When I got back, I left a message for Brian Goldberg to go ahead and call the press conference for one o'clock, that I was in.

"Go, team," I said to his machine.

PART TWO

oVer-under

ten

hese are some of the things that happen to you in the first two weeks of owning even half of your very own professional football team:

1) You manage to survive your first formal meeting with all the microphone- and notebook-carrying graduates of Twink School.

"What qualifications did you pick up in Las Vegas that might help you now that you're running the Hawks?"

That one came from an adorable boy who'd introduced himself as Chip Somebody from CNN/SI. He seemed to have left Twink School right after he'd learned how to smirk.

"Tell the truth," I said. "Are you really from CNN/SI, or is this a school project?"

That actually got a laugh. You only have to be around the media for about five minutes to realize that they all hate each other the way the Jews hate Arafat.

Chip started sulking right away. "Is that an answer?"

"Nah," I said. "But that question wasn't for me, it was for all your pals."

He started to come at me again and I made a motion like I was signaling for a timeout.

"Listen," I said. "I played football, which automatically makes me more qualified than half the windbags in this league. And I'm Tim Molloy's kid. You have to make a modest wager on me just on bloodlines alone."

A little tough guy from the Madison Square Garden television network jumped up. He had a dese-dose accent and no neck. I'd seen him the night before. Every time he got excited about a three-run homer or the winner of the eighth race at Saratoga, he stammered.

"B-b-b-but you don't know nothing about running a team," he said.

"Neither did Steinbrenner when he bought the Yankees," I said. "How'd that work out for everybody?"

The hunky black guy who was like a hood ornament on the NBC pregame show casually got to his feet in the front row. He was wearing a three-piece summer suit, spats, and a watch fob.

"I'd rather like to ask you a football-related question," he said in a slow deep voice.

I said, "Okay, but you'll have to speak even more slowly than you already are."

"How do you plan to meet A.T.M.'s contract demands with your team already $10 million over the cap and so many of the accelerated bonuses scheduled to kick in next season?"

I looked over at Pete Stanton, leaning against the wall in the small theater they used for press conferences like these at Molloy Stadium. Pete winked. He had told me before we started that if anybody tried to sound informed about the salary cap, they were full of shit, that even he didn't understand the cap. The only people who did, he said, were the geeks that every team hired and who spent their entire working days staring at computer screens the way kids stared at video games trying to figure out a way to get James Bond out of the locked room.

"A.T.M. has a contract, last time I checked," I said.

"His agent says the market has changed and that contract is no longer satisfactory to either him or A.T.M."

"His agent, according to my general manager, attempts to renegotiate every time we move the first-down markers."

"So," the hunky dude said, "you're indicating that you have no plans to renegotiate at this time?"

I gave him the kind of sincere look I usually saved for a million-dollar line of credit.

"We don't renegotiate contracts around here anymore."

"After Liz Bolton met with Donyell last week, she said that she was keeping her options open."

Donyell Webster was A.T.M.'s fourth agent in just his third year of pro ball. A.T.M. had been asked one time where they'd met and he'd said, "School." When it was pointed out to him that Donyell was twenty years older than he was, A.T.M. said, "I meant drunk-driving school."

"The option on renegotiations just closed," I said. "I always told myself that if I owned the team, that guys wouldn't treat contracts like some napkin they autographed in a restaurant. Well, now I own the team."

"What about what Liz said?" Vicky Dunne asked.

"Liz didn't get the memo yet," I said.

Vicky nodded as if to say, okay, she'd played straight girl. "What memo is that?"

"The memo to Donyell and all the other Donyells that they don't run the Hawks anymore, and I do."

Brian Goldberg leaned over the microphone to tell everybody that we were going to take two more questions, and as he did he leaned close to my ear.

"Mayday," he said. "Dive, dive."

2) You meet your coach and are finally compelled to inform him that he works for you and not the other way around.

Vince had left after practice the day of the press conference because he had to shoot another television commercial for Mercedes. According to Brian Goldberg, Vince Cahill also had endorsement deals with a cell phone company, Campbell's Soup, the *Daily News*, a clothing line geared to fat guys like him, and a chain of fast-food restaurants of which he was part owner, called Vince's Vittles. He also had his own weekly television show on Channel 7, and a Monday night call-in show on WNUT, one of the six all-sports radio stations now operating in the New York City area.

He came in the next morning before meeting with his coaches. As soon as we shook hands, he went right to the heart of his presentation, as if I was part of some corporate group that had paid $35,000 so Vince could motivate us all to take next year's earnings to an all-time high while holding the line on overhead.

Vince told me he didn't want to see me around "his" field or "his" locker room.

He said that it was rich boys like me who were trying to ruin pro football the way they had America.

He said that it made him sick to see owners coming down to the locker room and making speeches to the players when most of them had never worn a jockstrap or a protective cup in their goddamned lives.

On the other hand, he said, he had no problem with his "close personal friend Jerry Jones" being the kind of hands-on owner he was with the Cowboys, since Jerry had bought the team with his own hard-earned money and not had it fall into his lap like some kind of goddamned titty dancer at a topless bar.

"Lap dancer," I said. "They call them lap dancers, Vince. They squirm around and then you pay them according to how good they make you feel. That's the way sports should work, don't you think?"

I had the air-conditioning cranked all the way, a habit from Vegas summers. Even with the windchill factor in the old man's office near freezing, Vince's speech had left him red-faced. He was wearing a gray Hawks sweatshirt a normal-sized person could have used as a comforter. His hair and bushy eyebrows and mustache were the color of a tangerine.

"You stay away from my team," he said.

"Your team?" I said mildly.

"Listen, kid," he said, "don't sit there in your daddy's chair like you and me are on some kind of equal ground here. You're talking to somebody who's won two fucking Super Bowls."

"Somewhere else," I said.

"What's that supposed to mean?"

"It means I've been doing a little research, just to satisfy my own curiosity. You know how many coaches have ever won NFL titles with two different teams?"

"I try to save the trivia for my radio show," he said. "If you don't mind too much, I've got work to do."

But he didn't get out of his chair. He ran a hand distractedly through his orange hair, but after he did, the hair looked exactly the same as it had before. It was like some miracle both of coloring and what had to be industrial-strength gel.

I said, "One coach has won with two different teams, Vince. Old Weeb Ewbank. He did it with the '58 Colts and then with Namath's Jets. That's it, the entire list, going all the way back to leather helmets and Papa Bear Halas. And since television invented the Super Bowl, nobody's won Super Bowls with two different teams."

"I don't have to listen to this shit," he said.

"My father thought he was buying the Super Bowl when he bought you," I said. "I'm not so sure. You spend as much time grubbing for endorsement money as you do coaching this team."

"It's a free country," he said.

"When you own the team, which I understand is one of your ambitions, then it's a free country. But you don't own the team, at least not yet. I do. And as long as I do, we're going to do things my way. Or I'm not going to have any fun around here at all."

He got out of the chair. The process was somewhat like watching a pool toy inflate to its full size.

"Are we done getting to know each other?" he said.

"Just a couple more things: I don't want to read another quote from you about me in the papers. And if I ever see you second-guessing Pete the way they tell me you did last year when the season went to shit, you're fired."

He got to the door and turned around.

"Remember what I'm telling you," Vince Cahill said. "Nobody talks to me this way and gets away with it."

"I just did."

Billy says you have to make it clear from the start to the guy pushing the chips that he's not the one who owns the casino.

3) The NFL commissioner calls you into his office and lets you know that if you're selling, he's got buyers lined up all the way from his office to "21."

"Think about something, Jack," Wick Sanderson said. "Do you really want to pledge an asshole fraternity like this?"

This was the Tuesday before we were scheduled to open the regular season, at home, against the Saints. The NFL offices were on Park Avenue. To get to Commissioner Sanderson, which is what everybody in the NFL offices called him, I had to go through three security checkpoints, two p.r. guys, a personal secretary and what I was sure was a bodyguard.

Sanderson had an office that looked like the parlor in one of our honeymoon presidential high-roller freebie suites at Amazing Grace. When I finally made it there, he didn't waste a lot of time with small talk.

"You're going to be a tough sell, Jack," he said gravely. "I'm not going to sit here and lie to you. And I say this as the process has barely begun."

By process, he meant the financial reports I'd have to put together for him, at least one background check and possibly two, and a formal interview with the league's head of security. It's why nobody would be voting on anything until the Super Bowl. Oscar Berkowitz and the Hawks' lawyers had all told me the same thing, that it was just the NFL's way of covering its ass if they decided they didn't want me.

Wick Sanderson was wearing tinted glasses. He had a lot of gray hair and a nice tan and was plump as a cherub. Carole Sandusky once drank too much white wine at one of Billy's hot tub parties and confessed that when Commissioner Sanderson got too heavily into the Chardonnay himself, he liked to be spanked. His wife had stayed in San Francisco when he'd left his job as president of the 49ers to succeed Paul Tagliabue as commissioner. It gave the new commissioner a lot of play time.

"You really think I'm going to be a tougher sell than Vito Cazenovia?" I said.

"Well, now, that's an interesting question," Wick Sanderson said, and went to fix himself some cappuccino while he filled me in on what he said was the "real Vito Cazenovia story."

Vito was the owner of the Los Angeles Bangers, now in their fourth year of existence and finally a Super Bowl contender. Before the Bangers, there hadn't been an NFL franchise in L.A. since Al Davis had moved the Raiders back to Oakland, during that period when Davis was moving the Raiders up and down the California coast like they were the Ice Capades. But Vito finally solved the league's problem by offering to build his own stadium with his own money off the 405, and also agreeing to pay one billion dollars for the team.

Everybody knew the team's nickname was short for Gangbangers, though nobody would come right out and say it.

"Why should the NBA get to clean up on all the gun money?" Vito asked me one night, at the annual outing he had at Amazing Grace for both his cement and construction companies back in New Jersey.

Vito had started out in both businesses with his brother Antone. But Antone had died suddenly a few months after Cazenovia Bros., Inc., had just signed its first big thruway deal with the state. It happened near the Vince Lombardi rest stop on the Jersey Turnpike. They were supposed to be building a new exit there. Antone was standing behind one of their cement mixers. Vito was in front talking to one of his foremen. What happened next has been disputed ever since, but Vito said he heard the driver of the mixer, Arnie Oppenheimer, call him a "knuckle-dragging dago wop guinea bastard" because of a pay dispute, a charge Arnie Oppenheimer would later deny. At this point, Vito climbed up on the rig, threw Arnie out of there, and said he would pour himself. But his operating skills turned out to be a little rusty, which is why the huge machine suddenly lurched into reverse, killing Antone instantly in a hail of blood and flying body parts.

The police concluded that it was mere coincidence that Antone had been telling people he planned to sell his half of the company to a competing company owned by the father of his fiancée, Mary Margaret Accorsi.

Or that the accident occurred the day before Antone was to change his will, leaving everything to Mary Margaret instead of his brother.

"These things happen in the best of families," Vito explained much later to the *Wall Street Journal* in their first big profile of him. "A mixer goes into reverse, the rest of us must move forward."

When Tagliabue was still running the NFL, Vito had been rebuffed in attempts to buy the Tampa Bay Bucs and Cincinnati Bengals. Vito in those years told people that pro football was the only contracting business he knew about where the low bid always seemed to win.

But then Tagliabue retired and Sanderson said he had no choice, when Vito's bid for the Bangers was $325 million more than the syndicate put together by Billy Crystal and Robin Williams. At the press conference introducing Vito to the media, Commissioner Sanderson did become testy at what he said was clearly anti-Italian innuendo. He said it was sheer coincidence that what turned out to be a crucial Financial Committee vote in Vito's favor—belonging to former Saints owner Zoot Charlemagne—changed at the last minute after the oven in his suite at the Beverly Wilshire Hotel mysteriously exploded.

Behind his desk now, Wick Sanderson blew gently on the frothy steamed milk at the top of his NFL Properties mug.

"Vito's a little rough around the edges," he said. "But he's got a good heart."

"Let's face it, Commissioner," I said. "Compared to Vito, Billy Grace is a Trappist monk."

"Billy doesn't own the team. You do."

"I worked for Billy. Jump ball."

"Times have changed just since Vito got the Bangers," Wick Sanderson said. "It's like the old days around here, all of a sudden people are actually starting to worry about image again. And the people who don't want you are going to portray you as being some kind of pimp."

"You know that's a bunch of happy horseshit."

"Of course I do. But I don't get a vote, Jack. They think you're Billy's pimp, I'm their pimp." He sipped some cappuccino.

"Jump ball," he said.

"I think I'll just hang in there and see how this all turns out," I said.

"And that is your prerogative," he said. "But the purpose of this meeting is to let you know that there are people out there who would be willing to take the Hawks off your hands by the end of the business day."

He stood up, meaning the meeting was over.

"I am getting calls from some of the richest men in America. The world, really."

"Tell them the Hawks aren't for sale unless my brother and sister have changed their extremely small minds."

"Aren't for sale yet," he said, trying to sound ominous.

"I know gambling is a bad word around here," I said. "But you're just going to have to go ahead and spin the wheel."

"Our investigators say they're having a very interesting time in Vegas, Jack," he said.

"More interesting than you know," I said. "Billy fixed them up last night. Maybe you know their dates. You ever meet a couple of girls out there named Bambi and Thumper?"

4) Finally, this is what happens to you in the first two weeks you own the New York Hawks:

The president of your team leaves you a voice mail that she's quitting, her resignation effective immediately only because she can't date it yesterday.

"Bad news, Jack," Liz Bolton said. "I'm quitting the floor show. You'll have to find somebody else to carry the lead fan."

eleven

Big Tim Molloy's personal suite at Molloy Stadium, the luxury box to end them all, had changed somewhat in the years since I'd last been there.

Mostly into my dream house.

I didn't remember a lot about what his original suite was like when the stadium first opened, just that it was like watching the game in somebody's rec room.

The place had grown over the years, like some old lineman who no longer had to make the weight. The old man had taken over the box to his right, the one that used belonged to the late Steve Ross, the old Time-Warner chairman who'd checked out too soon with cancer. Then he got the one to his left, which Madonna'd given up after she broke off her romance with Tire Iron Timmons, that last year before Tire Iron found Jesus.

"I frankly don't think Jesus could have moved in on him the way he did if Tire Iron wasn't all fucked out," Pete Stanton had said.

So now the old man's box was broken up into three basic killer rooms:

Ross's old box looked like a television studio, with a wall of television monitors, a giant screen in the back, away from the field, and two rows of theater seats with their own laptops attached to them. There was also a bar, a kitchen, a full bath with Jacuzzi, and a weight room.

Madonna's former digs were more homey. There were big comfortable chairs in there, two wraparound sofas, oversized pillows scattered on the floor. Another home entertainment extravaganza built into the wall: a television screen, CD player, all manner of Nintendo and PlayStation in case there were kids running around. Another full bath. Pool table. One of those pop-a-shot basketball games.

The best, though, was the old man's private quarters, in the middle, where his original luxury box had been. This was where he'd watch the game when he was through slapping backs and shaking hands and making sure all the assholes he'd invited that Sunday didn't ever have an empty glass or suffer a single moment of low self-esteem.

There was the easy chair that had belonged to Frankie Molloy, one that he had restored every couple of seasons. There was the gold-plated cigar humidor that I was sure cost more than a backup tight end. Next to that was a chair that had Pete Stanton's name upholstered on the back, and one next to that for Liz Bolton.

No other chairs.

This was the war room.

The old man had his own wall of monitors, in case he wanted to check out what was happening in the Jacksonville–New England game. There was another wall of photographs, like the one he had in his office, including a giant black-and-white shot of Bubba and me after we upset Notre Dame, two weeks before my knee exploded.

I didn't remember the picture, or that I'd signed it:

"Dear Pop. Save a place for us in the backfield. Your son, Jack."

In the back was an old-fashioned soft drink machine, filled only with six-ounce bottles of Coca-Cola. There was the kind of popcorn makers you see at the movies. There was a skillet where the old man could make what he called his greasy-spoon hamburgers.

In the very front of the box, there was the hook where he'd hung Frankie Molloy's old camel topcoat. Next to that, in a trophy case, was my powder-blue Number 19 from UCLA.

I was standing in front of that when I heard the click of the lock and Liz Bolton walked in. I had asked her to meet me up here, figuring that neutral territory might enable us to have a conversation about her resignation that didn't turn into a soccer riot.

"You look right at home," she said.

"You know what I just decided?" I said. "This *is* my new home."

"Three rooms," she said. "Stadium view. It's actually a funny idea."

I said, "I'm serious."

"You're going to live here," she said. "In your father's luxury box. In the stadium."

"Yup. You think he has all the premier movie channels on all the televisions?"

"Probably not the ones you like," Liz said. "My understanding is that you only get Spectravision in hotels."

She came past me and sat down in the chair with her name on it, facing the field. She was wearing a white blouse and a black skirt. She sat there for a minute and then spun the chair around.

"You wanted to see me."

"Don't quit," I said. "Please."

"This is not negotiable."

"Everything is negotiable," I said.

"Not this."

"That goes against everything I've learned while getting my master's in Las Vegas."

She crossed her legs. No stockings.

I thought, Steady, soldier.

She said, "You purposely embarrassed me in front of the media. You sandbagged me with Donyell Webster, that pretentious little shit. You're here for twenty minutes and now you stand in front of everybody as if you're the voice of this operation." She shook her head. "You seem

to like getting off a good line, Jack. So here's one right back at you:
Fuck off."

"Listen," I said. "I'm sorry. I was out of line at the press conference. I
should have at least given you a heads-up about the way I feel about
renegotiating contracts."

She laughed, but not the way you would at, say, the Marx Brothers.

"The way you feel about renegotiating contracts? You? Who gives a shit
what you think about anything, Jack? You may be able to dazzle everybody else with your footwork, and whatever football knowledge you've
retained from watching *The NFL Today*. So save that material for what
I'm sure you see as a season's worth of sound bites. But I'm out of here."

She spun the chair back toward the field.

"What can I do to change your mind?"

"I believe there's an America West nonstop that leaves out of Kennedy
at one o'clock."

"Not happening," I said.

"Not staying," she said.

I shrugged.

"You run like a girl," I said.

I walked over and grabbed a Coke out of the machine, used the
opener. When I turned around, she was standing right in front of me. A
fire-breathing girl. In heels, she was nearly as tall as I was.

"Excuse me?" she said.

I took a step closer, so now everybody was in everybody's personal
space.

"I said, 'You run like a girl.' Everybody told me my father hired you
because you were smart and tough and didn't take anything from anybody, and now I show up and hurt your feelings and you fold your hand
as if you shouldn't have been playing with the big boys in the first place.
Everything you and Pete and the old man worked for was this season.
One roll of the dice. Hell, even I can see that. Bubba's got one more year
left, maybe, as a top guy. Tucker's not ready, A.T.M.'s in the last year of
his contract, next season we're capped out of the world, even if the cap is
going to go up because of the new network contracts. This is it, lady. This

is your chance. And now you're going to push your chair away? The old man would be very proud."

I started to take a swig from the bottle, but she grabbed my hand before I could.

That was when I was momentarily distracted by the zoom.

Zoom was what happened in the room when the subject changed to sex.

Nobody sounded an alarm when it happened. There was never any formal announcement. Sometimes it was real sex, right there on the spot, let's go. Sometimes it was a kiss or a flash of leg or the way somebody smelled or that she reminded you of somebody who had blown your doors off when you were nineteen and horny as a stud horse.

And sometimes it was somebody getting pissed off and grabbing your hand to maybe keep herself from slugging you.

Nothing ever had to come of it. Maybe only one person felt the little shock. But there it was now in the luxury box, in the air between Liz Bolton and me.

A whole shitload of zoom.

"You know what the funny thing is," she said quietly. "I was more a son to him than you were."

She was still holding on to my hand.

"You don't know what he thought about anything," she said. "You don't know what he thought about me, or what I thought about him. So don't act like you know. You can be king of the bullshitters with every-body else, Jack. Just not me. And not here, okay? Don't act like you know what it took for me to get up here, to sit at your father's right hand and look at the team we built, the one that was supposed to make him die happy."

She let go of my hand and poked me hard in the chest with a finger and said, "Don't."

From one of the other rooms, I could hear the chirp of a phone. One of the windows was open, so I could hear a mower kicking in down below.

"Okay, here's what I do know," I said. "I know that you don't want to walk away from a Super Bowl team any more than A.T.M. Moore and his agent do. I know that the old man didn't leave me this team because he wanted to run you off. And even the king of the bullshitters is smart enough to know about the snapshot you have to have been carrying around inside you when you decided to leave television and strap on a helmet."

"And what snapshot is that?"

"The one of Wick Sanderson handing you the Vince Lombardi Trophy after the Hawks have kicked somebody's ass in the Super Bowl."

She looked away to buy herself a moment of time. "The owner gets the trophy."

"Not if we win. We meaning us."

"Us."

"If we win, you get the trophy. You make the acceptance speech. You thank the Academy. I won't even be in the room."

She walked around the room, touching things, straightening a few pictures. Only a pig would have found himself staring at her ass.

"That's it?" she said, when she turned back around. "That's your trump card? You dangle your big moment at me and I fall into your arms and say yes?"

"I actually hadn't played it out all the way," I said. "But that would work for me. Yes."

"No."

"You know you've thought about it. How many women are ever going to fondle that thing in front of the whole frigging world? You're telling me you don't want to be one of them?"

She started to move around again, and I said, "Please don't rearrange anything else, you're starting to scare me."

"I'm going to want to think about this."

"You've already thought about it."

She went and leaned against the wall next to old Number 19.

"You know I hired an investigator, don't you?"

"If somebody sneezes in Las Vegas," I said, "I catch a cold."

"Don't you want to know why?"

"Not particularly."

"I wasn't trying to get something on you," she said, making a little brackets motion with her fingers around "get." "This was before your press conference. I just wanted to have my own information and make up my own mind and not find out things about you from the commissioner or Kenny and Babs."

"The devil children."

Liz Bolton smiled for real, finally. It was like somebody had hit the switch for the arc lights at the top of the stadium.

"Your father used to say they'd been raised by wolves," she said.

"Stay," I said. "It'll be fun. Sports can still be fun, right?"

"Jesus," Liz Bolton said, "the investigators were right about one thing."

"My remarkable sexual exploits?"

"They actually thought you were gay," she said.

"What were they right about?"

"That you're living in some kind of weird time warp."

I put out my hand. "Deal?"

She came over and hesitated and then shook it.

"Zoom," I said.

twelve

onyell Webster said he and A.T.M. would meet me at a steak joint in the West Village where the Hawks players got together every Wednesday. He said it was called Beef and he better give me directions, it could be hard to find down there if you didn't know where it was and accidentally took a left at the wrong gay bar.

"You like to dive into some prime every now and again?" Donyell said on his car phone.

"I sneak in a steak now and then when the surgeon general isn't watching."

Donyell cackled.

"Yeah, baby," he said, "that's what I'm talkin' about."

He must have had A.T.M. in the car with him, because now he put the phone on speaker.

"A.T.," Donyell said, "how 'bout you? You like your beef?"

"Yum yum," A.T.M. Moore said, and then both of them were laughing before the connection cut out.

The cabdriver got lost twice in the meat-packing district. Finally, he pulled up to what looked like just another warehouse until I saw the small neon sign with "Beef" written out in script. Underneath that was a lasso that I thought resembled a G-string.

They had to buzz you in.

"Jack Molloy," I said into the speaker. "Donyell invited me."

A minute later, the door opened and I was adjusting my eyes to the dim lights inside.

I looked around, then felt myself smiling.

"Oh," I said, though I couldn't even hear myself over the kill-everybody-and-everything roar of the rap music. "That kind of beef."

They had converted this particular warehouse into a huge, ornate strip club, twice the size of the main room at Amazing Grace. I could smell food, so it really was a restaurant as well. But my boys weren't here for the steak fries, I was fairly certain.

They were here for the yum yum.

There was a horseshoe-shaped bar that dominated the middle of the room. Off to the side, like lounges, were two small but brightly lit dance floors. On the one to the right, I recognized my second-year full-back, Jimmy T. Kirk, named after the commander of the Starship *Enterprise*. Jimmy T. Kirk was locked in slow, dirty dancing with a blonde who was big enough and healthy enough to bring Jimmy T. down in the open field, and who was extremely naked except for black fishnet stockings and spiked heels with little flashing lights attached to the back of them.

On the dance floor over to the left was a solitary redhead who was continuing a sultry strip from a nun's habit.

But even she stopped for a moment when she heard the loud cheer, over the music, for Raiford Dionne, who was chasing a girl the color of a Starbucks latte around the top of the bar. The light wasn't great over there and there was a thick haze of smoke between me and the action, but from where I stood, the only thing the Starbucks girl was wearing was a pair of shoulder pads and the football she was carrying under her arm.

"I do believe Raiford's about to record his first sack of the damn season," Donyell Webster said from my left, making his high-pitched voice heard over the mindless thumping of the music. "One of these days Coach Vince gonna figure out a way to get Raiford to chase Brett Favre the way he does beef."

Donyell laughed now and said, "Run, nigger, run."

Donyell Webster was maybe a head shorter than me, and dressed whiter than the yacht club. Blue blazer, white open-necked shirt, white v-necked sweater vest, cream-colored pants, saddle shoes. Round tortoise-shell glasses. I wondered where his pipe was. Another black guy trying to look like a WASP preppie. The preppies, of course, they went the other way. They wanted to dress black and talk black and give you all that black hand-jive like everything they said required directions back to the 'hood, even if it was in Larchmont.

For some reason, I noticed the chain to his pocket watch hanging from the front of his vest.

"Good evening, old spoke," I said.

Donyell grinned. "You callin' me a smoke?"

I leaned down so he could hear me better.

"The football fans of New York think our kids get together once a week to bond and sing a couple of choruses of the team fight song."

"They are bonding," he said. "Lookit Jimmy T. over there. My bartender girl's gonna have to throw water on him and Chelsea pretty soon, get them apart."

The big blonde was in a lineman's three-point stance now, picking what appeared to be a hundred-dollar bill out of Jimmy T. Kirk's zipper.

Donyell led me around the bar and through a door into what actually did look like a small dining area. There were maybe a dozen tables with the same red-and-white checked tablecloths you'd see at Pete's Tavern or P.J. Clarke's. The only difference was the waitresses, all of whom looked like the Playboy Channel. They wore aprons and nothing else, except what seemed to be some kind of sparkle on their bare chests.

"Don't worry about them leanin' too close to your chili cheeseburger," Donyell said. "My girls are so clean you could eat off them even if you *didn't* want to."

"This is your place, isn't it?"

"Mine and A.T.'s. Though nobody'd ever figure that out in a million years, readin' the lease."

I told him everybody should have a home away from home like this.

"Tell you how it happened," he said. "Me and A.T. was at the Palm one night. You know it? Up on Second? We was doin' what we always do on Monday night. Get ourselves some good beef, then move over to Scores afterward to kick back and look at some titties. And in the limo on the way over there, A.T. says to me, 'You know what we need, Donyell?' And I say, 'What's that, A.T.?' And he says, 'One place where you can get both kind of prime.'"

Donyell Webster made a gesture that took in both the front room and back room at Beef, and said, "Voilà."

It came out voy-la.

A.T.M. Moore was at a round table on the other side of the room, sitting back to the wall. He wore a white turtleneck, despite the heat outside, and a gold medallion around his neck that was the size of a hubcap. His hair was in those neat cornrows made popular by the guy on the Knicks who'd choked his coach. On the table in front of him, arranged as neatly as the line of scrimmage, were his cell phone, his pager, a backup pager, the case for his sunglasses, some kind of handgun, and a bottle of hand lotion, which explained the scent of jasmine.

After he shook hands with me, he casually uncapped the lotion and rubbed it lovingly into his palms.

"Gots to take care of my instruments," he said.

A waitress leaned close to A.T.M. as she set down some kind of pink drink with a parasol in it and said, "Don't forget to save some of that sticky for later, angel."

A.T.M. sipped some of his drink through a straw and said, "Yum yum."

I ordered a Scotch from her. Donyell ordered green tea with a shot of tequila on the side.

"We wanted to meet with you face-to-face," Donyell said. "That way we could present our GTHs in person."

I said I wasn't familiar with GTHs.

A.T.M. said, "Gots to Haves."

I ducked the waitress's breasts when she came back and sipped some of my scotch.

"What about your AGs?" I said.

"Never heard of no AGs," A.T.M. said.

"Already Gots," I said. "As in, already gots a contract."

Both of A.T.M.'s pagers were going off and his cell phone was making bird noises. He shut off the pagers and took the call, cupping his hand so we couldn't hear anything except the occasional "fuck" or "straight" or "fucking straight" when he'd raise his voice a little bit.

"Shee-it," Donyell said. "You got to know there's a problem with that deal."

"Yeah," I said. "You're not getting a percentage of it."

"Where you been, Jack? Don't you know that first contract ain't nothing more than both sides establishin' a bargaining position?"

I sipped more Scotch. From the front room, there was a burst of applause and then I could hear everybody chanting Raiford's name.

I mentioned to Donyell and A.T.M., off the phone now, that he must have finally caught the girl in the shoulder pads.

A.T.M. Moore shook his head.

"Boy strippin'."

"Raiford?"

Donyell said, "He must be takin' it off a little early tonight. This usually don't happen until he's had about a dozen of his parasol drinks."

A.T.M. said, "He get about a gallon of pink in him and he wants to show everybody his beef, you understand what I'm talkin' about?"

I walked over to the door to the front room. Just about everybody in there had moved close to the bar and were clapping wildly now for

Raiford, who I thought was showing impressive balance as he did one of those discus-thrower spins and flung his carpenter jeans toward a chandelier hanging over the dance floor where the girl in the nun's habit had been.

Raiford, I noticed, was as forgetful about underwear as his pal Elvis Elgin had been in college. But it was clear when somebody put one of the spotlights on him that he didn't need boxers or briefs as much as he did some kind of tool belt for his equipment.

A.T.M. was standing next to me.

"He'll settle right down now," he said. "Take a couple of girls into one of the Do-It Rooms."

He sipped some of his drink and smacked his lips. "You ought to go check out a Do-It Room 'fore you leave," A.T.M. said. "Pillows, waterbeds, mirrors all over the place. Replay cameras. Big screen. Pretty much everything except a floor."

I told him I couldn't believe how much the place reminded me of the Yale Club.

thirteen

e sat down for a few more minutes before A.T.M. went upstairs to his personal Do-It Room, but made no progress on their Gots to Haves. I had asked where Tire Iron Timmons was and Donyell said he was waiting in the car for A.T.M. to finish up with his allotted sin time.

"He just sit out there and pray that I run out of sticky sooner rather than later," A.T.M. said.

"Listen, guys," I said. "I'm telling you I'll take care of you after the season, when the contract's up. But I can't do anything now."

"They redid Jimmy T.," Donyell said.

A.T.M. said, "And Jimmy T. only in the second of a four."

Donyell said, "Front-loaded, too, 'stead of back."

Second year of a four-year deal, with a big up-front signing bonus.

I told him that was the old policy, the new policy had gone into effect as soon as I'd held my press conference.

"You sayin' no to me?" A.T.M. said.

He looked at Donyell. "He sayin' no to me?"

"Well," Donyell said, "my brother, it don't sound like he sayin' yes."

"I'm saying that you just have to wait a few months. If you have the year everybody expects you to have, which is the year you always seem to have, I will make you the highest-paid goddam player in history."

"You don't understand," Donyell said. "This ain't about the money."

That meant it was only about the money, even the guy holding the coach's microphone cord on the sidelines knew that.

"We clearly having a philanthropical disagreement," A.T.M. said.

I told him those were always the most painful kind.

"This about face," A.T.M. said

"Respect," Donyell said.

R-E-S-P-E-C-T, I said.

"That's what I'm talkin' about," A.T.M. said, nodding solemnly.

"You got to treat my man like a man," Donyell said, voice rising.

"Don't be *like* the man, though, trying to hold me down," A.T.M. said.

I told them both that sometimes all this man stuff confused the shit out of me.

"Just tell the press we've tabled this discussion until after A.T.M. leads us to the Super Bowl," I said.

"You got no Super Bowl team without me," he said.

"Man's right," Donyell said. "A.T.M. isn't just *a* man. He *the* man. Which is why you got to change your economic philosophy, which now been in place about forty-eight hours, according to my calculations."

"Donyell, work with me. Even if I did redo A.T.M., how long do you think it would be before Bubba was in my office?"

Donyell raised an eyebrow.

"You got money problems with that boy already," he said. "And they got nothin' to do with a redo on A.T."

"You mean because of his alimony?"

He made a big show of taking off the preppie glasses and cleaning them, then carefully putting them back on. "You wish."

"Meaning what?"

Donyell stood up. "Bubba's your problem, baby. A.T. is mine. You think about what we talked about here and you call me in the morning and then we'll see if we in the mood to practice or not."

A.T.M. collected his phone, pagers, gun, lotion, and left a hundred on the table for the waitress.

"Gots to have some yum now," he said.

I sat at the bar for a while, watching the floor shows, one of which involved three girls in referee outfits and involved some creative acting-out of various penalty calls.

Eventually the place began to thin out, as guys either left or repaired to the Do-It Rooms.

The bartender's name was Annie. It was on her name tag, which was actually attached to a white shirt. Her last name, she informed me, was Kay.

"Can I ask you something?" she said. "What's a nice owner like you doing in a place like this?"

"How do you know I own the team?"

"Because I own a television," she said. "I read the papers without moving my lips. I even listen to sports radio sometimes, if I'm feeling maladjusted."

I told her it was strictly a fact-finding mission.

"So it's not a breast thing," she said.

I told her I preferred the non-exploding kind.

Annie told me she used to date one of the Hawk players, a strong safety who'd been cut early in training camp. He'd gone home to Nebraska after that to save the family spread and said she could stay in the apartment they'd been sharing on West Street, which was paid for through the season. Now she was working here three nights a week and taking broadcasting courses at NYU. She said she was twenty-four, in case I was wondering. She had auburn hair cut nearly to her shoulders, green eyes, a splash of freckles across the bridge of her nose, and a smile that tried to stop your heart.

She said Donyell had asked her if she wanted to make extra money dancing, and when she said no, he said it was cool, she could work the bar.

I sat there through the last floor show, when she switched the music to jazz. We discussed the team's prospects for a while. I noticed Jimmy T. Kirk was the last Hawk in the place, sitting at a table talking to two dancers in perky flip haircuts who'd just finished a strip number to the old theme song from *The Mary Tyler Moore Show*.

He finally came over and asked Annie if she could fix him up a batch of pink to take upstairs.

"What's in that drink?" I said.

She looked at me gravely and said, "It starts out a strawberry daiquiri, then gets sweeter and more lethal from there. Raiford's the one who invented it, actually. He calls it his prom drink."

It was two o'clock in the morning by now. Annie had closed up the register and was counting her tips.

I asked her if she might like to go back to my place for a nightcap.

She looked at me for a long moment, clearly making up her mind about me.

"You live nearby?" she asked.

I told her where I lived.

"Far fucking out," she said. I guess she'd decided.

When we got back to the stadium, I had the security guy throw on all the field lights and Annie said far-fucking-out again and then I showed her my etchings.

fourteen

ater the next afternoon, A.T.M. Moore and Donyell Webster held a press conference at Kennedy Airport before boarding a British Airways Concorde to London.

Donyell had called Suite 19, which was the number of the old man's box, at a few minutes after eight in the morning. Annie had answered the phone.

"Fifty-yard line," she said brightly.

Then she nodded and said, "One moment. I'll see if Mr. Molloy is available."

She mouthed Donyell's name and handed me the phone, then went off to do coffee things.

"You thought about our proposal?" Donyell said.

"Don't you mean ultimatum?"

"C'mon, Jack, we talkin' here about the universal language of love."

"My answer's the same this morning as it was last night. You've got my word I'll take care of you after the season."

"My man say he got a problem with waiting."

"You know what they say, Donyell. The first step towards recovery is admitting there *is* a problem."

Annie must have set Mr. Coffee's timer the night before, because she came over wearing only my favorite Yankee t-shirt and handed me a coffee mug.

"Once we go, we gone," Donyell said now. "You think you the man now, Jack. But you only playin' at it. Your old man was the man. He would've had this handled before it ever got to the staredown."

I sipped some coffee. "Donyell, I'm not awake enough to play man with you."

He said, "Well, get a pen, I'm gonna give you a number you better hold on to."

I fumbled around next to the bed and found one next to some stationery with the Hawks logo on it.

"Shoot," I said.

He gave me a long number, and when I asked him what it was, he said it was A.T.M.'s international pager number and hung up.

At Kennedy they said it was this contract dispute that had forced A.T.M. to reexamine his passion for the game.

"He need time for reflection and contemperation," Donyell said.

Someone asked A.T.M. how long he planned to stay in London and he said, "Until I get tired of Big Ben and the Louvre and all like that."

He slipped on his Oakleys and turned his San Antonio Spurs baseball cap around on his head. On television you could hear someone from the crowd of reporters call out one last question.

"What's the real reason you're retiring from football?"

"One word," he said. "Jack Molloy."

He'll be back," I said. "Imagine how shocked he's going to be when he finds out they moved the fucking Louvre."

We were in the conference room next to Liz's office. Me. Liz. Pete Stanton. Brian Goldberg. The first order of business for Pete was deciding how he wanted to fill A.T.M.'s roster spot. He said he could look at the waiver wire again, but he'd done that earlier in the week when all the teams in the league had made their last cuts, getting down to the number of players, fifty-three, we were allowed to carry on the active roster for the regular season. Or he could just move somebody up off the active roster.

He had just been with Vince Cahill. Pete said Vince spent most of the meeting talking in fairly graphic terms about cutting me up into small pieces and then scattering the parts from the team plane when we flew to Miami to play the Dolphins in our second game of the season.

Brian said they'd finally just shut down the switchboard because of the overload of calls from angry fans.

"I asked the operators to log the more interesting death threats," Brian said. "Compared to some of them, Vince's plan almost looks like a mercy killing."

When we'd first sat down, Brian had asked if I wanted to hold some sort of press briefing, just so we could get our side of the story out.

"Oh, why don't you, Jack?" Liz said. "You have such a winning way with the press."

She'd been snippy with me all morning, perhaps having something to do with walking into Suite 19 just as Annie was coming out of the old man's shower singing the second verse of the Hawks fight song.

"He'll be back," I repeated. "Pete says if he doesn't, he has to give back six million in bonus money."

"Maybe you're right," Liz said. "But by the time he figures out we're serious about asking for the bonus money back, we could be 0–2."

Pete said, "The Cowboys started 0–2 one time when Emmitt Smith held out, and they still won the Super Bowl."

"They had Troy Aikman at quarterback," she snapped. "We don't even have our best guy starting because everybody's afraid to tell Bubba the Drunk he's washed up."

"You really think Tucker's better?" I said.

"Duh," Liz Bolton said.

The season started in about seventy hours. When I'd come into the conference room, Liz and Pete and Brian were listening to WNUT, to get their own handle on fan reaction, as if shut-ins calling the radio was some kind of scientific polling. Some host with an air-raid-siren voice was screaming that A.T.M. flying east meant the Hawks would start flying south on Sunday.

His partner chuckled and said, "That's a good one, Rat."

"What are our options in the short term?" Liz said to Pete.

He had a bunch of printouts in front of him. He said, "We can bring up Gwyneth Moses from the practice squad, of course. I thought the kid had a good camp. I think Vince only cut him in the end because he's queer."

"A gay wideout?" I said.

Pete nodded. "We managed to keep it quiet so far, but he took up with our radio colorman during mini-camp."

"What else?" Liz said.

"There's always DeMarquis Queens. The Rams cut him Monday."

"DeMarquis is out of the big house?" Brian said.

Pete pulled a newspaper clip out of the stack in front of him. He said it was from the *L.A. Times*, and explained that DeMarquis—who'd once been a first-round draft choice out of Liberty University, the Reverend Jerry Falwell's school in Virginia—had finally had his conviction on gun-running overturned by an appellate court. The judge said that while it originally appeared as if DeMarquis, whom sportswriters had nicknamed "Guns of Navarone," had masterminded the purchase of automatic weapons from Algerian nationalists, his Sixth Amendment rights had been violated with the original search of his Hollywood Hills garage.

Once DeMarquis finished his time-served on a previous rap, for stalking a neighbor, one of the female co-stars of *The Jamie Foxx Show* on the WB network, he was free and clear to resume his pro football career, which had already included two trips to the Pro Bowl in Honolulu.

In the newspaper story, DeMarquis said that he loved America and whatever part of the Constitution it was that made him a free man again.

We were actually having a serious conversation about whether or not Vince Cahill was more likely to want a gay wide receiver or Guns of Navarone Queens when Kenny and Babs showed up.

A re you completely and clinically *insane?*" Babs yelled. "Is there some kind of record for team-destroying you're shooting for, Jack?"

"Did you want to do it this week or were you actually waiting until we played a couple of games?" Kenny said.

Sometimes they fell into old habits and dressed alike. This was one of those days. She was wearing a white blouse, khaki-colored skirt, penny loafers. He was wearing a white shirt, khakis, the same style loafers, beige suspenders that actually looked wider than Babs's arms.

"We had planned on honoring Daddy at halftime on Sunday," Babs said.

"Or will you be busy trying to fire a few of our defensive linesmen?" Kenny said.

"*Line*men, Ken," she said. "Not linesmen."

I said, "We're working here, sis. Or perhaps you hadn't noticed."

Babs put a hand on one of her bony hips and laughed.

"Work?" she said. "I thought work for you was making sure the girl was delivered to the right suite at the hotel."

Kenny waved the piece of paper in his hand triumphantly, if a bit girlishly, as if he had just scored a touchdown.

"We're actually here to show you this," he said.

It was a printout that somebody had just made off the Internet, of an Associated Press bulletin. I noticed there was a Las Vegas dateline. The headline read this way:

"New Hawks Owner Linked to Game Fixer."

"What's that?" Pete Stanton said.

I handed him the story.

"Not what," I said. "Who. Tommy 'Ferret' Biel."

"Okay?" he said. "I'll bite. Who's Ferret?"

I told him he was the guy who meant that somebody had decided to play dirty.

Somebody had decided to bypass Billy Grace and go right after the old Jammer.

fifteen

It was all in there, a different kind of sticky. The bad kind.

There was the point-shaving scandal at Notre Dame that Ferret had helped mastermind. They'd brought out all the old material from when he'd been one of Pete Rose's bookies in Cincinnati, back in those days when Pete supposedly had bookies on twenty-four-hour call.

The story reminded anyone who had forgotten that it was Ferret Biel who had tried to peddle bats that he swore under oath Joe DiMaggio had signed for him on his deathbed, even though Ferret, in his haste to get them on the market, had dated them two days after the Yankee Clipper had finally passed over.

"It was the medication," Ferret said on the witness stand. "Sometimes the Clipper, God rest his soul, would think it was 1941 and he was still in the middle of his hitting streak. So he was a couple of days off. What, that's some kind of federal offense?"

Just state, as it turned out.

He had disappeared for several years after the DiMaggio scam and then turned up in a brand-new incarnation, running card shows in Las

Vegas. To the amazement of practically everyone, Billy and me especially, the shows seemed to be first-class and strictly legit. Ferret's nickname had always seemed to give a lot of weasels and lizards and iguanas a bad name, but he swore up and down the Strip that he was a changed man, that he'd even sworn off legitimate gambling at the various sports books in town, including ours.

"Jammer, I'm telling you, I've twelve-stepped myself right out of the old toilet," he said in my office one day.

I told him that Gamblers Anonymous really did work when people were sincere about it.

Ferret Biel said, "I mean, once you get past the hand-holding and the bullshit about a Higher Power."

He'd been there begging for Billy to let him use our main ballroom for his biggest show yet, for the thirtieth anniversary of the 1969 Mets, the 1969 Jets, and the Knicks of 1969–1970 all winning titles.

"You're a New York guy," he said. "If you don't want to do it for me, do it for Joe."

Namath.

"Do it for Willis."

Reed.

"You want to see the great Tom Seaver over at the Bellagio?" he said, referring to the place Wynn kept after he sold the Mirage.

He had slicked-back hair, pig eyes, skin as white as copy paper. He wore nice suits, cream-colored on this day, that always looked as if they belonged to his older brother. He had gone a little heavy on cologne, which explained why my office had started to smell like the spray counter at Bloomingdale's.

"Ferret," I said, "you are still the most transparent person I've ever met in my life."

He put out what I was sure were sweaty palms and said, "Hey, Jammer, I am who I am."

He swore he'd been completely clean since his last brush with the law, when he was caught stealing the sports bras the United States women's soccer team had worn when they won the World Cup at the Rose Bowl in

Pasadena. Ferret had tried to hide in a locker, but finally the lack of oxygen and the excitement of the bras caused him to pass out and come crashing to the floor just as Mia Hamm was taking a phone call from President Clinton.

"You can't find it in your heart to give a second chance to your old buddy Ferret?"

He constantly talked about himself in the third person, as if he were one of the athletes whose signatures he was peddling for big green.

"You give me the De Niro Room," he said, "and it will send a message to everyone that I'm back."

I asked what had happened to all the money he had stolen and scammed over the years.

"Especially," I said, "the score you made when you got all those fine scholar-athletes from South Bend to actually dump the FedEx Orange Bowl."

"The lawyers take the big bite," he said. "And God-almighty, who'd've known that the DiMaggio family would turn out to be such bad fucking sports."

Ferret shrugged inside the oversized sports jacket and nearly disappeared.

"The rest of it?" he said. "Hey, even lowlifes like me like to live high."

So we let him use the De Niro Room for the show. He made money, we made money, and that was the last I'd heard from him. Now here we were on the wire together, the story making it sound as if Ferret and I were closer than Butch Cassidy and the Sundance Kid. Next to the copy were two old pictures, one new one.

One had Ferret and me, flanked by Dave DeBusschere from the old Knicks, and Joe Namath.

The other picture was the famous one of Ferret Biel in the hot tub at the Fountainbleu in Miami, with the entire starting backfield from the Notre Dame football team and two do-me girls Ferret had recruited from a topless bagel place he'd found near South Beach.

The new picture had a betting slip with my name on it, suggesting that I had bet $100,000 on the fixed FedEx Orange Bowl game.

"The story says I had Notre Dame and the under," I said. "Even the old man would never bet the Catholics up that big, even on a sure thing."

Nobody in the conference room said anything for what seemed like an hour and a half. Kenny and Babs got tired of waiting for me to start wailing and throwing myself about, and left. I was thinking that everybody at least felt a lot better about A.T.M. going over the wall when Liz Bolton said, "Could somebody explain to me what this all means?"

"Somebody who doesn't want me to get the Hawks got to the Ferret, is what it means," I said. "The question is who."

I told Pete and Liz to do whatever they needed to do about replacing A.T.M., that I had to go make an important phone call.

I called the Four Seasons. Billy and Vinny and Johnny had already checked out. I remembered Billy saying something the day before about flying back to see Cher open at Amazing Grace so he must have left early. I tried him on the cell and got no luck there, which meant they were already airborne. The only time you couldn't reach Billy on the cell was when he was at thirty-five thousand feet or getting laid. Or both. I finally called the pager number that allowed me to talk to a human, and told the woman who answered that it was urgent that Mr. Grace call me from the plane.

I wanted him to send Vinny and Johnny over to Ferret Biel's place as soon as they landed, so that one of them could choke the truth out of him while the other took notes.

Right before they drew straws to see which one of them then choked the life out of the little bastard.

sixteen

erret Biel had disappeared.

"We are checking all the previous rocks under which he might previously have hidden," Billy said from Vegas the next day.

As soon as they'd landed, Billy had sent Vinny Two and Johnny over to the condo Ferret had bought near Shadow Creek. The do-me girl who'd answered the door, who gave her name as Inger, said Ferret had left town the day before, like, you know, in a hurry?

Vinny reported that Inger was practically blond, about six feet tall and spoke with a Winter Olympics accent.

He asked where Ferret had gone and she said she didn't know, but if they wanted to come in they could all have a glass of wine and talk about it.

Johnny asked if Ferret had said how long he might be away and Inger said he might have, but when he got nervous like he did yesterday, she couldn't understand a word he was saying.

She said if she remembered anything else she'd give a call and then gave them her pager number.

Billy said, "We'll treat this like he ran out on a little bit of a bill. Which means we'll find him, it just may take some time."

He asked how the papers had handled it.

"Like I stole all the welfare checks," I said.

"You know," Billy said, "you always seemed like such a popular kid when you worked for me."

He said he'd be in touch.

Even with the old man gone, Kitty had decided to go ahead with her annual Welcome Home Dinner for the team at the Plaza. She always staged it the Friday night before the home opener, with the proceeds going to her charity-of-the-moment, which this year was the Gay Men's Health Crisis.

"I couldn't help thinking how much fun it would be watching those cute boys from the GMHC go all weak at the knees over some of our hunky-monkey defending backs," she'd said when I walked in, before she went off to work the room with a vengeance.

We were at the VIP cocktail party in the Terrace Room for coaches, players, wives and so many celebrities it looked like they'd emptied out the Hamptons early this year. I had been standing off to the side, sipping a Scotch and arriving at the conclusion that it had become impossible in sports to decide which ones were the players' wives and which ones were do-me girls out for a night on the town. Kitty spotted me and came sweeping across the room, finishing the last of her champagne, putting her glass on a waiter's tray and then grabbing another one in the same motion. She was wearing a low-cut crimson gown that made me think she'd had some front-end work done and was wearing enough jewelry to open a branch office of Harry Winston. As usual in settings like this, she was perkier than a debutante.

"Jack, you scamp," she said breathlessly, "I thought I'd lost you."

I told her I was just hanging around long enough to watch the President and First Lady do the inaugural waltz.

"I think just about everyone's here," she said. "I frankly don't know how Cindy and Neil are going to have enough space to list all the luminaries in the *Post* tomorrow."

She pointed out the mayor and the police commissioner, talking with some actress whose name I couldn't remember but who looked as if she'd had her nose broken a couple of times. I'd been out of Vegas only a week and already I was forgetting names. There was Bob Wright from NBC and his wife, Kitty said. They were talking to the Brokaws. The governor and Libby had just called to say that the helicopter from Albany had been delayed by fog, but they were on their way. Donald Trump was there with a brunette I could have sworn had served me drinks at Beef, chatting up Maury and Connie. Oh God, Kitty said, Larry King's wife is preggers again!

They were all there, a society class of twink, like some repertory company of twinks, because jock-sniffing had evolved over time into some kind of society art. In the old days, when the old man hit town with money in his pockets, these people wanted to be photographed with the other swells at places like the Copa and the Stork Club and the old Rainbow Room. Now it was ballplayers, any kind of ballplayers. But mostly the Hawks. The Knicks hadn't won anything lately. The Yankees had finally stopped winning everything. The Giants hadn't won shit since Bill Parcells had left and neither had the Jets. Hockey was a video game; if the Rangers disappeared, maybe twenty thousand people, tops, would notice. The Hawks were the hot team. They were glamorous in New York now the way the Giants had been in the fifties, when the do-me girls Frank Gifford took to hotels were still his age and the rest of them, Pat Summerall and Kyle Rote and Charlie Conerly and Dick Lynch, ran through the big-city nights the way they ran through the NFL. The old man had never gotten over those Giants, even if they'd won only one championship, in 1956. They'd won once the way the old Brooklyn Dodgers had, and he didn't care. Gifford had become one of his best friends, even after he married Kathie Lee. Summerall was my godfather. When I was a kid, I played catch in the park with Alex Webster.

Memories of the fifties made the old man get more sentimental than half a bottle of Irish whiskey could, once he got to talking about how everything was better in those days, football and theater and television and the city and the goddam United States of America. The only subject that made him weepier was my mother, who had died of cancer much too soon.

"Molloy," he'd say, after his fourth absolute last nightcap, "you've got to promise me that if you ever find yourself the right girl, the way I did with your mother, and you're ever feeling flush, take her to Paris. I always promised I'd take your mother, and then I managed to put it off long enough, becoming such a goddam success, that when I finally went, I went alone."

I hadn't been listening to Kitty and she hadn't noticed. I finished my drink and did what I was certain Big Tim Molloy must have done hundreds of times as she was taking him through the entire Social Register: I told her I was going to the bar. But before I could, she clamped her big-diamond hand on my wrist, said there was somebody I just absolutely had to meet, and then started leading me through the rabble like she was Vonteego D'Amore, our All-Pro center.

Babs and Kenny were talking to some guy who had his back to me, but quickly excused themselves when they saw me coming. Babs whispered something in the guy's ear and then all I could see of her was her shoulder blades disappearing like tail fins on an old Chevrolet Impala.

"Allen, you scamp," Kitty said. "I thought I'd lost you!"

He was about my height, maybe an inch or two taller, with an old-fashioned crew cut and nerd glasses with thick black frames. Even in formal clothes, he had his trademark red and blue Sharpies sticking out of the breast pocket of his tuxedo jacket. Even if you didn't know a microchip from a cow chip, you knew this was Allen Getz himself.

Or Allen Getz What He Wants, which is the way he had been known to most of the civilized world since *Time* had used that headline in making him their Man of the Year a few years before. Really, he was Getz.com and he was still the richest and most powerful dot com of them all. Somehow since the early 1990s, he had managed to maintain the biggest inventory, the lowest prices and every book ever written, even, as he told *Time*, all the ones "with those icky toilet words in them." At the high end, his catalogue and web site read like Neiman-Marcus and at the low end, an old five-and-dime store. Somehow he had managed to become one of the ten wealthiest men in the world over the last decade, even if no one could show a single quarter when Getz.com had ever turned a profit.

I knew he was in his late thirties, single, and still lived in some remote part of New Mexico near where he'd built his first warehouse. But I'd read in one of the tabloids a few days before that he'd moved into a new triplex at 71 East 71st, on Park, one of the best buildings in town.

I only knew that because I'd grown up there.

"Jack," Kitty said, "I'd like you to meet my dear dear friend, Allen Getz."

She dropped my hand and took his, like a trapeze artist going from one Wallenda to the next.

"Golly," he said, giving me a full-pump handshake, "it sure is nice to finally meet Tim's son."

"You knew my father?"

He gave Kitty's bare shoulder a squeeze and it gave her a reason to press her tits into him a little more.

"Thanks to this gal right here," he said.

I told him my stepmom certainly was an amazing woman, knowing Kitty liked me calling her stepmom as much as she liked her butt beginning to drop like the big Waterford ball in Times Square on New Year's Eve.

"Neat party," Allen Getz said. "I was just telling Kenny and Babs that I mean, wow, I felt like I was in the middle of a feature on *Entertainment Tonight*."

I mumbled something about how festive it all was.

He said, "This whole thing makes me more excited than ever about this swell opportunity with the Hawks, which I really, really think is going to be win win for everybody involved."

Kitty suddenly got that frantic look she'd get when a better dress suddenly appeared on her radar.

"Is that Bobby and Blaine Trump over there?" she said in a voice that seemed to have jumped a couple of octaves. "Blaine said she would just scratch my new eyes out if she didn't get to meet you, Allen."

I quietly said to him, "What opportunity would that be, exactly?"

Kitty shrieked, "Oh . . . my . . . God! Mo Jiggy showed up after all!"

That part wasn't a diversion. The rapper had just walked into the ballroom with what looked like an NBA starting five of bodyguards. Mo Jiggy himself was wearing what looked to be a white Philadelphia 76ers home jersey under his black morning coat, baggy blue surgeon's pants and ballet slippers. He also had one of those new cell phones with the earplugs and the microphone dangling from a cord underneath his chin. On his arm was Kelli Ann Gonzalez, the former Miss America now starring on the television show *Baywatch: The New Millennium*.

Kitty tried to pull Allen Getz in Mo Jiggy's direction, but I had my hand firmly on his arm now.

"You mentioned a business opportunity with the Hawks," I said.

He said, "Your brother and sister didn't tell you?" He looked down at Kitty. "You didn't tell him, Kitten?"

I said, "Tell me what?"

"About renaming the stadium."

I looked at Kitty and then at him and then back at Kitty, who seemed to want to be anywhere in North America now except right here with Allen Getz and me.

"Which stadium?"

"Yours."

"Mine already has a name."

He stammered a bit and then said, well, gee, it probably was going to have a new name if Kenny and Babs decided to take the hundred mil.

Across the ballroom I could see Mo Jiggy air-kissing the mayor's wife and then giving Cardinal Moriarty a handshake that looked more complicated than the whole Bible in sign language. They'd done a piece on Dan Rather a couple of nights before, showing the cardinal baptizing Mo Jiggy at the man-made lake he'd had built for his swans in East Hampton.

I took a deep breath and let it out and said, "The twins are thinking about selling you the naming rights."

"It's real early, but it kinda looks that way," he said. "They said they weren't ready to give up their half of the Hawks just yet, but that this would be a neat way for them to lay off some of those pesky estate taxes."

Kitty was gasping again because Liza Minnelli, who had put on a few since she revived *Cabaret* for Billy last year, had just showed up.

"Getz Dot Com Stadium," I said.

"Field," he said. "Getz Dot Com Field. Kind of catchy, don't you think?"

Allen Getz had moved in fast, I had to give him that. He must have talked to Wick Sanderson, and Sanderson had told him that he had no shot getting my half, at least until after the owners' vote. So he'd gone straight for the twins, probably with Kitty's help, willing to pay a hundred million, over however many years, just to get his foot in the goddam door.

Didn't you tell him, Kitten?

She must have had something going on with him while the old man was still alive, which would have put Allen Getz into a club about as small as the Army Reserve. Maybe it was just a way of Kitty hedging her bets. If she played her cards right and the computer geek was willing to hang in there, she could be back to being First Lady of the Hawks by next season.

Allen Getz Fucking Field.

I thought: Over my dead fucking body.

I finally spotted Kenny and Babs near the podium from where Kitty would welcome all her dear dear friends once she decided they had enough suck-up and face time with her hunky monkeys. Kenny saw me about the same time I saw him, and did what he'd pretty much done since we were teenagers and he'd burned a cigarette hole in the old man's leather chair and blamed it on me:

He ran like he was the anchor leg of the asshole relay.

And I would have followed him all the way to Central Park South and then into the park and all the way to his summer house on Shelter Island, if Bubba Royal, frustrated about the sudden line coming out of the men's room and drunker than a bachelor party, hadn't picked that particular moment to piss into the sink Kelli Ann Gonzalez was using to freshen up.

seventeen

ccording to Kelli Ann, Bubba was originally quite courtly when he walked into the ladies' room. She said he called her "Hon" and complimented her on what he described as an eye-catching dress, which consisted mostly of straps and material so flimsy you could see the tattoo "Almost There" right below her pierced navel.

"But before I knew it," she said to reporters later, "he unzipped his pants and pulled out that . . . thing and just started going and going. And going."

Kelli Ann added, "I've never seen anything like it in my life, unless you count Death Toll."

Death Toll was Mo Jiggy's horse.

Kelli Ann finally cut short her fascination with Bubba and began to scream in the soprano that had pretty much clinched the talent contest for her at Miss America.

Kitty's Welcome Home Dinner for the Hawks disintegrated rather quickly after that.

Mo Jiggy, for obvious reasons, instantly recognized some of the notes Kelli Ann was hitting, even over the screams of some of the other women in the ladies' room, among them the eleven o'clock anchor at Channel 4, Tina Brown of *Talk* magazine, Raiford Dionne's wife Luscious, the girl-friend of one of the deputy mayors, and the noted lesbian photographer Marty Fisher.

"The rest of them came out of their stalls and saw old Trigger doing his thing and all I could feel in the room was a lot of love," Marty said on NY1 later when they interviewed her and Luscious Dionne, who said the only stream she'd ever seen like that was underneath her whitewater raft.

As soon as Kelli Ann came charging out of the ladies' room in her familiar babe-lifeguard sprint from *Baywatch*, heading back down the marble hallway toward the Terrace Room, Mo Jiggy yelled "Go! Go! Go!" at his security, who all produced guns on cue, as if the training sessions were over and this was some kind of code red.

There would be the suggestion later that in all the confusion that followed, some of our players pulled out guns of their own from beneath their tuxedoes, waving their carry permits as they did. But since everybody in the room from the police commissioner on down was a big Hawks fan, there was nothing more than speculation in the television news reports that night and in the morning papers.

I had followed the general noise and confusion out into the hall, passing Kelli Ann Gonzalez as I did. I got to the ladies' room in time to see two of Mo's guys on either side of the door like the stars of *Law and Order* ready to go into the apartment after the bad guy. The rest of them were in a crouch position facing the door as Bubba came out, zipping up and saying to someone behind him, "Thanks, Hon, but that wasn't nearly even close to a record."

One of Mo Jiggy's guys came from behind Bubba and threw him up against the pink-colored wallpaper. The other one started to bring the butt handle of his gun up to the side of Bubba's head, when I interrupted him with a rolling block that made my bad knee feel like it had that day against the USC Trojans.

That gave Bubba enough time to disable the guy holding him with a soccer-style kick to the balls.

The rest of the Hawks showed up then.

The last thing I saw before a lot of the crowd fell on Bubba and me was Raiford Dionne holding Mo Jiggy up off the ground, Mo's ballet slippers kicking wildly in the air.

Raiford said, "Sing me one of your bibbity-bobbity-boo cop killer songs now."

Wick Sanderson announced a one-game suspension for Bubba the next day, which meant he would miss the opener, the commissioner explaining that this was his second ladies' room of the preseason, which put him over the league limit.

Bobby Camby strained a quadriceps muscle trying to pull Kelli Ann Gonzalez off Raiford Dionne, but when he tested it in light pads the next afternoon at practice, pronounced himself ready to go against the Saints.

"Bitch blindsided me with some kind of kick-box move," Bobby Camby told Brian Goldberg, when he was getting taped up. "Somebody better tell her that getting' down with Jiggy gonna be a faster career-ender than all that weight she startin' to put on."

I shut off all the phones in 19 and slept in. Annie finally let herself in about noon and spread the papers all over the bed with a flourish. It turned out the *Post* and *News* had both used the same picture on the front page, the one that made it look as if Bubba and I were trying to crawl our way out of a formal-wear Million Man March.

It was also one of those days when they both decided to use the same headline:

"HAWKS PISS AWAY OPENER" is what both tabloids said.

eighteen

The average operating profit for a team in the National Football League at the start of the current season, I had discovered as part of the crash course Liz and Pete had been giving me all week, was $30 million a year.

The thirty-four teams now in the league were worth more in some cities than others, but even owners who didn't know if a football was blown up or stuffed with feathers, as Bill Parcells had once said, were guaranteed a profit of at least $30 million before anybody called heads or tails on the opening Sunday, at which I had somehow arrived as half-owner of the New York Hawks.

The Hawks, even with the old man doing everything he could to keep ticket prices in a general area where regulation fans didn't have to take out a second mortgage to come to the games, made $40 million in ticket sales alone, after what even the consumer advocate people described as only modest increases over the last five years. Pete said that my father used to tell him that he knew enough rich assholes already, he didn't need to fill his stadium with fifty-five thousand more every Sunday.

We made another $10 million a year in local radio rights from WNUT, the official Hawks station.

Concessions brought in another $8 million, even though the old man wouldn't allow the sale of beer after halftime.

Advertising, parking and other miscellaneous shit brought in another $15 million. If Kenny and Babs had their way, the miscellaneous, maybe as soon as this season and every one of the next ten seasons, would include $10 million from Allen Getz.

That was if I couldn't properly find a way to slow down negotiations between Getz and my brother and sister.

Before anybody even opened the doors the first Sunday after Labor Day, every single team in the National Football League picked up $85 million from network television. That included international money as well as domestic, because now even people in London and Paris and Rome and Munich were watching American football on Sunday. But most of the money came from ABC/ESPN, Fox, NBC, CBS.

Our partners.

"I asked one of the geniuses one time why they paid us this kind of money," Pete Stanton had said. "And the guy said, 'You can't rent today's game, that's why.'"

The player costs wiped out the television money. Eighty-five million in, eighty-five million out.

The cost of actually running the business, all the overhead that went with it, was about $25 million in the modern NFL. It was more expensive in New York just because everything was more expensive in New York.

When you added everything up, the league average for total operating expenses came to about $100 million, give or take a few chips. The total revenues, on average, were $130 million.

Average is the key word here. We made a lot more with the Hawks because of the luxury boxes.

"That's where you put your whales," Billy Grace said.

Whales were what we called the highest of the high rollers in Vegas. Whales were why the Bellagio wanted to be better than the MGM Grand, and why Kirk Kerkorian bought the Mirage from Wynn and why Billy

Grace wanted to have better digs and better suites and better everything than all of them. Everybody had the same tables in Vegas, the same limits, the same odds. The Strip was three and a half miles long and you could walk in a casino at one end and never go outside until you came out the other end, through Amazing Grace. There would be security cameras on you the entire way, because that was the town now, along with all the improvements and all the theme-park special effects.

One thing hadn't changed: the biggest of the big spenders. Whales made all the difference.

The old man made more money off his luxury boxes than anybody else in the league. Over at Giants Stadium, where the Giants and Jets both played their home games, they cut the take from their boxes three ways: the Giants got a third, the Jets got a third, the state of New Jersey got a third.

Tim Molloy, who built his own stadium, got it all. His house. House money. He understood the concept as well as Billy Grace or anybody else in Vegas ever could. There was no fixed ceiling on any of the thirty suites, any more than there was any real limit on the lines of credit Billy gave out to his whales. With the whales, it was whatever they wanted, or needed. With the old man's suite owners, it was whatever he decided they'd be willing to pay. I remember him telling me once when he was about to get into Winged Foot that if he ever owned his own country club, he'd run it this way:

No initiation fee.

No uniform annual dues.

No waiting list.

No membership committee.

Just him.

"Take that bullethead who owns the movie stores, for example," he said.

He was talking about Wayne Huizenga, then the Blockbuster Video king. This was before Huizenga bought the Dolphins. His name was actually pronounced High-zenga, but the old man never did get it. It's "Farve" for Brett Favre. I was sure my father called him Favor to the end.

"Say somebody like Hugh-zinger wanted to get into my club," he said. "He'd say, 'How much initiation?' I'd say, 'Half-a-million.' That would be my Hugh-zinger price, just because I don't have much use for the fellow. But say somebody like The Kicker moved back from Dallas and he wanted to join."

Pat Summerall had always been The Kicker to him. When he wasn't Old Number 88.

The old man said, "Before he stopped drinking, I would've only asked him to cover his bar bills."

His philosophy was to be fair with the people in the stands and then go upstairs and say to his whales, "Okay, this is a stickup." The high-end suites went for as much as a million dollars. The old man used to tell Liz Bolton he just imagined he was selling condominiums, in a choice location. If he didn't like your business, you were out. If he didn't like your politics, out. He'd turned down one former governor, two former senators, and one former secretary of state, all Republicans. He turned down most rock stars and had only gone for Madonna because Kitty had begged and Madonna had promised to show up for games in regulation clothes. Nobody knew what anybody else was paying, because you signed a secrecy clause in your contract with the team. Your price was your price. If you didn't want to pay, the old man moved on to somebody else.

On the day he died, he was clearing $20 million a year, sheer profit, on the suites. It was one more reason why the Hawks had just been rated the top value in the NFL, ahead of the Cowboys. We had a contending team, packed houses in a stadium we owned, and whales crawling all over the place at the loge and mezzanine levels behind the tinted glass.

I stood on the field at ten-thirty in the morning, less than two hours before the Hawks would play the Saints, and looked around as the first fans began to make their way to their seats. And for a few minutes, I didn't worry about Allen Getz or Bubba Royal or the evil twins or whatever scum vermin it was who'd gotten Ferret Biel to sell me out. I listened to the rock-and-roll songs I'd ordered to replace Mo Jiggy's rap on the sound system—Aretha, Temptations, Four Tops, old Supremes, Chuck

Berry—and saw the first of the Hawks, without pads, come out of the tunnel at the other end of the stadium from where I was and begin light-tossing the ball.

God, as Frankie Molloy would always tell my father on Sunday morning, was good.

"It's actually still a pretty good game when you can wrestle it away from the big bank accounts and their tiny little peckers," someone next to me said.

Josh Blake, named after the legendary Negro Leagues catcher Josh Gibson, was our offensive coordinator and, according to just about everybody I'd talked to, the coolest guy in the entire organization, after Pete Stanton. He was thirty, handsome, black, a former All-America quarterback from Michigan who'd passed up a Rhodes Scholarship because he wanted to play pro football. He'd been drafted in the first round to replace Bubba someday, in the days when Tucker O'Neill was still in the second row of the boys chorale in Jesus Loves You, Utah, or wherever it was he'd come from. But then he got hit just as he was bringing his arm forward in a late-November game against the Bills his rookie year. He was only in there to mop up in a game the Hawks were winning by four touchdowns, but he decided he wanted to show off his arm, and it was as if somebody ran his rotator cuff through a shredder. He hung around for four seasons as a safety and special teams guy, even made the Pro Bowl as a special teamer his last year.

Then he started drawing X's and O's for Gadge Kopka, Vince's predecessor with the Hawks, and it turned out that Josh Blake's X's and O's were so much better than everybody else's that you could practically dance to them.

Now he was coming to the end of the line with the Hawks, unless Vince Cahill either packed it in or suffered some kind of massive coronary one morning on the treadmill. Josh Blake had been officially designated as the boy wonder of coaching, even though nobody could actually call him *boy* in the newspaper without a picket line immediately forming.

It didn't seem to hurt him terribly that he was the color he was and not another fat white guy in a sweater.

"How do you know I'm not one of those big-bankroll, little-dick guys?" I said.

Josh Blake grinned and said, "The word on you, especially with what I've seen coming out of Suite Nineteen in the mornings, is that it's the other way around."

Annie and I had spent the last three nights there getting to know each other a lot better.

"So how do we look?" I said. "Isn't that what owners are supposed to ask?"

Josh Blake smiled. He looked even younger than he actually was. He wore an old-fashioned Hawks letter jacket, the kind with leather sleeves, and pressed chinos and plain white hightop sneakers. His hair was cut so close it looked as if it had been spray-painted on.

"You should see your brother," Josh said. "He even gets in the pre-game prayer circle."

"It probably gives him a sense of belonging," I said.

"Your sister, too," he said. "Elvis Elgin thinks she's got a crush on him. Or at least a fascination with certain parts."

I briefly imagined Babs disappearing underneath Elvis Elgin like a Kleenex tissue.

"Can we throw it today?"

Josh said, "Even without A.T.M., we think our speed guys can beat their outside guys. I'm just hoping we can get something out of Guns of Navarone."

We had signed Guns of Navarone Queens late the night before, after the league had received assurance that his probation had been wiped out when he got his conviction overturned.

"Everybody knows Tucker's got more arm than Bubba," Josh said. "But it doesn't mean squat if he can't show it off."

He nodded toward the other end, where Tucker O'Neill was throwing one perfect spiral after another to one of the ballboys.

"Tucker would like nothing better than to throw for five TDs and about four hundred yards today and then hint afterward that Bubba Royal is older than the T-formation."

"Does Tucker hate Bubba that much?"

"Bubba's just in his way, is all. So while Tucker's position in public is that we're all God's children, he wants Bubba to drive his car off the Triboro Bridge on his way to practice someday."

He said he had to go get with his receivers coach. I shook his hand and wished him luck and told him to tell all the guys to do it for their schools.

Josh Blake said, "Hell, our boys are looser than their own morals, baby. We all know that even if we lose, everybody's going to put it on your ass, anyway."

I had stayed around the locker room long enough to hear Vince Cahill's pregame speech to the team. I lost count somewhere in the middle, but I was pretty sure he had used the word *fuck* seventy-two times in a twelve-minute presentation.

The last part made me bite down so hard on my knuckle that I drew blood.

"Those fuckers in the other locker room want to beat your fucking asses because of one thing," he said. His face was so red against the orange hair, all of that set off against his blue Hawks sweater, that he brought a sunset to mind. "They want to beat you because you're the New York Fucking Hawks and they're fucking not."

Vince took a deep breath and then said, "Okay, chapel in two minutes."

Annie Kay was waiting for me upstairs when I got out of my private elevator. She was also in Hawks blue, a summer dress that showed off just enough of her legs and the rest of her long freckled amazing self. She said she'd gotten to the box about an hour before and had been mingling the way she imagined her personal hero, Kitty Drucker-Cole Molloy, surely would have.

"How is it inside?" I said.

"It's a good night at Beef, just without a lot of the ambience," she said, and kissed me chastely on the cheek.

I asked her to give me a read on the mood in there and she said excellent, if you were the kind of positive-type person she was, that the people who thought I was in over my head far outnumbered the ones who thought I was trying to get back at my father by destroying the team.

Unfortunately, Big Tim Molloy didn't like to put things off. So he had sent out tickets and passes to the opening game about a week before he died. I didn't have to worry about Suite 19, nobody besides Liz and Pete and Annie and me would be allowed in there once the game started. But the other rooms in the extended box were like some sort of celebrity oil spill from the Welcome Home Dinner, all of whom had recovered from the excitement with Bubba and Mo Jiggy. There were even some of the old man's friends I recognized, from business and television and politics and church and just all around big-guy-ness, who actually seemed more interested in watching the game than being seen.

I noticed when I got upstairs about fifteen minutes before the kickoff that somebody had allowed a television crew from NBC in there. The hunk from the pregame show, Brock Cleveland, said they were looking at doing a sensitive piece about the "pall hanging over this box and this day, even though we all know that Big Tim Molloy is looking down from his new digs in the sky."

I said to Brock Cleveland that I certainly wouldn't want to be quoted on something like this, but that I was always fascinated when people started taking me through a dead guy's normal day.

Kenny and Babs had their own box, Suite 17, four or five doors down the hallway at about the 35-yard line. I assumed Kitty was there with Allen Getz. I had told her that if I laid eyes on him he better have changed his plans about the naming rights, or start hoping that you could buy a new set of teeth from Getz.com. Brian Goldberg was upstairs working the press box, but he said that if more gunplay broke out, I should definitely page him.

I pretended I was still the Jammer and tried to mingle as best I could. I saw Pete Stanton standing over near the putting green and he made one of those crossing gestures that are supposed to scare off vampires. Liz

Bolton was standing near the game seats in front, back to the field, chatting with Michael Douglas and Senator Chuck Schumer. Don Hewitt, the producer of *60 Minutes*, was in a group that included Steinbrenner, Chris Rock, Spike Lee, and Rosie O'Donnell.

Ol' Dirty Bastard, one of Mo Jiggy's rival rappers, had his arm around Martha Stewart.

Wick Sanderson was chatting up Carole Sandusky, whom I'd flown in for this occasion, even if she'd been instructed not to tell the commissioner that beforehand.

Carole winked at me, then leaned down and kissed Wick Sanderson on the top of his head, like Mommy getting ready to send him off to school. I'd told her to call me later with any information she'd picked up while she had him over her knee.

Annie said, "Is it like this everywhere in football today?"

"Pretty much," I said. "But it's like Big Tim always told me: The only problem for everybody else is that they're out of town."

Pete Stanton said that the first luxury boxes were at the Astrodome in Houston in 1965, when that became the first indoor stadium. The eighth wonder of the world, they called it at the time, but Pete said that was before the invention of the modern players' union. At about the same time, Dodger Stadium put in some celebrity seats down at the field level, where you could watch Cary Grant and Doris Day and Frank Sinatra eat popcorn and cheer for Sandy Koufax. But it was the late Edward Bennett Williams, the big-shot Washington lawyer who ended up buying the Saints, who had first turned the whole idea of an owner's box into some football version of Hef's Place. The camera would pan over to Williams's box at old Robert F. Kennedy Stadium and you'd see presidents sometimes and vice-presidents and cabinet members and network anchors and Kay Graham and little Georgie Will, squeezed in there like this was the last lifeboat off the *Titanic*, knowing they were getting a lot of face time on CBS, and knowing something else, much more important: This was the glamorous place to be on Sunday afternoons, like some A-list Georgetown cocktail party.

Pete had made his way over to where Annie and I stood, surveying the rabble. In a Westchester lockjaw voice, he said, "Lovely party."

I told him I'd had all the color and pageantry I could handle, it was time to go kick some Saints ass.

It was Hawks 7, Saints 7 at halftime when Bobby Finkel, the Saints' owner, stopped by Suite 19, uninvited, to say hello, as if this were some sort of protocol for hot-shit owners like us. He wore a blue pin-striped suit, spit-polished black loafers with cute tassles on them, over-sized wire-rimmed glasses with a rose-colored tint to them, and was holding a cigar that was bigger than he was, which was about five-three, five-four.

"Oh, look," Pete Stanton said under his breath. "It's Tom Thumb."

Finkel had a bodyguard with him I thought I recognized from some-where. Then Bobby Finkel said that if I was from Vegas, hey, I had to know his main man, Edge.

I did. He had once been the biggest draw for the Wrestling Universe Federation (WUF), which was headquartered in Vegas, along with its hit television show on the WB network, *Tuesday Night Testosterone*. Billy had let them shoot *Tuesday Night Testosterone* at Amazing Grace the first two seasons it was on the air, but eventually decided it looked bad when the wrestlers had bigger breasts than the girls in the shows.

"You helped put Andy Stein Tyrone on the map," I said to Edge.

Andy Stein Tyrone was the founder of WUF and North American dis-tributor of several designer steroids still masquerading as diet supple-ments in Tyrone's chain of health food stores.

Edge gave me an aw-shucks nod. He was about twice Bobby Finkel's size, had blond hair pulled back into a ponytail and wore a white t-shirt that showed off a massive upper body and what appeared to be about a twenty-seven-inch waist.

"He's my driver now," Finkel said. "You can't be too safe these days in my line of work."

"What, dwarf undercover cop?" I said, but he didn't hear me. He had taken too deep a pull on his water and had gone into a coughing fit.

"I'm a celebrity now, what can I say?" Bobby Finkel said, when he finally got his breath back. "What, only Mo Jiggy-boo needs security?"

"You guys moved the ball pretty well," Liz Bolton said. "I like your quarterback."

The Saints had signed Toby Luckett in the off-season after his much-publicized stay in rehab for amphetamines, painkillers and dietary supplements. Bobby Finkel said, "I was just saying to Edge here that being a speed freak hadn't affected his arm at all."

When Finkel smiled, it was somewhat like a shark opening up to show us his teeth. "The bastard cried like a baby when he asked for a second chance. How funny is that? Most of these guys have no freaking clue."

Toby Luckett had gotten hooked on the painkillers the previous season for the Vikings, playing the last four games of the regular season and the wildcard game with a broken bone in his left leg.

Finkel jerked his head toward the bar area and Edge nearly ran over there to get him a bottle of designer water. He brought it back in what seemed to be record time and Finkel took a swig. "Sonofabitch," he said, "this stuff runs right through me. I must have peed ten or fifteen times since the opening kickoff already."

Liz Bolton was so fascinated by this information that she said she had to go make an important phone call.

Bobby Finkel turned to Pete and said, "What'd you think of the first half, big guy?"

Deadpan, Pete said, "You tell me, Bobby, you've been around this game a long time." If you didn't count the preseason, this was Bobby Finkel's first official game as owner of the Saints.

Finkel either didn't hear or simply ignored Pete, because he was trying to take in everything in Suite 19 at once, including Annie Kay, who was sitting on the couch with her legs crossed, nervously flipping one of her sandals, studying the first-half stat sheet, occasionally stopping to make some sort of mark on it with a ballpoint pen. I had noticed during the first half that Liz Bolton ignored every sharp observation Annie made about the game and generally tried to keep an entire time zone between them.

"I better not let Muffin in here," Bobby Finkel said. "My wife. The fabulous Muffster. Jesus, if she ever gets a look at the inside of this freaking place, I'm going to have to spend more money decorating our suite than I paid for that fat slob I've got at nose tackle. You see him in the first half? I want to see one replay where he actually got up out of that crouch that makes it look like he's taking a dump."

Only Edge laughed.

"These freaking guys," Bobby Finkel continued, gesturing toward the field. Players from both teams had come back out for the second half. "My coach, the lovable goober? I mean, where did he coach before the Saints, Deliverance State? The first day I got the team, even before the Finance Committee approved me, I sat down with him and said, 'I didn't get into this business to lose.' You know what he says to me? 'You better get used to it.' Freaking guys. They wouldn't last five minutes in e-trade."

Annie was up at the front row of the box, opening windows.

"Sorry about your father," Bobby Finkel said to me. "He seemed like a nice enough old guy."

Before I could say anything, he said, "I'm outta here. Gotta go pee again. Nice chatting with you."

He nodded at Edge, who opened the door, checked out the hallway, and Bobby Finkel left.

Pete said, "You know what's rather frightening? He's one of the more evolved of the new guys."

Annie smiled brilliantly and asked which Pinter play I thought Edge liked best.

About a minute later, Boogie Wise, the Saints kick returner who'd recently been featured on the cover of *Sports Illustrated*'s annual Tattoo Issue—he wore a Speedo bathing suit and showed off a tattooed chest that featured the likenesses of all eight of his children—returned Benito Siragusa's kickoff ninety-seven yards for a touchdown.

It was 28–28 in the fourth quarter when Vince Cahill got an unsportsmanlike conduct penalty for bumping an official after a critical pass interference call against Guns of Navarone Queens. The controversy the next day wasn't as much about the call as the allegation from the guy who'd made the call, Ike Werner, that Vince had suggested that he'd obviously left Hebrew school before they got to the part about pass interference.

Vince didn't help himself later when he asked, "I thought his people were known for a sense of humor. Hell, Shecky Greene is one of my best friends."

That was the end of the Hawks drive that looked as if it might tie the game with four minutes to go. On the Saints' next play from scrimmage, Toby Luckett hit Boogie Wise for a seventy-seven-yard touchdown pass to put their team back ahead, where they would stay.

We had one last chance. We were at the Saints' 48-yard line, fourth-and-ten, half a minute to play. Tucker O'Neill had just called our last time-out. As soon as Pete Stanton saw the formation, he said, "Gadget play."

Liz nodded. "A.T.M. made Vince call it 'Big Sticky' in the playbook for some reason."

Pete said, "Quarterback takes a one-step drop and throws it to A.T.M. on the side, at least when he's not off seeing the world. It looks like a pass, but it's actually a lateral if they run it right. As soon as A.T.M. catches it, he steps back and throws a bomb to whatever wideout we've got on the other side of the field."

The two of them were standing, so I did, too.

I said, "Has it ever actually worked in a game?"

"Nah," Pete said. "But goddam if it didn't work like a charm in practice when A.T.M. was still here."

The whole stadium was up now, sounding like a runway. If we hit the play, we tied the game, sent the whole thing into overtime. It occurred to me that even for somebody who used to make fun of the old man for living and dying with the Hawks the way he did, the moment was ridiculously exciting. This was the moment I usually watched from the sidelines in the casino, some guy letting a pile of chips ride on one throw of the dice, or one turn of the dealer's card.

"The old man was right," I said to Pete, grinning. "This shit is better than sex."

"Not even close," he said.

I could hear Annie saying something like "Ex*cuse* me?" just as Tucker stepped back from center the way Pete predicted he would and threw over to his right where Guns of Navarone Queens was waiting for the ball.

Through clenched teeth, Liz Bolton said, "Step . . . back."

Tucker's throw seemed to travel right along the midfield stripe. It was a little low, but Guns of Navarone fielded it cleanly and straightened up and then threw the ball as far as he could down the left sideline to where Quadripro Cleveland was about two yards behind the Saints defense.

Quadripro held on for the touchdown and then performed his familiar pagan ritual dance in the end zone, the highlight of which involved him humping the ground and then taking a puff of an imaginary post-sex cigarette.

"I can't lie, I get a kick out of that one," Annie said.

"Imagine that," Liz said, turning her head slightly, just as Pete Stanton seemed to say about a dozen curse words in a row and threw down his game program.

The last word he said was "flag."

"Goddam," Liz said, "they're going to say it was a forward goddam pass."

Pete said, "They're going to the replay."

Liz said, "They'll never reverse."

Pete said, "I love this fucking rule. If the zebras are only a little bit wrong, the call on the field stands. But if they really really suck, then you've got a chance."

Annie said it sounded exactly like the Supreme Court.

"Who the hell in this organization keeps voting for this stupid rule?" Pete said.

"You," Liz said.

The line judge had ruled that Guns of Navarone was in front of the point from which Tucker had released the ball. The rules only allow you to throw one forward pass per play, which meant that Guns of Navarone's pass to Quadripro Cleveland was illegal. Which meant no tying touch-down for the Hawks, unless the official checking the replay on the field camera used for plays like this decided the line judge had clearly made a horrible tragic mistake.

"I'm telling you," Pete said, after watching the replay they were showing on NBC, "we've got no shot."

The lead official came back on the field, clicked on his microphone and said, "The call on the field stands. Illegal forward pass. Five yards from the spot of the original catch. Repeat fourth down."

We repeated fourth down. Tucker threw one up for grabs in the end zone. Guns of Navarone had the best shot at it for us, but the Saints' rookie safety, Cassius Bietch, batted the ball away.

The clock said 0:00. The scoreboard said Visitors 35, Hawks 28. We were 0–1. It was only the opener, but I already felt busted.

"The French have a word that covers this," Pete Stanton said.

"*Qu'est que c'est?*" Annie Kay asked.

"Shitfuck," he said.

nineteen

nnie said she'd promised one of the other bartenders she'd
work for her. She said that Donyell's man, Funk Dat, who
managed the place when Donyell was away, had decided
this season to open on Sunday nights after home games, or
early away games if the Hawks were somewhere close like Washington or
Philadelphia. She said she'd probably have to close up, so she'd call
tomorrow. Pete said he was going downstairs to his office and start calling both Donyell and A.T.M. on their cells, international cells, international pagers. If he couldn't reach them that way, he was going to try
London information and ask if they had any listings for After Hours joints.

Bubba had called Suite 19 from the locker room and said he was
going to be at The Last Good Year later, but first he'd promised Martha
Stewart that he'd stop by the new bistro she'd opened on the West Side
near Café des Artistes, called Public Offering, in honor of the killing she'd
made on Wall Street a couple of years before.

"I'm startin' to think that old girl wants to run her hands over Bubba
the way she does those ferns and things on her TV show," he said.

Billy called after Bubba and said that if I already had my head in the oven, he'd call back, but he wanted me to be the first to know that the day wasn't a total loss.

I told him I'd love to know how and he said, "Because I bet so big on the over, I think my hands are cramping up from that carpet tunnel thing the dealers get sometimes."

One of the ways you could bet pro football was with something called the over-under. Vegas, and then the bookies, would establish a number that was supposed to be the combined number of points two teams would score in a game. Then you had to decide whether they would score more or less. The over-under number for the Hawks-Saints game had been fifty, which he decided was insanely low, even with Bubba and A.T.M. not playing.

I mentioned that it sounded pretty noisy in the background for six o'clock Vegas time.

"We decided if we were going to properly share your pain, we might as well start the postgame buffet early," he said.

A lot of his guests must have hit the hot tub already, because I heard a sound like waves crashing and then a lot of squeals and laughter.

"Hey," Billy Grace said, "you know who turned out to be kind of a cute kid? That Inger. You know, the one with Ferret Biel? She called Vinny yesterday and said she was lonely, could she come out and play?"

"Any Ferret sightings, by the way?"

Billy said that Inger remembered him taking an overnight trip about a week ago, but he wouldn't tell her where he was going. She still hadn't heard from him and was saying now that she hoped the little shitweasel never came back.

"If Bubba plays, we score on that last drive," Billy said.

"We're urging him to keep Big Bubba in his pants this week," I said. "The entire organization feels that's an excellent blueprint for success against the Dolphins."

"It's like I always told you, " he said. "Don't lose sight of the fundamentals." There was another squeal of laughter and Billy said, "Gotta go, kid. Surf's up."

I came out of the bedroom and Liz Bolton was still in the same seat from which she'd watched the game, a fresh drink next to her. She swiveled around and said, "I know you've got cigarettes in here somewhere, give 'em up."

"You smoke?"

"Only after gut-wrenching, heartbreaking losses at home."

The Marlboros actually belonged to Annie, though I didn't mention it to Liz, who hadn't been thrilled that we'd set up a chair for Annie here in the war room. I grabbed the old man's lighter from next to the cigar humidor he kept on top of the bar, fixed myself a Scotch, and then Liz Bolton and I sat and looked out at what was still known as Molloy Stadium, the field completely empty now except for four boys, probably coaches' sons, playing a game of tackle football near midfield.

The only sound was from the blowers the workmen were using to clear garbage out of the aisles.

On the other side of the stadium, two levels up from where we sat, I could see sportswriters pounding away at laptops. As I watched them, the phone rang. I thought about not answering it, but thought it might be Pete. It turned out to be a columnist from the *Daily News* named Gil Spencer, who said he had the inside line because Tim Molloy had given it to him. He said he wasn't going to wear my ass out, he just wanted to ask a couple of questions. I told him one, he was interrupting what was going to be a rather lengthy cocktail hour. Spencer said, okay, he'd keep it simple and asked how much I thought we'd missed Bubba and A.T.M.

"I know it's a dumb question," he said. "But, hey, asking them is a living."

I told Spencer I couldn't speak for everybody else, but I missed them both the way I missed making out with Ellie Rhodes in the backseat of my old man's Seville.

"Any thoughts about changing your long-held policy on renegotiation?" he said.

"Nah."

"I figured. Can I give you a piece of advice?"

"Sure."

"Don't listen to WNUT for the next several years."

I told him that my listening habits hadn't changed since high school, that Imus in the Morning gave me all the information I needed, then I shut the radio off for the rest of the day.

When I hung up, Liz said, "Ellie Rhodes?"

"She plays the spunky sister now on John Ritter's new sitcom," I said. "I read in *People* or somewhere that she likes girls now."

"And how do you feel about that?"

"My position is that after me, there was nowhere else to go in heterosexuality except down."

Liz Bolton said, "Losing really sucks, doesn't it?"

"Worse than Ellie," I said sadly, and she laughed for the first time since I'd met her in the hallway with Pete.

We sat there drinking and smoking. The kids left the field and the blowers stopped blowing. Someone switched off the field lights and just left on the smaller ones set above the upper deck, which gave off a halo effect. We switched from Scotch to a bottle of the old man's Remy.

"Don't tell me," she said. "Ellie was a cheerleader."

"Push 'em back, push 'em back," I said. "Way back."

"Me, too," Liz said.

I turned and looked at her. "No way."

"Way," she said, handing me her empty glass. "I was a good girl, then I strayed."

She'd gotten her first on-air job when she was still at Stanford, with a television station in San Jose. She was a junior. The spring of her senior year, on a lark, she sent an audition tape to ESPN in Bristol, Connecticut. The guy in charge of hiring watched the tape and faxed her back immediately with the following message:

"You start as soon as we get back from our honeymoon."

She hated the job from the start, no matter how many times the people in charge told her how much the camera loved her. By the time

she was twenty-five, she was already tired of those same executives hitting on her, the athletes, all the single guys in the media and about half
the marrieds. Mostly she got tired of standing on the sideline at places
like Soldier Field, on Sundays so bitterly cold they should have had bob-
sled runs, and talking about absolutely nothing.

She stood up in Suite 19, holding an imaginary microphone, staring
into an imaginary camera, bobbing her head slightly from side to side.

"I spoke to him at halftime and he's still maintaining it was just an
over-the-counter diet pill," she said. "Back to you, Boomer."

She took a year off in New Mexico, then came back and reinvented
herself in management at ESPN.

"What is it again that you call on-air talent?" she said.

"Twinks," I said. "Or talking hairdos. All the back-to-you's."

"I decided I was going to be the boss of all of them," she said.

She quickly made her way up, then out of Bristol. When she wanted
to move to the ESPN offices in New York City, they let her. When she
wanted to move over to ABC, after Disney bought both ABC and ESPN,
they let her do that, too. She ended up marrying the boss twink right
ahead of her at ABC, Ian Bolton, executive producer.

The marriage lasted nineteen months, four days, twelve hours, she
said. By then, she'd made the decision to leave for Fox.

I told her it certainly sounded like a storybook romance to me.

She gestured again with her empty glass. If she was getting drunk, she
wasn't showing it, other than becoming a little more careful holding the
curves on some of the longer words. If I looked at her when she was
speaking, that meant I didn't have to look at the way she kept crossing
and uncrossing her legs on the table in front of us.

Liz said she was the last person in maybe the entire company to know
just how many production assistants and interns Ian Bolton had screwed.
She finally caught him with the twenty-four-year-old stage manager for
Monday Night Football at the Four Seasons in Boston when she decided
to surprise him one night before a Patriots-Colts game in Foxboro.

"It was actually kind of interesting watching him turn into a country
western lyric right before my eyes," she said.

"Which one?"

She grinned. "'Who you gonna believe, me or your own lyin' eyes?'"

I asked her why she kept his last name, and the grin disappeared as quickly as it had arrived. "Because I had fucking well earned it," she said.

I put on *The Gentle Side of Coltrane*. We moved back out of the game seats into what was the living room of Suite 19. I couldn't remember later which one of us sat down first on the couch, or how we got as close together as we did.

Somewhere out of the liquor and the lateness of the hour and the quiet except for John Coltrane's alto sax, she said, "I didn't sleep with your father."

"No one said you did."

"Bullshit," she said. "Everybody says I did, behind my back anyway. But I didn't."

"Okay, then."

"Okay."

"He started out as my boss and ended up my best friend. Okay?"

"Okay."

She had put down her drink. When she turned to me, her eyes were very wide.

"Okay, then," she said again.

I would be as unclear later about who kissed whom at that point as I was about a lot of what happened next. Just not all that happened. I just knew that things developed very quickly and we never made it back to the bedroom, which is why we were still in the living room with only Frankie Molloy's topcoat covering most of Liz and hardly any of me when Annie Kay, who'd finished much earlier than she thought she would, decided to surprise me with a cheerleader's outfit she'd borrowed from one of the dancers and a great big thermos of chilled pink.

twenty

nnie Kay took it pretty well, all things considered.

I didn't hear her come in, and only awakened when I heard the door close behind her. She had apparently only stayed long enough to leave notes for both Liz and me, Liz's sticking out of her purse and mine taped to the bathroom mirror.

Liz's simply said, "To Little Miss Hard to Get: I know more football than you do. Best, Annie Kay. P.S. If you're as young as your bio says you are, your tits shouldn't be starting to sag this way."

Mine read this way:

> Dear Jack,
>
> Every time I start to think you guys aren't all the same something like this happens and I am reminded that of course you're all the same. I have to confess, I briefly considered dousing you both with pink and then setting you on fire, but I am too young and have too much ahead of me to spend the rest of my life in women's prison. So I will just leave you with this:

Fuck you.

Stronger message to follow.

Annie.

Liz wordlessly showed me her note as she was leaving at about eight in the morning. This was after we each had played the morning-after game of "How the hell did my clothes get up *there?*" She said she was going to sneak down the freight elevator, hopefully get to her car without being spotted, then come back to work in a couple of hours having completely forgotten that any of this ever happened.

"Not only did it not happen," she said. "It can never, ever happen again. Is that clear?"

I told her it was good for me too, darling.

Billy Grace had always told me that with guys, it's mostly about the sex, with women it had to be more fucking complicated than setting the timer on the VCR.

Kenny and Babs stopped by my office Wednesday morning. Babs was wearing so much tennis white she looked as if she were on her way to Centre Court at Wimbledon. Kenny was still in his workout clothes, a white towel around his neck. Two or three days a week, he liked to go down to the weight room and pump iron with the big sweaty athletes and pretend he was a jock himself, even though the only varsity letter he'd ever earned at Choate was in dressage.

As usual they'd walked in unannounced, walking right past my secretary, Delores, as if she were the lawn jockey outside "21."

"Have you by any chance heard from Wick Sanderson yet today?" Babs said.

I told Kenny that the last contact I'd had with the commissioner was before he went off Sunday night to play School Detention with a mutual friend of ours from Las Vegas.

"Very funny," Kenny said.

"Not if you play it right," I said.

He had a plastic bottle of water in one hand, some kind of thick manila folder in the other. I wondered whether that was actual sweat on the front of his gray HAWKS t-shirt, or whether he'd given himself a little spritz before he came in just to make himself look more manly.

"Ken and I met with some of the Finance Committee members yesterday over at the league office," Babs said. "The commissioner said if we talked to you before he did, that you should be expecting a call from Donnie Mack Carney. He's going to be in town later in the week and wants to meet with you."

There were more owners' committees and subcommittees in the National Football League than there were branches of the federal government. There was the Competition Committee and the Television Committee and the Rules Committee and the Expansion Committee and the New Stadium Committee and the Finance Committee, of which Donnie Mack Carney, the Baltimore Ravens' owner, was chairman. The newer owners generally politicked to get a spot on the Television Committee, because there wasn't a rich guy alive who didn't get hard watching network executives beg like dogs at the back door.

But Donnie Mack's Finance Committee ultimately decided who got to own NFL teams and who didn't. There were seven owners on the committee, counting Donnie Mack himself. If four decided they didn't like you, your ass never made it to a vote of all thirty-four owners, no matter how much money you had. In all the years that Donnie Mack had been chairman, no one the Finance Committee had ever recommended, including Vito Cazenovia, had ever failed to get the two-thirds majority needed to get into the club. Mostly because nobody wanted to tangle with Donnie Mack.

At the time the old man died, he had a seat on the Finance Committee. In the old days, before they had started rewriting the league constitution, I would have automatically taken his place. Not anymore. The morning after the world knew that Big Tim Molloy had died, there was a conference call with the six surviving committee members and it was decided, by a unanimous vote, to give his spot to Corky DuPont III, the Jets owner and renowned hot air balloonist.

I said to Babs, "I thought nobody was going to do anything about anything until they all got together at the Super Bowl."

"Officially, they're not," Kenny said. "They're still going through the process with the reports and background checks. But they're not too thrilled with the publicity you get sometimes just by showing up for work."

Babs said, "Basically they wanted to ask Kenny and me just what the hell has been going on around here since daddy died."

Kenny said, "They asked us if there was any chance that you'd consider selling, to a buyer of their choice, before we had to go through a long and painful confirmation process."

"Which is something for you to consider before you sit down with them," Babs said.

Kenny said, "Unless you've reconsidered about selling to us."

To both of them, I said, "How about you tell me who your investors would be first?"

"Oh, please," Babs said. "We could put something together before lunch if we had to."

I asked her if I could change the subject for a second.

"What?" she said impatiently.

"I thought you gave up tennis after Dad caught you popping the assistant pro from West Side Tennis in the back of the limo that time?"

"Ha ha, Jack," she said. "Ha ha ha. You are such an incredible cutup. You just keep getting off those clever lines of yours while everything around here turns to sludge, okay?"

I remembered Liz Bolton, who'd been avoiding me the way she would a process server, getting close to me on the couch the other night, brushing some hair away from my eyes, saying, "Okay?"

Babs said, "You know what the real joke here is? That Daddy, who was so smart about everything else, could have been such a complete jackass when it came to you." She made a snorting sound. "Jackass Molloy."

"I forget," I said, "which one of us is considering selling the old man's name to some dot com head who moved in on his widow before they even had the pictures arranged on the top of the casket?"

Kenny said, "Keep changing the subject, Jack, so you don't have to talk about how it's taken you less than a month to become this big an embarrassment to the team, to the league . . ."

". . . and especially to this family," Babs said. "Some things never change, do they?"

It had been war for as long as I could remember, the two of them coming out of the womb aligned against me, the whole thing eventually turning into the most vicious two-on-one game ever played. I wasn't like them, they weren't like me, they weren't anything like the old man, as far as I could tell. Every time they'd see me screw up in some way, or get into another stupid fight with the old man over girls or smoking or grades or just general teenaged jacking around, they'd see another opening and try to move right in. Only they never could. Not only did the old man not seem to love either one of them very much, he didn't even seem to like them. He had no idea how to handle a daughter, even if Babs was the twin who at least had some real balls. Then after my mother died, he had shipped Kenny off to Choate the first chance he got. The excuse he gave for letting me stay at McBurney was that I'd been a football star from junior high on, and it wouldn't be fair to ship me off to preppie prison just when the college recruiters were starting to come around.

When it came to my football career, the old man wouldn't have let the National Guard get in the way.

Babs? There wasn't ever a chance that she was going anywhere besides the Manhattan private school of her choice. The one and only time the old man raised the subject of boarding school with her, she immediately stood up, stuck two fingers down her throat and threw up right at the dinner table, glaring at him the whole time.

"Okay, Daddy, your call," she said. "The Karen Carpenter thing or Spence."

The singer had died of anorexia. Spence was where all her girlfriends were going.

When I'd left for Vegas, they were sure he'd turn to them at last. They were the ones working for the team. They were the ones who hadn't abandoned him. Only it still didn't happen. He still had no use for Babs, or her cutout Goldman Sachs husband, or their girl. He still thought Kenny was the same whiner and complainer he'd always been. He let them have their piece of the Hawks, as a way of letting them have a piece of him. He was pretty much doing what he'd always done: giving them money because he knew he couldn't carry off even pretending he actually cared for them.

"You know what I really think he was doing, having the will this way?" Liz told me that night in Suite 19. "Hedging his bets. They'd been competing with you their whole lives. So he made the Hawks the grand prize. Strongest Molloy wins."

In my office now, Kenny quickly walked across the room and dropped the folder he was carrying, one stuffed with Nexis Lexis printouts, on my desk and then retreated to a spot about three feet inside the door.

It was all in there: the various tabloid headlines. The stories and columns they'd pulled up from sports sections all over the country about me running off A.T.M. All the lurid shit about Mo Jiggy and Bubba. The rumors in the gossip columns the last couple of days about Liz Bolton and me. The long piece *Sports Illustrated* had done about Ferret Biel, using him as an example of what the writer said was "a lower life-form that has become a virus in big-time sports."

There was the coverage of the Saints game, including the column Gil Spencer had written in the *Daily News*, the one in which he asked his readers whether or not what they thought what had been going to be a Super Bowl season for the Hawks had already been completely sabotaged by all the chaos and controversy and general frivolity created by the character known in Las Vegas as Jammer Molloy.

"They also call him Jam Up in Vegas," Spencer wrote. "He's legendary out there for being someone who makes things work. Only the opposite has happened now with a football team that was his father's whole life. It has taken Jack Molloy about twenty minutes in New York to turn into a twenty-car pileup. Sometimes even the most anticipated seasons end three hours after they begin."

Spencer's last line was "Sometimes father doesn't know best."

Finally, there was the story in that morning's *Times* quoting a series of anonymous management sources who said that twenty-four owners would vote against me if a confirmation hearing were held right now, and six would vote for me. The others said they were reserving judgment, just because they couldn't make themselves believe that somebody who had worked for Billy Grace as long as I had could be this much of a screwup.

"Bitsy Aguilera had more support than this when we found out she was inheriting the Chargers," one owner said. "And most of us thought she got the team by having somebody blow up her husband's Evinrude."

"Corky DuPont gave me that file," Kenny said. "He said if it was that thick after one game, by midseason it was probably going to look like the Warren Commission report."

Corky DuPont, who'd gone to Choate with Kenny, had bought the Jets from the Hess estate for three quarters of a billion about five years before. To get the team, he'd beaten out Hunt Throckmorton and Whip Prince. The Throckmortons had invented television remotes, the Prince family those little cards you used at tollbooths. The newspapers at the time had a field day with the competition for the Jets, because Corky, Hunt and Whip had not only grown up together in Upper Saddle River, New Jersey, but had also attended Princeton together, tried to go around the world twice in the same balloon, were a regular summer golf foursome at Shinnecock Hills in Southampton, hated real work the way Joe McCarthy hated Commies, and had sat together underneath the basket at Knicks games for as long as anybody could remember.

When it came time to close the deal, after the other two weren't willing to go past seven hundred million, Corky had shown up at Wick Sanderson's office and written the commissioner a personal check.

"For the last time," Kenny said. "Let us put a group together."

"As long as we're involved," Babs said, "then at least it's the devil you know."

I told her that she was being much too easy on herself.

Kenny said, "Please don't insult us by saying you're holding on to the team for Daddy's sake, okay?"

I clasped my hands behind my head and considered what it would actually take to properly insult Kenny Molloy.

"We're only telling you what the other owners are going to tell you," Babs said, leaning down and brushing something off the toe of a canvas sneaker so white and clean it looked as if it had just come out of the box.

I looked over at the little screen attached to my phone where Delores could instant-message me if she thought it was important, or if she thought I needed rescuing from some kind of hostage situation. She was telling me now that Donnie Mack Carney was on hold.

I stood up wearily and told Kenny and Babs they had to leave, if we kept talking I might get confused and start thinking I was the asshole.

twenty-one

Donnie Mack Carney had made his fortune in Christian broadcasting, both television and radio. He had even founded Carney College on the eastern shore of Maryland, known to heathens everywhere as Virgin Atlantic; it was generally acknowledged that Carney College made the Rev. Falwell's Liberty U. look like a giant ongoing keg party in comparison. By the force of Donnie Mack's personality and the size of his righteous war chest, he had become a major force not only in the God wing of the Republican party but in the National Football League as well. He had started out producing some call-this-prayer-line-right-now salvation show in Armpit, Alabama, and slowly built his Heaven on Earth Network (HEVN) into what had essentially become a third political party, especially when senators or congressmen or even presidents didn't kiss his big diamond pinky ring or his fat rear end fast enough.

Donnie Mack had never been an ordained minister himself, but his son, Bobby Ray Carney, had replaced Billy Graham as the most famous preacher man in America. Donnie's wife Coral, who'd been the lead singer in a country group called Bible Belt Babes—and, according to a controversial *Vanity Fair* article a few years before, kind of a fun girl at a party—before they met and fell in love, was now the No. 1 gospel singer in the country. Her group sang at the revivals that Donnie Mack produced for his son, the biggest of which were held in NFL stadiums all over the country, including ours. Liz said that the old man wasn't very happy about that, but that nobody said no to Donnie Mack Carney.

"Donnie Mack told your father and me one time that it was a funny thing, he opened up his Bible and sometimes people's sins had a way of spilling out," Liz Bolton said. "After that, Tim just referred to him as the Godfather of Soul."

Liz said the reference had nothing whatsoever to do with James Brown.

Donnie Mack had bought the Ravens from Art Modell, who'd moved the team from Cleveland and gotten one of the sweetheart deals in the history of the NFL to do it. Modell got a new stadium, almost as many luxury boxes and suites as the old man had at Molloy, and a lease that gave every owner, except Bitsy Aguilera, erections you could have used as the bottom of the goalposts.

Even with all that, Modell was drowning in so much red ink the sportswriters in Baltimore started calling it the Red Sea when Donnie Mack started negotiating with him to get the team.

Brian Goldberg had showed me a few of his favorite articles from that time before I went off to lunch with Donnie Mack. The best quote turned out to be from my father, in a column Dave Anderson wrote in the *Times*.

"If you can't make money owning a pro football team, then you're someone who could f— up Windows '98," Big Tim Molloy said in the paper of record.

Donnie Mack, whose headquarters for HEVN were located in Annapolis, Maryland, bought in for a little with Modell, then a little more, finally had the team all to himself. He had hired one I'd-like-to-thank-the-Lord coach after another and still hadn't managed to make the playoffs or even have a winning season. But it didn't seem to bother him, even if the Ravens hadn't quite turned into the cash cow he thought they'd be despite the highest ticket prices in the league and the fact that he had apparently shaken down every major church organization in the country except B'nai B'rith when it came time to pony up outrageous sums for his luxury boxes down there. Liz Bolton said there'd been some suggestions in the *Wall Street Journal* lately that his empire wasn't as strong as it once had been, but Donnie Mack said those were just the instruments of the devil and financial-district New York Jews.

Over time, the other owners had become as frightened of Donnie Mack Carney as they were of empty seats. Even the media was afraid, which is why no one even made it an issue anymore that the entire Ravens roster was composed of born-again Christians. Win or lose, they'd all congregate at midfield with the Christians from the other team when the game was over, and the music would play Coral Carney's music over the loudspeakers, and suddenly a Baptist church would break out.

I noticed a comment in a *Baltimore Sun* story from one of the Ravens' wide receivers, a black speed guy from Grambling named Ecclesiastes Woody. After a loss to the Falcons one day, he was overheard in the locker room saying, "Some of the niggers on this team could think about doin' that Praise Jesus jump when the damn ball's in the air, know what I'm sayin'?"

Donnie Mack had him traded to the Lions the next day.

It was understood around the league that if you tangled with Donnie Mack, on almost anything, you could start counting the minutes when you could look outside your window and see somebody picketing near Gate A for some godless practice or another in your organization.

Brian Goldberg said that I could have met with the other members of the Finance Committee—Corky DuPont and Bobby Finkel—the way Kenny and Babs had, but it wouldn't have gotten me anywhere, the only one with any real juice was Donnie Mack.

"Good luck," Brian had said, when it was time to go. "Convince him you're not Satan, win valuable prizes."

———

We met at the Post House, on 63rd between Park and Madison. It was owned by the same guys who owned Smith and Wollensky's, the other best steak joint in town. If you didn't count Beef, that is.

It was a bright, loud, big-city place. I found Donnie Mack Carney at a table in a back corner of the room, set behind a small brass railing. A few feet away, there were two well-dressed young guys in gray suits to go with the two I'd seen standing at the end of the bar when I'd come in. All of them had earpieces. The two in the back had set up their table so they could take in the whole room at once, in case anybody tried anything funny with the lemon pepper chicken.

I was starting to think I was the only owner in the league without muscle.

He was wearing his trademark lavender suit, white shirt, solid white tie. There was a solid gold crucifix in his lapel, matching the diamond one set into his pinky ring. He had a pile of white hair and a bushy white mustache.

"Well, well, well," he said in a booming voice, after Nick, the maître d', showed me to the table. "The controversial Mister Molloy."

He tried to give me his fund-raiser handshake, but I managed to slide my hand up his wrist a little.

I smiled at him and said, "Save me, Donnie Mack."

He laughed.

"Even I may not have the power to do that," he said. "Sit yourself down, son, order yourself a drink."

I noticed that he had a four-olive martini in front of him the size of a wading pool. I ordered a Scotch. It was too early in the day for me, but I didn't want to insult him and make him drink the beast he had in front of him alone.

"Sorry about your father," he said solemnly. "He was one of the best Catholics I ever knew."

I couldn't tell whether he was that sad about the old man going to his reward, or being Catholic.

"I know he thought a lot of you," I said.

It was total bullshit, of course. My father had always had trouble with the Born Agains. He used to say that you got one birth, one death, ten commandments, seven sacraments, he didn't need anybody changing the goddam math on him now.

Donnie Mack waited for my drink to arrive, and then as soon as it did, he took a big swallow of his own, closed his eyes and smiled.

"When they were thirsty," he said, "He gave them drink."

He stabbed an olive now and ate it. "Tell me something, son. How is it that people act as if you're the worst public relations disaster in this league since O.J.?"

He had gotten right to it, so I gave him the speech I'd prepared with Brian. I told him that I hadn't enlisted on this deal, that I'd been drafted the day I heard the lawyers read the will. I told him that I knew how much I'd disappointed my father with the life I'd been leading in Vegas, and that I wasn't particularly proud of that. But, I told him, my father still had enough confidence in me, and my love of the Hawks, to leave the football end to me and not my brother and sister.

I told him that the easy way out would be for me to sell the team.

I told him that I knew I had made some mistakes so far, but I was learning from them.

I promised him that I would show him in the time before the vote that I was capable of doing the job my father obviously wanted me to do.

At the end, I heard myself saying something I hadn't prepared and that surprised me by nearly dying in my throat about halfway into it. Maybe because I actually meant it.

"Who knows, Donnie Mack," I said. "Maybe I can finally be the man my father thought I could be, despite a mountain of evidence to the contrary."

He sat and listened to it all, head back, eyes half-closed, his face showing me nothing, only stirring himself when he wanted to take another sip of his drink.

Neither one of us said anything when I finished, and then Donnie Mack Carney suddenly started laughing loudly enough that I was sure they could hear him out at the bar.

"Son," he finally said, wiping tears from his eyes with his napkin, "they told me you were a bullshitter, but no one told me you were gonna be this good."

"Excuse me?"

"I'm impressed, is all I'm saying. You could talk the stink off a horny evangelist."

He made a praying motion with his hands toward our waiter, who headed off toward the bar on a dead run. When the kid, Seamus, came back with another martini, Donnie Mack drank some of it and then said, "You know you're sitting on the crown jewel, don't you, son?"

He was talking about the Hawks, of course. I told him everybody seemed to be in agreement that the Hawks might be the most valuable property in sports.

"And you know what you do with a crown jewel, right?"

"Make sure you don't lose it?" I said.

"Praise the Lord and pass the gin," he said.

"I'm trying here, Donnie Mack. I'm trying."

"Well then, son, you've certainly got a mighty interesting way of showing that," he said. "Because from where I sit, it seems to me you've been doing everything in your power *to* lose this team. I guess what I'm here to ask you is when exactly that's going to stop?"

I said, "I'm not going to sit here with the most powerful owner in the whole damn league and say that I haven't made mistakes. I know I have. But I also know I've still got a few months left to turn this thing around. I'm just asking you to not just go on first impressions and give me a chance."

He laughed again and slapped the table this time.

"Lord have mercy, Jack," he said. "If I just went on first impressions, I'd've already marked you lower on the food chain than an agent."

When I replayed the whole conversation later for Pete and Liz, I would remember him talking for about half an hour straight then. Donnie Mack Carney told me about his wife, the five sons they'd raised, about how he'd built HEVN by the grace of God and his lawyers. He bragged that not a single current member of the Ravens had ever been divorced or fathered a child out of wedlock, even though fathering children out of wedlock seemed to be the national pastime now in some of your other Third World sports. He quoted First and Second Corinthians, Acts, and two books of the Old Testament I'd never heard of. I couldn't decide whether he was drunk on Beefeater or the Holy Spirit or both. He told me two or three times how much he loved my father. If he didn't, he said, we wouldn't even be having this meeting.

Near the end, he got down to it and asked if I'd consider selling if I wasn't forced to.

I told him, No sir, I wasn't selling, I was going to play the hand all the way out.

He asked if I'd read the story in the *Times* about the other owners. I told him I had, and asked if he thought they had the numbers right.

Donnie Mack said that even the New York City *Times*, which was more liberal than one of your gay groups, got something right occasionally.

"You don't have the votes, son, in committee or out," he said.

I told Donnie Mack I could get them.

"And how do you plan on accomplishing that?" he said.

"It's sort of what I do," I said.

"This isn't Vegas, Jack," he said.

"Actually," I said, "it's a lot closer than you think."

He leaned forward then and said that since we were talking man to man here, he was going to give me one more piece of advice, whether I wanted it or not.

"Son, I didn't get to where I am in this world without watching my business," he said. "Doesn't matter whether it's the business of the Lord or television or whatnot. I know that Mr. Wick Sanderson is the commissioner of this league now, but he's weak and a sinner and don't even try to deny it, I know what goes on when he's with you and your friends out there in Las Vegas. So there's more people starting to think that I'm the real commissioner of your NFL, and to me that's an awesome responsibility, like I go first to one church on Sunday morning, then another on Sunday afternoon."

I thought: He actually believes this shit.

"We'll play this out," he said, "because those are the rules. But if a real good offer comes along before the end of the process, one from a fella you think old Donnie Mack Carney might approve of, you think about grabbing it, you hear?"

Then he said the Lord, He worked in mysterious ways, and I said that I would certainly drink to that.

twenty-two

ere is how we went to 0–2 against the Miami Dolphins in the middle of a South Florida rainstorm that started out looking like just your average epic disaster movie and ended up looking like the end of the world:

With the score 13–10 for the Dolphins, a minute and thirty left in regulation, Raiford Dionne managed to knock the ball loose from the Dolphins' rookie running back, Second Story Johnson. Second Story, Gil Spencer had explained to me at halftime, was so named became of an incident his senior year at Auburn when he broke an ankle, and cost the Tigers a share of the SEC title, when he jumped out of the athletic director's office with a DVD player under his arm.

Gil Spencer said Second Story actually had a pretty funny line when his mother showed up to post bail.

"I don't want nobody tellin' me ever again that the damn ground don't cause a damn fumble," he said.

It wasn't the ground this time at Pro Player Stadium, it was the rain, and Raiford Dionne taking a big old swing at the ball from behind, as

Second Story tried to turn the corner for what would have been a first down that ended any chance we had to come back and tie the game or win it.

Then we had one timeout left and a first down of our own on the Dolphins' 20-yard line.

Somehow, after two running plays, one miraculous scramble by Bubba Royal and two intentional incompletions, we had fourth-and-goal at the Dolphins' one, with 0:17 showing on the clock. Bubba called our last timeout and came over to the sideline to talk to Vince Cahill and Josh Blake about whether to try a field goal, which would have tied the game, or go for the win with a touchdown.

Josh Blake took me through it later on the team plane, right before all hell broke loose.

Vince said, "Kick the damn ball and we'll take our chances in overtime. The worst thing that happens is a tie."

Josh said, "Coach, too many things can happen with a kick. Let's have Bubba punch it in on a sneak and we can win this sonofabitch right now before we all get into the Ark."

"Their boys in front got no footing and no fight," Bubba said. "Goddam, Vince, if we can't make a yard, let's all of us start wearing panties instead of cups."

"You boys aren't listening," Vince said. "We kick the fucking thing."

Josh said, "You're wrong, Coach. You're asking for a good snap, a good hold, and then for Benito to be able to get his plant foot down on Biscayne Bay."

Benito Siragusa was our Italian-born kicker.

Vince got in Josh's face then and gave him one of his dumb catchphrases, screaming to be heard over the storm. "Don't tell me about the pain!" he said. "Just show me the baby!"

Bubba stepped in between them. When he did, Vince tried to shove him out of the way. These were the pictures that everybody would see replayed later about a hundred times on television: Bubba taking off his helmet, using the back of his bloody right hand to wipe the rain out of his eyes, then using the same hand to grab Vince Cahill by the front of his rain slicker.

What nobody except Josh Blake, standing there in the middle of all kinds of storms now, could hear was this:

"You ever put your hands on me again, you fat fuck, I will shove a yard marker up your fat ass."

On the television in the press box I heard Matt Millen say to his broadcast partner Dick Stockton on Fox, "See, there's the kind of spirited relationship you see sometimes between a veteran quarterback and a veteran coach."

The ref finally came over and said that if everybody was through acting out, maybe Vince could decide whether or not he was going to send the kicking team on the field.

"Hey, Angelo," Vince said, turning to Benito Siragusa, "get out there and pretend you and the other dagos have a chance to win the World Cup."

As soon as Pete saw the kicking team start running through the mud, he started stuffing his game notes into his battered leather valise.

"Benito's people have an expression that covers this," he said.

"Shitfuck?" I said.

"No, that's French," he said. "The Italian is no fucking way."

The snap never made it to Tucker O'Neill, the holder. Our long snapper, Turk Sloat, had the ball slip on him as soon as he started to move it back through his legs, and then watched helplessly as it went sliding through the mud before coming to a dead stop about two yards short of where Tucker was kneeling.

Tucker dove for the ball, managed to get control of it as he got to his feet, yelling "Hot, hot, hot" as he did, which is what you're supposed to do when there's a bad snap on a field goal or extra point. At that point, the blockers on the outside, if they're paying attention, run to an open spot downfield and become pass receivers. The kicker, with the play in front of him, is already supposed to have done the same thing.

Benito Siragusa did just as the special teams coach had always told him to, and ran to the left flat, and would have been wide open to receive

Tucker O'Neill's pass if his soccer instincts hadn't betrayed him. Because instead of reaching out to catch what was a remarkably accurate throw from Tucker in light of what had now become hurricane-like conditions, Benito suddenly elected to head the ball in the direction of the Dolphin goalposts, in the style of the legendary Italian soccer star Baggio, his hero growing up in Palermo. Making solid contact with his helmet, Benito propelled the ball about fifteen yards down the field, where it ended up in the hands of one of the Dolphin deep backs, who fell into the mud as the clock ran out on his team's victory.

Everyone thought that was the last real excitement of the day until Bubba Royal tried to strangle Vince Cahill on the flight home, right about the time the pilot informed us that if we looked out the left side of the airplane, we could see our nation's capital.

It was acknowledged around the National Football League that the New York Hawks had the most luxurious team plane. Team planes, actually. We leased a 737 stretch for the shorter flights to places like Boston and Cleveland and Detroit and Washington. For longer flights we had a vulgar new 777, as long as the airports could handle it.

The outside of the big one was painted in Hawks colors, and the inside, as even respected publications like *House and Garden* agreed, looked like something that belonged in the Sultan of Brunei's fleet.

Over the last few years, team planes had inspired the same sort of ugly competition among sports owners that luxury boxes had caused in the eighties and nineties. Our veteran strong safety, Nike Evans—he'd legally changed his name from Norbert as part of his shoe contract when he'd come out of Maryland as the most famous two-sport star since Deion Sanders and Bo Jackson—told me that the first time he'd seen the inside of the City Hawk, which is what my father had nicknamed the 777, he'd immediately called his wife on one of his cell phones.

"I said, 'Maybelline, forget about taking the kids to DisneyWorld on school vacation, we're just goin' to the team plane this year.'"

I was sitting with Nike and Bubba and Pete Stanton in the lounge area, complete with the piano players the old man would borrow from the Algonquin Hotel for road games. The lounge was about halfway back in the plane and separated the coaches' cabin from the various sections where the players were. It was adjacent to the screening room, where the more industrious members of our team, or just the suckups like Tucker O'Neill, could sit and study game film on the way home.

If nobody wanted to watch the game, some players generally locked the door and watched X-rated movies that usually had "Suburban Housewives" in the titles.

No one wanted to watch the Dolphins game, especially after we'd sat on the runway at the Fort Lauderdale airport for two and a half hours waiting for the storm to finally subside. Mostly, everybody just wanted to drink and bitch about Vince going for the field goal and pop the pain pills that were being passed around by the flight attendants the way they would the honey-roasted almonds on a commercial flight.

Maybe it was because I'd been away from my own brief career at UCLA. Or maybe it was because of the convenient amnesia that all ex-players managed to develop the longer they're retired. But it had been a while since I had seen—and heard—firsthand how the first few hours after a game turned the team plane into a flying veterans' hospital.

Raiford Dionne had just come up to the lounge to pick up another industrial-sized glass of pink, then shuffled past us as if he'd misplaced his walker.

Bubba watched him go and said, "You know what people manage to forget about the good old days? How much they fuckin' hurt."

He said he had to go take a piss and maybe chat up one of the new flight attendants.

"And don't worry, Bubba," he said to me. "I'm plannin' to do one first, then the other."

"Thank-ee," I said.

It was about ten minutes later that we heard the shouting from the coaches' cabin.

When we got in there, we saw that Bubba was warning people off with the bottle of Johnnie Walker Red he had in his left hand. His right hand was around Vince Cahill's throat. Josh Blake was standing a few feet away from Bubba. The other coaches were in their seats. As soon as Pete and I got inside, Pete told Josh, who was clearly part of the drama, to stay right where he was and for the rest of the coaches to get the hell out of there.

When they were gone, he shut the door behind us and locked it.

"The fewer people testifying, the better," he said.

Vince appeared to be breathing, but his face was the color of ketchup.

"Take it back," Bubba said.

He wasn't the aw-shucks boy from Mayberry RFD anymore. I'd seen him like this a few times before, always in college, never over a girl or a game, always over something he decided was personal.

"It doesn't matter," Josh said to Bubba. "Let it go."

"Let *it* go?" Vince sputtered. "Tell him to let *me* go, for chrissakes!" Then he made a sound like a kid blowing bubbles with his straw.

"Take it back, Hon," Bubba said, with the same quiet menace in his voice.

". . . fucking has-been" was the best Vince Cahill could manage.

Bubba tightened his grip and shoved Vince's head back hard into the carpeted wall behind them.

"Wrong answer," Bubba Royal said.

"Hey, bud," I said.

He knew it was me without even turning around. "Hey," he said.

"Well, sonofabitch, if we don't seem to have ourselves a situation here," I said.

Bubba smiled with everything except the Newman-blue eyes that had a way of making all the girls in the room go weak at the knees, and sometimes about half the guys.

"You was always the smart one," he said.

I said, "You promised no more bar fighting until after the Super Bowl."

"Well now, Jack, I don't want you to think no less of me than you already do," he said. "But I lied."

"You want to tell me about it?" I said.

"You tell," Bubba said to Josh Blake.

"You don't have to fight my fights," Josh said. "This is between coach and me."

"You tell Jack or I will," Bubba said, and so Josh told me that he'd been demoted from offensive coordinator, that Vince had decided he'd call the plays himself from now on.

"All of it," Bubba said. "Take your time. Ain't nobody goin' nowhere."

Josh told all of it then:

After the game, Vince had told the reporters that he and Josh and Bubba had all agreed on kicking the field goal instead of going for it on fourth down. But then, when everybody was dressed and ready to start boarding the buses, Gil Spencer caught up with Josh. It was one of Vince Cahill's rules that none of his assistant coaches got to talk to the press. But when Josh heard Vince's version, he decided to tell Spencer the truth, not trying to make it a controversy, just wanting to set the record straight.

He tried to be casual about the whole thing, finally saying, "It was our usual democracy. Vince's vote won."

When Spencer went back to Vince Cahill for a response, telling him what Josh had said, this is what he got: "No fucking comment."

Vince must have waited until he'd had a few drinks on the runway and then a few more on the plane before he called Josh out on what he called an act of disloyalty. Bubba happened to be walking back from the front of the plane, still carrying his personal Scotch, when he heard Vince saying that Josh wasn't offensive coordinator anymore.

Josh seemed as if he wanted to leave it there, but now Bubba said, "He told Coach Blake he could go be somebody else's house nigger if he didn't like it."

I moved slowly up the middle aisle to where Bubba had Vince. I said, "Why don't you let me handle it from here?"

"When he takes it back."

"Let coach go, so I can ask him a question," I said.

Bubba Royal let him go.

Vince Cahill rubbed his neck where Bubba had been holding him and said to Josh, "I've changed my mind. You're fucking fired." Then he turned to Bubba and said, "And you're suspended without pay."

Nobody said anything until I said, "No."

Vince Cahill tried to move as far away from Bubba as he could in the small space between his front-row seat and the wall and said, "What's that supposed to mean, no? No what?"

"Did you say what Bubba says you said, Vince? And before you answer, let me remind you that there's a lot of witnesses, and I sign every one of their goddam paychecks."

Vince watched Bubba while he talked to me.

"It was locker room talk, is all. Heat-of-the-moment bullshit. You walk through a football locker room nowadays, all you hear is nigger this and nigger that. It's just part of it."

I said, "It's part of it when Josh says it to Elvis. Or Raiford. Or Bobby Camby. Or Nike. Not when you say it."

I reached over and gently took the Scotch out of Bubba's hand, took a swig out of the bottle, handed it back to him.

"Anyway," I said, "no means no, Vince, not that you've got a real good handle on the word, from what the secretaries say. No, you're not taking Josh's job away. And no, you're not suspending Bubba."

"You better take another look at my contract," Vince said. "I have final say on my staff, and in all disciplinary matters. So you can kiss my ass, okay, junior?"

"You don't have a contract anymore," I said.

Vince wanted to know what that was supposed to mean, and I said, "It means you're fired, Vince. When the plane lands, clear out your office or I'll have somebody do it for you."

I turned to where Pete Stanton was standing near the back door to the cabin and saw him smile at me and make a little punching motion in the air and mouth the word "Yes!"

"Who do you think you're going to get to replace me?" Vince said.

I nodded at Josh Blake and said, "Him."

PART THREE

upon

further

review

twenty-three

e won our first two games under Josh Blake, beating both the Eagles and Cowboys on the road. Bubba threw three touchdown passes in each game and even ran fifty yards for a touchdown against the Cowboys, on what he said afterward was the longest quarterback draw he'd run since UCLA.

"Man, I didn't think I was gonna make it," he told Chris Berman and Tom Jackson on *NFL Prime Time*. "It was the power of imagination that got me to the promised land."

Berman asked him how that worked, and Bubba said that he pretended one of his ex-wives was chasing him.

"Which one?" Berman said.

"Which one you want?" Bubba Royal said on television.

So we were 2–2. The same sportswriters and radio guys who had pissed all over me for firing a legend like Vince Cahill just two games into a season had fallen head-over-heels in love with the New York Hawks all of a sudden. That kind of flip-flop was as easy as ever for them; the tricky part was not giving me any of the credit for the turnaround. I finally concluded that Josh Blake must have been the first coach in NFL history to hire himself.

"Here's how it generally works with these assholes, once they decide to drop the hammer on you," Pete Stanton said. "Anything good that happens, somebody else did. Anything bad is your fault."

I told him that I had pretty much figured that out for myself. The media, except for a handful of guys who actually seemed to get it, were more fickle as a group than teenaged girls, and even less sure of themselves. If they were wrong in yesterday's paper, they acted as if somebody else wrote that piece-of-crap article. And they were all ready to change their minds by tomorrow if they'd shopped around and found an opinion they liked better than their own. Reading the papers and listening to radio stations like WNUT and WFAN since I'd been back in town, I remembered something the boxing promoter Bob Arum said one time in Vegas after being caught in a lie so outrageous it should have had tin cans attached to its back bumpers.

"Yesterday, I was lying," Arum said. "Today I'm telling the truth."

The day after I'd had Vince Cahill's fat ass escorted out of Molloy Stadium by security, I was "Jack the Ripper" in the tabloid headlines. Two weeks later, headed into the Giants game at what was still called Molloy Stadium—Wick Sanderson had put a hold on any negotiatons about the naming rights until the owners' meeting—I was at least back to being a colorful and unpredictable rogue.

The morning after we'd gotten back from the Cowboys game, Pete and Tire Iron Timmons had flown over to London to see Donyell and A.T.M. By now, A.T.M. Moore had become a bit of a celebrity over there, even signing on as a color analyst for BBC 4's NFL Game of the Week on Sunday nights. The week before, the *Post* had reprinted an interview A.T.M. had given to one of London's biggest Sunday papers, *News of the World*, about how he loved going to some of the important test matches in cricket.

"You people play less defense than the f—ing Vikings," he told the writer. "Somebody gets ahead 542–3 and then it rains for three or four f—ing days before the other team catches up around tea time on Thursday. Then some m—f—er hits one of those foul balls that gets everybody wavin' their crucifix flags, and somebody wins by a widget."

Wicket, the writer corrected him.

"Yeah, whatever," A.T.M. replied. "I mean, what's up with that foul ball s—t, anyway?"

When asked if he missed the Hawks in particular and football in general, A.T.M. said he did get homesick occasionally for certain aspects of American life he had to admit he'd taken for granted, like *SportsCenter* and all the titty channels you could get on DirecTV, but that on the whole he felt himself adjusting nicely to life in the United States of Kingdom.

"If it was easier to get the scores," A.T.M. concluded, "I might actually think about deporting myself permanently."

They asked him what he missed the least about America, and he said, "You people over here familiar with a bitch woman named Oretha Keeshon?"

Pete and Tire Iron were making the trip so they could remind Donyell in person that if his client wasn't back on the Hawks' active roster by the Monday before our tenth regular season game, the league would officially put him on its inactive roster and A.T.M. would blow his entire $4.5 million salary.

Pete said he was bringing some persuasive graphs and color pie charts to help show A.T.M. that he was going to burn more money than Oretha ever did. And even after he had, his ass would still belong to us.

Tire Iron was going because I'd called him in and showed him a copy of his own contract with the Hawks, pointing out that if A.T.M. wasn't back for the second half of the season it was going to take a miracle comparable to the loaves and fishes for any of Tire Iron's bonuses to kick in.

"The church needs the money," Tire Iron said of WHUP.

"A.T.M is certainly letting a lot of people down," I said.

"It's not just me," Tire Iron said.

"Think of the children," I said.

"I'm starting to get a little bit of a red ass here just thinking about it," Tire Iron Timmons said, clenching and unclenching his fists.

I reminded him that even the Lord got angry sometimes.

Annie Kay had not returned any of the phone calls I'd made since she found Liz Bolton and me in Suite 19. I finally went down to Beef on a night when I knew she'd be working, and just sat down at the bar and ordered a drink. She lingered for a few minutes after serving it to me and we made some small talk, as I tried to ease into an apology. But when I turned my head to bum a cigarette out of Jimmy T. Kirk's pack of Kools, she poured a fresh pitcher of pink all over me.

"There," she said, "now I can finally let these feelings go."

When Jimmy T. came back from the men's room, he looked at me and said, "God*dam*, boss, you look like a condom."

Liz Bolton and I, on the other hand, seemed to have fallen slightly in lust, but only on Sunday nights. The rest of the time she acted as if nothing had changed between us; anybody who didn't know what was going on and only saw us interacting at the office would think she had as much feeling for me as she did for the Domino's deliveryman. But she was considerably friendlier when we were behind locked doors—I had had a new Medeco installed after Annie Kay's surprise—in Suite 19. After we won the Eagles game, Liz said she had promised to meet some people in the city right after the game, then showed up at 19 later with a pizza and two bottles of champagne.

When we'd polished off the pizza and were halfway through the second bottle of champagne, she stood up and asked if Wounded Soldier/ Naughty Nurse was a real game.

I told her it was if you played it right.

In the morning, she told me she'd brought a change of clothes this time, because of the inbound rush-hour traffic on the Deegan.

"I've got a new secret route to my office," she said.

"It's a small price to pay for happiness," I said.

Billy Grace said he was working every owner he knew, especially the ones for whom he'd extended what he called "various and sundry courtesies" at Amazing Grace over the years. He said that the ones who didn't have heads shaped like the pyramid at the Luxor—it was one of the newer hotels on the Strip—were starting to get the message that any help they could give me with the Finance Committee members would be considered a great personal favor to Mr. Grace.

"Talking about the sundries always seems to get their attention," he said.

He said he was trying to think of some creative ways to fuck with Allen Getz's stock, but hadn't come up with anything yet.

"Eventually, what I'd really like to do is just do a face-to-face with the asshole and ask him an important question," Billy said on the phone one night.

"What kind of question?"

"I am just going to ask him if pursuing the Hawks is a path he really wants to go down."

"You want to shake down the eleventh-richest man in the world," I said.

Billy said that notion was insulting to a legitimate businessman like himself. "I just feel this is a moment in Allen's life when he really ought to get an education in the Vegas way."

I had started learning the Vegas way the first day I'd gone to work for him, after saying goodbye to the old man for good.

The Vegas way was knowing how much you were willing to lose before you placed your bets.

We had that particular conversation the Thursday night before the Giants game. Before we both hung up, I asked him if he'd heard anything about Ferret Biel. He told me the same thing he'd been telling me for weeks, that Ferret was somehow managing to keep a lower profile than Michael Jackson after those pesky allegations about the little boys.

It was the next morning that Ferret called me at the office and said he was in town for a couple of days, would I like to get together?

Ferret said on the phone it wasn't that he didn't trust me, because he still considered me a dear personal friend despite our recent misunderstandings. But he wanted to meet me in a public place and he was going to bring a couple of friends along in case I still had what he called anger-management issues where he was concerned.

"You don't have friends, Ferret," I said. "You just have fellow forest creatures."

"Listen, Jammer," he said, "I can understand how you still might be a little hurt . . ."

"Hurt?" I said. "Hurt is what I plan to do to you, you little shit-weasel."

"See, that's why I felt the need to bring friends along," he said. "I just want to explain a few things, is all. As a way of clearing the air and whatnot."

I told him I looked forward to that, and said I would meet him at The Last Good Year around 9:30, that was as early as I could get out of a Boys Club of New York dinner at which Brian Goldberg was forcing me to serve dais duty.

It was actually closer to ten when I broke away from former governor Carey and from the cardinal, who had taken me through the first four games of the season like an assistant coach breaking down game film.

When I came through the door at The Last Good Year, Joe Healey said, "Your dates have arrived."

Healey still looked the way he had for as long as I'd known him, like the young Jackie Gleason, just minus thirty or forty pounds. He had that kind of round Irish face, dark eyes full of fun, a mop of black curly hair. His father had been the congressman from the section of the Bronx where Yankee Stadium was located. He loved the Hawks, and needed hardly any encouragement to sing our fight song (*"Fly above the sky-line/Kick in the end zone door/Soar, Hawks, soar!"*—Kitty had commissioned it from a precious young composer she'd met a few years ago through Steve Sondheim) when he had enough Canadian Club and ginger ale in him. But the Yankees were his team. He had been to the last forty consecutive Yankee home openers, even going AWOL from Fort Dix during basic training to keep the streak alive at sixteen. They'd thrown him into the stockade for that one when he got back. Lieutenant Maybee, his commanding officer, had told him as he locked the cell door that Healey was the type who would turn his back on his fellow soldiers in battle.

"Begging your pardon, sir," Healey said, "but only if the Yanks were in the Series."

It got him sixteen days instead of the eight Maybee was originally going to give him.

We had been friends all the way back to high school. And I'd always known Lieutenant Maybee was wrong about Joe Healey, that he was foxhole-loyal.

"I got your back," he said. "One of the guys waiting for you looks like a bridge troll, but he's got a couple of furniture movers with him."

I told him that forewarned was forearmed and to have Little John bring me back a Scotch, that watching the cardinal pound drinks for the last couple of hours had made me even thirstier than usual.

Ferret Biel's friends were both Chinese. Both had crew cuts, hoop earrings hanging from their right ears. The one on the left, closest to me, wore a bright red Lacoste shirt and had a tattoo on his forearm that read "PUNK." Ferret introduced him as Ling. Ferret said the other guy's name was Chew. His most prominent tattoo was peeking over the open collar of his black Lacoste and said "PAIN," with what looked like a barbed-wire fence extending out from the "P" and "N" and going all the way around his neck for what appeared to be miles and miles.

I pointed at Chew and said, "I get it. Pain in the neck, right?"

He said, "Whatever. Yeah."

Ling just grunted.

Ferret said they didn't mean to be unfriendly, they mainly just spoke martial arts.

Our table, Ferret's and mine, was about ten feet away from where Ling and Chew were sitting. Ferret had extended a hand in greeting when I'd first walked in, and I'd ignored it. Now he tried again as I sat down and took a sip of the drink Little John had brought. This time I just studied his right hand, curious, as if trying to understand cubism.

Ferret sat with his back to the wall, creep style, and was even edgier than usual, trying to take in the whole back room with his pig eyes at once, drumming the fingers of both hands on the table. He was wearing black suit, black shirt, solid black tie. From all the television sets in the place, I could hear Tim McCarver talking about the Yankees, which was always fine, because McCarver was still the best in the business, even if the Mets had been dumb enough to lose him to Steinbrenner while I'd been away.

"Why'd you sell me out?" I said.

Ferret laughed nervously in his high-pitched voice, hee hee hee, and said nothing had changed, I still got right to it, didn't I?

"I got you back in the game in Vegas," I said, "and the very first chance you get, you punk me over a bet we both know I didn't make and wouldn't make."

I leaned forward a little, and as soon as I did, I could hear Ling and Chew making scraping noises with their chairs.

In the mirror behind Ferret, I could see Joe Healey standing at the door to the back room with three waiters, Healey nodding at me, smiling, gesturing with the Mickey Mantle autographed bat he kept behind the bar, letting me know he had everything handled.

"Tell your boys to relax," I said. "I just came here to find out who wanted me set up. Then I'm out of here, believe me."

"I can't, Jammer," he said in a whine. " 'Cause, like, well, I gave my word."

I stared at him.

"Your *word*?" I said. "You know what your word is, Ferret? Gimme."

"That's a very hurtful thing for me to hear."

He drummed his fingers even more loudly on the glass tabletop.

"It has to be somebody who wants the team," I said. "So who is it? My brother and sister? Allen Getz? Some mysterious asshole I don't even know about yet? What, somebody decided he needed more ammunition against me than everybody has already?"

Ferret Biel made a motion that meant his toothpick-thin lips were sealed.

I stood up.

Ling and Chew immediately did the same. I noticed that they were both wearing shiny black workout slacks and high-topped wrestling sneakers. Maybe they were going over to Gold's Gym later to take turns bench-pressing Ferret.

"Now I am out of here," I said.

"Wait!" Ferret said. "Just because I can't give you the information you want doesn't mean I don't have information you can use." He nodded at Ling and Chew, who sat down.

"Maybe if I do you a favor," he said, "you can do me a favor, and call off Billy so's I can go home."

"Home to Inger," I said.

"Hey," Ferret said. "You know Inger?"

"I don't," I said. "But Billy's kind of sweet on her all of a sudden. She mention to you he's letting her spin the roulette wheel on the show?"

The Game Show Network taped a week's worth of *Problem Gambler*, hosted by Tony Orlando, at Amazing Grace on Mondays and Tuesdays. The two contestants had to bet their own money on a series of casino games. The only way they were eligible to play is if they showed up with a notarized statement showing they had cleaned out their checking accounts, and were willing to bet it all on the show.

If they ended up with the grand prize, we'd double their winnings as a parting gift. If they lost everything, we had a counselor from Gamblers Anonymous on hand who would take them directly to their first GA meeting.

I said to Ferret, "Billy says she's a natural."

"Not blonde," he said, in a snippy way.

I sat back down and said, "Let's play this another way. If you can't tell me who, tell me why."

He ran his tongue across his lips in a way that did justice to his nickname and told me that he'd had some rather nasty reversals lately, and explaining how nearly three-quarters of the rat-bastard '86 Mets had backed out of a show on him at the last minute, blowing an entire sold-out weekend in Tahoe. "Which, as you can probably imagine, cost me a pretty fucking penny," he said. Then, because of what he swore was a mistake at the printing company, he sent out a release that said he had a limited supply of the last official signed photographs from Joe DiMaggio, from the final game of his fifty-six-game hitting streak in 1941.

"Can I help it if some numbnuts pops in the wrong disk?" he said.

I told Ferret that he had to let go of Joe D. once and for all now, that the Yankee Clipper, dead or alive, had caused him nothing but heartbreak.

Yeah, he said, it was pretty much a wrap now on the Clipper's estate ever showing any kind of sense of humor.

"So you had to write another big check to them," I said.

Ferret said, "Big enough to be a zip code in Alaska."

Anyway, he said, a party who obviously knew a lot about his friend Jammer Molloy came to him representing another party who was very interested in doing whatever it took to get the Hawks away from Mr. Molloy. Ferret said that I seemed to be doing a pretty good job of giftwrapping the Hawks for somebody else by myself, but this party said that there was maybe a way to create what he called a little "creative shit" to move the whole process along. Ferret said he told the guy, forget it, I was his friend. At which point the first party said that the second party was paying to pay a princely sum for a few more days of big, bad headlines. Ferret asked the guy what he meant by princely sum and was told one hundred thousand dollars.

"I'm not gonna lie to your face, Jammer, I have too much respect for you," he said now in The Last Good Year. "But in that moment, I was not as loyal to you as I could have been."

No kidding, I said.

"But," he said, "and this I believe is a significant breakthrough, I swore to myself that if I took this money and used it to get over, I would find a way to make it up to you if it was the last thing I ever did."

Because of our friendship, I said.

Ferret said he knew what I was doing, using sarcasm to mask the hurt I was obviously still feeling toward him.

Ferret said he'd get back to the guy, he had to think it over, and then came up with the story about the Orange Bowl, knowing how much anything related to game-fixing would spook the league. The morning the story moved on the wire, he went out to get the *Las Vegas Sun* and there on the doorstep, underneath the paper, was the hundred grand, in hundred-dollar bills. There was a note inside saying that if Ferret could pass a lie detector test after the owners' meeting at the Super Bowl that he hadn't revealed the name of his benefactor to anybody, even Inger, there would be another envelope with his morning paper, filled with another hundred thousand.

"I don't have to tell you that second large could mean a whole new beginning for me," he said.

Amazingly, I was starting to notice sweat stains even on a black collar.

"You said you had something else for me," I said.

Ferret leaned forward now, lowering his voice. The Yankee game must have ended, because McCarver had been replaced by Sinatra singing "All of Me." Ferret motioned for me to lean closer.

"One of your players is doing some business," he said.

"Betting games?"

He nodded.

"Our games?"

Another nod.

"With both hands," Ferret Biel said.

I asked him which player, and now he smiled.

"Bubba Royal has gone back to his old ways."

In The Last Good Year, I asked Ferret what that was supposed to mean, his old ways?

"Jammer," he said. "You think you and Bubba are the only ones who know he dumped the USC game and gave you that war-hero limp?"

Ferret was a little vague on details, just that there had been a call from a bookie in New York to another bookie that Ferret knew, because Ferret seemed to know everybody. Then another call to one of the sports books out in Vegas. When enough calls like that are made, eventually flags go up on The Strip and it starts to look like the plaza in front of the United Nations. Somewhere in this phone tree, Bubba Royal's name came up. So now I knew what he knew, Ferret said. The story was out there. If he'd heard it, then the league was going to hear, he just wanted to give me a heads-up.

I sat there for a few minutes, thinking about what he'd told me, and finally told him I'd call Billy when I got home later. He said that he'd been wondering why he couldn't get Inger on the phone, no matter what time of the day or night he called.

He said, "She's really on *Problem Gambler?*"

"There's already some talk she might get a shot at escorting the contestants to the soundproof booths on *Twenty-One*," I said.

He didn't even try to shake my hand this time, just told Ling and Chew to finish up their rum-and-Cokes, that they were leaving. He told me I didn't have to worry about him telling anybody else about Bubba, and then did the lips-sealed thing again.

"I'm sorry I couldn't tell you more," he said. "But I told you a lot, right? Right?"

Right, I said, and then told him I'd walk him out, I wanted to see if I could go find Bubba somewhere.

Ferret's limo was parked right out front. There was another stretch right behind it, looking like its twin.

That was the one that had Elvis Elgin and his posse inside.

twenty-four

he size of a player's posse usually depended on whether or not they were married or single, how big a mansion they'd built for themselves in Harrison or Rye Brook or Greenwich, how much serious cash they were willing to throw around on walk-around guys, and—most important of all—how much they'd bought into the general macho rap notion that if you didn't have as many walk-around guys as somebody like Mo Jiggy, you were some kind of candy-ass.

"Remember how guys used to say when we were kids that if you had big hands or big feet that meant you had a big thingy?" Pete Stanton said.

"Did I ever mention that I wear a size-ten shoe?" I said.

"Now it's the size of your posse," Pete continued. "I think that kid Iverson on the 76ers is the leader in the clubhouse these days, but we've got guys around here who aren't too far behind."

"What do they all do?"

"One guy drives the main car," he said. "Then they got another guy to drive shotgun on that car. A third guy sits in the back with somebody like Elvis and plays Nintendo 64 with him on the way to wherever they're going, or handles the incoming and outgoing cell phone calls. There might be one more guy squeezed into the way-back with the snacks, the Cheez Doodles and sixteen-ounce bottles of Mountain Dew and so forth. Then, of course, you've got your backup car, with your backup driver and backup shotgun-rider. And in Elvis's case, shotguns *means* shotguns."

"No kidding?" I said. "Big guns to go with all the little guns?"

Pete said, "Like one of those old Sam Peckinpah westerns."

"And they all live at the same house?"

"That's where they chill and whassup each other until the Hawk Girls arrive," he said. "I drove up to Elvis's place in Greenwich, down the street from where Mel Gibson lives? It looks like the White House on steroids."

When I'd told Pete where I was going and that Ferret had said he was bringing friends, Pete had suggested I might want to talk to Elvis Elgin. I went down to the locker room after practice and told him what I thought the deal might be and he said, "You want us to help you keep it real, yo." I said, something like that. He reached into a leather bag in front of him and sorted through three or four cell phones until he found the one he wanted. He said that he and his boys were going to be club-hopping later before they went to Beef, what time did he need them? I told him no later than ten o'clock, just in case Ferret and I finished early, and then told him where The Last Good Year was on 50th.

Elvis said his boys loved live-action shit like this, how much *NBA 2000* could they play?

Then he punched out a number on the cell, waited a few seconds, and said, "Whassup?"

As soon as they saw Ferret and me follow Ling and Chew out the front door of The Last Good Year, they came tumbling out of the back limo so fast Ling and Chew never had a chance. All of the guys in Elvis Elgin's posse wore baseball caps turned backward, hooded sweatshirts that seemed to be about nine sizes too big, baggy painter's pants and various brands of hundred-and-fifty-dollar sneakers. I assumed the shotgun guys were the ones in the long leather coats who used only one arm while the other guys cuffed Ling and Chew.

All of Elvis's boys nearly convulsed laughing when Ling and Chew yelled "Hah!" and then got back-to-back the way they'd obviously been taught at black belt school.

"Yo, Jackie Chan?" one of Elvis's boys said to Chew. "That some of your Benihana shit?"

Chew nodded grimly.

Elvis's guy pulled out his gun and said, "This here a Glock. You and Bruce Lee still want to go first?"

Ferret tried to run at that point, but I had him by the back of his designer sports jacket.

Elvis was just leaning against his limo, all his gold jewelry and the gold in his teeth glinting brilliantly in the Manhattan night, dressed in white v-necked t-shirt, baggy denim shorts and shower slippers that had the logo of And1, his sneaker company, in some kind of neon lettering on the part where he Velcro-ed them.

"How long you want us to detain the bitches?" Elvis said.

"I shouldn't be too long," I said.

Elvis's boys threw Ling and Chew into the back of Elvis's limo and I dragged Ferret Biel down the alley between The Last Good Year and the Ray's Original Pizza next door and sat him down on top of a garbage can.

"Now," I said, "why don't you tell me who paid you to set me up. And whatnot," I added, giving him a shove against the brick wall behind us. Ferret was making the hee hee hee sound again, only this time I was worried he might start bawling.

"Jammer," he said, back in his whiney voice, "cut me some slack, I got the second large riding on this."

I grabbed his black tie and lifted him off the top of the garbage can.

"Actually," I said amiably, "you have a ride with Elvis riding on this."

We both looked down toward the street, where Elvis waved with the sixteen-ounce Mountain Dew he was drinking. Behind him, I could see the stretch rocking back and forth a little bit. He knocked on the window, which went down automatically, and someone handed him what looked like a bag of chips.

The air went out of Ferret now.

He said, "Allen Getz."

"What he wants," I said.

I let Ferret go and told him to start practicing for his lie detector test, not that he needed much practice. I also told him that if I saw Ling or Chew again, it would be Billy Grace's posse piling out of the car next time.

Then I wished him good luck with Inger, telling him he was going to need it now that the kid had stars in her eyes.

When I got back to Suite 19, I went into the cabinet where the old man kept his scrapbooks on my short-lived career as a college football hero, and opened to that USC game. There was the Jim Murray column in the *Times* about Mountain Montoya and me, and the picture of me being carried off, then the sidebar the *Times* ran the day after my surgery, quoting me as saying that I'd be back and the doctors basically saying it must have been the drugs talking.

That was the day Bubba finally came to see me at the UCLA Medical Center. He was in the room only about five minutes when he started blubbering like he was watching the end of *Old Yeller* and confessed that he'd taken a dive in front of Mountain Montoya, and that he'd been betting on our games all season.

"I never did nothing to cost us a game, Bubba," he said. "You gotta believe me."

He said there were a few other players involved, but that he couldn't tell me who they were. I told him that I was wearing a cast that felt like it was made of concrete and had enough Percodan in me to sedate a wild horse, so I didn't give a rat's ass about anybody else, I just wanted to hear about him.

He started crying again then and said, "Goddam, it was pussy, Jack. You want the truth, there it is. I ain't even turned twenty-one yet and I can already see that I'm gonna put more money into pussy than I ever will into one of them long-range IRS accounts."

IRA, I told him.

"You know what?" he said. "It don't frankly matter either way."

He said he had one girlfriend in an apartment off-campus. I told him I knew about her, a song girl from Honolulu whose first name was Jenny and whose second name sounded a lot like macadamia. He said, Yeah, Bubba, but you don't know about the one from Pepperdine I just knocked up and the high school girl over in the damn Valley who said she'd tell her parents first and KNBC second about the big college football star if I don't keep her in enough dope to start her own cartel.

Then, of course, there was the annulment from the captain of the cheerleaders he was still paying off back home in Louisiana.

He blew his nose and told me that even with what some of the boosters were paying him, the overhead was starting to eat him alive.

Apparently, he'd gotten drunk one night at The Ginger Man when it was just him and the bartender about two in the morning, and the bartender, who'd played some ball for UCLA himself once and now had a small recurring part in *The Young and the Restless*, said that he might have a friend who could help Bubba Royal out.

The friend turned out to be someone Bubba already knew, a sleazy UCLA booster hanger-on named Milt Samuels who'd made about ten fortunes with an L.A. rental car outfit known as Cheap Heeps. Milt had finally sold the company when he was in his mid-sixties and devoted himself after that to sucking around star athletes at UCLA and breaking every rule about gifts and handouts to college football players the NCAA had ever written up. When he wasn't busy with all that, Milt Samuels spent the rest of his time promising UCLA cheerleaders and song girls he'd get them into the movies, if they'd just come to his parties, and pose for the odd photograph. Samuels was grotesquely overweight, had gray hair that he wore much too long, and no matter how much money he paid for his clothes at Bijan, they never seemed to cover as much of him as you wanted them to. The first time I'd met him, at our annual athletic banquet, I said to Bubba Royal afterward, "You ever wonder who gives Milt the creeps?"

Milt Samuels liked to gamble even more than he liked to watch the cheerleaders rub suntan lotion on each other at his swimming pool, and what he mostly liked was sure things. He told Bubba all that, and told him he'd basically cover all his existing money problems. In return, all Bubba had to give him was five games a year.

And his soul.

Bubba asked him what that meant, "give" him five games a year, and Milt Samuels said, "What do you think it means, Gomer?"

Bubba said he couldn't possibly do it himself, that he might need help with a holding penalty in a big moment, or a pass interference, or even a fumbled snap on a kick. Milt Samuels said not to wear him out with a lot of details, just give him a number. Bubba said he could handle it with one offensive lineman, one defensive back, and either a defensive tackle or linebacker who could plausibly blow an assignment or two on key third-down plays.

And even with that, Bubba told Samuels, he still couldn't guarantee that we'd cover, or our opponent would cover, in a given game. Bubba explained to him that you could have everything set up prettier than a homecoming queen, and then a zebra could throw a flag and you were completely screwed.

Milt Samuels said, hey, even odometers weren't an exact science, as he'd discovered fairly early on at Cheap Heeps.

"Give me five games and maybe we hit three," Milt Samuels said. "You'll be in the clear, I'll have a little fun, and you can still ride in the Tournament of Roses Parade."

Bubba got $50,000 a game, but only if the game went the way Milt Samuels was betting it. If Bubba had a particularly strong opinion that a point spread was way out of line, and the Bruins were not only going to cover but run all over the other team, he would ask Samuels to bet some of the $50,000 for him.

He said he had hit three games out of four with two weeks left in the regular season. Our second-to-last game was against Stanford, a twelve-point underdog. They were called the Cardinal now—the tree-huggers made them change the nickname from the Indians—and they never had a chance to win the game that day. Bubba threw for two touchdowns and I ran for two and everybody thought Bubba was just being careless when he fumbled a snap from center at our own 22-yard line with seven minutes left to play. Stanford took it in from there, and it was 28–17 for us, which meant we were going to win easy and they were going to cover, which is exactly what Bubba Royal wanted.

Except that we couldn't move the ball on our next series, and then Stanford couldn't move, and they weren't desperate enough to go for it on fourth down from deep in their own territory. So they decided to punt, a short, line-drive punt that our flashy sophomore kick returner, Baddoo Greene, caught on the dead run at midfield; he picked up some blockers when he cut to the left sideline and returned it all the way for a touchdown.

Now it was UCLA 35, Stanford 17, and suddenly Stanford wasn't going to cover a cow turd, as Bubba said in my hospital room.

In fact, he said, he nearly blew his cover as Baddoo Greene went flying past our bench. Seeing that Baddoo was clearly going all the way, Bubba suddenly took off his helmet, flung it to the ground and yelled, "Cock-sucker!"

It was his misfortune to be standing next to our coach, C. O. Jones, at that time.

"What the hell's eating you?" C. O. Jones said.

Thinking more quickly than he usually did in moments like these, Bubba said, "Damn, coach, thought I saw a clip."

Everybody's bets were saved four plays later when our safeties—only one of whom was out there on a Milt Samuels grant—collided on the desperation pass that gave Stanford its last touchdown. The final score at the Coliseum was 35–24 for UCLA on the scoreboard, 36–35 Stanford in Bubba's pocket.

The last serious action of the season was supposed to be the USC game the next week. We were ahead 13–10 in the last minute, and everyone was sure that with USC about to call its last timeout, Bubba would just kneel down a couple of times and run out the clock. Except that one of the student managers had told C. O. Jones that not only was I just two yards short of gaining a hundred for the game, but that my father was in the stands watching.

C. O. Jones had been dreaming about coaching in the National Football League longer than he had been feeling up secretaries in the Athletic Department.

"I told C. O. that we were already in the damn Rose Bowl, why risk a fumble," Bubba said. "But he looked me in the eye and said that your daddy had traveled all the way across the country and he deserved to see his son crack the century mark. God Aw-mighty. Crack the century mark? I got USC and four points and he's standing there talking to me like he's Keith Fucking Jackson."

We are on the USC six. C. O. had told Bubba to run a draw, but I'd had a tendency all day to look like Jim Brown on the draw, so Bubba came back to the huddle and called for a sweep right, a play USC had been stuffing all day.

And they would have stuffed it one last time if Jack Molloy hadn't reversed his field and taken it the other way. Mountain Montoya held his ground at right defensive end, but as I got near the front corner of the end zone, I had a blocker.

Bubba.

He took his dive there. Mountain Montoya put his helmet to my knee and hit it the way wrecking balls hit condemned buildings. That was what Bubba Royal meant when he cried for the first time and told me that he owed me one.

He swore in the hospital room that day, before he brought one of Jenny's song girl friends in to show me what she was wearing under the candy-striper outfit he'd rented for her, that he would never bet another football game as long as he lived.

"On my daddy's grave," he said, with his hand on his heart.

It wouldn't be until much later, at the tenth reunion of that Rose Bowl team, that I would discover that Bubba Royal's father could have been any enlisted man stationed at the Army Air Corps base outside Baton Rouge, Louisiana, in the spring of 1964.

"Trust me, Bubba," he'd said.

He'd leaned over and kissed me on the forehead, then opened the door and gestured that it was okay for Jenny's song girl friend, Rhonda, to come in now. "Do it for your school, Hon," he said to her. When Bubba was gone, Rhonda locked the door behind him, then smiled as she looked at my clunky white cast, attached to the wired contraption hanging from the ceiling.

"Well, okay," she said that day, showing me the black underthings she was wearing underneath the candy-striper clothes. "Somebody else gets tied up around here for a change."

twenty-five

I decided to wait until after practice to talk to Bubba Royal about what Ferret Biel had told me. I would have preferred waiting until the next eclipse of the sun, the way he'd been playing since Josh Blake had become head coach of the Hawks, but I had to know.

I owe you one, Bubba, he'd said.

Trust me, he'd said in the hospital room that day.

It was one thing for him to roll over the way he had for Milt Samuels when he was a dumb kid, that's what I'd always told myself. Every time he'd get drunk enough after that in some bar near campus, he'd swear again that he'd learned his lesson, that he wasn't never gonna cheat on the talent God had given him. And once he got to the pros, he didn't even have to worry about Milt Samuels trying to slither back into his life. Samuels died during Bubba's rookie season with the Hawks, when a mysterious fire swept through his Brentwood home. Luckily, his new bride, a former UCLA cheerleading captain known simply as Skye in her days there, was at the exercise studio, Killer Bod, her husband had opened for her, one that would eventually become a nationwide chain after her generous inheritance.

"Everyone who loved Milt begged him not to smoke cigars in bed," Skye Samuels said at the time. "Me, his bookies, all the cheerleaders and girls from the escort services who had spent so many happy hours at his pool parties."

So Milt Samuels had died with his secrets and Bubba had gone on to have what many experts already felt was a Hall of Fame career, even without the Super Bowl appearance that most of the other immortal NFL quarterbacks had on their résumés. If he was willing to risk all that, then it meant he had gone through money faster and more frivolously than my lunch date for that same day, Kitty Drucker-Cole Molloy.

The old man used to say that a blowtorch couldn't take the numbers off a Visa card the way his second wife could.

I had called her as soon as I got to the office that day. She said she was in the middle of a session with her personal trainer—"Franco, *stop* that!" she said at one point—and asked if I could call her back in forty-five minutes, she had a small window before her deep-tissue massage therapist got there.

I said I was actually just calling to see if she might be free for lunch, even on short notice.

"Well, aren't you the sweetest boy," she said, then groaned. "Call me back."

The last thing I heard before she clicked off was a slapping noise and some giggling and them my stepmother saying in a husky voice, "When did we start doing this part without the lotion . . ."

She called me back an hour later and told me that I was in luck, that Debby Norville had just canceled and why didn't I come over there and we'd eat in.

"There" was the triplex at the corner of 67th and Central Park West that Tim Molloy had bought his bride as a wedding present when she informed him that there would just be too many icky ghosts and memories for her at 71 East 71st. The old man had to actually buy two apartments in the old brownstone to make sure Kitty had all the space she said she wanted and the penthouse view. The whole deal, I recalled, had cost about as much and taken about as long as renovating Yankee Stadium in the old days.

It was one of those elevator deals where the doors opened and you walked right into the place. I was only in there for about fifteen seconds when Kitty made her entrance, sweeping down the spiral staircase, wearing some kind of strapless lemon-colored dress, looking as if there'd been just enough time for her after the massage to undergo a complete makeover.

"Kisses, kisses, kisses," she said, then gave me the kind of full-court bosom-thrust she'd always given me, whispering into my ear, "I know what you're thinking, you bad boy, but these babies are still all mine."

I told her she was a monument to clean living and whatever she was paying Franco and the deep-tissue guy.

She showed me out to the terrace, one with a view of the park that had swept away more than a few flight attendants and aspiring actresses when Big Tim and Kitty happened to be on another cruise in Alaska or around the tip of South America. The one time I'd taken Ellie Rhodes there, in an old-times-sake date before she moved to Hollywood for good, she'd taken one look at the view, turned around and said, "Well, at least you give good park."

There was a new houseperson, whom Kitty called Toi. Toi had shiny black hair that fell in severe bangs and what seemed to be vaguely Polynesian features, and wore a pressed white jacket and black satin slacks that came to the top of the ankles. Toi was barefoot, showing off toenails painted a violet color.

Kitty said she'd like a Bloody Mary and I said I'd have the same. When Toi disappeared through the sliding glass doors, I said, "I don't mean to pry, but is Toi a boy or a girl?"

Kitty sighed and said, "How many times has that poor confused child asked himself the same question?"

We sat there awhile and sipped our drinks and stared out at one of those pictures of the dream New York while Kitty engaged in a nonstop stream of extremely small talk about this opening and that fund-raiser for young playwrights and the truly soul-enriching work she was doing with the new shelter at St. Bart's and had I been over to see Michael Feinstein at the Algonquin since I'd been back, that only people from out of town still thought it was so trés trés chic to see Bobby Short at the Carlyle.

She said that she was absolutely thrilled with the way the team had played since I'd gotten rid of that awful Vince Cahill and praised me for giving a second chance to Guns of Navarone Queens, who she said had better hands than Karl.

"Let me guess," I said. "Your masseuse."

"He's a little weak with English," she said, and made a motion with her hand as if fanning herself. "But those hands speak about seven languages."

It was when Toi came back with our refills that I said to Kitty, "Tell your boyfriend to lay off me."

She gave me some rapid blinking with her ridiculously long eyelashes and said, "Well, Jack, dear, I'm sure I have no idea what you're talking about."

We were both sitting facing the park. I turned my chair toward hers just slightly, so I was facing her, and took her hands in mine, and then leaned forward so our faces were almost touching. It's worth mentioning that even though I had always thought she was sillier than a French farce, I was inside her force field now, which meant I could feel the full force of everything that had put my father at the head table of the Old Fools' Ball.

"Kitty?" I said.

She nodded slowly.

I said, "We need to cut the shit now, okay?"

I'm not sure what she thought was going to happen, but whatever disappointment she felt that I wasn't going to finally make a move on her, was gone in a few more blinks and then she was looking at me with cat eyes. When she tried to pull away, I squeezed a little harder on her hands as a way of telling her to stay where she was.

"I don't know if I can hold on to this team or not," I said. "But tell Allen the geek that if he doesn't stop fucking with me I will make sure he doesn't get it if it's the last thing I do."

"How about this?" she said. "How about you tell him yourself?"

She tried to give her perfect hair a little toss, but it was going to move when Central Park did.

"You're in over your head," she said.

"That's what they're saying," I said, "all over town."

"Think about it," Kitty said. "The prodigal son against Allen Getz? Jack, dear, what kind of odds would they have for a fight like that out in Las Vegas?"

I found myself smiling again, just because we had finally gotten down to it now. It was just the two of us. She didn't have to play the grieving widow or flirtatious stepmom or crazed charity Nazi woman.

With me on this terrace was the dead-eyed sharpshooter who'd bagged the old man on her last safari and was now looking to bag Allen Getz.

I said, "I would like to say that the grief counselors have worked wonders with you."

She let that one go like a batter taking a strike.

"Despite what you might think," she said, "Allen and I are just good friends. He recently lost his mother, you know. We're both very needy right now."

I'll bet, I said.

"You're going to think what you want, anyway," she said.

"Tell me something, Kitty," I said. "Why does this guy want the Hawks so goddam much?"

"Because he does, Jack," she said. "Haven't you learned anything sucking around people like Allen Getz? What do you call them in Vegas? Your whales? Before he gets what he wants, he wants what he wants."

"Why does he want this particular team?"

"Because he does," she said. "It's not any more complicated than that. He has the best plane his money can buy. He has the best yacht. Now he wants the best team money can buy. There are thirty-four of these toys in the whole world. Only three of them are in New York, except two of them aren't in New York, they're in New Jersey. That leaves the Hawks."

She waved her hand dismissively. "Please don't try to apply the sort of logic you would to a normal person."

Kitty made "normal" sound like "diseased" or "crippled," something like that.

Toi was on the other side of the glass. Kitty turned and made a motion like she wanted a cigarette. Toi brought a long one out, stuck it in her hand, lit it, then stood there waiting to find out if Kitty wanted him to smoke it for her as well.

"I know you think I put him up to this somehow," she continued. "But I didn't. He decided on his own, and quite some time ago, that he wanted the Hawks. He'd been talking to your father about buying the team for more than a year."

I said, "Bullshit."

"Fine, Jack. Bullshit. But how would you know, really? Your father had started to give up on your ever coming back. You still can't see that, but then you were always such a self-absorbed shit, weren't you? You think your father loved the Hawks this much for himself? Well, guess what? He didn't. They were always supposed to be something he could share with *you*. Something he could pass down to *you*. Only *you*, Jack, you didn't want them."

Kitty Drucker-Cole Molloy said it was funny, if you really thought about it. The only reason I'd inherited the Hawks is that she kept convincing Tim Molloy he shouldn't sell them, sure that the longer he held on to them and the longer I stayed away, the better the chance that he would leave the team—or at least half of it—to her.

"Then your father had to make a complete mess of everything," she said.

"By dying," I said, "and leaving what you thought should have been your half to an absent, self-absorbed shit like me."

"At least when poor Emilio Aguilera had that tragic, tragic accident on his boat, *his* affairs were in order."

I said, "You mean, he left the team to his trophy wife."

"If they're not going to do that," Kitty said, blowing out a jet stream of smoke, "what the hell is the point?"

She stubbed out the cigarette now and stood up.

"Forget about marrying this bastard, even if I have to admit marrying *is* what you're good at," I said. "Why not just adopt him?"

She acted as if she didn't hear the last part. "He is so young, in so many sweet ways. I've been able to help him in so many ways, including some suggestions about how to deal with you. You'd be surprised at how much your father knew about you."

"You really believe you can get him down the aisle, don't you?" I said.

"I do," Kitty Molloy said. "What a nice way for us to conclude our little chat, with my two favorite words in the entire English language."

She stood there as if holding a bouquet, eyes glistening.

"I do," she said again.

twenty-six

Bubba Royal said it was a goddam stinkin' shitbird lie and he'd swear to that on the head of his sweet little angel baby girl.

I asked Bubba which baby girl, since there was league-wide speculation that he might have more illegitimate children than an NBA small forward.

We were on the field about half an hour after practice. The rest of the players were gone by now. Josh was down near the tunnel leading to the locker room surrounded by the regular beat writers who covered the team. A few yards away, obviously waiting for him to finish, was Vicky Dunne. She had her cameraman with her, and a young woman who looked an awful lot like Annie Kay.

"Who told you a stinkin' lie like that?" Bubba said.

He was wearing the red bib over his regular jersey that reminded the defense to keep their lousy hands off him in practice after he threw the ball.

"Ferret Biel," I said.

He spit out the Gatorade he'd been drinking, as if even the mention of Ferret's name was like dumping chemicals into it.

"Jesus Crimminy, Jack, who you gonna trust?" he said. "A lyin' sack of shit like that or me?"

"The way I trusted you against SC that day?"

"That's hittin' me so far below the belt, now it's my knee should hurt," Bubba Royal said in a wounded voice.

I told him I just wanted to know where we stood here, once and for all. He could look me in the eye and tell me that he was clean, that Ferret Biel had some kind of new agenda here, was working some kind of new angle. Or he could come clean and tell me he was doing business, just like Ferret said he was, in which case I was going to make sure that he wouldn't be able to get a football job in the fucking Arena League.

Bubba had been sitting on the field in front of the bench. Now he got into a kneeling position, as if he were preparing to stand up. But then he just stayed there, hands on his knees, as if he were too exhausted to move. I thought of the famous photograph of Y. A. Tittle the old man had in his office, Tittle at the end of his career with the Giants, helmet off, blood trickling from the side of his bald head, at the end of a day when the Saints had kicked his ass.

The old man's copy was signed by Tittle himself:

Dear Tim,
Get out a year early instead of a year late.
Best always,
Yelberton Abraham Tittle.

I told Bubba to get up or Vicky Dunne was going to come running over and want to know why he had assumed the prayer position and was facing Mecca.

He slowly pulled himself up and sat on the bench, fussing with the straps on his helmet.

"I've done a lot of shit in my life I'm ashamed of," he said. "I did somethin' to you that day I got to carry around as much in my heart as my damn memory long as I live. And I ain't gonna insult you by sittin' here and sayin' that I don't have the goddam shorts again. I do. God help me, but I do, after all the money I made in my life. But what I'm gonna tell you right here and now is true: The last bet I ever made was with that pukeface Milt Samuels."

"So you're saying Ferret made this up?"

"I can't tell you somebody didn't give him my name," Bubba said. "Maybe there was some late money come in. And can I tell you that there isn't a single guy on this team placin' a bet here and there? Fuck no. It'd be like me tellin' you nobody goes lookin' for a jump-start pill about a quarter-to-Sunday-afternoon."

I went over and crouched in front of him, feeling my sneakers sink into Tim Molloy's lush green grass.

"You're telling me on our friendship that you don't bet."

"That's what I'm tellin' you."

"People think you do, you know that. Even people who don't know about Milt Samuels."

"People think you're a career fuckup," he said.

He looked past me now, squinting into the last sun over the stadium. "Hey," Bubba said. "Isn't that Annie from Beef down there with Vicky?"

I told him if it wasn't she had a sister who was just as much of a heartbreaker.

Bubba said, "Jimmy T. said she poured a big pitcher of drinks on you the other night. Jimmy T. also mentioned he didn't think it was because you were some kind of piss-poor tipper."

I grinned at him and tried to sound as much like him as I could. "Goddam, Bubba, it always come down to pussy, doesn't it?"

Tell me about it, he said sadly; there ought to be a fixed interest rate on it.

We sat there and talked about the team a little bit, how he was sure we were going to smack the Giants around on Sunday, how Josh was actually talking to the players again and how much that had changed an atmosphere in the locker room that had become more toxic under Vince Cahill than a Jersey waste dump. Bubba said that he actually thought the Hawks might be turning into the team they were supposed to be, and how before this season was over, we were going to be the number-one attraction in the whole damn league, all the way to what those jerkoffs in the media still called the ultimate game. Finally, he fixed those blue eyes on me, serious now, and said, "You gonna pull this deal off or not?"

"You mean hold on to this team?"

"Become a force to be reckoned with," he said, "in pro football, the right-wing theater of America."

I told him that the forces of evil were not only still lined up against me in a nickel package, but were starting to show some zone blitz.

"But I got chips left," I said.

"Figured you did," he said. "Maybe your daddy knew you better than you know your own stubborn self."

He asked when I was going to give him A.T.M. back: If he had A.T.M. on the other side from Guns of Navarone Queens, he'd put up points faster than the Knicks. I told him Pete and Tire Iron Timmons were over in jolly old England efforting that even as we spoke. Bubba wanted to know if A.T.M. was still set on renegotiating and I told him he probably was. Sometimes you got to compromise, Bubba Royal said, and I told him funny, that's the same thing Big Tim Molloy used to say to me.

We both saw Vicky Dunne, her camera guy and Annie Kay walking toward us. Bubba groaned as he stood up and said, that's it, he was out of here, just the thought of talking to Vicky today made his balls ache. He gave a courtly bow to Vicky and Annie and jogged toward the locker room, helmet in his right hand, going down the center of the field and then through the goalposts, the last of the sun hitting him like a spotlight, following him until he was through the tunnel, Bubba Royal in that moment still looking like everybody's All-America.

———

Vicky Dunne said she understood that I'd met her new intern from NYU, Annie Kay? I didn't know how much Annie had told her about us, so I just said, "Hey, Annie."

She was wearing tight jeans and a tattersall-checked shirt with the sleeves rolled up and made Vicky Dunne look like her aunt.

"Mr. Molloy," she said, extending her hand. "So nice to see you again."

"Call me Jack," I said.

She said she couldn't, she'd been taught to be respectful of her elders.

Vicky, who'd been busy with her microphone, asked if I minded if she asked a few questions on camera. I noted that her hair had gone spikey now and was Lucille Ball–red, matching her blazer and her lips, which seemed to be getting bigger every time I saw her.

"Football or business?"

"Football business," she said.

They set up. I asked if she wanted me to look at the camera or her and she said her. Annie handed her a notebook, then went and stood behind the camera guy, a tall white guy who'd decided to give up on hair and had gone bald.

"Speed," he said.

"I'm with Jack Molloy," she said. "Jack, is it true that Allen Getz is interested in buying the Hawks from the Molloy family?"

"Word travels fast," I said. "The only problem is that the Hawks are not for sale."

As usual, she acted as if she hadn't heard a word I'd said.

"And if he does buy the Hawks," she said, "that he plans to bring back Vince Cahill as head of football operations?"

Very slowly, I said, "Liz Bolton and Pete Stanton run the football operations for the Hawks, whom the Molloy family has no intention of selling to Allen Getz or anybody else."

I looked past Vicky Dunne and said to Annie, "Is it who or whom?"

She looked over toward Yonkers.

Vicky said, "Okay, we're still rolling. Sources within the organization say you're resigned to the fact that you'll never get enough votes to keep the team."

"Which sources?"

"What?"

"You said you had sources within the organization," I said.

"I can't reveal . . ."

"Except there aren't any sources in the organization, there's just Liz and Pete and me, and we only talk to you on the record, it's sort of a rule I passed that gets your ass fired if you break it."

She looked down at her notebook and said, "I have one more question, unrelated to the sale of the team."

"A team not for sale," I said.

"Is it true," Vicky Dunne asked, "that you are conducting an internal investigation about the recurring gambling problems . . ."

I walked past her and said to the bald camera guy, "Okay, stop tape."

He looked at Vicky. So did Annie. So did I.

Now I said to Vicky, "Tell him to stop tape or I will take his camera away from him."

The bald camera guy said, "Hey," then we all looked at each other a little more and then Vicky said, "Why don't we all take a little timeout here?"

"Why don't we?" I said, and motioned for Vicky to come join me on the field. She started to say something and I put a finger to my lips and gestured toward the Hawks logo at midfield. When we were out of earshot of either Annie or the camera guy, I said, "We're not going to talk about gambling allegations now or ever. If you mention it to anybody else or attempt to go on the air with it, then I am going to cut you off here."

"My, my," she said. "That sounds like a threat."

I thought of Billy and told her that I didn't make threats, just promises.

I said, "I will make sure that not a single member of this football team talks to you."

"I'll go to the league . . ." she said.

"Go. When you come back, you won't get another one-on-one with the players, with the coaches, with me or Liz or Pete. You need access in your business the way the rest of us need oxygen. If the network comes to me, I'll tell them that the only way the new policy will change is if you're off the fucking beat and they send some new twink to take your place.

"Now," I said, "who gave you the gambling?"

"You know I can't give up a source," she said.

"In the White House press corps, they can't," I said. "On the cop shows, they can't give up a source. Here it will be fine, I promise."

"I can't," she said, and now I was afraid she might cry.

"Your call," I said, and got about five steps away.

"Vince," she said.

I came back and said, "Vince? Why?"

"I don't know. He said if I wanted it, there it was."

"He's really in bed with Getz?"

"Says he is."

"He mention a guy named Ferret Biel?"

"No. He just said everything he was telling me was solid, that I shouldn't be afraid to go with it."

Billy was right, the NFL was starting to make Vegas look like church in comparison.

I told Vicky if she heard anything more from him, to call me. She wanted to know why she should help me out after I'd just said so many really shitty things to her and I said, "Because I'm the guy who owns the team and Vince is a slob with an ax to grind."

I put my arm around her and told her that I was glad we'd been able to have this frank and open dialogue, that it was crucial for a management person like myself to keep the lines of communication open with the media.

"You're our conduit to the public," I said.

"Fuck off," she said.

I told her that when we had speed again to ask me if it was true that Pete Stanton and Tire Iron Timmons were in London with our old friend A.T.M. Moore.

I said, "Vicky, your sources are as good as ever. Pete and Tire Iron have been there since Monday. We're all keeping our fingers crossed that maybe we're all about to get through this impasse and get A.T.M. back here where he belongs."

While Vicky put headsets on and checked the sound, I said to Annie Kay, "You think Vicky has ever seen *All About Eve*?"

"You mean where the young ambitious girl tries to knife the bitchy diva in the back? Hell, no."

"Have one drink with me tonight," I said quietly.

"Got a date," she said.

"With who?"

"Whom," she said.

"Okay, whom?"

"None of your business," Annie Kay said, when she saw Vicky looking at us. "Listen, I'm still working two nights a week at Beef while I try to improve myself. If you show up some night, I promise not to slime you."

She started to run to catch up with them, then stopped and came back to me, kneeling as if she'd dropped a pen or something.

"What did you say to Vicky over there at the old midfield stripe?" Annie said.

I told her.

"She gave it up that easy?" Annie said, her face suddenly flushed with excitement.

I nodded, thinking it was still early in our relationship, but that this was as overheated as I'd seen her wearing all her clothes.

Annie Kay threw a fist in the air and said, "She is *mine*!"

twenty-seven

e beat the Giants that Sunday, even though we lost Nike Evans for the season in the process. Nike—who had started to play both offense and defense in the absence of A.T.M.—got caught from behind on a post pattern and tore up so many parts of his knee with the word "collateral" attached to them that it sounded as if his reconstructive surgery the next day should have been done by the head of the mortgage department.

We beat Arizona on the road the next week, somehow surviving four interceptions by Bubba Royal in the process. If I wasn't such a trusting soul—and the oddsmakers hadn't made it a pick-'em game—the last one would have made alarms go off. It was supposed to be a fourth-quarter screen pass to veteran backup fullback Redford Newman—Brian Goldberg wrote in Newman's bio that he was so named because his parents loved both *Butch Cassidy and the Sundance Kid* and *The Sting* so much—but ended up in the belly of Mountain Montoya himself, playing out the string with the Cardinals that season. We were ahead 13–0 at the time and Montoya's touchdown would turn out to be the only one the

Cardinals would get all day in a game we'd finally win 16–7. The over-under on the game was thirty points, so I couldn't see where Bubba handing the Cardinals a gift touchdown at that point could have helped out anybody. So I just wrote the play off to one of those dumb-assed decisions Bubba would make sometimes, had always made, as if his head was anywhere except in the game he was playing.

On the plane going home, he came up and found me in the lounge, having a celebratory drink with Pete and Brian.

"I know what you was probably thinkin' after I give it up to Mountain," he said.

"I'd forgotten the sonofabitch was still in the league," I said.

Bubba looked at me hard and said, "I didn't look before I threw, is all. Rookie mistake."

Okay, I said.

"Just wanted you to know," he said.

I asked him if he wanted to join us for a drink.

Bubba said, "I'd eat that bastard's underwear before I'd ever give him a game," and went back to play cards with Elvis and Raiford and Redford Newman.

Pete and Tire Iron had flown straight through from London to New York to Phoenix to make the game after spending the week with A.T.M. Pete said relations between A.T.M. and Donyell were clearly strained, that it was Pete's feeling that A.T.M. was ready to say fuck it and come back and play, but that Donyell was still deep into what was essentially a rap about how this was another example of *the* man holding *his* man down.

"Did he call me Whitey?" I asked.

Pete said he came close a couple of times.

He said, "Donyell's determined to play this thing right out until the week before the deadline. At which point, he believes you will fold. He said, and I quote, 'If the Hawks go down, Jack Molloy goes down like a prison bitch with them.' End quote."

Pete said he thought about defending me, but just told Donyell how powerful his imagery was instead.

In the lounge, I said to Pete, "But you think A.T.M.'s ready to play?"

Pete said that A.T.M. was worried about Oretha, as always, fearful that if his money was cut off until after the season, she might go after one of his houses. Pete said that A.T.M. loved his five houses as much as he loved the cars he hadn't totaled yet and his dozen Rottweilers, currently residing at his estate in East Hampton, about a mile or so from where Mo Jiggy lived. He also had places in Rancho Mirage, California; Jupiter, Florida; and a hunting lodge in northern Michigan just because he had heard Muhammad Ali was up there somewhere. A.T.M. told Pete that Oretha knew that the lodge in Michigan was his favorite, because that's where he went to find his peace and solitary.

At the last meeting Pete had with A.T.M. and Donyell, he said he dropped the hammer on them, said I wasn't bluffing, and that A.T.M. better get his ass on the right side of the Atlantic. He said he left them sitting in the bar of the Savoy, Donyell dressed in so much tweed Pete wondered if tweed boxer shorts made your balls itch, the two of them bickering like an old *Honeymooners* episode.

Two weeks later there was an item in Page Six of the *Post* saying that their sources in London said that A.T.M. Moore was considering making an agent switch—it would have been the fourth or fifth of his short career, depending on whether or not you counted Oretha Keeshon— to Mo Jiggy.

"Mo Jiggy, rap agent?" I said to Pete in his office.

"Don't laugh," he said. "He has two sports clients already. There's this kid Sharif Mustafa O'Rourke, a shooting guard for the Dallas Mavericks, he just got a seventy-million-dollar extension, and Johnson Johnson, that four-hundred-pound defensive tackle for the Saints."

Pete reminded me that not only were Mo and A.T.M. neighbors on Gin Lane in East Hampton, but that A.T.M. had been telling anybody who wanted to listen for years how one of his dreams was to be either a rapper or an action star in the movies.

"You think Mo Jiggy can actually deliver this kid?" I said to Pete.

Pete said that once you took away the earrings, the tattoos, the neck-laces, the hundred-thousand-dollar diamond ring Kelli Ann Gonzalez had given him as an engagement present, and the mysterous death of his for-mer business partner Fat Load, he actually thought Mo was a pretty sharp guy for the way he'd marketed himself and, more important, the way he'd managed to avoid what Pete called the National Rap Star Death Toll.

"I know one other thing that might be helpful," he said.

"What?"

"Mo Jiggy wants a luxury box here more than he wants Kelli Ann," Pete said.

I told him I'd have to run it by Kenny and Babs, but that I could prob-ably handle that, as long as Mo promised to have A.T.M. back in uniform by our tenth game, against the Redskins in Washington.

Our ninth game was against the Philadelphia Eagles at Molloy. I was wondering if Allen Getz would have the balls to show up with Kitty. He hadn't returned any of my phone calls and had skipped the last couple of home games; I knew because I kept looking for him in Kitty's box. She said he was either in New Mexico or St. Bart's. Or was it Tokyo, with all his new little friends over there? She did say she'd passed on my various messages to him and that Allen was genuinely wounded that I thought he would use such vulgar tactics.

"You don't know how truly sensitive this man is," Kitty said.

By then I was marking all time in my life by our schedule. Before the Eagles game, I had lunch one afternoon at the Four Seasons with Corky DuPont III and Bobby Finkel, who lived in the city and only commuted to New Orleans a couple of days a week on Saints business. Both of them assured me that no matter what I might have heard, they were going to keep an open mind about me, especially now that they knew Allen Getz was lurking.

"Hey," Bobby Finkel said, "you think I'm going out of my way to help someone whose dot com is bigger than mine? My ass."

Corky DuPont, who looked like a bigger and only slightly more robust Woody Allen, said, "We're not opposed to new money, Jack, don't get us wrong."

Bobby Finkel said, "Corky says my new money feels old."

I said to Corky, "What about if it's Dad's money?"

Corky said, "Nothing wrong with Dad's money ever, as far as I'm concerned."

When he talked about Dad's money, he sounded like Bubba talking about pussy.

While we were finishing up that day, while Edge went to get Bobby Finkel's car, Corky DuPont III said, "But we would, all of us, appreciate something, Jack."

"What's that?"

"Could you find a way not to spend as much time on the front page as one of those rap people who look as if they should be tending to my grounds?"

I told him I'd work on it, making a mental note as I did to add Elvis's posse to the Suite 19 pass list the day we played Corky's Jets; that way everybody could get to know each other.

It was the Saturday night before the Hawks-Eagles game. Somehow Annie Kay and I still hadn't managed to have that drink we'd talked about, despite a few false starts. But I'd called down to Beef and she was supposed to be coming in around nine o'clock, so I thought I might wander down later, maybe even catch a couple of the floor shows.

I hadn't talked to Liz Bolton for a couple of days, not since she'd informed me she had been watching from her office when I was on the field with Annie that day.

"I don't share, Jack," she said.

I told her I wouldn't expect her to, especially with a catch like me.

"I don't even share desserts," she said.

"I didn't know we were going steady, Gidget," I said.

Then I told her what was technically the truth, that nothing was going on between Annie and me, and hadn't been going on since she'd walked in on us that night, and that despite what Liz thought she'd seen, Annie still considered me a lower life-form than an amoeba.

"I watched you watch her leave," Liz said in the old man's office, as if that explained everything. "You didn't stop staring at her ass until she was in the parking lot."

I got to watch Liz leave right after that, staring at her ass until she was all the way past Delores's desk and through the reception area.

Now I was back in the old man's office, the swivel chair facing the field, feet up on the windowsill, smoking one of his cigars, looking at my watch and thinking there were just fourteen hours until kickoff.

So it had taken less than half a season for me to need these games like every serious player I'd ever seen in Vegas needed the action. I was hooked. I was on the inside now and I liked it, and if I told myself anything else, I would have been kidding myself worse than all the guys up and down the strip, from the ones pumping the slots to the whales in the private rooms, telling themselves they would walk away anytime they wanted to, no problem. I knew why every owner in the league wanted to get into the club, and stay in the club; why they wanted to decide who got in with them and who didn't. Owning one of these teams was the newest and most expensive designer drug. Opium, but certainly not for the masses. And there were no damaging side effects, not a single one, as long as you could handle the losing and the bad press that came with it without wanting to hide under your bed. Four preseason games, sixteen regular-season games, then the playoffs in January if you made it that far. Twenty times a year, maybe more, you got to be what anybody with any jock in him ever wanted to be: captain of the varsity.

All of us, even the ones like me who'd gotten into the club on a pass, got to feel like players on the field, even from up in the luxury boxes. We got to feel like we were in the game, without ever having to take a single goddam hit or end up at the bottom of the goddam pile.

If the team won, we walked around the locker room afterward and took as many bows as anybody. If the team lost, it was somebody else who did it. If the team kept losing we could fire somebody, or cut somebody, or make a trade. Players got hurt, players got old, coaches and general managers came and went. Owners were forever, covered like stars now, treated like stars. It had started in baseball as far as I could tell, with guys like Charles O. Finley of the old Oakland A's, and right after Finley came George Steinbrenner, who for nearly thirty years in New York had been a headline and controversy machine.

After that came all the children of Steinbrenner, in all the major sports.

All of a sudden, you had Jerry Jones down on the sideline for Cowboys games, standing a few yards away from Jimmy Johnson or Barry Switzer, yelling at players, slapping them on the ass, bitching at the refs, leading the cheers sometimes, doing everything except wearing one of the designer headsets and talking to the assistant coaches upstairs like a pilot talking to a control tower.

Along the way, the media figured something out: how much every one of these people loved the sound of their own voices, and how likely they were to say almost anything. And when some nitwit in the papers or on the radio, or one of the twinks doing the games, would want to know why the owner was getting involved this way, they'd all say the same thing, from Donnie Mack Carney to Corky DuPont to Big Tim Molloy:

It's my money.

Now what?

From my first week, Liz and Pete and even Brian Goldberg had been explaining the finances to me, showing me how owning any team, but particularly this team, was like owning the First National Bank of Football, explaining how even with a salary cap you could still pay and over-pay your stars, as long as you could get as many guys as possible at the bottom of the roster to work as close to the minimum as possible.

"You pay your high-end guys and screw your low-end guys," Pete said, "and basically do everything in your power to completely wipe out the middle class."

I told him it sounded somewhat like the Republican Party that way.

Liz explained an old tax law from the seventies that allowed you to assign half the purchase price of a pro sports team to player contracts, and then amortize a sweetheart deduction like that.

"Say somebody like Allen Getz did get the whole team for a billion dollars," she said. "Under the law, he could write off nearly five hundred million of that from his operating income over the next five years."

Even I could figure it out from there.

"Reduce your income," I said, "reduce your taxes."

Liz said, "And your critics—and they are legion—say that even the simplest decisions in blackjack make your little head hurt."

Pete said, "If you play it right on a billion-dollar purchase, you can get a deduction of a hundred million on the football team and use it to lay off income from your other businesses if that's the way you want to go."

"The trick," Liz said, "is being able to prove that the value of your contracts equals fifty percent of the purchase price." She smiled. "But that's why we've got more accountants around here than we do assistant coaches."

"It's our posse," Pete said, "they just carry pocket calculators instead of Sig Sauer nine-millimeters."

With all that, it still wasn't the money, not where we sat. Ballplayers said it wasn't about the money and it always was. But owners already had all the money, old or new, oil money and media money and real estate money and dot com money. Or inherited money. Corky DuPont had inherited his, I had inherited mine. Our friends knew us as Corky and Jammer, but our nicknames really should have been "Thanks Dad."

Even with Thanks Dads like Corky and me, it wasn't the money or the tax breaks or the way every politician in town wanted to go down on us if we even hinted we were unhappy.

It was the action.

It was exactly the kind of action people had always come to Vegas or Atlantic City looking to find, the rush of being a player, of putting it all on the line, as Bubba once said, "when the money is on the fucking table." You didn't have to sit through five-hour baseball games, or wait for another tattooed kid to dunk the ball in the NBA, if somebody named Vladimir hadn't just stepped back to make a three-pointer. Some rich guys wanted to own movie studios, but who wanted to wait a year or more to find out whether you'd flushed a couple of hundred million on Kevin Costner or the new Arnold Schwarzenegger epic about saving the world?

All you had to do in football was wait for next Sunday. New odds, new action. New game. Everybody starting clean. Pete said the old man used to talk all the time about having one of the seats at the only table worth talking about, if you really wanted to have any fun in this world. Now I was in that seat, smoking one of his cigars, drinking his Scotch, counting the minutes until my team played again, wondering how long it was all going to last.

Or how long I wanted it to last.

"Molloy," I said out loud in the empty office, "I have met the enemy. And he is me."

The old man had told me from the time I was a kid that it was perfectly fine to talk to yourself as long as you at least listened once in a while. I poured more Scotch and noticed that half the bottle was gone and wondered if I was starting to get drunk.

Because when I looked at the field now, I saw an old man down there, a little hunched over, his back to me, walking slowly along the 20-yard line at the east end of Molloy Stadium.

He had what looked like a cigar in his hand and seemed to be talking to himself as well.

twenty-eight

took the press elevator down to field level, then walked down the long hallway toward the tunnel, my footsteps so loud and spooky that I felt like one of the stars of those movies where everybody except the stars got stabbed by somebody wearing a *Phantom of the Opera* mask.

As far as I could tell, the victims always said the exact same thing right before they got it:

"Jenny, is that you?"

I made my way past the visitors' locker room, past the X-ray room next to it, past the room where the officials dressed, past the Hawks' locker room. Opposite that were a handful of choice parking spaces, for Kenny and Babs and Liz and Pete. There was one for me, even though I didn't have a car in the city. I noticed that somebody had painted over Vince Cahill's name, just left "Head Coach" on the wall above where Vince used to park the free Mercedes he got as part of his deal.

I gave a little salute to the night security guy, an ex–NYPD detective named Red Gellis, who'd been with my father, in different walk-around-guy jobs, for about thirty years.

"I got us tomorrow and lay the six," he said.

I told Red that gambling was sinful and as potentially lethal as the illegal narcotics he used to take off bad guys, but that sounded like the right way to bet Hawks against the Eagles.

The old man on the field was still down at the other end, walking toward the end zone now. I jogged toward him, and when I got to the five-yard line I said, "How you doing?"

When he turned around, I saw that it was Arnie Browne.

"Hey, kiddo," he said.

"Uncle Arnie."

He was the owner of the Eagles and had to be pushing eighty by now, his Albert Einstein hair flying all over the place as usual, his bow tie hanging crookedly from his collar, his seersucker suit looking as if he'd been sleeping in it. The tip of his trademark cheap cigar was hanging from his lower lip, which had as much spit on it as a basset hound's.

"What are you doing out here by yourself at this time of night?" I said.

He took the cigar out and wiped the spit away with the sleeve of his jacket, which had so many tobacco stains on it he looked as if he'd taken a bullet there.

"Having a visit with your father," he said. "But now I've got company who won't let me go on and on like some old fool." He put an arm around my shoulders and said, "Walk with me, son."

He was my father's best friend in football. The last time I'd seen him had been at the funeral, and he'd told me that day that he and the missus were finally going to take that cruise around the world they'd been putting off, that too many people had been dying on him lately, and he frankly didn't know when he'd be back. But he'd worked it out that they ended up in London and spent a week there and then he'd taken the Concorde back that day because he decided he wanted to see the Hawks game. His wife, Margie, was out with friends, but he'd pleaded jet lag and then he said he was wandering around the suite they always got at the Pierre and he got to thinking about the old man and he told them to call him a damn town car and here he was.

"Me and your father and old Well Mara, we're the dinosaurs," he said. "We didn't get into this business to get our pictures in the damn newspaper."

He had won the Eagles in a card game, or so legend had it, after he'd made it back in one piece from World War II. His family ran a trucking business from near the Villanova campus, and Arnie was supposed to take it over if he made it home. He did, with more medals from June 6, 1944, than he had room for on the front of his tunic. Only now he didn't want to run the family trucking business, at least not yet. After all the dying he'd seen, he wanted to live it up for a while.

I remembered him sitting in the old man's den at 71 East 71st one night when I was still at McBurney, not long after my mother died. It was about the time when they'd started the big debate in the NCAA about whether or not freshmen should be eligible to play varsity sports in college. Arnie Browne said he'd read a damn quote from Digger Phelps, the Notre Dame basketball coach in those days, wondering whether an eighteen-year-old kid could handle the combined pressures of academics and athletics.

"Yeah," he said to my father and me, "when I was eighteen and on my belly at Normandy, I remember thinking to myself, 'Arnie boy, you sure are lucky not to be facing the dual pressures of academics and athletics.'"

But he made it back to Philly and threw himself a party that he told me once lasted about three years, and then one night the party made it to a high-stakes poker game at a friend's apartment overlooking Rittenhouse Square. One of the players in the game was a flamboyant local character named Ziggy Gethers, the owner of the Eagles.

He'd bought the Eagles right after the war with some of his trust fund money, the rest of which went into a series of movies starring whichever starlet he was screwing at the moment. Now he was almost out of money, and when he got ahead early in the game he started to think that perhaps Arnie Browne's trucking money might be a solution to his severe cash flow problems. But then Arnie started to come on and finally it was six-thirty in the morning and Arnie bet everything he had, nearly ten thousand dollars, on one last hand. Ziggy tried to put up the contract of a singer-dancer named Adele he was going around with at the time, saying that beyond Adele's potential in show business, she had skills worth at least ten grand, if you spread them out over time.

Arnie always loved to tell the next part.

"I told Ziggy I already had a girl. My little Margie."

Ziggy's last marker was the Eagles. Arnie called and Ziggy turned over two pair, queens high. Arnie had a full house, jacks over lucky sevens, and he was suddenly in the pro football business. And had been in the pro football business ever since. So were his four sons and two daughters and any grandchild old enough to help out around Veterans Stadium. Now my father was gone, and he and Well Mara were the two grand old men of the NFL. Arnie, when he wasn't off seeing the world with Margie, still came to practice every day, still went to his office. Still signed the damn paychecks. He had expanded his interests over time to include horse racing, and had even had a Kentucky Derby about ten years before with a horse named Ziggy's Mark.

I noticed he'd aged even in the two months since I'd seen him last. It took us a while, but we finally made it back to the locker room end of the field. Arnie wanted to know if there was a place nearby where we could go have a civilized drink and catch up and I told him, "My apartment."

He said the town car was at the top of the ramp, but I told him we weren't going to need it and then told him where I was living these days.

He slapped me on the back and said, "I used to worry that you were a little slow out of the chutes, kiddo. But you always did have that flair, just like your father."

We went up to Suite 19 and I filled him in on everything that had been happening while he'd been away. Some of it he knew, because he said that his Margie didn't go anywhere anymore without her damn laptop, and that the *International Herald-Tribune* was still a pretty good read, if you weren't in a hurry for something like a damn box score. He said one of his boys had told him on the phone one day what that prick Getz was trying to do. I told him about my lunch with Donnie Mack Carney, whom he described as the proprietor of the Jesus Shopping Network, and somebody whose bullshit should be believed only as a last resort. Then he reminded me that he and my father had been the ones to form the Finance Committee in the first place, back in the late sixties, and that he'd fought to get me the seat even if I was technically on probation as an owner, but he couldn't make it fly, and Corky DuPont III replaced the old man.

"So there's me, Donnie Mack, that midget from the Saints," he said. "That's three. Then you've got Al Davis from the Raiders and the fat kid from the Patriots who bought the team with his wife's money from those sanitary napkins."

He was talking about Barry and Nancy Teitlebaum. Her father's Brockton, Massachusetts, company had invented the easy-glide tampon and spun that off into one of the most profitable feminine-hygiene operations in North America. Barry, a lifelong Patriots fan who'd worked on the team's stat crew while at Brandeis, was the one who convinced his wife to take the company—Easy Pass—public and then used the killing they made to buy the Patriots.

"That's five," Arnie Browne said. "That leaves Jerry Jones and Bunky."

"Corky," I corrected him. "Corky the third."

"Aw," he said, "who gives a good crap, one way or the other?"

Excellent point, I said. He gestured at me with his glass, his hand trembling as he did. He said that of course I had his vote and that Al Davis would do anything to piss the league off, that was just his nature, so that probably meant two votes. And when it got down to it, Jones would go for me, too, because as much of a publicity-hound pain-in-the-ass as he was, he was a loyal sonofabitch, and my father had voted for him at a time when a lot of the other owners on the Finance Committee acted as if a descendant of the Beverly Hillbillies was trying to get the Cowboys.

"If somebody abstains," Arnie said, "which has happened in the past, the commissioner is supposed to break the tie. You have any idea which way he'd vote?"

I said, "It will probably depend on Donnie Mack Carney. If he goes against me, then the commish will have to ask himself if he's more scared of the religious right or a do-me girl from Las Vegas named Carole Sandusky."

I told Uncle Arnie about Carole, and not only the power she seemed to have over the commissioner of the National Football League, but her rather extensive collection of cassettes. "The kid loves home movies," I said. "She always has."

"Bless her heart," he said.

"Whenever Wick Sanderson even thinks about breaking it off with her, she holds up one of the cassettes and says two words that bring him around every time," I said. *Inside Edition.*"

He sat there for a while, talking about what he thought Corky DuPont and Bobby Finkel and Barry Teitlebaum might do, telling me a story about the first time he'd met Teitlebaum, and how Teitlebaum said he wanted to ask a football question. What? Arnie'd said. Which position hits the hardest? Teitlebaum said. Arnie Browne laughed at that one, until the laugh broke apart into a rheumy cough that started to sound like the onset of TB. When it ended, he leaned back a little more on the couch, his worn Nike walking shoes up on the coffee table, the tumbler of Jack Daniel's balanced underneath his bow tie. I was briefly afraid he'd fallen asleep. Then he was wide awake again and talking again, as much to himself as to me.

"I liked this league a lot better when we'd settle whatever damn thing we had to settle with a good steak and some whiskey," he said. "Before the money got crazy and all the wonder boys came around, thinking that the history of pro football started when they got interested in it. I was standing in the back of the press box one time with your father, rest his soul, and I said to him, 'You have any more fun now than you did before these shitbirds started throwing this kind of money at us?' And you want to know what my friend Tim Molloy said? He said, 'I liked it better when it was ours.' "

He started to straighten up, but couldn't manage it by himself. I went over and took his drink out of his hand and helped him up. He was still my height, but now there was nothing to him, it was like picking up sticks. He said, "Kiddo, in the end it's all going to come down to whether Donnie Mack Carney wants you or not."

"What do you think?"

"It depends on how much he thinks is in it for him. He can talk about Christian charity 'til he's blue in the face, but everybody knows he'd try to talk an old cripple out of his Social Security check."

"What could I possibly have that he wants?"

"We got a little more than half a season to find out, don't we?"

Arnie laughed, started to cough a little bit and said, "Hell, maybe he wants the Hawks."

"He's already got a team," I said.

"Poor old Carroll Rosenbloom had the Colts, but he decided he wanted the Rams more," he said.

I looked at him, trying to decide if he was just busting my chops, the way he had my whole life, or whether he was serious. "You're kidding, right?" I said.

"Just rambling, kiddo," he said. "It's what happens when you're this old and this drunk."

He said that Margie Browne had been telling him that his senior moments were starting to last about a month.

When we got out to the parking lot, I hugged him and told him how much I'd missed him, and how much the old man loved him.

"I think your daddy knew you'd be able to handle the football," Arnie Browne said. "Hell, anybody hasn't had his first stroke yet can do that. What I don't think he knew is how you'd handle the rest of it."

The driver, a tall Indian guy who'd introduced himself as Vijay Day, opened the back door of the town car and helped Arnie Browne in.

"You know," I said, "maybe I was right and the old man was wrong. Maybe I'm not cut out for the football business."

"Jesus, Mary and Joseph," Arnie said, suddenly exasperated. "Wake up, will you, kiddo? You're not in the football business anymore'n I am. You're in the family business."

twenty-nine

e lost 20–17 to Arnie Browne's Eagles the next day, dropping our record to 6–3, ending our winning streak at six games. Guns of Navarone Queens let two sure touchdown passes slip through his hands, then Bobby Camby and Redford Newman did the same thing in the last minute, and Josh Blake had lost his first game as the Hawks' head coach.

A lot of the sellout crowd at Molloy Stadium spent the last few minutes of the game chanting A.T.M.'s name. There was a huge banner in the upper deck that read this way: WE WANT MOORE, BUT WE'RE GETTING JACK INSTEAD. The section directly in front of Suite 19, knowing that I was in there after all the newspaper stories and television pieces about my new digs, turned when the game was over and gave me the finger as a group, looking more festive and organized than fans at college bowl games did with their colored cards.

All in all, a magical day.

Which is why, Mo Jiggy was telling me the next morning at our power breakfast at the Regency Hotel on Park Avenue, that he had decided to reach out to me this way.

Mo had dressed down for the occasion. He was wearing brushed denim overalls, no shirt, the classic red suede Puma sneakers Clyde Frazier used to wear for the Knicks in his prime, wraparound Oakley sunglasses; he'd brought only one cell phone and one pager.

He'd shown up at the Regency dining room, known officially as 540 Park, with two of the boys from his posse and one of his own Rottweilers. When he did, the maître d' had said in his faintly French accent, "I am terribly sorry, zhentlemen, but we require a tie at 540. And, of course, no pets."

I was seated close enough to the door to hear Mo giggle and say, "Yeah, right" as he moved past him.

The maître d' tried to put out a hand and gently stop Mo from going any farther. That's when the ranking posse guy, Montell, took the maître d's hand and placed it on the bulge right near the "8" on the front of his road-blue Knicks Sprewell jersey.

"Pet this, okay, Pierre?" Montell said.

"Jean-Claude," the maître d' said, and then Montell said, "What, we're gonna do *Crossfire* over every fucking thing today?"

Mo Jiggy had waited until his egg-whites-only omelette had arrived before getting to it.

"A.T.M. is ready to play," he said.

"If I were any readier for him to play, you'd have to hose me down."

"The problem," Mo Jiggy said solemnly, "is face."

"That old thing," I said.

He speared a tiny piece of omelette and popped it into his mouth. "I'm officially his agent of record now, you know that, right?"

I told him Pete had gotten the call from Gene Upshaw, the head of the Players' Association. "What happens to Donyell?" I said.

"Donyell will be relocating to the west coast offices of Toe Tag, Inc., my production company."

"Donyell pretty happy about that?"

"I don't care how he feels," Mo said. "I'm just interested in what the boy is going to say. And what he's going to say is that he thinks this is a tremendous opportunity his good friend Mo Jiggy has given him to widen his range of interests in a new and exciting field."

I drank some of my coffee and said, "Can I ask you something? What happened to the Public Enemy Number One jive-ass I'll-cut-you Mo Jiggy I see interviewed all the time on MTV?"

Mo smiled, showing off a discreet gold tooth, off to the side, front left.

He said, "You know what one of my teachers at McBurney told me one time?" He nodded then, as a way of saying, yeah, we'd both gone to McBurney, wasn't that a coincidence? "He said, 'Maurice, you're only in trouble in this world when you start to believe your own material.'"

"Which teacher?"

"English. Paul Doherty."

"A hot shit when I was there, too."

Mo lapsed into his bad-guy voice and waved his hands a little bit and said, "Taught this dude all he know about dat iambic pentameter shit." Then he said that the trick for the two of us was to get A.T.M. back into Hawks blue without it looking as if he'd come crawling back to Massa Jack.

"That's your end," Mo said. "My end, of course, is making sure that A.T.M. keeps his mouth shut better than he did at all those colleges he went to about the money you just passed him under the table."

Across the room I heard a threatening growl, and saw Mo's Rottweiler straining at the leash Montell was holding, baring his teeth at a table that included former Donald Trump, former senator Alfonse D'Amato and the mayor. Two of the beefy rogue cops the mayor traveled with—Ling and Chew with badges—reluctantly started to get up from their own table, warily eyeballing the Rott the whole time.

"Sit!" Montell snapped.

One of the cops exhaled loudly and said, "That's better," and Montell said, "I wasn't talkin' to the damn dog."

At our table, I said to Mo Jiggy, "What money under the table?"

He looked at me. "The money in the suitcase the guy brought to A.T.M. at the Inn on the Park, London, England, last night."

"What guy?"

Mo said, "A.T.M. said the guy called himself Vinny One. He said he was a friend of yours who'd sort of retired to England a few years ago."

Vinny One, I said.

"A.T.M. said he was funny, had a lot of interesting stories."

"How much money?"

"Five."

"Million? This guy Vinny One just showed up at A.T.M.'s hotel with five million dollars in a suitcase?"

Mo said, "He called first."

It occurred to me that I hadn't heard from Billy Grace in a couple of days, but that wasn't unusual, it meant he could be playing a pro-am in Dubai or hiding out in the Dominican with an Inger, or maybe in Beverly Hills having some neck work done. Billy worried about a saggy neck more than he did about his grosses sometimes, it was why he wore so many white turtlenecks even in summer.

"Mo," I said, "I have no idea what you're talking about."

He put his palms up. The only jewelry he was wearing was the big rock from Kelli Ann, one big enough to have "Gimme Mo" written across the top in diamonds.

"Okay, Jack," he said. "You don't know about Vinny, you don't know about the money. I'm cool on that."

I just decided to go with it until I could talk to Billy.

"You add the five million to the four-five I'm already paying him," I said, "and now he's the highest-paid receiver in the league."

"There you go," Mo Jiggy said.

We kicked around some ideas about the best way for him to announce he was coming back, and why, and some of the ways I could be the one doing the bowing and scraping. I told him I'd heard he was interested in getting a luxury box at Molloy, and he said he'd heard that there weren't any available and I told him I thought we might be able to work something out before the season was over.

Then he said that before we wrapped up, he wanted to ask me a question, one McBurney guy to the other, about something that had been bothering him.

"How long are you going to let Allen Getz mess with you this way?" he said.

I told him I didn't see as how I had much choice, that whatever he was trying to do, it wasn't going to matter in the end if I had the votes.

"But the more he makes you look bad," Mo said, "the harder it is for you to get the votes. It's why you ought to think about getting him to back off a little bit."

"What, threaten him with a hostile takeover?"

Mo Jiggy raised his hand like a kid in class, as a way of telling our waiter he wanted more green tea. "Money never scares guys like that," he said. "You take some off them, they find out a way to get more. My friend The Donald over there? He was nearly busted a few years ago, now he's bigger than ever. You ever see *Citizen Kane?* My favorite movie of all time. Remember that scene where he tells the guy, 'I lost a million last year, I'm going to lose a million this year, and if this keeps on for thirty more years, I'm going to have to sell this paper'? You know that one?" The waiter put the tea in front of him and he blew on it gently, the heat briefly steaming his Oakleys. "It's like that with somebody like Getz, only we're talking in billions instead of millions. I deal with CEO guys like him all the time, guys who own the record companies and the studios. I like to meet with them myself, show them I'm not the Notorious Tupac or something. And the more I meet them, the more I'm convinced there's only one thing in the whole world that really scares them."

I grinned. "Erectile dysfunction?"

"Dying," Mo Jiggy said.

I told him I appreciated him caring this way, but I frankly didn't think I could knock off Allen Getz, though I'd noticed that there were people in rap who saw that as a successful business plan.

"I'm not talking about killing him," he said. "And don't believe that garbage about the way Fat Load died, it was his brother who did it, after he found out him and Fat were both screwing the same cousin."

"I'm glad you cleared that up," I said.

Mo Jiggy said that the way to deal with Allen Getz was to fuck with the boy's mind a little bit, make him think something bad could happen to him, and then motioned for Montell to come over, and leave the dog.

PART FOUR

big sticky

thirty

 few days later, after A.T.M. had finally ended things with a waitress he'd met at the Hard Rock Café, we sent the team plane, the big one, to pick him up at Heathrow Airport. Jack Molloy and Tire Iron Timmons and Mo Jiggy were eastbound passengers along with Jim Nantz and his crew from *The NFL Today* and Pat O'Brien with his own crew from *Access Hollywood*. O'Brien was Mo's idea, him trying to make A.T.M.'s return seem more like some kind of show biz event, but he was crestfallen when O'Brien didn't bring along his co-host Nancy O'Dell.

"How *Baywatch: The New Millennium* missed a blondy girl like her, I'll never know," he said sadly.

On the flight home, A.T.M. told Nantz and O'Brien the same thing he'd tell every sportswriter and twink and radio nitwit in the days leading up to the Hawks-Redskins game, that it was Jesus' love that had kept him strong throughout this terrible ordeal, and love of football that had brought him back.

"The Lord made me a football player for a reason," he said, "and I don't believe it was just to keep up on my [bleeped out for air] child support."

A.T.M. said that he finally decided you couldn't put a cash value, no matter how much of it was deferred, on the handful of Sundays he might have left in his career.

I was pretty sure Mo Jiggy had given him that line in the customs area.

A.T.M. also said that life in London had been more educational in just a few months than several of his colleges had ever been, but that he eventually found himself getting bored watching cricket and soccer.

"I mean, try watching Manchester [bleeped out for air] United beat them Rockingham Hot Spurs two-[bleeped out] nil one more time," he said on-camera to Jim Nantz.

He also mentioned to Nantz what a no-good bastard Vince Cahill was and always had been, and that if Mr. Jack Molloy hadn't made what he considered a brilliant switch to Josh Blake, he would never have played another down for the New York Hawks.

Mo Jiggy raised his eyebrows when he heard that one.

I shrugged. "That one was mine. Fuck Vince Cahill, okay?"

Pat O'Brien asked A.T.M. about the status of his contract renegotiation.

A.T.M. said, "Straight up? I've had a lot of time these past few weeks to make stock, and I finally decided that Mr. Molloy will do the right thing by me, same as his dead father did."

Then he asked O'Brien if they could take a break so he could have his afternoon shot of what he called that Jim Gray tea he'd come to like so much.

Before A.T.M. had done either interview, Mo Jiggy had made it abundantly clear to him that if he ever mentioned the five million Billy Grace had sent through Vinny One—"I got tired of standing around with my dick in my hand waiting for you to figure this out for yourself," Billy'd explained—he, Mo, would personally call Oretha and tell her about the sudden windfall he was holding back from her and the lawyers.

"Did you mention the kind of penalties the league imposes on guys who cheat on the salary cap the way we just did?" I said.

Mo said, "Wouldn't have mattered none. Other than that Bobbitt guy got his pecker chopped off by his missus, I've never seen a man more afraid of a woman than he is of that Oretha."

The last thing that A.T.M. said in both interviews on the plane was that none of this could have possibly happened without his friend and mentor, Mo Jiggy, now the greatest sports agent in the world, the way he was the greatest entertainer who hadn't been shot up in a drive-by yet or, as A.T.M. put it, permanently killed.

A.T.M. Moore caught the tail end of our practice after we landed and then had full practices the next two days before catching two touchdown passes on Sunday as we beat the Redskins. He caught another one when we beat Houston and three more the next week when we beat Donnie Mack Carney's Ravens, including one of his patented one-hand jobs in the corner of the end zone against the Ravens' lone defensive All-Pro, safety John Three-Sixteen Vaughn. Vaughn was one of the tallest safeties in the league at six-four, and he and A.T.M. went up together. Then Three-Sixteen Vaughn did what normal people do, which meant he came down.

A.T.M. stayed up there.

The refs would call pass interference on Vaughn, who was clearly holding on to A.T.M.'s right arm when they were still up there together. It didn't matter, because A.T.M. reached up and caught the ball like some hunky kid reaching up on the beach to pluck a Frisbee out of the air.

The 19–7 victory meant we had a record of 9–3 and everybody around the team was thinking we might run the table to 13–3 over our remaining four games of the regular season. But then A.T.M. suffered a groin injury between the Ravens game and our rematch with the Giants, which we lost in overtime. Then we lost to the Patriots on Monday night, the week before Christmas, putting us back into a first-place tie with the Jets, with two games to go.

Tire Iron said he thought A.T.M. really might have injured his leg the night he took a couple of dancers from Beef named Venus and Serena up to his Do-It Room, but that there wasn't nothing nobody could do about it now, and promised A.T.M. would be ready for the playoffs, even if he had to shoot him up with cortisone himself.

"You know what's a miracle which you could put in the Bible with your loaves and your fishes?" Tire Iron said. "That the boy didn't get into those London tabloids one single time over sticky, even with that ho from the Hard Rock he decided he was in love with."

I told Tire Iron that Bubba Royal and A.T.M. Moore really ought to write a book about sticky someday.

"Yeah," he said. "Be the first one either one of them read besides the playbook."

I've figured out what Allen Getz is doing," Mo Jiggy was saying in Suite 19.

This was a few hours before our game with the Jets, the second-to-last game of the regular season, both of us with records of 9–5, two games ahead of the Giants and Patriots in the Pete Rozelle Division, first place on the line.

"It's like those push polls used in political campaigns by some of your more prominent right-wing-nut Caucasian politicians," he continued. "They call up some prospective voter and they say they'd like to ask a few questions, then they say, 'But before I do, I would be remiss in not mentioning that my opponent likes to do the nasty with farm animals.' Or like that. Getz is doing the same thing with you, the way I see it. His people must feel that if they get enough negative shit out there about you for the other owners to read or hear about, enough of it will stick eventually."

Mo was wearing his home white Bubba Royal jersey, Number 6, a Hawks cap turned around backwards, starched denim jeans, and Nike football shoes with rubber cleats. He had his Oakleys hanging from a string around his neck. His shaved head looked smooth and shiny as a marble.

"You're sure Getz is coming to the game today?" Mo said.

"I called Kitty again this morning with a bogus charity question and she said he was," I said. "Your guys are clear on the drill, right?"

He made fists with both hands and patted his knuckes together.

"The boys are downstairs chillin'. I paged them before, just as a dry run, and they made it up here in three minutes thirty-seven seconds."

Mo's full posse, with Montell and his top lieutenant Denzell, was downstairs in my office, all of them watching a bootleg video of the new Jackie Chan movie. They had two of Mo's Rottweilers—he'd named them Regis and Kathie Lee, Kathie Lee being the meaner of the two, he said—with them, so I'd put one of the security elevators on hold, in case any of the dogs needed to go outside.

The Jets were ahead 14–13 in the second quarter when I sent Liz Bolton over to Kitty Molloy's suite. She was supposed to tell Getz that I had an important matter to discuss with him and could he come over to 19 for a few minutes at halftime? Then she was supposed to hang out with the commissioner in his suite until I called and told her the coast was clear and she could come back.

What Allen didn't know or need to know was that the only guests in 19 on this day were Pete, Liz, Mo and me.

"Allen got a posse?" Mo said.

If he did, I told him, he was very discreet about it; I hadn't noticed anybody with him the night at the Plaza when Bubba had shown Kelli Ann his.

"All she could talk about for weeks," Mo Jiggy said afterward.

Because it was such an unsettling experience, I said.

"Nah, wasn't that," he said. "Girl said he was hung like goddam Secretariat."

The buzzer at the front door rang about five minutes later. When I opened it, I saw that Allen Getz did have two guys with him. They looked like a couple of personal trainers on loan from the gym, both of them wearing navy jumpsuits and sneakers. I nodded at them and they nodded at me and we all stood there nodding at each other like old-fashioned bobblehead dolls, until I said to Getz, "I'd like to talk to you in private, if that's okay."

Getz said, "Gee, I don't know, Jack. Ty and Randy don't even like me to go to the men's room alone."

I thought: I'll bet.

Then I put a hand on his shoulder and said, "Allen, it's a luxury box. At a football game. With luxury boxes on either side of us and Ty and Randy standing outside at the door."

He looked past me. The only person he could see was Pete, who smiled and waved.

I said to Ty and Randy, "Can we send something out to you? An energy shake?"

Allen Getz said to them, "Don't move away from this door, okay, guys?"

They nodded again, even more vigorously than before.

I showed Allen Getz in, discreetly hitting the switch that locked the door behind us, then took him through my living area and into the room on the other side where I usually stashed the guests on Sunday. That's where we had the assorted tasty treats, souvenir Hawks caps, Hawks pennants, game programs, a self-serve bar, stacks of Sunday papers, Montell, Denzell, three enlisted men from the posse and the two dogs, Regis and Kathie Lee.

Mo had pointed out that Kathie Lee was the one with the knife scar near his right eye.

"Kathie Lee's a guy?" I'd said, and Mo had looked at me quizzically and said, "Your point being?"

I closed the door to my living quarters behind me now and heard a growl as I did, unable to determine immediately whether or not it came from the posse or one of the dogs.

"Down, boys," Montell said to somebody, casually waving his hand. The rest of the posse guys were wearing the uniforms belonging to various members of the Portland Trailblazers' starting five and paisley headbands. Montell was still in his Sprewell, with an even bigger bulge than usual next to the 8.

Allen Getz stared at Montell, then the dogs. In that moment, he seemed a much better bet to wet the carpet than either of the Rotts.

"I think I'd like to leave now," the CEO of Getz.com said.

"Come on, Allen," I said jovially. "You just got here."

"This . . ." He cleared his throat. "This is *not* funny."

"Humor is so subjective," I said.

"I could scream right now for Ty and Randy," he said.

"I wouldn't."

"Why not?"

I told him that Montell had just gotten through telling me how much loud noises upset the dogs.

O kay," Allen Getz said. "What's this all about?" He had his legs crossed and kept playing nervously with one of the tassels on his Top-Siders, at least until Montell unhooked Kathie Lee from his leash. When the dog came over and started sniffing him, Getz carefully put his hands in his pockets and seemed perfectly willing to leave them there until the dog died of old age.

"He must smell my cat," Getz said.

"Uh-oh," Montell said.

"Uh-oh, what?" Getz said.

Montell acted as if he didn't hear him and went over and fixed himself a sandwich. Kathie Lee finally got tired of sniffing and just plopped down with a loud snort at Getz's feet.

From across the room, Montell said, "Yo? Smile at him once in a while?"

In a tinny voice, Allen Getz said to me, "*Please* tell me what this is about so I can get back to Kitty's. I don't want her to worry."

"Why'd you decide to jerk me around this way?"

"Kitty said you already asked her the same thing."

"Now I'm asking you," I said. "You always do business this way, trying to slime the other guy?"

"I don't know what you're talking about."

"Sure you do."

He uncrossed his legs in slow motion, so as not to stir Kathie Lee. "It's no secret that I'd be interested in the Hawks if you're not approved. It's why I tried to get the naming rights, even if that hasn't, you know, unfolded as quickly as I would've liked. The rest of it, the mean allegations you made in front of Kitty, are just you being paranoid."

"I don't think so," I said. "I think somebody you trust told you this was the way to play it. And somebody is telling you where to dig for dirt on me."

Getz seemed to gather himself briefly, even if it was somewhat difficult for him to be a rugged captain of industry with his knees up on the couch now and his arms hugging them.

"In the real business world," he said smugly, "you use the tools available to you."

"Somebody knows an awful lot about me," I said.

"Duh," Getz said. "Your life is pretty much an open book, Jack. One with plenty of dirty pictures in it, I might add."

"Who's helping you? Is it somebody in Vegas?"

We all looked at Kathie Lee now, mostly because he was making farting noises that sounded like a series of small explosions.

"My people—" he said, when the dog finally finished.

"You have people who know people like Ferret Biel?"

"—are very thorough," Allen Getz said.

From outside, even through the closed windows of the suite, we could hear a roar from the Molloy Stadium crowd, which had to mean that the Hawks were taking the field for the second half, still trailing the Jets by a point.

"I'm going to remind you what our motto is at Getz dot com," Getz said. "Knowledge is power."

"No shit," I said, "I hadn't heard that one."

"You'll see," he said, trying to sound both vague and threatening at the same. "Or read. Or hear."

Considering the fact that he was alone in a room with Mo's posse and two Rottweilers who hadn't been out to the parking lot since early in the first quarter, I had to admit that Allen Getz was showing some surprising spunk.

"Well, I'd sort of like what my friend Mr. Jiggy"—Mo turned around from the front row of the middle room and saluted sharply—"calls negative campaigning to end, Allen. It's not only upsetting to me, but to my friends. And you can see for yourself how tense it's made the animals."

"Yo?" Montell said. "You don't want a tense Rott, believe you me."

Denzell said, "They start to question so many fucking things."

"You never know what they might do," Montell said. "Where they might show up."

"Second half about to start, in case anybody's wondering," Mo Jiggy called out.

I gave a look to Montell, who came over and put Kathie Lee back on his leash. I stood up and grinned at Allen Getz, looking sporty in his tweed jacket and pink sweater and brown cords. He had three Sharpies in the breast pocket of the jacket, pink to match his sweater.

He was also sweating like Elvis Elgin during two-a-day workouts in the summer.

"That's all you wanted to say?" Allen Getz said, carefully getting to his feet himself.

"Well, I would like to add one more thing," I said. "No one in this room wants to see, or read, or hear another fucking thing from you until the vote at the Super Bowl."

I clapped my hands, which was a mistake, because Regis and Kathie Lee started snarling now and trying to pull Montell and Denzell toward Allen Getz, who was frantically trying to scramble over the back of the leather couch.

I said, "Oops."

The posse guys left first, with the dogs. Out in the hall, Montell said to Ty and Randy, "What the fuck *you* lookin' at?" Allen Getz was right behind them. When he got about twenty yards away, I made a loud barking noise, which made him wheel around in terror.

"Just kidding," I said, and went back inside to watch the second half.

thirty-one

 had asked Montell if he and the rest of the posse guys wanted to stop by Corky DuPont's box with me, but he said they'd had about as much fun scaring the jiggy out of white people as they could stand for one day, they just wanted to go back downstairs and watch the end of the Jackie Chan. After that, Mo was taking them all to the Knicks-Celtics game at the Garden.

"Like Mo says in his song 'Celebrity Row,'" Montell said. "So many effin' games, so little effin' time."

I told him I could practically feel myself starting to dance to it already.

We finally won, 26–14, even though a snowstorm no one had predicted came blowing in out of nowhere about halfway through the third quarter. Guns of Navarone Queens had gone out with a knee right before halftime, and without him and A.T.M. in the lineup and with the snow coming down hard, we had to run the ball the rest of the way and the Jets couldn't do a thing to stop us. We even started running some old-fashioned option plays, the kind Bubba used to run at UCLA, with

Bubba rolling out and Bobby Camby as the trailer. Pete mentioned he didn't know we even had the option in our playbook and it turned out we didn't, that Josh Blake had just drawn them up at halftime.

In the locker room afterward, Pete said to Josh, "You know when the last time was Vince Cahill made an adjustment like that at halftime? When Nancy Reagan was still president."

So with one game to go, we had first place to ourselves. That meant that if we could win next Sunday on the road, against the Falcons, we'd have a first-round bye in the playoffs, and then home field for the conference semis and, if we won that, the conference finals.

Next stop after that was the Super Bowl.

I stopped by Bubba's locker and he asked if I wanted to join him at Beef later, there was a couple of dancers he'd heard about down there that A.T.M. told him he had to see.

"Names are Venus and Serena," Bubba said. "He says that if all you know about women's doubles is lesbian in the ad court and lesbian in the deuce court, these girls will turn you right around."

I told him I might see him down there later, if I finished studying for my psych test on time.

The truth was that Pete Stanton wanted to talk about what we were going to do about wide receiver for the Falcons game, since the pictures from Guns of Navarone's MRI had turned up looking like some kind of complex irrigation map and he was probably gone for the season. So when the locker room cleared out, we went back upstairs to Suite 19 to kick some names around. Pete asked Liz if she wanted to join us, but she said she was having dinner with her ex-husband in the city, that if he didn't agree to give her more time at the summer house in Sag Harbor, she was going to have her lawyers pull his tongue out by its roots.

"Sweet kid," Pete said, when she was gone. "It's that Doris Day quality."

Pete said that he thought our best bet to replace Guns of Navarone this late in the season was an ancient ex-Hawk named Sherman Fountainblue who'd been cut loose by the Cowboys at midseason and had never hooked on with anybody else. Pete said Sherman always needed an extra check, because he'd had more trouble with women in his life than Bubba, and probably had fathered more kids.

Sherman Fountainblue, according to Pete, had once even tried to organize a Father-Illegitimate Son touch football game during training camp.

It turned out that when Sherman had come out of Clemson, his rookie contract was the first Pete had ever negotiated as the Hawks' general manager. The kid was a second-round draft choice, and announced to Pete that he didn't want to bother with an agent, he was going to represent himself.

"Why should I give four percent to some agent when I can give it to the boy me and Shirrelle just had?" he said at the time.

Pete asked if Shirrelle was his wife and Sherman Fountainblue said, no, that Charrisse was his wife, Shirrelle was just a school friend.

They scheduled a meeting after the draft and Sherman flew up from school and finally agreed on the dollars, which meant the last order of business was a signing bonus. Sherman asked for $50,000 and Pete said fine. He came around the desk to shake hands, saying that he'd have the lawyers draw up the contract, that Sherman would probably want to at least have a lawyer look it over before he signed it.

Sherman shook his head.

"I can't take this deal," he said.

Pete said, "Why not?"

And Sherman Fountainblue said, "Because you gave it to me."

Excuse me? Pete said.

"If you gave it up that easily, you must be fuckin' me," he said, and left, and the next day there was a real agent in Pete's office, accusing him of trying to fuck Sherman.

"I gave him the years he wanted, I gave him the money he wanted, I gave him the bonus he wanted," Pete said.

The guy said, "Well, I hope you're proud of yourself."

In Suite 19 now, Pete said, "Sherman's always in better shape than an exercise girl on TV, he knows the offense, and I believe he'll bust his ass for us if we give him a chance to make the big game."

I only made Pete promise to call if Sherman wanted to negotiate this deal himself. He said he would, then said he was going home to worry about next year's salary cap and who we were going to have to cut, whether we won the Super Bowl or not; that's what he made himself do when he started to get too happy.

He left and I fixed myself a drink and watched some of the highlights on ESPN as I read the Sunday papers left on the coffee table where Allen Getz had been sitting. When the doorbell rang, I thought it might be Liz Bolton, that she'd decided to blow off old Ian for me.

I opened the door and said, "Gidge, is that you?"

It was Annie Kay.

She said, "Who's Gidge?"

"Gidget," I said. "You never heard of Gidget? Sandra Dee in the movies, Sally Field on television. I think there might have been one other girl in the movies."

"I'm glad we cleared that up," she said, brushing snow out of her hair and off the front of her black topcoat. "Are you going to ask me in?"

I did, and locked the door behind me, just in case Liz Bolton showed up later with urges.

I told Annie Kay that I had been actually planning to stop by Beef later, not only to see her, but because of what I had to admit was a growing curiosity about Venus and Serena.

"It starts out as a tennis deal," she said. "They're wearing these little Fila dresses and carrying oversized Prince rackets. But from there it degenerates into your basic lick fest."

Some men apparently found that entertaining, I said, and did they perform any night except Sunday?

"I admire that you're honest enough to admit you're a pig, Jack," she said. "I really do."

I asked Annie if Venus and Serena were black and she said no, but they were trying to pass.

"They spend more time at the tanning salon than I personally think is healthy," she said. "Though the beads in the hair are a nice touch."

She had cut her hair since I'd seen her on the field with Vicky Dunne, but had longer bangs than she did before, which somehow made her look younger than she already was, and made me feel older. She asked for a glass of Chardonnay. When I came back with it, she had kicked off the hiking boots she'd been wearing because of the weather and had curled up her feet underneath her on the sofa. I was playing Getz. Stan, not Allen.

I told her about my meeting with Allen earlier, including our own version of the Westminster Dog Show.

"They're not really named Regis and Kathie Lee," she said. "You're making that up."

I said she could page Montell if she wanted to ask him, I had six or seven different numbers for him.

"I have a couple of announcements to make," she said.

"You already dumped me," I said.

She ignored me and said, "I'm quitting Beef. Vicky got me an associate producer's job at Fox Sports Net. I'll be working with her pretty much full-time. And the best part is that when she can't be somewhere, I can go with the crew and do the interviews for her, even if that doesn't get me on-camera yet."

I lit a cigarette and said, "You're too smart, about practically everything, to carry her water for very long."

"That's very nice, but you can stop sucking up, because I've decided to forgive you."

"That's very generous of you. But I meant what I said." I went and brought the bucket with the wine bottle in it and put it on the table in front of us. "Are you still going to be taking classes?"

"Yeah. It's going to take some creative scheduling, but my professors are being pretty good about it."

"Cool," I said.

Annie Kay got up and refilled her own glass. Behind her I could see the snow still falling against the dimmed lights of the stadium.

She said, "Who's going to replace Guns of Navarone?"

I smiled at her. "Is this off the record?"

"Of course not."

"Pete's probably on the phone with Sherman Fountainblue right now."

"I thought he might do that," she said, nodding. "He already knows the plays."

"That's exactly what Pete said."

Now she smiled at me over her wineglass, her eyes full of fun, and said, "God, I'm good."

Getz became Miles Davis. The snow kept coming. Every once in a while, I could hear a phone ring in the other room and ignored it. Annie wanted to know what was happening with the other owners since the last time we'd really talked. I told her what Arnie Browne had told me and said that, ultimately, who the hell knew until everybody got in the room in Phoenix? Off the record, she wanted to know how I got A.T.M. to come back and said that it was my powers of persuasion, and that was my story and, goddam, I was sticking to it.

Annie said that while she was initially pissed about Liz Bolton and me being so completely stupid about her, she had come to a couple of conclusions. One, I was a man, after all, which meant an invertebrate about women, and, two, I'd eventually come to my senses and decide she wasn't my type.

"You love football," Annie said. "She doesn't."

"She says she does."

"She *likes* football, don't get me wrong," she said. "She likes being one of the guys, the way I like being one of the guys. And she knows football pretty well for a girl. But she'll never love it the way you do, and you do love it, despite whatever messed-up issues it created between you and your dad."

I said something profound, like, Oh?

"Me?" Annie said. "I loved football even before I saw it as a way into the land of twinks and show biz. Even when I was a kid."

"You're not now?"

"I *always* had better cards than my brothers," Annie Kay said. "Always."

"That's it," I said to her, taking the glass out of her hands and putting it on the table. "Take me."

She kissed me first, and things developed fairly rapidly from there. Much later, when we'd finally made it to the bedroom after so many false starts they nearly had to call off the race, I said to her, "What was your name again?"

She propped a head up on her elbow and brushed away the new bangs and said in a husky voice, "You can call me Venus," then gave me a move she swore was from the Venus-Serena floor show at Beef, but I just thought was a case of her showing off.

We were both still awake, sharing a cigarette and watching the snow, when I said, "You never told me what your other announcement was."

"I know," she said. "But if things developed the way I wanted them to develop, I didn't want us to get sidetracked before we got to the sticky. That's what A.T.M. calls it, right?"

"Oh, yeah," I said with gusto.

"So what's the other announcement?"

She sat up in bed.

"In the world of big-time journalism," she said, "they would call this burying the lead. But I'd been missing you."

Now I sat up and brushed some of the bangs away and kissed her on her forehead. "You're only human," I said.

In the half-darkness, making no move to cover her amazing body, Annie loudly blew out some smoke and then said, "My favorite bookstore in Manhattan is the Madison Avenue Bookshop. It's on 69th and Madison, across from the old Westbury Hotel."

I told her I knew the neighborhood.

"Well, I was there yesterday afternoon, just wandering around, and when I was finished, I realized how close I was to 71 East 71st, and how you'd told me one time that was the building you grew up in."

"I know there's a point you're getting to," I said.

"There is," she said. "So I walk over to Park and and walk up a couple of blocks to the building, and just as I get there, this huge limo pulls up and these two cute guys who look like male cheerleaders get out, and then Allen Getz gets out right behind them."

I told her I'd met the cute bodyguards, they were named Ty and Randy.

Annie said, "Then one other person got out of the car."

"Don't tell me," I said. "My amazing stepmother."

I could see her shake her head, then let me know deeply she had buried the lead.

"Liz Bolton," Annie said. "Bitch on wheels."

thirty-two

On the phone, Billy Grace said, "I'd like you to keep something in mind: Girls lie sometimes, especially about other girls."

"Not this girl," I said.

Meaning Annie Kay.

"So what you're saying is that your team president, the one with the legs, might have gone over the wall?"

"There's lots of reasons why she could have been in Getz's car, but none I can come up with seem too innocent to me, unless Allen Getz has started up a Park 'n' Ride program for big-time sports babes."

Billy said, "I thought you gave her everything she wanted. And I do mean everything."

I told him the Sherman Fountainblue contract story. Maybe, I said, she wanted more than everything the way Sherman did.

"I know that guy!" Billy said. "He's the one who named all his kids Sherman, right?"

The boys were Sherman, I told Billy, the girls were Shermayne.

"I love it when they do that," Billy said.

In the background, I could hear a female voice calling his name. "I gotta go, Inger's awake. She likes to fool around first thing in the morning or sometimes she stays pissed off all day."

He asked me what he could do to help with Liz Bolton, and I told him. Billy said he'd see what he could do, and get back to me.

I was pretty sure he waited to hang up the phone until I heard the following:

"Holy shit! Look what the room service waiter has under his apron. . . ."

Billy got back to me the Monday after we'd beaten the Falcons to finish 11–5 and clinch first place in the Rozelle.

Liz Bolton was on the phone when I let myself into her office, doing a lot of "uh huh uh huh uh huh" to whomever she was talking to, chin cupped in her right hand. She was wearing one of those headsets with a microphone attached to it, leaving her other hand free to doodle, her rather graphic phone art usually running to hangings and stabbings, depending on which league executive she had on the other end of the line.

When she noticed me, she put a hand over the mike and said, "Marketing veep from the league. We're going over playoff crap."

Winter had settled in on New York; ever since our game against the Jets, the temperature had consistently been in the twenties, and the weather twinks were hysterical that another storm front was on the way. I had tried to work out in the weight room earlier, but this was one of those mornings when what was left of my knee was barking the way Kathie Lee the killer Rott had at Allen Getz. After I helped myself to what I knew was Liz's house blend from Starbucks, I sat down across from her and stretched the leg out and waited for her to stop bullshitting the marketing veep from the league, somebody named Chip.

When she was done, she took off the headset and jammed the sleeves of her gray sweater up over her elbows. Liz, I had noticed, did a lot of dark gray. I'd read somewhere it was the "new black." What was wrong with the old black?

"We start off with where the logos are supposed to go on the 'NFC playoff' caps," she said, "and end up talking about how Chip's wife doesn't understand him anymore."

"But he thinks you do."

"You bet." She buzzed her secretary outside and told her over the speaker to hold all her calls, and said, "So to what do I owe this visit?"

She had this way of widening her eyes when she focused herself on you, looking almost surprised. Like: Oh, it's you.

"You never told me," I said. "How'd it go that night with Ian in the Battle of Sag Harbor?"

"He got June and July, I got August through Labor Day. Major victory." She smiled. "But why am I thinking you didn't come down here to talk about my summer house?"

"I've been wondering about something," I said. "When you told me the story of your life that time, you told me that you went off to find yourself in New Mexico before you came back to ESPN as a boss. You remember that?"

"Did I say it was New Mexico? We had had a lot of wine by then, as I recall."

"Yeah, you definitely said New Mexico," I said. "But you didn't say what you did while you were there." I lit a cigarette. "So what did you do there?" I smiled. "Better yet, who'd you do it with?"

There had been a hundred meetings like this in Vegas, my previous life, when I was the Jammer and I had someone across the desk from me who knew he or she was bare-assed caught. A blackjack dealer who'd decided all the security cameras were going to miss him getting cute. A bartender who thought he was being even cuter and that nobody would notice how he was ringing up only every second or third drink when things would get really busy on fight night. Even girls from the shows who thought they could go into business for themselves in some of the lounges and that Billy and I wouldn't pick up on something like that.

Sometimes you had to draw them a picture before they finally gave it up, sometimes not.

Nobody had to draw Liz Bolton a picture. She picked her glasses off the desk in front of her and folded them neatly, just to give herself something to do with her hands, then carefully put them back down.

"So," she said.

"Do me a favor, okay?" I said. "Do not even attempt to bullshit me now. If you do, you'll be out of here faster than Vince Cahill was and I will then speed-dial around this fucking league telling people what you did and who you did it with."

"Do you want the long version or the short version?" she said.

Knock yourself out, I said.

She had rented a place in Santa Fe. She knew some friends from college there, and one of them worked in upper management with Allen Getz, and one night she met Getz himself at a party. She had been there a couple of months by then and was bored already, and found him cute and needy in a nerdy sort of way. He was also hornier than a teenager. Before long, they drifted into an affair. It took him about a month to start talking about marriage, but she made it clear it wasn't going to happen. Then he started offering her just about any position at his company she wanted. She told him she didn't want that, she still wanted to be queen of sports or the networks, she was just taking a timeout, exercising like a maniac, doing some writing, deciding exactly what she wanted to do next.

A few months later, ESPN called, at which point she broke things off with Allen Getz, much to his regret. The rest, she said, was her own dreary history. She didn't see Getz again until he started talking to the old man about buying the Hawks. They decided there was no point in letting on, to Big Tim Molloy or anybody else, that she and Getz had been a big sweaty item in a previous life.

"I stayed out of the conversations he had with your father," she said now. "I didn't give Allie any advice one way or the other—"

"*Allie?*" I said. "Jesus, kill me now."

"I didn't give Allen any advice, I didn't try to sway Tim," she continued. "Mostly because I never believed your father would sell this team in a million years, no matter how angry he was with you. All I told Allen, from the beginning, was that the Hawks, in my opinion, were the greatest single buy in all of sports. And if somewhere down the road there was a chance to get them, he sure as hell should."

Then Big Tim Molloy had died. And all Liz Bolton knew at that time was that the prodigal son black sheep of the family—her original stated opinion of little old me—had gotten the team. *Her* team. That's when Allen Getz showed up on the arm of Big Tim's widow. Liz said she didn't know when Getz had started fooling around with Kitty and she frankly didn't give a shit, because she knew that ultimately it didn't matter.

Liz and Kitty Drucker-Cole Molloy happened to be in almost perfect harmonic convergence about one thing:

Allen Getz wanted the Hawks because he fucking-well wanted them.

"He wanted to make sure of two things," she said. "One, you didn't get the team. And two, that he was first in line with the league and the other owners once you were out of the way."

"He asked you to help him," I said. "The old man was gone and the only person you needed to be loyal to was yourself."

"Yes," she said.

"Was getting me into the old sack part of the deal?"

"No," she said. We stared at each other for a moment, nobody giving ground, then she said in a softer voice, "No."

"I was just looking for a clarification."

She sent Getz after Kenny and Babs first, thinking he might be able to rich-slap them before they really knew what hit them, even if it wasn't their half that really interested him. They'd told him they weren't selling, certainly not until they saw how things played out with me. It was Liz who then came up with the idea of offering to pay a ridiculous amount for the naming rights just because—quoting the old man to him—that at least got him a seat at the table.

She told him how the Finance Committee worked, how an old church lady like Donnie Mack Carney was going to hate any hint of scandal, how there was always going to be a handful of weaklings on the committee who did whatever Donnie Mack told them to do. Basically, Liz told Allen Getz that it probably wouldn't be the worst thing in the world if the bad publicity that I'd gotten when I first inherited the team continued for as long as possible.

Throw enough shit against the wall, he said to her.

"Rich guys're as influenced by what they read as the rest of us," Liz Bolton said. "Sometimes more than the rest of us."

"Those weren't your investigators in Vegas back at the beginning," I said. "They were his."

She nodded.

"You gave him Ferret."

Another nod. I asked her why she'd quit that time and she said she knew she was taking a chance if I called her bluff, but that if I talked her into staying, I'd trust her more than I did before.

I said, "And what were you going to get out of all this? Other than some nights of almost indescribable pleasure?"

"Ten percent of the Hawks if Allen ended up with them."

Just like that.

"And what does Kitty get?"

"Kitty?" Liz said. "She gets to be Mrs. Allen Getz. The schmuck is actually in love with her."

"Ten percent of a billion-dollar property is a nice haul."

"Only if you're not the sort of schmuck who turns it down."

"You turned it down," I said.

"Yup."

"Sure you did."

"You told me not to bullshit you. I'm not. I may be certifiable. But I am most definitely not bullshitting you."

"Anymore."

"You want to beat me up a little more, beat me up," she said. "I deserve it. The whole time I was coaching Allen, I kept telling myself that the worst thing that happened to you was that you'd have to sell, which meant you'd walk away with what? Four hundred million at least? It's

248 / mike lupica

not like your father hadn't taken care of you, okay? Even if you lost, you won. Then you show up and acted like you were in this for laughs, starting with that first press conference, when you had to show everybody what a character you were. And then before I knew it, A.T.M. was gone and we were 0–2 and I thought it might get worse from there."

"Even after we had our little talk."

"Even then."

"You were going to let me ruin one season," I said. "But just one."

She smiled. "Then shit happened."

"Like us."

"We happened. The season happened. It wasn't anything Allen did. It was everything that was happening *here*. The fun everybody started to have around here once Vince was gone. I never would've had the nerve to fire Vince that way, it was like something a fan would've done in the heat of the moment. But there was a part of me, even the next day, that knew it was the right thing, even if I wasn't going to admit that to you." She shook her head. "Bottom line? I started to think it might not be such a hot idea betting against you."

It was Allen Getz's idea to get Vince Cahill on board, thinking it would be a great public relations move to bring him back if he did get the team. It was Cahill who gave Getz the shit on Bubba. Liz told Getz they didn't need it, but Cahill had already leaked it to Vicky Dunne by then.

Liz said, "Allen and I finally had lunch the day before the Jets game. We went back to his apartment afterwards—he's got this new place on East 71st?—and I told him his offer was certainly a generous one, but he was on his own the rest of the way."

Nobody said anything now.

Josh Blake had given the guys a couple of days off, since our first playoff game wouldn't be until the Sunday after next, against the winner of Saints vs. Jets in the first round of the playoffs. So the field was empty at mid-morning. I got up and walked around the desk and stared out at the place through Liz's window, imagining what Molloy would look like and sound like for that first playoff game here, maybe a black-and-white day like this one, like one off the old man's wall or out of his scrapbooks, him standing next to Frankie Molloy, Frankie in that topcoat, the old man in his own, probably covering his church clothes.

Liz said, "You might not believe this, but I felt lousy about all of this from the start."

"Part owner," I said. "I can see how that would turn the head of even a sweet kid like you."

Across the way, I saw A.T.M. Moore in his blue Number 84 and gray sweats jogging slowly up the stadium steps. The doctors had given him clearance at the end of last week to start running again, telling him to go easy, but that he would be a hundred percent for the playoffs.

He was something to watch even running up stairs.

"I was going to tell you myself," Liz said.

I turned around. She had turned her chair around, so now she was the one facing the field.

"Were you?" I said.

"I was," she said. "I didn't want to be sitting up there in your suite during the playoffs and still feel like . . ."

"A scummy turncoat weasel traitor bitch?"

"Listen, I'll make it easy for you," she said. "You don't have to fire me. I'll resign."

"You want that on your résumé? The president of the team who resigned two games before the Super Bowl?"

"As opposed to the team president who got herself fired two games before the Super Bowl?"

"I'm not firing you," I said. "And you're not resigning."

"I'm not," she said. "Why is that?"

"I could tell you that it's because I believe you," I said. "And I could tell you we had a deal, about you getting presented the old Lombardi trophy, and how I hardly ever break a deal. All true. Just not the real reason."

"Which is?"

"Which is that I now have a marker with you, and a big one."

Liz said, "You're not kidding."

I said, "You owe me."

I left her sitting there and walked down the hall, thinking of something Arnie Browne had told me that night before we'd played his Eagles at Molloy.

Then I made a stop I should have made a long time ago.

Two, actually. I'll tell you about them later.

thirty-three

The old man would have loved the way we did it against the Saints in the first round of the playoffs. He would have loved it more than anybody in the place.

Just because he would have understood it better than anybody except Pat Summerall, who was there doing the game with John Madden on Fox.

The old man's favorite story about Summerall was from 1958. It was the year the Giants finally lost that sudden-death championship game to the Colts at the Stadium, a game credited with putting pro football on the map and giving people something they liked to watch on television almost as much as westerns and rigged game shows. But a couple of weeks before that, the Giants had to beat the Cleveland Browns on the last day of the regular season to tie the Browns for the Eastern Conference championship, and set up a one-game playoff with the Browns the next week. And Summerall, Old Number 88, won that one with a field goal in the snow that was somewhere between forty-eight and fifty-two yards,

252 / mike lupica

nobody's sure to this day because it was snowing like a sonofabitch in New York that day, and by the end, nobody could see the yard lines, just the scoreboard saying that Summerall and the Giants had won, 13–10.

Vince Lombardi was a Giants assistant coach in those days, in charge of the offense, and he used to butt heads with Summerall, at least according to the old man. The reason was that Lombardi knew it was Summerall who was the leader of the pack when the Giants would start running around Manhattan at night, leading the league in those late nights I'd always heard about.

"Your godfather and his friends would often be coming in about the time Saint Vincent was heading off to seven o'clock Mass," was the way Tim Molloy explained it.

So Lombardi had no use for Summerall and the feeling was mutual. But after Summerall kicked the ball and was through being mobbed by his teammates on the sideline, he looked down the field about twenty yards and there was Vince Lombardi, standing by himself, homburg pulled down tight over his glasses, arms folded in front of him, staring grimly into the snow.

Summerall couldn't resist. He went down to Lombardi and said, "What'd you think of that?"

Lombardi, not even looking at him, snapped, "You know you can't kick it that far."

Summerall, when he told the story himself one night in the old man's den on 71st Street, laughed and said, "He was probably right." But it was the most famous kick in New York football, until Benito Siragusa's against the Saints put us into the NFC championship game.

It snowed the way it had for Summerall, even harder than it had against the Jets. It snowed as hard as I'd ever seen it snow in a football game that wasn't being played in Denver. It was still snowing when Benito kicked what the television cameras were able to prove was a 58-yard field goal with four seconds left to beat the Saints, 10–9.

On television, Summerall deadpanned to John Madden, "I've got to admit it, John. Benito's is bigger."

We had scored our touchdown early in the game when Sherman Fountainblue, playing on special teams (and providing immediate dividends on our short-term investment toward his extensive family planning for all the little Shermans and Shermaynes), fell on a blocked punt in the Saints' end zone.

We'd give up a safety later when the Saints blocked one of ours. Winky Huang, our punter, was trying to kick out of our end zone, when he slipped on the snow and did a Rockettes-like kick and the ball went back over his head and nearly made it into the stands.

It was 7–2, Hawks, early and stayed that way into the fourth quarter, when the Saints somehow managed a seventy-eight-yard touchdown drive, Boogie Wise finally managing to cross-country-ski his way into the end zone on a reverse.

It was 9–7, them, with three and a half minutes to play. Tucker O'Neill had been in at quarterback since the middle of the second quarter, Bubba Royal having suffered a mild concussion when blindsided by Johnson Johnson. He'd been in the locker room ever since, telling our trainer fascinating and sexually explicit stories about some of his female professors at UCLA.

He would occasionally look up at the game. When he saw Boogie Wise doing his Dirty Boogie dance in the end zone, Bubba grabbed his helmet and came jogging back on the field in what Gil Spencer would describe as a scene out of an old forties college football musical.

And maybe it was.

In conditions more suited for the Iditarod than football, Bubba took us down the field, even though his teammates would remark later that he would occasionally lapse into calling out a formation from his old UCLA playbook. The play that everybody would remember—at least before Benito Siragusa's historic kick—was one Bubba pulled from his own glory days. He was facing a third-and-long at midfield, less than a minute to go, and called for a rollout pass to A.T.M. on the sidelines. Only he slipped pulling away from scrimmage and the play broke down completely and Bubba was forced to scramble the other way until, in desperation, he somehow managed to throw the ball to Redford Newman.

Behind his back.

Redford made the first down by a margin so small he would describe it later as the length of his former agent's dick.

But Bubba couldn't advance the ball any farther, and finally we were at the Saints' 40-yard line, four seconds left. Bubba could either chuck a prayer to A.T.M. in the end zone. Or he could let Benito try one from fifty-eight yards, even though the longest field goal of his career was fifty-two.

Josh sent the kicking team out.

In Suite 19, Pete Stanton said, "I've got everything we've ever tried to do here riding on a guy who calls me Il Duce."

I opened the windows in 19, because it was snowing so hard now I figured I'd be able to hear if he made it even if I couldn't see.

The little bastard kicked it through. The kid running the message board somehow was able to digitally re-create the Italian flag, though I thought it looked more like a Gucci loafer. Underneath that, this message kept flashing "Hawks 10, Saints 9."

In the locker room afterward, Bobby Finkel came in with Edge to congratulate me, if somewhat halfheartedly.

"I'm twenty million over the fucking cap," he said. "I let it all ride on this season. And I lose to Pepe the Waiter."

We were in the championship game, which was played in almost summer-like conditions the next Sunday in Molloy against Arnie Browne's Eagles, and turned out to be an anticlimax after the heroics of Bubba and Benito the week before. Bubba threw three touchdown passes to A.T.M., one to Sherman Fountainblue, ran for two others, and we blew their doors off, 42–10.

We were in the Super Bowl against Vito Cazenovia's L.A. Bangers, who had won three straight upset games on the road as a wildcard team.

On the field at Molloy after we beat the Eagles, A.T.M. Moore spoke, I thought, for all of us.

"One more win," he said, "and I'm goin' to [bleeped out on fast work by our p.a. man and the guy in the Fox truck] Sea World!"

This was after the Eagles game, by which time championship Sunday at Molloy had already turned into the Monday of Super Bowl Week.

I had been celebrating since the game ended. There had been a players' party at Beef to which Mo Jiggy and A.T.M. had invited me, and where I saw for myself that Venus and Serena were a much more impressive family act than the Judds. After that, Annie and I had wandered up to Elaine's to meet Billy Grace and Inger, then to The Last Good Year, before finally making it back to Suite 19.

And after a rather heroic romantic effort from Mr. Jack Molloy considering the amount of Scotch I had consumed as I'd gamely made my way uptown, I left Annie sleeping soundly and put on some old UCLA sweats and running shoes and made my way downstairs to Big Tim Molloy's office.

Where I took one of his last Cubans out of the humidor and poured myself a glass of his favorite brandy and sat down behind his desk one last time.

Where I raised a glass to my favorite picture of the two of us, from a Saturday at Baker Field at Columbia when I was still playing at McBurney, my uniform full of dirt and what looked like some dried blood, the old man holding my helmet in the air like a trophy.

"Well, Molloy," I said, "you finally made the big game."

I smiled to myself.

"*We* finally made it," I said.

I drank some brandy.

"One more win," I said, "and we're goin' to fucking Sea World!"

I laughed and kept laughing and then for the first time since the old man had died, for what I swore would be the one and only time, I finally dropped my guard.

And cried.

thirty-four

n the past, I had only gone to the Super Bowl to drink and chase after the Bad Girls and Very Bad Girls who always seemed to descend on the host city in the same locust-like swarm with media people and corporate sponsors. On occasion I had been there as the Jammer, organizing parties for some of Billy's whales, showing them around Miami or New Orleans or Beverly Hills when the game was in the Rose Bowl, making sure they were on the pass list for the best parties and shows, even importing a Bambi or Thumper from Vegas if the situation called for it, scamming tickets left and right.

Now I was on the inside.

Brian Goldberg said that from the time our team plane landed until the ball was actually kicked off at the Cardinals' new stadium—the Charles Keating Memorial Coliseum—I would be expected to do the following:

Attend six thousand media functions.

Make myself available for a sitdown with an old friend, Al Michaels, since ABC was televising this year's game.

Prepare the remarks I wanted to make to the Finance Committee when I gave my State of the Jammer address.

Find out exactly where I stood with its members, who would be voting on Saturday.

And oversee a major production Mo Jiggy and I had prepared for the Hawks players, even Raiford Dionne, whom Mo had finally forgiven for holding him upside down at the Welcome Home dinner at the Plaza.

What had started out six months ago with the reading of the old man's will would finally play out at pro football's version of the Mardi Gras, with even more drunks and assholes.

The Hawks had taken over the Arizona Biltmore, the classiest old hotel in Phoenix, the original structure built by one of Frank Lloyd Wright's sidemen, Albert Chase McArthur. I knew that because the old man loved the place, used to take us there sometimes in the winter. So I remembered the stained-glass skylights off the main lobby, and marble bathrooms and fountains and grounds and wrought-iron pilasters. I knew how William Wrigley, who owned the joint once, had gotten himself so excited about the blue-and-gold tiles at the bottom of one of the pools that he'd bought the company that made them. And I knew how just about every American president since Hoover had stayed there at one time or another. So when the league gave us a choice between the Biltmore or the Phoenician, I grabbed the Biltmore, mostly because that's what the old man would have wanted me to do.

"The Wrigleys didn't know shit about baseball," he used to say. "And I was never a gum guy. But they built a nice goddam hotel."

So we were all there: front-office staff, coaches, players, families, in addition to Mo Jiggy and both his posse and band. Some people were staying in the main building, and the rest of us were scattered around the grounds in cottages. Mo had six cottages in the back for himself, Kelli Ann Gonzalez, the musicians, Montell, Denzell, and the Rotts. Kenny and Babs and their families were in the main building. Annie and I had a vulgar two-bedroom cottage near where Mo and Kelli Ann were staying.

The Biltmore had waived its no-pets rule after Montell and Denzell talked to the manager.

"Took about five minutes," Mo Jiggy told me later. "Boys made some opening remarks, and before long Mr. Mendoza—he's the manager—was into that 'mi casa es su casa' shit."

Billy and Inger and the Vinnys and Johnny Angel had their own floor in the main building.

Brian Goldberg had decided to stay at the media hotel downtown, the Hyatt Regency, so he could be on twenty-four-hour call for the New York media.

"There's only like two hundred sports-talk shows set up downstairs," he said. "You should come over sometime and take a walk through. If they think you might make a good guest, all you see are hands reaching out like you're Mother Teresa and they're Calcutta."

Kitty and Allen Getz were staying out at The Boulders in Carefree. At home or on the road, she was a spa junkie, and The Boulders won.

After we'd all settled in on Monday night, we turned the living room of my cottage into a war room. Annie was there, Pete and Liz, Mo and Billy and me. Mo and Billy had sent Mo's posse, the two Vinnys and Johnny, to the hotel bar, where they were scaring people around them half-to-death and getting better acquainted.

"They'll mostly just compare Glocks and Sigs and shit," Mo said.

Before they'd left, I'd finally gotten to meet Vinny One. He looked an awful lot like Vinny Two, except for the eye patch.

"Thanks for all your help in London," I said to him.

He gave me a blank look with his good eye.

"I was never in London," he said, and walked off across the lawn to catch up with the rest of the guys.

Billy stood next to me, beaming as he watched him go. "You can't teach that," he said.

Mo nodded.

"You got to be born with it," he said.

In the cottage now, Billy said he thought I had three solid votes on Thursday: "My dear friend, Al Davis," Jerry Jones and Arnie Browne.

"From what I hear," he said, "we're dead in the water with the tampon twins."

Barry and Nancy Teitlebaum of the Patriots.

"Why don't they like me?" I said.

"It's me, actually," he said with a pissed-off wave of his hand. "Turns out there was a problem one time with her old man."

Since "problem" with Billy could cover so much territory both inside and outside the law, I asked him what kind of problem.

"He said he got rolled by a couple of our nannies, which was total bullshit," Billy said. "Threatened to go to the papers with it, even though that would have meant blowing his cover with the lovely Neva."

Nancy Teitlebaum's mother, as alive now as she was then.

"What finally happened?" I said.

"I had Vinny talk to him."

"Which one?"

"One," Billy said. "Who got a little carried away, though why the guy made such a big deal, considering the advances that had already been made in knee-replacement surgery, I'll never know."

Three votes to one, I said.

"Three-three," Billy said. "I don't think you've got Corky DuPont or the midget who owns the Saints."

"Gee," I said, "I thought Bobby Finkel and I were buddies."

"He's still pouting about the way your team beat his team," Billy said. "It's as simple as that. And now that you end up in the Super Bowl, Corky's worried that he might never get to finish in first place ever again, which he thinks makes him look bad with his daddy, Corky Junior."

"You always hate to see that happen," Pete said.

Billy Grace, who'd just come in for a swim and was wearing his white complimentary Biltmore robe, said, "So you mean it could all come down to Donnie Mack Carney?"

Pete said, "Okay, we're dead."

Mo shook his head sadly and said, "Deader'n Fat Load."

Billy asked who Fat Load was and Mo gave him the story bumper-sticker fashion, telling about the problems Fat and him started to have with their label, Fat's cousin LaDonna, and finally the shooting outside The Forge in Miami.

Billy patted him on the shoulder and said, "At least there was closure."

Liz said we needed a couple of more buckets of ice from outside, and Annie, who'd promised to be nice, said she'd go with her. "I'm a gracious winner," Annie'd said before everybody arrived. "But I *am* the winner!" she whooped and then went through Quadripro Cleveland's entire touchdown dance, including humping the rug at the end.

Once a lady, always a lady, I'd told her.

In the cottage now—Annie'd already taken to calling it Suite 19½—Pete said, "You said you got along all right with Donnie Mack that day at the Post House."

"It was either me or the gin," I said.

"Do they vote on your brother and sister the same time they do you?" Billy said.

"Yeah, but it's only a formality with them," I said. "There've been some stories that the other owners are worried about the fact that we're supposed to be the most dysfunctional family going, but nobody believes those're grounds to take out blood relatives who have pretty much been a part of the operation since they got out of college."

"Okay, then," Billy Grace said, "anybody got any ideas how we could leverage the Holy Ghost? 'Cause if you do, I'm all friggin' ears."

Nobody did, so we all sat around drinking and smoking for a while, until the private phone line I'd had installed suddenly chirped. It was Brian Goldberg calling on his cell from the Hyatt, asking me if I had the television on, because if I didn't I better turn it on right now, to CNN/SI.

I did that.

Standing at a podium that had "Hyatt Regency, Phoenix" on the front were Donnie Mack Carney and Allen Getz.

". . . nothing's on paper yet," Donnie Mack was saying, "but we just wanted you guys and gals to know first that Getz dot com is about to buy itself a little slice of HEVN."

Donnie Mack put his arm around Allen Getz now and took his voice up a couple of decibels.

"Because isn't it high time," he shouted, "that Jesus Christ had the best web site?"

Getz put his head down, trying to look humble.

"Praise the Lord," he said.

"Jesus *dot* com!" Donnie Mack Carney said, dominating the picture in his three-piece lavender suit, raising both hands over his head.

In front of the television, I said, "Say hallelujah."

"Say amen," Mo Jiggy said.

thirty-five

I am not here," Commissioner Wick Sanderson of the National Football League said. "I am not here, none of us are here." He giggled nervously, loosening his tie a little bit. "This place doesn't even exist.

"So there's really no problem, is there?" he said, talking mostly to himself now.

We were in an elegant old home on Thunderbird Trail, which was the road feeding into the Arizona Biltmore. I'd rented the place for the entire week. Billy had told me about it; he'd stayed there the first time there'd been a Super Bowl in Phoenix, when the game was played at Sun Devil Stadium in Tempe, the Cowboys beating the Steelers that year. Some friends of the Wrigleys had built the brick Colonial in the thirties, but it was one of the later owners who'd added the spacious ballroom facing the back of the property, one that Alice Cooper later had soundproofed when he'd briefly lived there in the early eighties. Alice, who hadn't been born again yet, wanted to bring his own band around for parties and not have the neighbors, which included Ronald Reagan's in-laws, bitch about the noise and think he was a bad person. Alice, not the Gipper.

We were in that ballroom now, watching the floor show.

By "we," I mean an exclusive guest list consisting of Commissioner Sanderson, Annie Kay, most of the New York Hawk players, and Mo Jiggy's band.

The floor show was Venus, Serena and Billy's friend Inger.

Venus was wearing a tennis halter top, high-heeled shoes made to look like tennis sneakers, nothing else. Serena was wearing the matching bottom from the outfit, the same sneakers. They were in the process of undressing Inger, who had agreed to do a cameo as the chair umpire. So most of the Hawks players were up on their feet, clapping rhythmically to the beat of Mo's band while Mo rapped his way through a song he had written especially for the occasion, called "McEnroe, Yo."

. . . can't believe you called me out,
Blind white fool,
Incompetent tool,
Got half a mind to blow
Your fuckin' brains out.

"What?" I said to the commissoner over the music and noise. "You don't like the way we've re-created the Café Carlyle?"

Sanderson said, "Maybe ABC can do a remote from here on their pregame show. They've only got eleven hours to fill this year."

On the dance floor, Elvis Elgin and Raiford Dionne and Bubba had gotten into the act now, rescuing Inger before Venus and Serena toppled the umpire's chair, ending at the same time all of Ferret Biel's nasty innuendo about whether Inger was a real blonde or not.

She was, as it turned out.

Wick Sanderson was still talking to me, but was watching Inger, who loved the spotlight as much as Billy told us she did. "What did you say you called this place?"

Beef West, I said. I explained that it was my way of letting our boys blow off a little steam after they'd done all their media and looked at as much film as any sane person possibly could, and generally protecting the organization and the league for what had historically been the number-one downtime activity for Super Bowl participants: Soliciting undercover cops posing as hookers, sometimes right up until game time.

The married guys who wanted to see the floor show were technically at a team meeting until ten o'clock, and would have to leave then to get back to their wives. The single guys could stay until midnight, which was Josh Blake's curfew for the week.

The married guys' playbooks were arranged alphabetically on a table near the door; they could pick them up when they left like party favors.

Wick Sanderson said, "You're sure nobody besides your people can get in or out of here?"

I reminded him that Montell and Denzell had been waiting for him at the front door, with Regis and Kathie Lee, when his limo had pulled up in the driveway.

"We don't foresee any real problems with gate-crashers," I said.

"You make a good point," the commissioner said.

This was Tuesday night, and I was scheduled to address the Finance Committee late the next afternoon. I'd called Wick Sanderson at the Ritz-Carlton and told him I needed to talk about Donnie Mack Carney and someone the newspapers were now calling Allen Getz Saved.

"What happened to all the rules about cross-ownership you talk about every time the Finance Committee screws some cable TV baron out of a team?" I said.

There was a roar from the dance floor, where Venus and Serena's basic act had now turned into a game of keep-away with Venus's halter.

"Clothes by Fila," Annie Kay said admiringly from across the table. "Bodies by God."

"Allen Getz doesn't own a team," Sanderson said. "If you don't own a team, cross-ownership isn't an issue."

"Doesn't own a team yet."

"That sounds pretty pessimistic to me," he said, and looked over to the door as he did every few minutes, waiting for the front of Carole Sandusky to come through a couple of minutes before she did. "From what I'm hearing, the Finance Committee vote could go either way."

I said to him, "Did you know that Donnie Mack was looking around for investors?"

Sanderson said, "Carney College turned out to be more of a drain than he thought it was going to be." He sipped from the glass of pink Annie'd urged him to try, noting that it tasted like Bazooka bubble gum with a bit of a kick. "And," he continued, "Donnie Mack didn't do nearly as well as the analysts thought he would with that spin-off network, HEVN Classic."

"C'mon, Wick," I said. "Are you going to sit by and let Getz buy the election this way? And after he does, then what do you say about one end of this partnership owning the Ravens and the other half owning the Hawks? Rewrite the rulebook again?"

"Hey," Wick Sanderson said, brightening a little. "We do it all the time with replay."

Mo Jiggy had put down his handheld microphone now and was in the middle of the dance floor, bare-chested underneath a leather vest, bent over an amazingly limber Serena and the two of them grinding away.

Annie Kay said, "And I waste three hours a week on spinning classes."

"Seriously, Jack, what do you want me to tell you here?" the commissioner said. "All they've done is announced they're merging. I issued a release saying that if and when the merger goes through, and if at that time Allen Getz is involved with a team or attempting to get involved, then at that point of course the league will look into it. You want me to take on the biggest dot com going and the biggest God guy, on spec? Just because they called a press conference? Give me a fucking break. They're your problem for now, not mine. Have you noticed who the other owner in the Super Bowl is lately? Vito the Back Hoe? I'm waiting for someone to point out on Page A1 of *The New York Times* that this bastard has buried more Italians in his life than Mount Vesuvius."

Then he told me something I already knew, that if I showed up in Phoenix needing Donnie Mack Carney to put me over the top, that I was probably screwed from the start.

The commissioner finished the last of his pink now with a smack of his lips, then stood up to wave at Carole Sandusky, who'd apparently even created a stir with the dogs as she entered, Montell and Denzell furiously trying to pull them away from her and stop their barking and carrying on.

Annie Kay looked over at where the commotion was in the ballroom and said, "Wick, is that your date, or is the second show about to begin?"

Brian Goldberg, p.r. man to the stars, said that once before I died—an event he expected to happen any day now, according to the coverage of the Finance Committee vote he'd been reading on-line—I had to see the players be interviewed by the media at the Super Bowl.

Because there was only one week this year between the conference championship games and the Super Bowl, what was known as Media Day was occurring on Wednesday morning at Keating Coliseum, the Hawks being made available on the field first, then the Los Angeles Bangers an hour later. Annie said she'd be there, too, with Vicky Dunne and their crew, and she'd see me over there. Technically, she was staying at the Hyatt with the rest of the media. But as soon as she was finished editing Vicky's tape at night, she'd come over and find me at the Biltmore. Then, much later, after we had finished groping each other like a teenaged soap opera, one of Mo's guys would drive her back to the Hyatt so she could be there for her morning production meeting with Vicky.

"You're telling me that Vicky doesn't suspect about us?" I'd said to her at Beef West, after Wick Sanderson and Carole Sandusky had gone back to his place.

"As far as I've been able to ascertain, Vicky's interests are these," Annie said. "One, career advancement. Two, career advancement through sexual favors, if necessary. Three, her hair."

Brian drove me out to the Keating Coliseum, which had been built behind the Scottsdale Princess. I'd asked Billy Grace if he wanted to go with us, just for sport, but he said that Ferret Biel, of all people, had been leaving messages for him at the hotel, and that he wanted to have what he described as a "heart to heart" with him once and for all.

"Heart to heart" with Billy covered almost as much territory as "problem" did.

"Not to worry," he said on the phone. "It's like with kids, there's just a point where they finally have to understand something."

"Such as?"

"Such as limits," he said, and hung up.

What the league basically did on Media Day was scatter players all over the field and then let about a thousand or so members of the media have at them. When the gate at the loge level of Keating was finally opened, the media then came filing in; it was impossible to know whether it was them making the mooing noises, or the players.

Brian and I were up at the top of the stands, watching the scene from up there, the media scattering and running once they hit the field, trying to get a good spot in front of whomever it was they wanted to talk to about the big game, and generally feed the monster that was Super Bowl Week.

"This is pretty much what the photo ops in hell will be like," he said.

"I read the papers and watch television like a loyal American," I said. "Nothing ever happens at Super Bowl Week until one of the players goes looking for a blow job."

"You can be very negative sometimes," he said. "You know that?"

Josh Blake and the bigger stars like Bubba and A.T.M. had their own podiums set up for them. Some of the other guys would just sit in the first row of the stands. Even Pete Stanton, I noticed, had drawn a crowd.

We watched for a while and drank coffee Brian had gone off and found somewhere, and I finally said let's go down on the field, trying to quote Teddy Roosevelt about how only the man in the arena understood something or other.

"No bombshells today, okay?" Brian Goldberg said, saying he thought Josh might need him. "Just give 'em the old razzle-dazzle."

Vicky saw me first, and then before long there were about fifty people with me, near the goalposts at the west end of Keating. I answered all the questions, many of which were in English.

Was I worried that this game between the Hawks and the Bangers might be my last official function as owner of the Hawks?

If it was, I asked, did that mean I couldn't go to the scouting combine and wear a stopwatch around my neck?

How did you really get A.T.M. Moore to come back to the Hawks before he lost the whole season?

Easy. I just did what Bitsy Aguilera of the Chargers would have done. Offered to marry him.

Seriously, Vicky Dunne said.

Okay, okay, I said, I'll come clean. I paid him with cash under the table, look how well that worked when he was in college.

Rat, one of the hosts from WNUT, jokingly asked if I was going to bet the game.

I looked offended and said, People gamble on pro football in this country? How long has that [bleeped for radio] been going on?

Gil Spencer wanted to know what my father would say about this game if he were alive.

Give the points, I said.

Vicky was the one who pointed out that Phoenix restaurant owners and club owners were complaining that off what they'd observed on Monday and Tuesday night, the Hawks were keeping a very low profile.

What, she asked, have they been doing in their spare time?

I winked at Annie Kay and said that a number of them had expressed an unusually high interest in the Australian Open tennis tournament, whose second week was traditionally Super Bowl Week.

They like *tennis*?

My guys love Venus and Serena, I said. What can I tell you? A lot of them say they've even seen them play in person.

It went like that. I was telling everybody I was going to give Vicky a one-on-one, mostly because Annie had asked me to, when I heard the yelling from across the field.

Brian Goldberg came running.

"You better come quick," he said. "Oretha Keeshon—A.T.M.'s former sweetie?—just showed up with a crew from MTV."

Oretha was a six-foot, light-brown, perfectly proportioned goddess woman.

She had one of those short haircuts, not quite a girl crew cut but cut that close to her scalp. She was wearing a white dress that showed off perfect specs in the area of chest and legs and ass. Somehow the color of the skimpy sundress only seemed to make the color of her and the size of her, her all-around presence, more dramatic.

I said to Brian Goldberg, "She was a graduate assistant? Where, Halle Berry University?"

She had pushed her way to the front of the crowd at A.T.M. Moore's podium. I noticed A.T.M. was already cowering the way Dirty Harry's victims used to, right before he didn't read them their rights.

"So, bitch face, we meet again," Oretha said in a loud voice.

"'Retha," A.T.M. said meekly, "this ain't the proper time or space, you know what I'm talkin' about?"

"Oh," she said, hand cocked on her hip, playing as much to the media as she was to A.T.M., "I've known what you're talkin' about for a *long* time. I know *all* about your sorry ass. That's why I'm here to change your nickname today to what it ought to be: L. P. Moore."

Somebody in the crowd behind her, trying to be helpful, said, "Long Playing?"

Oretha turned around, hand still on her hip, and gave everybody a contemptuous look. "Late Payment," she said.

The Reverend Tire Iron Timmons, who'd been standing behind A.T.M. on the podium, had quietly come down and was standing next to Oretha's MTV cameraman, a tall skinny kid with a wispy goatee and his long hair in orange- and lemon-colored braids.

Tire Iron took a step forward and put a gentle hand on Oretha's arm.

"Back off, God Boy!" she snapped.

She could even back up Tire Iron.

" 'Retha," A.T.M. said. "You come any closer to me, you'll be in violation of that constraining order."

There were, I noticed now, a lot of summer blazers with official league name tags attached to them and guys in yellow "Event Security" nylon windbreakers in the general vicinity of the podium, though none of them seemed in any hurry to tangle with Oretha Keeshon.

Brian whispered to me, "Were you planning on turning on the charm anytime soon? Say, before the draft?"

I told him I didn't want to sound as if I was stuck or anything, but Oretha was a fucking grad assistant?

Oretha turned to the camera guy in the braids and said, "I'll ask my questions now, you keep the camera on bitch face here."

Oretha frankly didn't need a camera of her own, because every other camera at Charles Keating Coliseum was now trained directly at her.

She looked down at some notes and said, "Okay, question number one: In which area do you think you're weaker, blocking or child support?"

A.T.M., doing his best to stand his ground, said, " 'Retha, please. Talk to Mo. He'll tell you straight up, we just movin' some money around . . ."

Oretha turned to the crowd and said, "The boy's always been good at movin' *somethin'* around, you know what *I'm* talkin' about now?"

Some of the women reporters in the crowd smiled and clapped now, and I heard a few of them say, "Uh *huh*."

I said to Brian, "Look at that, they've dumped him for a better quote."

Oretha said, "Okay, question number two."

A.T.M.'s mike was still open, and I was sure I heard something that had "kill this bitch" in the middle of it.

"Question number two," Oretha said again, even louder than before. She smiled. "And please remember you've got all your lifelines left, you no-account sonofabitch. Which means you still can phone one of your little whore friends."

Oretha's impression of Regis even made me smile, as much as I was trying to feel A.T.M.'s male pain.

"Okay, here it is: Do you feel as if you will be able to exploit L.A.'s matchup zone as well as you have your goddam *wife?*"

"Ex-wife," A.T.M. said, leaning forward to the microphone, his "Moesha" baseball cap pulled down to the top of his sunglasses.

"Like you're gonna be an ex-damn-Hawk if anybody finds out the real reason . . ."

"Hey, Oretha," a voice said.

Mine.

I had moved up to the front of the crowd and was now standing directly between her and A.T.M. I put out a hand and said, "Jack Molloy? Owner of the Hawks?"

The interruption seemed to throw her for a second, the scene suddenly not going exactly as she had planned it, or played it out in her mind. So she made a motion to her sound person, a woman, that said, cut.

"Oh," she said, trying to look bored. "The fuckup."

"You've heard about me, then?" I said, playing a little bit to the crowd myself now.

"Don't come around tryin' to get in my business," Oretha said.

"Now, that is some coincidence right there," I said. "Because business is exactly what I'd like to discuss with you."

"And what is that supposed to mean, exactly?"

I glanced over my shoulder at A.T.M., who looked so happy and relieved not to be talking to Oretha any more I thought he might cry.

I put my arm around Oretha now, gave her shoulder a little squeeze and said, "Now that you've vented, how about we talk about maybe some money changing hands. Would that be okay?"

thirty-six

I asked Oretha if she was really working for MTV and she gave me a look and said, "Why the hell not? You ever see some of the pieces that bitch Downtown Julie Brown used to do from the Super Bowl?"

We were in the backseat of the limo I'd rented, on our way back from Keating Coliseum. I told her that the driver would drop Brian and me at the Biltmore, if that was all right, and then drive her over to the Hyatt, where she was supposed to meet up with her crew. She said, fine with her. I then asked if she wouldn't mind terribly staying the fuck away from A.T.M. until my team had every chance to win itself the big game on Sunday.

Oretha sighed, bored, and said that was fine, too, as long as I wasn't messing with her when I'd gotten to the part about some money eventually changing hands.

"You mess with me, I *will* find a way to mess with you," she said. "Or *which* you, as A.T.M. would say. You understand what I'm talkin' about?"

Oretha and Brian were sitting facing the driver, I was facing them in the stretch, hoping that she'd cross her legs sooner or later, which she now did. Brian looked as if he'd just witnessed somebody else unwrapping his favorite birthday present, making no attempt whatsoever to look away.

"Oretha," I said. "You can ask anybody in Vegas, I've never faded anybody in my life. You're just going to have to trust me."

Oretha said, "Oh yeah, that's what I want to do. You're a man, I got something you want. Let me get right into my trusting mode."

I said, okay, let's try this another way, and asked for some kind of ballpark figure on what it would take for her to lay off until A.T.M. got his new contract, at which point he was on his own with her as far as I was concerned.

We had gotten off Scottsdale Road now, made the turn onto Lincoln, on our way to 24th Street.

"I know A.T.M.," she said, dodging the question. "No way he comes back if you don't pay him to come back."

I said to Oretha, "What if I did?"

"How much you cough up on the boy?"

It took an effort not to smile. "Are we negotiating already?"

She smiled brilliantly and said, "How 'bout I get some of what you give him?" She nodded and said in a throaty voice, "How 'bout you give me some of *that*?"

We rode in silence the rest of the way, finally coming up Thunderbird Trail past Beef West and then into the Biltmore's driveway, where there was a stampede of doormen trying to get the back door open first.

As I got up out of my seat, Oretha leaned forward and kissed me on the cheek, then made a little growl and bit my ear.

"See you *real* soon, Jack Molloy," she said.

"Oretha," I said, "good luck at convent school, okay?"

I got out first and Brian followed me. The doorman was starting to close the door when I leaned my head in, Lieutenant Columbo asking one more question.

"Oretha," I said. "Tell the truth now: You really had to cut a deal with A.T.M. to get him to marry you?"

With a trace of melancholy in her voice, she said, "The Lord may have blessed the boy with a gift for football. But he wasn't ever gonna be the brightest bulb on the Christmas tree."

Then she told the driver, let's get a move on, she had a damn voice-over to do.

I was scheduled to address the Finance Committee in a conference room at the Ritz-Carlton at three in the afternoon. I wore the new beige summer suit Annie Kay had picked out for me, a pale-blue oxford shirt from Brooks Brothers, rep tie, my new brown suede loafers with the rubber soles. I even wore socks.

Brian waited in the living room of the cottage while I changed; he said he had some time to kill before he went over to the Hawks' practice at Arizona State. I kept yelling and cursing from the bedroom that going over to the Ritz was just a waste of *my* goddam time, that everybody in the goddam room had already made up their goddam minds.

"If you blow them off now," he called back, "then we might as well put a bow around the Hawks and hand them to Getz right now."

"Allen Getz can kiss my ass," I yelled.

Brian said now I was talking, I sounded almost as intimidating as Oretha Keeshon.

Donnie Mack Carney was at the head table when I got there, dressed casually, wearing a lavender golf shirt from Carney College instead of a suit. Al Davis and Jerry Jones sat to Donnie Mack's right, along with Arnie Browne. Across from them were Corky DuPont III, Bobby Finkel and a third guy who had to be Barry Teitlebaum, tampon king. Teitlebaum looked like Bobby Finkel's fat little brother. He had one of those crew cuts that was like a giveup on a receding hairline, and a lot of worry lines in his forehead, as if wondering why his bushy black eyebrows had gotten all the hair. He wore a lemon-colored sports jacket, a navy knit shirt underneath with the collar turned up, as if he were really here for a meeting of the Greens Committee.

Donnie Mack took charge right away, passing out the financial report the league had done on me, the initial background check, the follow-up check, and the transcript of the interview about my Vegas years that had been conducted, with both a tape recorder and stenographer, by Bill Brendle, the head of NFL Security.

Brendle had tried to look more serious than a Fed, but had turned out to be a pretty funny guy. After he'd asked questions for over an hour about what it was like being the Jammer, he'd closed his notebook, stuck his pen in the pocket of his shirt and said, "One favor?"

Sure, I said.

"If you ever go back there, please take me with you."

When everybody had the reports in front of them, Donnie Mack tried to lighten the mood by saying that in light of everything that had happened with the New York Hawks this season, both on and off the field, he couldn't decide whether this committee was in the presence of a rock and roll star or just some kid who'd managed to take over the principal's office.

Al Davis, dressed in a white windbreaker and wearing wraparound sunglasses, said, "All I know about this kid is that his team is still fuckin' playing."

"Which," Jerry Jones said, "is more than I can say for the rest of us." He looked across at Barry Teitlebaum and said, "You fire your coach yet?"

Teitlebaum shook his head. "They say I can't until the girl's parents decide whether or not to press charges."

"Let me know when they do," Jones said. "I might be interested."

Donnie Mack cleared his throat and said he hated to interrupt this fascinating chitchat, but did anybody have any questions for young Mr. Molloy?

Barry Teitlebaum actually raised his hand and asked why I'd decide to move into Suite 19 and I told him, "Rent-controlled apartment, New York City."

That actually got a laugh around the table, if a small one.

Teitlebaum then wanted to know about the circumstances surrounding the firing of Vince Cahill and I told him everything, no jokes now, from the conversation on the sidelines to the lies to the reporters to the scene on the plane.

"He used the 'n'?" Barry Teitlebaum asked.

"You know," Al Davis said, "like Corky does when he thinks he's tryin' to be one of the fuckin' guys."

"I resent that," Corky DuPont III said. "Ask any of the boys on my team. They love me."

Bobby Finkel asked about Ferret Biel and the hundred grand I was supposed to have bet on the FedEx Orange Bowl. I told him it was a setup, that the league had determined the betting slip was a phony, it was all there in Bill Brendle's report, that only a handful of sportswriters looking to get through the day had bought into Ferret's bullshit.

Jerry Jones said he didn't have a question, just an observation.

"I just want to go on record as saying that I've liked Jack's style from the start," he said. "Reminds me of when I was running around this league with my nuts on fire. Hell, we need some new blood in this league, young studs like Jack who don't feel's if they have to check with their lawyers and accountants every time their gut tells them to drill a damn hole."

Bobby Finkel said, "Ooh, Texas oilman talk. I think I'm getting a chubby."

"Be his first in a long time, from what I hear," Jones said, poking Al Davis with an elbow.

"Is that a shot at the Muffster?" Finkel said.

"Sweet Jesus, Bobby," Arnie Browne said. "You really are an annoying little shit, aren't you?"

Arnie slowly got to his feet now. He didn't seem to have changed the wrinkled suit since I'd put him in the car that night at Molloy. He seemed to have lost a little more weight, gotten even more stooped. The only way to stop his hands from shaking was to put his cigar on the end of the table and stuff them into his pants pockets.

"Now I'd like to say my piece," he said, "if everybody would shut their pieholes."

They all shut their pieholes.

"I frankly don't give a crap what's in those reports," he said. "And I've been sitting here trying to figure out how there can be this many agendas on a committee this goddam small, pardon my French." He came up with a shaky hand now and pointed it at me, at the other end of the long table from Donnie Mack. "All I know," Arnie said, "is that this kid is what owners in this league used to be like, before we started letting in all these little boys who need a search engine to find their way to the goddam crapper. Is he a gambler? You bet he is, just like his father was, my friend Tim Molloy. And you want to know something else? He isn't afraid. He isn't afraid of sportswriters, he isn't afraid of the radio. And whatever happens in here, he isn't afraid of us. Does he fight with his brother and sister? Bet your ass he does, because that's what brothers and sisters do. My dear friend, Well Mara, used to fight with his nephew when they each had half of the Giants, and all they finally did was win two goddam Super Bowls. Now this kid who some of you think is unfit to have a seat with the rest of you at the Tightass Ball might win one his first time out of the blocks."

A coughing spell hit him then, one that even made my chest hurt. When Arnie managed to catch his breath with the aid of an inhaler, Al Davis helped lower him back into his chair.

"There isn't one of us in this room who wouldn't change places with him this week," Arnie Browne said, leaning back as if even that short speech had exhausted him. "And we still might end up voting him out on his ass." He made a harrumphing sound. "Then pretty soon we'll be in another conference room someplace hearing why we should be voting in Donnie Mack's Jews-for-Jesus friend Getz."

"That's out of order," Donnie Mack said. "And none of your business."

"Isn't it?" Arnie Browne asked.

"Maybe we should stay on point here," Donnie Mack Carney said, "and hear what Jack himself has to say."

I took a sip of water and stood up.

"There's really only one thing I want to say," I said. "The Hawks have always been in the Molloy family, and they're going to stay in the Molloy family."

I walked back to the conference room door and opened it.

"I even brought along much better Molloys than me to tell you why."

Kenny and Babs walked in then.

I had talked to them individually, first one office and then the other, the day I'd confronted Liz Bolton. They were the two stops I'd made afterward. Then we'd met later for dinner at The Last Good Year, just the three of us in the back room, having a talk we should have had about twenty years earlier with the old man sitting across the table from us.

I told them what Arnie Browne had told me about being in the family business, not the football business.

I told them we could keep hammering away at each other with body punches the way we had our whole lives, and that when we were done, a pissant like Allen Getz was going to walk off with the team the way he had walked off with the adorable Kitty Drucker-Cole Molloy.

"That gold-digging bitch," Babs said.

Her, I said.

"She had to be sleeping with him while Daddy was still alive," Babs said.

If she wasn't, I said, you could throw all her past performance charts right out the window.

I told them the truth that night, that I didn't know if I even wanted to stay around whether we made it to the Super Bowl or not, but that if that's the way I decided to play it, it was sure as hell going to be my call, not Getz's.

I said that if I were the two of them, I'd hate my guts too, that you'd have to go to the Jackson Five or somebody to find someone who could beat me out for the shittiest sibling award.

I told them that it didn't take Dr. Laura to see that we were the same old dysfunctional sitcom family, even with the old man gone.

I finally told them that maybe our last best chance was to take the bastards on together.

"It sounds like a noble gesture," Babs said. "But what does it mean if we can't get the votes?"

"Maybe nothing," I said. "But at least they can't give us any bullshit about how we'll never be able to get along, and how that will eventually paralyze the organization. I also think a unified front from us'll make it a little harder for them to say you guys can stay but I'm out of there."

"Before this turns into *Touched by an Angel*," Kenny said, "I've got to ask a question: Why should we put ourselves on the line for you, after all the grief you've given us in our lives?"

"Because I'm willing to put myself on the line for you."

Babs said, "What does that mean?'

I reached into the pocket of my trusty blue blazer and pulled out the letter I'd had Oscar Berkowitz, Billy's lawyer, draw up for me.

"It means that if I don't get the votes," I said, "I'll announce that I've already agreed to sell the Hawks to the two of you, in a letter dated last month, and you can tell them that if they try to sell my half out from under you, you will sue their fucking asses."

"We'd win and Allen Getz would lose," Kenny said.

"Blackjack," I said.

"Blackjack Molloy," my sister said.

In the limo on the way to the Ritz-Carlton, Kenny'd said, "You still don't believe you'll ever have to use that letter we all signed, do you?"

"Nope."

"You still believe you can get four votes?" Babs said.

"Yes," I lied.

Kenny and Babs waited outside while Donnie Mack ran the meeting and all the questions were asked and Arnie Browne made what was a long speech for him and I made my much shorter one. Then I opened the door and they came walking in and said contrary to what the fine members of the committee might have heard, it was the Molloys against the world now.

Or words to that effect.

I did what I have always done in moments of great stress, which meant going downstairs and waiting in the bar. Billy always said Lady Luck looked there first when she wanted to tap you on the shoulder, pretty much the same way the best hookers did.

On our way back to the Biltmore, Kenny said that Donnie Mack had gone somewhat ballistic after I'd left the room, reminding both Kenny and Babs that their ownership had never really been an issue with the committee, and that they ought to think long and hard about it becoming an issue this close to the vote.

At which point, Babs had said, "Is that some kind of threat, Donnie Mack?" She looked over at Arnie Browne then, and said, "Does that sound like a threat to you, Uncle Arnie?"

Arnie Browne said it sure sounded like a threat to him.

Donnie Mack said he was just making an observation, in light of what he saw as a grandstand play orchestrated by their brother Jack. Then he asked Kenny and Babs to sit down while he took everybody through my background reports.

At one point, Barry Teitlebaum had said that the whole thing read to him like a "Joan Collins novel."

Babs said she thought about correcting him, telling him he meant Jackie Collins, right? But then she wasn't so sure he did.

"Well," I said, "at least the opposition is well read."

"Jack, be serious for a minute," Babs said. "Please?" I noticed she actually had some color for a change, but it could have been the soft light in the back of the limo. "Because Donnie Mack couldn't be more serious."

"Did he say they were going to vote on us separately still?" I said.

They both nodded.

"He's afraid it would look funny if they change what had been their plan all along," Kenny said.

I asked what he thought his pal Corky was going to do.

"He said outside the conference room that he's keeping an open mind, and he wants to think about everything that happened today a little more, but he seems more scared of Donnie Mack than he is of Corky Junior."

He said he was going to meet Corky later for a drink after a big ESPN cocktail party, and that he wasn't giving up. Babs said she was going to see if it was worth working on Nancy Teitlebaum, even with the family grudge against Billy Grace.

When we got to the Biltmore and Babs was out of earshot, I told Kenny that if he could get Corky turned around, there was an address on Thunderbird Trail he might want to check out once he got Ashley and the kid in bed.

Annie had left a message saying she was working later than she thought, and would meet me in the lobby bar down near Wright's restaurant around eleven if she could make it. I'd eaten dinner at Wright's with Pete and Liz and Brian Goldberg, all of whom told me that practices had been going fine, that A.T.M. was running as well as he had since he came back from London, and that even Bubba Royal seemed to be getting his proper rest, managing to finish his business in the Do-It Rooms at Beef West and make curfew every single night.

"Okay?" Pete Stanton said, after the first round of drinks had arrived. "That's the small talk. How did things go with the hated Gang of Seven?"

I described the room and said that the side of the table to Donnie Mack's left didn't find me quite as charming as I had hoped.

Liz said, "You? Not charming? I find that difficult to believe."

"Al and Jerry and Arnie Browne don't scare," I said. "Al had as much to do with building the league as anybody, just because of the way he forced the merger in the sixties. Jerry? He won his three Supers, and if he never wins again, he knows he built one of the great teams of all time. And even dying doesn't scare my uncle Arnie. But the three dinks on the other side of the table look like they're going to wet their pants every time Donnie Mack looks their way."

I said I was tired of talking about them, let's talk about the game. There was going to be a game on Sunday, right?

We did that for a while, then Pete and Liz said they were going over to the ABC hospitality suite at the Hyatt, just to pay their respects to the moguls over there. One of the bartenders came over and said a Miss Kay had called, she was still working, she'd see me at the room. Brian and I sat and drank for a while, bullshitting about the season. He finally left about eleven, saying he might wander down Thunderbird Trail for Venus and Serena's last show.

"I have to level, though," he said. "The thrill has gone out of that a little bit now that I've seen Oretha."

"Give her a call," I said. "She's probably always wondered what it would be like to do it with someone who looks like Opie."

"Maybe it's her idea of kinky sex," he said.

"Maybe you could go up on her," I said.

I paid the check and walked back across the grounds to the cottage, thinking a little more about the meeting at the Ritz, thinking that was a show one of the eight thousand sports networks should put on the air, just so the fans could see what sports was really like on the inside, how George Halas and Paul Brown and Art Rooney and Arnie Browne and my old man had given way to Barry Teitlebaum and Bobby Finkel and Corky.

I sat in the living room of the cottage and put some Miles Davis on and was there with a brandy and a cigarette when I heard the knock on the door a few minutes after midnight.

I said it was open, then: "Let's skip the small talk tonight and go straight to the sex parts."

"Okay," Billy Grace said, slamming the door behind him, "but you gotta promise to be gentle."

"I thought you were somebody else," I said. "By the way, you don't call first anymore?"

"You had them put a no-calls on after midnight," he said. "We need to talk."

"I can't even begin to tell you how tired I am of talking," I said.

"Okay, then," he said, sitting down on the sofa across from me, setting down the bottle of grappa he'd brought with him, then lighting a Camel. "I'll talk, you listen."

He smiled with teeth he'd had whitened the year before by some dentist in Vegas who'd charged him two grand a tooth. Now when he was happy he opened his mouth and out popped the brightest lights on the Strip.

"Ask me where I been?" he said.

I did.

"I just come back from a very productive talk with our friend Ferret Biel, who I finally hooked up with and who I am starting to think is a very misunderstood figure, one with untapped potential."

"Ferret's only untapped potential involves an inevitable stretch doing two-to-five somewhere."

"That's what I thought, too. Until he told me about this friend of his who used to run girls at Caesars, but who was eventually forced to relocate at the request of the vice squad of the Las Vegas Police Department, and who ended up running an upscale escort service here, called Homewreckers, Inc."

Billy stopped and asked if I wanted some grappa and I told him it had always tasted to me like Murphy's Oil Soap. Suit yourself, he said.

"This friend," Billy continued, "always told Ferret to give him a call if he was ever in town. So now Ferret was in town, he gives the guy a call, feeling a little needy since Inger is with me now. And the guy gets all excited, saying he can't believe Ferret called, he's been thinking of him because he needs Super Bowl tickets all of a sudden, and he remembers how Ferret used to be with tickets when they were both in Vegas. He says if Ferret can come up with tickets, he can have any girl he wants this week, free of charge."

Billy always told stories at his own pace, as if we had all night, as if we were back in Vegas and there weren't any clocks in the casinos. I could tell this one wasn't going to be any different. I told him to keep going, I was listening, while I got up and switched CDs, from Miles to a Brubeck–Paul Desmond duet.

Billy kept going with his story. Ferret said he couldn't believe the guy didn't have contacts of his own. The guy said, well, he thought he did, but one of his best customers, in town for the game, had come up short. Ferret says, who? The guy says he couldn't tell, Ferret should know that. Just that it was somebody who should have been more grateful, having been set up the night before with the best-looking girl he had, a dead ringer for Tyra Banks. Ferret asks his friend, how many tickets does he need? The answer is ten good ones. Ferret laughs at him now, according to Billy, saying, ten? For the Super Bowl they're playing on Sunday? You must be shitting. His friend says he wishes he was, he knows how nuts it sounds, but he owes somebody at the D.A.'s a huge favor. So there it is, ten tickets, is there any way Ferret can help him out? Ferret says he can't promise anything, but he'll see what he can do.

I said to Billy, "Remember the time you came up a dozen short in Miami, the Thursday before 49ers against the Bengals?"

"You told me the tickets are always out there," Billy said. "You just have to know where to look."

It turns out Bitsy Aguilera—the Chargers' owner? Billy said—used to dance in the chorus at the Desert Inn in the old days, and was an old friend of Ferret's. Bitsy'd decided to skip the game and spend the weekend at home with her new boyfriend, a room service waiter she'd met at the spa at La Costa. So she came up with six for Ferret, then he bought four more from the Bangers' quarterback, JaRon Lashon, for whom Ferret had occasionally placed a discreet bet ever since JaRon had starred at UNLV.

"We're moving up on a happy ending," I said. "Right?"

"Bet your friggin' ass," Billy Grace said. "Ferret calls the guy back, says he wants to deliver the tickets in person. Which he does. Now his friend's showing him pictures of the showstoppers, saying pick one out you like. At which point Ferret says, for ten tickets, there's got to be a bonus. The guys says, how much? Ferret says, tell me who you set up with Tyra Banks. He's the Ferret, and he's got to know, he's got this feeling it's going to be good. Swears he won't tell anybody. Again the guy says, no can do. Ferret says, okay, there's no telling how much he could sell primo tickets like these for, he's sure he'll be able to scalp them for a pretty penny."

"Let me guess," I said. "That's when the guy gave it up."

"Not *it*," Billy said smugly. "Who."

"Okay. Who?"

"Mr. Franklin Sutton."

"Who the hell is Franklin Sutton?" I said.

"Donnie Mack Carney's Jammer," Billy Grace said. "That's who."

"Tyra wasn't for Franklin, was she?" I said.

Billy Grace shook his head slowly, side to side, held up his glass of grappa in the form of a toast.

I started to laugh then and Billy said, what's so funny? And I told him, sonofabitch, he'd been right all along, Lady Luck turned out to be a hooker after all.

thirty-seven

Before Billy left, he said that the escort service was a nice chip to have but it didn't mean anything if Donnie Mack decided to remain celibate the rest of Super Bowl Week. Even if he didn't, Billy said, we had to figure out a way to catch him in the act.

"The Ritz is crawling with owners," Billy said. "So he must have some kind of drill going."

I reminded him then that I was the Jammer, and had invented drills like that.

"You said he had security," Billy said.

"Not like ours," I said.

"Meaning the Vinnys and Johnny."

"And Montell and Denzell, and even Lassie and Rin Tin Tin if we need them."

We sat around until he said he'd had enough grappa. I asked him where Inger was and he said she'd decided to do one more set with Mo's band over at Beef West.

"You can take the kid out of Iceland . . ." he said, his voice trailing off.

Thursday was when I was supposed to sit down with Al Michaels out at Keating Coliseum. Before that, Mo and Annie and Billy met me for a late breakfast out by the pool that had once driven old man Wrigley so wild.

I told them how I thought we should play it. When I was done, Billy called Vinny One on the cell and told him to go over and have a chat with Peter Fairchild, the guy who ran Homewreckers, Inc.

"Tell him how much we want him on board," Billy said.

Montell and Denzell were swimming laps in their Speedo briefs, showing off their abs and tattoos. Mo told them to get dressed, put what Mo called their grand jury clothes on, and get over to the Ritz to check out logistics.

Montell, dripping wet, grinned. "We only call that shit logistics in the daytime," he said.

"After dark, we change the ter-mi-now-*low*-gy," Denzell said, rubbing about a half-bottle of some sweet-smelling lotion all over his upper body.

"Just call it what it is," Montell said, smiling. "Scene of the crime."

Billy nudged Mo. "I almost get choked up," he said, "watching the torch get passed to a new generation like this." Then he explained that his plane was landing in the middle of the afternoon with the rest of the crew I said we'd need.

When we were done, I still had about an hour or so before I was supposed to leave for Keating. Annie, who'd worked all night editing a long piece Vicky had done on Bubba, had been given the morning off, didn't have to be back at the Hyatt until the middle of the afternoon. When we were back inside the cottage, she said, "You think a scam like this will actually work on somebody as powerful as Donnie Mack Carney?"

She was wearing a Phoenix Coyotes sweatshirt over her one-piece black bathing suit. We'd only been in the sun a few days and already her hair had gotten lighter.

"It'll work," I said. "Mostly because it better fucking work."

She wanted to know if I'd told Pete or Brian and I said I hadn't, that if the whole thing turned to toxic waste somehow, the fewer people who knew the better. Annie said that made sense to her and then went about the living room closing shades before she put the "Do Not Disturb" sign on the door.

Then she came back to where I was standing and took off her Coyotes sweatshirt and the straps of her bathing suit.

"You look tense," she said, giving her wet hair a little shake.

"I'm actually fine."

The bathing suit was now halfway off, down to her waist.

"You're right, now that I think about it," I said, helping her get out of those wet things as any gentleman would have. "I'm a bundle of nerves."

Over the rest of the day, the two Vinnys and Johnny Angel baby-sat Peter Fairchild of Homewreckers, Inc. When I got back from the interview with Michaels, Vinny Two called the cottage and filled me in, saying that originally Fairchild—whose real name, he admitted to Billy's guys, was Paulie Spadafora—said he couldn't possibly be involved in something like this, his reputation would be absolutely ruined if news of this ever got out.

On the phone, Vinny Two said, "I finally had to give the guy a shake and say, 'What is this, fucking Sotheby's? You're running girls here, for Chrissakes.'"

Then he explained to Fairchild that Mr. Grace, whom he certainly must remember from Las Vegas, would consider it a personal favor if Fairchild could, in Vinny's words, make this particular occurrence occur. He said he thought Johnny helped everything along by walking around Fairchild's office and dropping anything that looked expensive.

Fairchild had promised to call Franklin Sutton later in the week, it turned out. So he called with the Vinnys and Johnny sitting there and said that he was trying to book the rest of the week, things got pretty hectic as everybody got closer to the game, would Mr. Sutton's employer be requiring any further assistance from Homewreckers?

Sutton called back a couple of hours later and said as a matter of fact, his employer would actually like another appointment with Shakeera, the girl he'd had the other night. Would Friday night be all right? Fairchild, on cue, said that Friday would be fine, but that Shakeera had been called away to Los Angeles. No problem, though, he had someone else in mind who made Shakeera look like some kind of deformed gnome.

Vinny Two told me all this over the phone, because he and the others were going to stay with Peter Fairchild and make sure he didn't give us up the way he had Donnie Mack Carney.

Franklin told Peter Fairchild he'd send a car around 9:30 to pick the girl up, that his employer had a function to attend in downtown Phoenix, and that he wouldn't be able to get back to the Ritz until about ten himself.

I knew the function because it was the same one I was attending, the commissioner's party, being held this year at the Bank One Ballpark where the Arizona Diamondbacks played their games. This was Wick Sanderson's annual festival of vulgar excess for about a thousand or so of his closest friends from the host city, from the league, from the media, and the army of gate-crashers and hangers-on who somehow always showed up at events exactly like this, in any sport, from big fights in Vegas to the Super Bowl, even though the evening felt somewhat as if you were trying to run with the bulls at Pamplona.

I mentioned this to Pete Stanton on the way into Bank One, and he said, "Yeah, but except in our case it's bullshit instead of bulls."

It was one of those expensive modern ballparks where they could even have the roof open or closed. It was beautiful weather in Phoenix, and so they had it open on what felt like a summer night, and somehow that seemed to fit the theme of this year's commissioner's party, built around an old-fashioned Frankie and Annette beach movie, even though the closest beach to where we were all standing was probably in Tijuana.

The league had dropped a ton of sand on the tarp in the infield, and brought in the Beach Boys to perform, which Annie said was like watching old people have sex. There was also a stage with Frankie and Annette look-alikes, and a lot of dancing girls in bikinis. The lights of the park made it as bright as the middle of the afternoon, so everybody was presented souvenir Super Bowl sunglasses when they entered.

Pete said it was even dumber than last year's extravaganza when we all settled into our beach chairs in the VIP section near the pitcher's mound. Annie said, "What was last year?"

Pete said, "V-J Day."

We had finally gotten tired of walking around and having people who I knew wanted the Hawks to get shellacked on Sunday wish me luck. I had posed for some pictures with Vito Cazenovia and Wick Sanderson. I'd chatted briefly with Spencer of the *Daily News*, who wanted to know, gun to the head time, he said, how I thought the vote was going to go, and if I even still gave a flying fuck.

I told him I liked my chances. Gil said, "You're the only kid in the whole class who does."

"Well," I said, "you know what they say?"

"What do they say?"

"The prayer meeting ain't over 'til the fat phony sings."

At around nine-fifteen, I saw Donnie Mack Carney and a young guy with him who had to be Franklin Sutton himself head for the tunnel behind home plate, trailed by the two security guys I remembered from the lunch Donnie Mack and I had at the Post House.

I turned to Annie Kay and said, "You're on, kid."

We waited until they had disappeared through the tunnel and then followed them out to the parking lot. She was wearing what she had described as her Vicky Wannabe clothes: cotton blazer, white blouse, long skirt.

"This *will* work, right?" she said, when we were in the limo.

It'll work, I said. Annie said that if it did, if everything went as planned, what was I going to tell Donnie Mack? I said I was just going to explain the Vegas way.

"I forget," she said. "Which way is that?"

"The one where you've got to decide how much you're prepared to lose."

Montell and Denzell and the rest of the posse guys were waiting for us near the service entrance at the back of the Ritz. They had all dressed down for the occasion, in baggy official-merchandise Super Bowl sweatshirts and baggy jeans, black Army boots. I asked Montell where the dogs were and he said that I saw what happened at Beef West the other night, something came over them when they saw girls without their clothes on.

"Plus," Denzell said, "they get in unfamiliar circumstances, yo? They got to mark their territory, and you can't get them to stop 'til they finished with their business."

Montell said they'd already been upstairs and checked things out, and that the man had three adjoining rooms, like I said he would.

I said, "One for his boys, one that's like customs, then the party suite."

Montell said, you the man. I asked him where the camera crew was that Billy'd had flown in from Amazing Grace, and he said they were waiting for us upstairs. In the freight elevator on the way up, Annie said to me, "You're completely in your element, aren't you?"

I kissed her on the top of her head and said, "First time all season I've felt like I was on my own turf."

"I thought you used to get people out of jams, Mr. Jammer?"

I told her not always, then I told her how much practice I'd had over the years with variations of the play we were about to use. Annie wanted to know if it had a name.

"The old bump and run," I said.

Annie was brilliant, as she would be the first to admit afterward. Donnie Mack's security guys never had a chance. Donzell, in a superb Prince Charles imitation, said, "Room service," and as soon as the door opened, the fact that our posse had the numbers—and much bigger guns—turned out to make all the difference.

Franklin Sutton was in the room next door, eating Jiffy Pop popcorn and watching a dirty movie on Spectravision, when Donzell and Montell went in there, followed by Annie and the camera guy and sound guy from Amazing Grace's game show, *Problem Gambler.*

Sutton was pretty cool, considering. He shut off the television, set the bowl of popcorn on the table next to him and took a sip of his Diet 7-Up. I was the last one into the room.

"You're Molloy, aren't you?" he said. He was blond, blue-eyed, wide-shouldered.

I nodded.

"I told him he was underestimating you," he said.

"People often do. I believe it's my disarming nature and nonconfrontational management style."

Franklin Sutton, straightening his tie, putting his loafers back on, said, "Is there any way I can not be here?"

I said sure, that Montell would have one of the posse guys walk him downstairs, just to make sure he didn't call anybody.

"You just tell the man you went downstairs for a pack of cigarettes," Montell said.

Franklin Sutton said, "I don't smoke."

Montell said, "What is it with you white people, you got to do point-counterpoint on every fuckin' thing?" Then he called out for Shaheen to get over here. Shaheen was the smallest and youngest in the posse, but I'd noticed by now there was no connection between a posse guy's stature and the size of his handgun.

On his way out the door with Franklin Sutton, I heard Shaheen saying, "One of your muscle boys? Ralph? I think maybe he come down with some of that incontinent."

Before Franklin Sutton left, he handed over the key to the suite, which worked on the inside door as well as the one in the hallway. I asked Annie if she was ready and she said she was.

"When you're good," Annie Kay said, "you're good."

And she was.

Just not nearly as good as Oretha Keeshon was.

thirty-eight

uch later, Oretha would say, genuinely pissed, "Well, we took our sweet-assed time, didn't we? Let me explain somethin' to you: That 'ooh ooh ooh, baby let's take it slow' shit only goes so far, then even old Billy Graham wants to take out his business."

But when the crew came into the bedroom as if it was an ambush by Mike Wallace and *60 Minutes*, Annie shouting, "Ann Kay, Fox Sports New York!" Oretha played her part to perfection.

"I *tol'* you," she snapped at Donnie Mack Carney, who seemed to be in the early stages of some sort of stroke, "cameras was gonna cost you extra."

She was standing next to the bed now, making no attempt to cover breasts that were everything I could have hoped they'd be, and so much more.

"You said straight sex, Rev," she said to Donnie Mack, looking straight into the camera now. "I didn't know we was here to shoot a god-damn sequel to *Boogie Nights*."

"This . . . this," Donnie Mack Carney sputtered. He was desperately trying to get his white belly and other parts of himself back inside what looked to be a black silk kimono. "This . . . is what they did to poor Frank Gifford!" he finally managed.

He pointed a shaking finger at Rick, our laid-back cameraman in his Hawaiian shirt, and said, "You put that thing down."

Rick poked his head out from behind his handheld and pointed to an area right below Donnie Mack's belly where the kimono still wasn't doing its job and said, "You put *that* thing down."

Donnie Mack was leaning back against the headboard of the king-sized now, chest heaving, calling out, "Ralph? Pierce? Get in here."

It was about this time that he noticed me, leaning against the doorjamb. "You?" he said.

Oretha was standing next to Annie Kay, finally sliding an arm into a white terry-cloth robe, so she'd have something on besides her black panties.

Annie was interviewing her as she did.

"You were paid to come here and have sex with Mr. Carney?" Annie said.

Oretha was playing it scared and a little hurt for the moment. "He . . . he told me it wasn't even a sin," she said. "That it would be like a little slice of HEVN."

"*I am begging you to please shut up!*" Donnie Mack roared at Oretha.

Rick had the camera on Donnie Mack, but in what I felt was a nice touch, suddenly whipped the handheld around to Oretha and Annie.

"Oh?" Oretha said. "*Now* you want me to close my mouth." She looked at Annie then, like it was girl talk, and said, "You believe this shit?"

"You did this," Donnie Mack said to me, ignoring everybody else.

"Nah," I said, "you did it to yourself. Unless you've got a Bible that says it's okay to get it on with bad girls like Chocolate Spice here."

"Reverend Carney . . ." Annie Kay said.

"*I am not a minister!*" he said.

Rick, the cameraman, said, "I know, dude, you just play one on TV, right?"

Oretha said, "What night this gonna be on?"

Donnie Mack Carney got off the bed now, as Rick did the whipping thing again, more to irritate him than anything else. Donnie Mack walked over to the wall and shut off the dirty in-room movie he and Oretha had on their television, then double-knotted the kimono.

"You," he said to me again, more resigned now.

I shrugged.

"I need your vote," I said.

He said that maybe it was time for us to go into the living room, alone, and get down to it. I said that was fine with me, the crew could wait in here while we talked.

Oretha Keeshon said, "Talk, talk, talk. Where's my goddam money?"

W e're all human," Donnie Mack Carney said in the living room.

I told him I'd heard that one before, one time from the guy who now was his quarterbacks coach in Baltimore.

He was at the bar, like a fighter trying to gather himself in his corner. He'd stopped in the bathroom and decided to switch to a real robe. Now he was fixing himself what he probably thought of as a martini and looked more to me like an industrial-size glass of gin. When he came over and fell onto the sofa, he asked if he needed to worry about Ralph and Pierce and I said they were fine unless one of them had said something snippy in one of those moments when Montell and Denzell took the cloth room service napkins out of their mouths.

"You ever been married, son?" he said.

No, I said, not even any near misses.

He drank some of the gin and said, "Well, you're looking at somebody who's supposed to be the most married man in America. Coral Carney. Voice of an angel and the instincts of that big black girl in the other room. She's one of those who got to singing about Jesus and forgot about all the guitar pickers she spent time with." He was talking to himself as much as me. "This ever gets out, you know she'll be the one running what the newspapers like to call the Carney Christian empire?"

I could pretty much figure that out for myself, I said, and went over to the bar and fixed myself a Scotch.

"Allen Getz is going to be terribly disappointed in you," I said. "I hope you've already got something down on paper."

Donnie Mack said, "I may think with my pecker more than an old man should, but I've always been smart enough to get 'em to sign before they get a chance to change their minds."

"You were helping him from the start, weren't you?" I said.

"Pretty much. I told him I never thought your Miss Bolton—she's a pretty little thing, isn't she?—had her heart in it." He leaned his head all the way back on the sofa. "He just had to have the Hawks. I don't know whether it was your stepmomma who originally got him so worked up or not. Maybe he wanted the team from your daddy, the way he wanted her. But it was a toy he had to have. He kept saying that if we threw enough shit at you, enough of it would stick and you'd quit, that everybody said you never stuck anything out in your whole life."

" 'Til now."

"It's all pecker-swinging in the end, isn't it? Savin' face instead of savin' grace. For you, for me, for rich boys like Allen. How do I look? You made me look bad? I'll make you look bad. Whether you got yourself a team, or just trying to get one. I told him if he wanted a team that bad, I'd sell him mine." Donnie Mack stared into his drink now. "Which is probably what's gonna end up happening anyway."

"It was just a GTH with Allen," I said.

Donnie Mack asked what that meant and I said, "One of my guys calls it a Gots to Have."

From the other room, we heard Oretha call out, "How long are we supposed to sit here on our asses waiting for you two to *get to it*? This shit is turning into a damn retreat."

"Just another minute," I said to her.

"Talk talk talk talk *talk*," she said, and then I heard Annie laugh.

Donnie Mack said, where's Franklin, by the way? I told him Franklin wasn't here when we came into the middle room and he wouldn't have been able to do a damn thing to stop us if he had been, that Donnie Mack was already caught, and sometimes you were just caught, I'd learned that in all the years when I'd been Franklin for Billy Grace.

"When do I get the tape?" he said.

"When I pass. With flying colors."

"Don't worry," he said. "You'll pass my committee, son, now that you got my thing in a wringer."

"No, I meant after the full vote tomorrow afternoon."

"They never go against me," he said with a sigh. "I'm Donnie Mack Carney." He put the big glass up to his lips and discovered it was already empty. "You want this team that much?"

"I go back and forth," I said. "But I sure as hell wasn't going to let you and a punk like Allen Getz make up my mind for me."

"It might be a closer vote with the full ownership than you're gonna like," he said. "That's the way it usually goes when it's close coming out of Finance." I needed a two-thirds majority, which meant twenty-five votes.

Then I told Donnie Mack that it wasn't going to be a close vote coming out of his committee, because he was going in there tomorrow and make sure it was unanimous.

"Your faith will give you the strength of ten men," I said. "That and *Debbie Does Donnie*."

Oretha was dressed by now, in a summer dress, this one peach-colored, even shorter than the one she'd worn to Keating Coliseum to mess with A.T.M. Her matching high heels made her taller than me. When she came into the living room, she hadn't forgotten that I told her to play her call-girl part all the way until we were all in the limo and on our way back to the Biltmore. So she went and stood in front of Donnie Mack and stuck her hand out.

"Pay up, Saint Peter," she said.

"But we never . . ."

"Oh, sure we did, honey," she said. "What, you're gonna sit there and tell me you didn't get your ashes hauled tonight?"

I passed the Finance Committee six votes to zero, with one abstention, that belonging to Barry Teitlebaum, who said he did it out of respect for his dead father-in-law, who deserved better than ending a distinguished career in feminine hygiene limping the way he did because of what happened with Vinny One at Amazing Grace.

Kenny and Babs passed seven to zero, Barry saying there was no reason to punish them for his father-in-law's fall down those steps.

Later in the afternoon, the full ownership passed all the Molloys, one vote this time, by a count of twenty-eight to five.

I didn't ask what Donnie Mack Carney, looking a little pale on Saturday, I thought, had said to Corky DuPont III and Bobby Finkel to get them turned around in committee, and frankly didn't care.

When the votes were all counted, the league scheduled a five-thirty press conference in one of the ballrooms at the Hyatt. When I arrived there, I found Franklin Sutton, who apparently had taken up smoking, standing in the back. I handed him a manila envelope with a copy of the tape that Rick, our camera guy, had dubbed for me before flying back to Vegas.

"Is this the only copy?" Franklin Sutton asked.

"Yes," I lied.

Then I went up and stood next to Donnie Mack Carney, who roused himself for the media, introducing me as the "official owner of the New York Hawks, in the eyes of God and the National Football League, Big Tim Molloy's son, Jack."

I thanked him, and thanked his committee, and thanked everybody but the Academy, and then said, "Well, as my dear friend Donnie Mack was saying to me just last evening, this league certainly does make for some strange bedfellows . . ."

On Saturday night, we threw a private party—without players, who were supposed to be locked up in their rooms—at Beef West. Mo and his band were there, Kelli Ann Gonzalez, Mo's posse, some of the guys from Elvis Elgin's posse, who'd flown in the night before. Kenny

Molloy, having managed to shake loose from Ashley and the kids, was there, seated at a table with Venus and Serena.

Mo had even invited Donyell Webster and some of the people from Toe Tag, Inc., to fly over from Los Angeles. Donyell's clothes were no longer preppie now, completely Hollywood. Black t-shirt, black jeans, black Nike hightops, cell to his ear constantly. He even air-kissed Montell and Denzell without stopping the phone conversation he was having.

Inger had flown back to Las Vegas with the camera crew. There was a scheduling conflict for Tony Orlando, so *Problem Gambler* was going to have to tape two weeks' worth of shows on Sunday before the game, which meant they were going to have to start early in the morning. I was wondering if somehow Billy Grace might have been behind the scheduling conflict, because when I walked into Beef West, he was at his own table with the two Vinnys, Johnny Angel, and Oretha Keeshon.

When I got a drink in my hand and walked over to thank Oretha for about the hundredth time for the way she'd handled Donnie Mack Carney, I heard Billy saying to her, "Who gives a flying fart, vice-president of what? How about vice-president of *me?*"

Oretha got up to go to the ladies' room. When she was out of earshot, I said to Billy, "What about Inger? I thought you'd already moved up to what color BMW did she want?"

Billy watched Oretha shake her ass at him a little and said, "I got that Ferret on the plane with Inger. I told them they needed to get into some of that healing shit."

Annie was waiting at my own table with Pete Stanton and Brian Goldberg. We shouted at each other over Mo's music, until he announced that he'd written a special song in honor of Billy Grace and me called "Closure":

. . . mess which me,
I mess which you.
Let you dis me,
Look like a fool,

Fuck me? Uh uh. Fuck you.
Fuck me? Don't think so. Fuck you.

I went up to the stage when he was finished and gave him a hug and said I know it sounded corny, but by God, I still loved a ballad.

Then the two of us sang a rollicking version of the McBurney fight song.

That should have been the end of the night, except that Bubba Royal stopped by the cottage right before Annie Kay and I were set to break several existing world screwing records, wanting to explain how we were going to win the big game and asking for the last favor he was ever going to ask from me, swearing that it was the last time, on all that was good and decent.

PART FIVE

bubba, royal

thirty-nine

They gave us two suites at Keating Memorial Coliseum, both of them opulent enough in a Southwestern chic pension-fund-robbing way, neither one of them comparing very favorably with Suite 19 at Molloy Stadium. When Pete came into the area where he and Liz and I would be watching the Hawks try to take the Lombardi Trophy from the hated Bangers, he said, "Which room do you suppose old Charlie Keating paid for with savings, and which one with loans?"

It was going to be the three of us in here today the same way it was on game day at Molloy. The rest of our group—Billy, Oretha, Mo, Kelli Ann, the Vinnys and Johnny, Montell, Denzell, Regis and Kathie Lee—were next door. Babs and Kenny had decided they wanted to sit in the stands.

I asked Mo why he'd let the posse guys bring the Rotts, and he looked at me as if he didn't even know me anymore.

"It's the Super Bowl, Jack. You want them to stay back in the room and watch on TV?"

He shook his head. "You're really not a dog guy, are you?"

I'd walked around on the field for a while, the whole scene down there a wild, loud, colorful mix of pep rally, normal pregame warm-ups, floats, and an old-fashioned battle of the bands. Gloria Estefan and her group were in one end zone and when they'd finish a song, Britney Spears would start singing in the other. Because of a mix-up, they had both been originally invited to be the halftime show, but the league was saved the embarrassment of having to choose when Wick Sanderson stepped in and decided that halftime would be a twenty-minute highlight package of what the producers promised would be the absolute last performance of *Cats* anywhere, ever again, on the planet Earth.

I saw Gil Spencer of the *Daily News* over near the Bangers bench. The NFL, he said, allowed one pool reporter to be down on the field before the game, picking up what he called "C and P."

I asked him what that was and he said, "Color and pageantry. I looked into the eyes of some of the Bangers and you know what I saw?"

"Fear?"

"Well, yeah, that," Spencer said. "But mostly amphetamines."

About an hour before kickoff, I stopped by the Hawks' locker room. Josh Blake was sequestered with his assistant coaches, adding a few plays to the first twenty for the Hawks he liked to script before every game, the way Bill Walsh used to for the 49ers. When he saw me in the doorway, he grinned. "What would Vince say to the guys at a time like this?" he asked.

"Fuck," I said. "Like, a lot."

"Oh, yeah," he said, "I forgot."

He came over to me and put out his hand. I shook it, and held it. "How about we win this sonofabitch for my old man?" I said.

Josh Blake said, "How about."

I went over to Bubba's locker and said, "Hey, hoss, do it for your school."

"Ever' time," he said.

He stared at me hard with the blue eyes, looking remarkably clear-eyed, I thought, looking young, really, the way he had at the Cotton Bowl that time, the first time I'd ever seen him wearing Number 22 for the

UCLA Bruins, before he became Number 6 for the Hawks in your program, number one in your heart.

"Hey," I said, "you look like you actually got some sleep last night after you left us."

He was wrapping and unwrapping the tape on his left wrist.

"I did, Bubba."

"Well," I said, "it's a little late in the game to start that shit, isn't it?"

Finally, I went across the room to A.T.M.'s locker. He was rubbing some of his lotion on his hands, looking like a doctor making sure his hands were ready for surgery, the baby-blue receiver gloves he liked to wear on the floor next to his chair. He was wearing an old New York football Giants cap with the lower-case "ny" and sunglasses and the headphones that were attached to his DiscMan player. At his feet I could see the case for Mo Jiggy's latest CD from Toe Tag, Inc.'s record division, *Eff I Ruled the World*.

When A.T.M., who must have had his eyes closed behind the shades, noticed me standing there, I made a motion for him to take the headphones off.

"I just wanted to tell you I'm glad you came back, man," I said.

"Played all this time," he said. "Worked more colleges than one of those stand-out comedians. Couldn't take a chance on missing the yum."

I said, "That's what I'm talkin' about."

He looked at me, frowning. "You ain't seen 'Retha around anywheres, have you?"

She seemed to be busy falling in love with my old boss, I said.

A.T.M. smiled brilliantly and said, "That means there's nothin' but green ahead of me now."

I said, "Gots to have the big trophy."

"Gots to have," A.T.M. said, and then we did some kind of secret handshake that ended with us hitting our elbows together so hard I lost feeling in one arm for a moment.

I figured I could tell him another time that the five million Billy had given him in London would be coming out of his next signing bonus.

Maybe I'd wait until our own parade through the Canyon of Heroes, when there would be so much yum in the air.

Some would say afterward that it was the most dramatic ending to a Super Bowl since Scott Norwood of the Buffalo Bills, that poor bastard, missed a last-second field goal in Tampa in the early nineties and the Giants won the game, 20–19.

Others would talk about the day in San Diego when the Broncos upset the Packers and John Elway finally won his first Super Bowl.

Gil Spencer would write in the *Daily News* that the only thing he ever saw that could compare to the ending we got at Charles Keating Memorial Coliseum was that time when it was the Rams against the Tennessee Titans in Atlanta, the clock running out with the Titans on the Rams' one-yard line.

Rick Reilly wrote in *Sports Illustrated* that they were all wrong, that there was finally a game-ending drive in the Super Bowl that was even better than the one Joe Montana engineered that time against the Bengals in Miami.

That was afterward.

First came the last ninety seconds of the Super Bowl, from the time Bubba Royal and the Hawks, down to their last timeout, got the ball on the Hawks' six-yard line with the Bangers, four-point underdogs coming in, still clinging to the 20–18 lead they'd had since early in the third quarter. We hadn't scored a touchdown since the middle of the first quarter, when Bubba hit A.T.M. for fifty yards down the right sideline. After that, the Bangers had done the best job anybody had done at containing A.T.M. Moore since he'd come back from what he called his sabbathical.

The star of the game, so far, had been Bangers quarterback JaRon Lashon, who'd outplayed Bubba and everybody else, throwing for one touchdown, running for another, making sure his team controlled the ball and the clock for most of the fourth quarter. It was JaRon who even executed the quick kick on third down that caught the Hawks completely by surprise, the ball finally rolling to a stop on our six.

"A quick kick?" I said in our suite. "A fucking *quick kick*? When was the last time anybody quick-kicked? Would anybody like to tell me that?"

"The Polo Grounds," Pete said quietly. He turned to me. "Where's your lighter and your smokes?"

I said, "I didn't know . . ."

"I don't," he said.

I handed him Tim Molloy's Dunhill, which I always carried on game day for luck, and my Marlboros. Liz was already smoking. So we all stood there and smoked and prepared to watch Bubba Royal, at the age of thirty-eight, try to take one more team down the field.

On first down, he hit A.T.M. for twenty yards over the middle, then got everybody lined up and spiked the ball to stop the clock, knowing he would need his timeout later.

Minute and fifteen seconds now.

One of the plays that the writers would write about later and the twinks would all talk about on television came next, a quarterback draw that Bubba made up at the line of scrimmage. He took one step back, decided not to hand the ball to Bobby Camby, and ran straight up the middle of Keating to our 40-yard line before a forearm from Bangers All-Pro middle linebacker Air-Rick Chevrolay dropped him in his tracks.

Somehow, Bubba got right up, staggered back to where we were already in formation for the ball to be snapped, and hit Redford Newman in the right flat, Redford running out of bounds finally on the Bangers' 36.

Thirty seconds left.

Liz Bolton laughed nervously and said, "I mean, it's only a football game, right? It's not like anybody's going to die here. Right?"

"Right," I said.

She looked down at her hands and said, "I'm smoking two cigarettes, aren't I?" Pete and I nodded. She was still staring at the cigarettes in both hands. "Yep. Two. But I'm fine. Only a game."

"Shut up now, okay, Liz?" I said.

"Okay."

There was a procedure call against the Hawks when A.T.M. jumped the snap count, pushing us back to the 41. Then on first-and-fifteen, right before Air-Rick Chevrolay, on a blitz, tried to drive the 6 on Bubba's jersey right through him, Bubba threw one down the left, dead into the double coverage A.T.M. had been facing all day, and somehow A.T.M. reached back when the ball turned out to be underthrown and caught it with his right hand and stiff-armed the first safety that got in his way and made it all the way to their six-yard line now before he ran out of bounds with twelve seconds left in the Super Bowl.

"Kick the fucker now," Pete said grimly in the suite.

"I don't think so," I said.

"Why, because we had that bad snap before?"

I smiled at him and said, "Nah."

Pete Stanton said, "Would you mind telling me what is so goddam amusing?"

"I don't know," I said. "Sports. Life. History. Neat stuff like that."

Liz said, "How about this? How about we have our truth and beauty conversation after Benito *kicks the fucker?* Would that be okay with everybody?"

"We're gonna score a touchdown," I said calmly.

"And why is that?" Pete said.

I said, "Because, we do that, then Bubba covers."

Pete said, "I thought he told you he didn't bet anymore."

I told Pete what Bubba'd told me when he asked for the money to bet on the Hawks the night before.

He lied, I said.

Maybe Bubba appreciated the irony of the play he ended up calling to surprise the Bangers, and that surprised Josh Blake so much that he nearly came down with a case of what Shaheen the posse guy called that incontinent.

Bubba Royal called a sweep.

What he really called was the Hawks' version of the Student Body Right we used to run at UCLA, figuring that even if Bobby Camby got stuffed over on the right side, with twelve seconds left we'd still have time to call our last timeout and send Benito Siragusa out to kick a game-winning field goal.

Only, Bobby Camby picked out a rather unusual time to come down with the dreaded Wanna Be the Man Disease.

When the Bangers' defense came up and shut him down on the right, he suddenly reversed his field and started running to his left, obviously forgetting how little time there was left on the clock, how much time he was taking.

Seven seconds.

Six.

"Get . . . your . . . bony . . . ass . . . out . . . of . . . bounds," Pete hissed.

Except that as Bobby Camby ran left, there was no time for that. There was just him with the ball inside the five, planting and cutting toward the end zone now with one person in front of him, Bubba Royal. And Air-Rick Chevrolay between Bubba and the goal line.

Where Mountain Montoya of the USC Trojans had been a hundred years ago.

Bubba Royal threw the block this time. Bubba threw a rolling block at Air-Rick Chevrolay that took out his feet and flipped him upside down, and Bobby Camby could have walked the last couple of yards into the end zone that won the New York Hawks the Super Bowl, and got his quarterback even once and for all.

We were all doing so much dancing and hugging and secret hand-shakes in our suite at Keating Coliseum that no one noticed Bubba on the field, rolling around, holding what was left of his left knee.

This was after Wick Sanderson, his tinted glasses aflame with the television lights trained on him and the lights of Keating Coliseum in the Arizona night, handed Liz Bolton the Lombardi Trophy once I'd stepped aside; after Bubba Royal made the crowd at Keating go insane when he made his way to the podium on crutches and then, refusing help from Pete and Brian Goldberg, held his crutches aloft like a trophy and limped up the stairs to where the rest of us were.

He came over to me, tears in his eyes, and said, "The one I owed you, Bubba?"

I told him to forget it.

"This here was the one," he said.

This was after Billy Grace somehow found me on the field after the trophy presentation and told me—because why the fuck not? the old romantic said—that maybe there was a time when the old man had flown out to Vegas without me knowing it, not long after I'd moved to Vegas, and asked Billy to look out for me.

"Like you was my own," Billy Grace said, brushing some of the confetti that had magically fallen out of the sky out of one of his eyes. "Some bullshit like that."

"Like that," I said, and tried to hug him.

"Hey," Billy Grace said, backing off.

This was after I'd told Kenny Molloy that he was going to have to be in charge of the Hawks for a while, that being a big-time sports mogul had seriously cut into my hanging-around.

"How long will you be away?" he said, and I told him not any longer than the first Sunday of next season, just because I figured I'd missed way too many Sundays in my life already.

This was Annie Kay and me at midfield after she'd somehow broken away from a crazed Vicky Dunne for a moment, who she said was having some kind of live-shot meltdown trying to persuade anybody in a Hawks uniform who'd done anything in the game to talk to her on camera.

I said I'd go talk to Vicky in a minute, and Annie said generosity like that would be rewarded a thousandfold later on at the Biltmore.

I also told Annie she was going to have to ask Vicky for some time off and then told her what the old man, Big Tim Molloy himself, had told me a long time ago, about how you shouldn't wait when you were flush, you should take your best girl to Paris first chance you got.

Annie jumped into my arms and kissed me hard and said, "Hey, we can even find out for A.T.M. what happened to the Louvre!"

I had to shout suddenly to be heard over Mo Jiggy's voice singing from the p.a. system about so many games, so little time, and over the roar of the fireworks in the sky above the last Sunday in January, but I told her that first we'd have to make one other stop in honor of Automatic Touchdown Maker Moore.

"We're goin' to fucking Sea World!" I said to Annie Kay.